Ar

Uncommon

Johannes T.

Alexos Fox, an introverted academic and polio survivor, is naturally quite sad when the long-time butler of his household, the man who all but raised him, retires. He is not at all prepared for the old man's replacement: his exceedingly attractive and painfully tempting nephew.

Unbeknownst to Alexos, his old butler chose Henry Sutton hoping the two of them might marry their interests together, and the gentleman is as suspicious as he is entranced when the new butler comes to him with talks of a secret marriage between them.

M/M erotic romance, rated E, 100k. Set 1927, primarily in West Sussex, England.

Featuring themes of disability, chronic pain, piercings and tattoos, loneliness and isolation, bodily autonomy, class dynamics, a butler/gentleman relationship, joyful non-monogamy and casual sex.

Kink-wise, enjoy size difference, switching roles, burgeoning D/s dynamics and mild sadomasochism, the aforementioned piercings and tattoos, and a lot of bathing and massage.

An Uncommon Betrothal is a work of fiction created from the author's imagination. Any resemblance to living persons, living or dead, or resemblance to actual events, places, or names is purely coincidental.

Cover design by Johannes T. Evans.

An Uncommon Betrothal

Chapter One

For a man of sixty-six, it seemed to Alexos that Mr Sutton was a remarkably hale and healthy man. He looked a good many years younger than his age, could easily pass for a gentleman in his forties and not one approaching seventy, but for all his face was youthful, he was struggling more and more with his duties throughout a given day. Alexos didn't at all begrudge him his retirement, although it did of course make him a little sad – it seemed to him at times that Mr Sutton had raised him more than his nanny had, let alone his parents, and he would miss him desperately.

As it stood, he had employed the assistance of Betty, the cook's assistant, to help him carry the cake into the little servant's dining hall. He had baked it himself, even though Mrs Perry had wrinkled her nose at the thought of Alexos being permitted to spend an hour in her domain to make it.

"It's turned out very well, Mr Fox," Betty said when she laid eyes on it, seeming so genuinely surprised it was impossible to take it as a compliment. "Do you bake an awful lot?"

"When I can creep into the kitchen, not ruled over by its queen's watchful eye," said Alexos.

"It's your house," pointed out Betty, and Alexos gave a short laugh.

"That might be true," he said good-naturedly, "but what you'll come to understand, Betty, is that as much as it might be our house, Mrs Perry rules the kitchen, and we are but guests therein – just as Mr Sutton rules below stairs. Or did. Have you hold of it?"

"Yes, Mr Fox, I think so," Betty said as she pulled the take tray forward and rested it on her forearms to make sure she could hold it steady – Mr Sutton had no wife or children, but he had a lot of nieces and nephews, and Alexos had wanted to ensure it was big enough for him to take home to them – and the two of them walked together down the corridor. "You really can be quiet with that thing, Mr Fox, it took me ages to get my footsteps quiet on this tile."

"Fifteen years' practice has served me well in that regard, Betty," Alexos whispered back, and led the way down the cellar corridor and to the servant's dining hall, which Mr Sutton's office adjoined. It wasn't that it was a big house, merely that the cellar had been built very narrowly, so that it was a long way from the stairs down to here.

Alexos tilted his cane as he moved the same way that he did his foot on the downstroke so that he didn't make even the smallest shuffle or squeak, and he made a silent hand signal to Betty to stop short as he leaned slightly forward to look inside.

Mr Sutton, luckily, was sitting at his requisite place at one end of the servant's table, and Alexos had picked his moment well: it was a little bit after four, and as well as him and Mrs Perry, Mr Gill, his mother's chauffeur, was sitting at the table and playing cards with Tom Lloyd, the gardener. Young Becca, the maid, was up in London visiting her sister, but she would be back tomorrow, and Alexos knew that Mr Sutton would think nothing of leaving a piece behind for her.

He knocked crisply on the door, averting his eyes and waiting a few moments for everyone to collect themselves before he stepped inside – Mr Gill especially was very particular about his appearance in front of his employers, and as much as Alexos didn't much care about that sort of thing, he didn't want to upset anybody.

"Hullo, Mr Sutton, all," said Alexos, and waved them all to sit down again, which everyone did except for Mr Sutton, who remained on his feet. "I've a surprise for you."

"A surprise?" asked Sutton, and then Betty came forward with the cake and its candles, and the old man's bushy eyebrows raised up like black and silver caterpillars, his mouth falling open in a bright grin. "Oh, Mr Fox!"

"A parting gift," Alexos said, stepping in after Betty as she set the tray down.

Mr Gill and Tom clapped their hands together, although Alexos didn't miss the way that Gill subtly pushed his ashtray back with his elbow, as he had professed to Alexos' mother to have quit smoking four months back – not that he'd ever tell her. Mrs Perry leaned up in her seat, lifting herself off of her chair to oversee the bake with a critical eye.

"It looks alright," she said, which Alexos took as the fervent praise it was coming from Mrs Perry, and Mr Sutton stood to his feet to shake Alexos' hand, clasping it in both of his own.

"It looks *splendid*, Mr Fox, it's very kind of you. I don't know that we can eat it all ourselves, though."

"It's for the whole Sutton clan, really," said Alexos. "There's paper and string under the tray to tie it up with."

Mr Sutton beamed all the brighter, the apples in his cheeks showing with the wideness of his dimpled smile, and he reached up to deliver an affectionate pat to Alexos' cheek.

"I do hope you treat my nephew with the kindness you do me, Mr Fox," said the old man.

"I wouldn't dream of doing otherwise, Mr Sutton," Alexos promised, and gave everyone a neat bow of his head before he went back into the hall.

"You've to save a piece for Becky, Mr Sutton," he heard Betty say as he made his way toward the stairs. "Mr Fox was worried you might forget."

"As if I could," was the quiet, warm response, and Alexos did his best to ignore the pang in his chest as he made his way up the steps. He knew that the servants' stairs weren't really intended for him, but the knowledge made it no easier on his bad leg or either of his bad knees when he had to scale their steep incline, and once he came up into the hall he took a moment before he went to brave the main staircase and walk up to the library.

"Alex," said Mother. "Were you downstairs?"

"Only for a moment," Alexos said mildly, giving her a smile as he approached her, and they walked together into the salon, her fingers touching against his back. His mother was giving him one of her concerned looks, but unfortunately, these looks of consternation were rather the default whenever she was home. He was always somewhat desperate for her to leave again.

"Are you feeling alright?" she asked, with a note of anxiety in her tone.

"Yes, Mother," he said with all the assurance he could manage. "No cold, no fever, no illness whatsoever – I am as healthy and in my prime as I get."

She looked down at his cane, as though looking at it with enough scorn might make it disappear from between his fingers and burn the ache out of his joints, too – or at least burn out that her son made the weakness visible in the way he held himself.

"Your voice sounds rather hoarse," she said.

"It does," he agreed. "But I regret to inform you, Mother, that it always does."

She peered at him, her lips twisting into a little frown, her nose scrunching up in a way that he knew his own did, when similarly taken aback. "Does it?" she asked.

"Yes, Mother," said Alexos, and patted her shoulder as they sat down for tea. "Yes, it does."

* * *

By early that evening, his mother had departed again with Mr Gill at the helm, and Alexos was sitting alone at the window bench in the library, a hot water bottle resting on his knees. It wasn't a particularly cold spring evening, but his knees were bad today, and the heat did help – as did, of course, the martini resting on the table beside him, although he hadn't much touched it.

"Surveying the grounds, Mr Fox?" asked Mr Sutton as he stepped into the library, and Alexos turned to look at him, his lips parting.

Mr Sutton had his coat folded over his arm and his hat in his hand. Mr Lloyd had helped him with his bags, he thought, and Mr Sutton's eldest nephew, a stockbroker, was due to pick him up in his motorcar at any moment to ferry him home.

Home away from the Foxes' Burrow, as it were.

"Watching for your nephew's car," said Alexos.

"You needn't look so glum, lad," said Sutton, coming up to stand beside him, and Alexos forced a little smile. "You can write me."

"I wouldn't want to bother you."

"Nonsense," said Sutton, with a little shake of his head, and squeezed Alexos' shoulder. "Mr Fox, I have cared for you since you were a babe in arms and view you with the affection I do my own nephews. More, if Claude, Wentworth, and Gregory are to be counted into the matter."

"Well, they ought be, Mr Sutton," said Alexos. "They *are* your nephews, and I'm not."

"More's the pity," said Sutton with a soft sigh, and Alexos laughed quietly, stroking one of his hands over the hot water bottle in his lap, and with the other reaching up to pat the old man's hand on his shoulder.

"Which one is it you're sending to take over your mantle?"

"Harry," said Sutton, and then raised his chin, clearing his throat. "Henry Reginald, that is."

Alexos tilted his head, feeling his lip curl up in a half-smile. "*Reginald*? He's named after you?"

"It's not the only reason he's my favourite," said the old man, and Alexos laughed quietly. "He's a very capable young man, a few years older than yourself – and he was a Second Lieutenant in the Great War. He's close in age to yourself, but he's more than qualified to head the household, and he'll keep everything in fine working order for your father and for you, at such a time as you take your inheritance as master of the house. Truth be told, I think the two of you will be perfectly suited to one another."

"Won't he be disappointed?" Alexos asked. "I would have thought a young man in his prime should want a more interesting house to buttle for. You know, somewhere with a great deal of action going on, and an employer with a little more esprit."

"You've esprit in spades," said Sutton, almost scolding him.

Alexos tapped his fingers against the hot water bottle, listening to the watery tap it made. "Mother was disappointed not to meet him."

"Was she?" Mr Sutton asked, surprised.

"Well, no, I don't think so," Alexos said. "But she said she was."

"That was good of her."

"She does try to say the right things," Alexos said, and saw the twin lights of the junior Sutton's motorcar on the drive as he came up toward the house. "I'll go down with you," he said, standing up to his feet.

"Oh, Mr Fox, you needn't," said Sutton. "Your knees—"

"My knees hurt anyway," he said, vaguely waving one hand, and picked up his cane to walk with him. "You did warn our new Sutton of that, at least?"

"I've told him everything about you," said Sutton, pulling on his coat. "You will like him, Mr Fox."

"You might as well call me Alex, you know," said Alexos. "You're officially retired, now."

"Alexos," said the old man, and Alexos smiled to hear his full name – his parents had loved it on his birth certificate but hadn't liked it once they started saying it out loud. He did, though. He really did. "But that does mean you have to call me Reg."

"I couldn't possibly," said Alexos.

"Reggie?"

"Reginald," said Alexos. "I might just manage."

The old man laughed, and it was a wonderful sound, like a creaking door – Alexos would miss that laugh, as often as he usually heard it.

"Do you want me to tell Father you're departing?" asked Alexos.

"If you really want to," said Sutton. "But you know your father. He won't care."

"I'm glad you said that," Alexos said. "I didn't want to go up the stairs."

They laughed together as they walked down, and it almost made it all better, that the old man was going – and Alexos was glad he was retiring, because he really had earned it, as old as he was, and he was being selfish, really, he knew that. It wasn't as though he'd be alone in the house, anyway.

"You will like him, Alexos," said Sutton again. "I'm sure of it."

"You needn't make your retirement all about me, you know," said Alexos as they slowly descended the stairs. "You must think me an awful narcissist."

"My retirement isn't about you," said Sutton. "But my replacement is, no doubt about that."

"Thank you, Reginald. For everything."

"I'm not dying, lad," said Sutton. "Cheer up."

Alexos smiled as they came to the stair, and he picked up the cake by the box's string, following the old man out to the car.

"Hullo, Uncle," said the driver, waving a handsome hand wrapped in a handsome driving glove. The man himself was handsome too – Alexos had had a great many of Mr Sutton's handsome nephews inflicted on him over the years, and it seemed each one he saw was more of a painful temptation than the last. "You must be Mr Fox. He loves you more than he does most of us, you know."

The young Sutton winked a shining grey eye, and Alexos swallowed hard, trying to force down his blush as he gave a polite bow of his head, and handed the cake to Mr Sutton as his nephew pulled the door open for him.

"Safe home, Mr Sutton," he said, and made no more fuss of his farewell, hurrying back inside and closing the door behind him.

He allowed himself to think for a moment on the terrible allure of Benjamin Sutton, and then turned the key in the lock.

Collecting his martini from the library, he hurried fast to bed.

* * *

It was on Monday that Mr Sutton Junior came down on the train from Oxford, where he had for two years been serving as underbutler at a much larger country house. Alexos saw his suitcase in the hall as he walked from the library.

The Fox household had three stories: on the first floor was the library and Alexos' own bedroom, as well as the servants' bedrooms accessible from the back corridor, and on the second were his parents' and the guest bedrooms, and of course, his father's office.

He had always rather idolized his father's office.

It was a beautiful room, dominated by wide windows and a balcony that overlooked the grounds, adjoining onto the master bedroom. Tall, mahogany bookshelves covered every wall, filled to the brim with leatherbound volumes, globes, some of Mother's book covers printed on fine card, and framed photographs – and his father's medals, of course, awarded for his service in the Boer war. He'd served very well before he'd been sent home.

It had seemed to him as a child to be a room filled with magic, particularly as short as he had been for the longest time, with so much of the room out of reach – and particularly as, back then, his father would often carry him up the spiral staircase to the second floor, that he need not make the journey himself.

Now, ascending the steps, he did his best to ignore the painful, sticking ache the tall, narrow steps rendered in his knees, even as he gripped tight at the bannister to support himself. It didn't help that he hadn't slept well the night previous – his hips were worse than usual and they'd kept him up, and his whole body was thickly weighted with a pained fatigue.

His father's office door was ajar as he limped up the corridor, gripping tightly at his cane's handle.

"... two years, and of course, before the war, I was valet for Lord Loxley's eldest son, Mr Bispham."

"Oh, we needn't take pains over your curriculum vitae, Mr Sutton – anyone your uncle would recommend, we would of course be glad to snap up, let alone a man of the same bloodline. I believe he's spoken with you already about the house?"

"I have the maintenance schedule, the grocery order, the servants' schedule. My uncle informs me that in recent years the wine cellar has been neglected owing to his ailing vision, and he requested that I devote some time to setting it in order."

"Oh," Alexos heard his father say. "Well. I don't know about that, Mr Sutton. I don't drink wine."

"But I do," said Alexos, appearing in the doorway, and his father looked up at him with a little, absentminded smile. "As does Mother, and as do our guests, Father. Your aversion is not a universal one."

"My son, Alexos Fox," his father said affectionately, and Alexos stepped over the threshold of his office.

Harry Sutton, who had been standing in the open doors to the balcony and overlooking the grounds, stepped in from the bright sunlight outside, and Alexos' eyes took a moment to adjust to looking at him without the light skewing his vision.

His mouth, all at once, went very, very dry.

He had seen, over the years, quite a few of Mr Sutton's nephews. He had close to thirty nieces and nephews, owing to his having five brothers each possessed of apparently prodigious fertility, and many of these nephews were devastatingly attractive, not that Alexos went out of his way to dwell on it.

Really, he did his best *not* to.

It seemed as though every other day he read another case of a gentleman being tried and sentenced for some act of sodomy or other, and one of the few benefits of the relative isolation he had adopted for himself, lingering at home with his family and his research, was in avoiding any sort of temptation.

It wasn't yet a crime to *think* of men, though he tried his best not to, had no particular wish to add additional temptations to his day. But how could one not, when nephews like Mr Sutton's existed?

Of the nephews he'd met, Harry Sutton, it seemed to Alexos – at least it seemed to his breath, which had stopped fast in his lungs, to his heart, which was speeding its pace in his chest, and to his cheeks, which were burning – was the most tempting of all.

He was a tall man, two inches taller than Alexos himself, fat, with a broad chest and huge shoulders. Alexos did not know if his suit was tightly tailored or if it was simply that the style of the modern butler's suit was not intended for a man so incredibly packed with brawn: either way, he could see the way his sleeves tightened into the great bulk of his arms, his waistcoat and shirt barely holding back the wonder of his barrel chest, and most tremendous of all, his trousers.

The butler's legs were woefully – or perhaps, mercifully – obscured by the length of his tailcoat, but Alexos could see the way his trousers hugged in against his thick thighs and tightened in toward the ankle, so that his legs formed a sort of Bermuda Triangle, a dangerous territory one would like to perish within the borders of.

Alexos felt slightly light-headed.

"My uncle ever sings your praises, Mr Fox," said Sutton, putting out one beefy hand to shake. Alexos stared at it a moment – he was a tall man himself, but lithe, and although Sutton's fingers were the same length as his, his hand was almost twice the size of Alexos' own.

He had a strong, powerful grip as he shook Alexos' hand, his skin warm and dry and rough with scars, and as he withdrew his hand his thumb stroked incidentally over Alexos' wrist. It made his head spin, and he struggled to force the blood out of wherever it had wandered off to and back to his tongue, so that he could try to speak again.

"It's a pleasure to meet you," said Sutton before he could manage it.

"And... and you," Alexos said, more aware than ever of his own voice, which had a naturally slightly rasping quality that was only made worse, he knew, by the amount he drank.

Sutton had a low, fruity voice that sounded rather like how port would sound, Alexos thought, if port had a voice – it was Dionysian in its melody and its rhythm and its sheer intoxicating quality, and he swallowed hard, glancing to his father.

"You have everything all in order, I expect?" he asked.

"Almost everything," his father said. "I was explaining to Mr Sutton that your mother isn't often here."

"I am informed Mrs Fox is a novelist of tremendous aptitude and flair, Mr Fox," said Sutton as Alexos looked anywhere but his face, which unfortunately included his chest, thighs, and hands, all of which were too overwhelming with which to cope, and he busied himself moving to examine some of the old photographs on the wall.

The Alexos in the photos was a brightly smiling child, and Alexos had never failed to notice that in many of the photos his father displayed – owing to his mother's editing of them, he expected, more than a preference of his father's – his legs were somehow obscured, a blanket over his knees or his body behind a chair or a tree trunk, that the camera should not catch a glimpse of his braces.

"Quite," Alexos said. "She is often abroad, Mr Sutton. I'm afraid you shall have to make do with myself and Father most of the time."

"I'm sure I shall incur no trouble on your account, Mr Fox," said the butler mildly. "My uncle advised that each of the gentlemen of the house had business pursued within the bounds of the home."

"That's right," said Father pleasantly. "We own a small factory and have investments in a handful of other business, which I keep track of; Alexos is a student of classics, and is an author in his own right."

"Is that so?" asked Mr Sutton, in a voice which curled around the base of Alexos' spine and threatened to make its home there. "It seems in joining your household, Mr Fox, my reading list increases exponentially. Ought I presume that you have books in print too, Mr Fox?"

His father laughed.

"No, my head is for numbers, not letters, Mr Sutton – or at least, not words. I've always been quite at home with algebra. But Alex here, he writes exceedingly well."

"My father flatters. It was, ah, a pleasure to meet you, Mr Sutton. With my work in mind, however, I'm afraid I must back to the library."

"Won't you show me, Mr Fox?" asked Sutton, and Alexos whipped to look at him, feeling more colour rise in his cheeks.

Mr Sutton did not at all resemble his uncle.

Apart from his body, he had a square face, a sharp jaw with a cleft in his chin, and a heavy brow, and he had a healthy, handsome colour to his face, but not the apple red his uncle carried in his cheeks. His hair was a tawny brown, neatly combed, and he had forest green eyes which were heavily lidded and decorated with long lashes. Mr Sutton had a sort of exacting gaze that Alexos felt he could dissipate, melt, or otherwise liquefy under, and he was liquefying swiftly under it now, because Mr Sutton's gaze was fixed on him.

"No," Alexos heard his own hoarse voice say. "I'm afraid I simply have— far too much work to be getting on with. See you."

He moved so fast he lost his balance, putting his cane down with the wrong foot, and his left knee buckled when it took all of his weight unexpectedly. He let out a hissed cry of pain, and as he crumpled to one knee, the great figure of Mr Sutton came in behind him, gently grasping him by the elbows and lifting him up.

A great bear of a man, he exuded warmth, and Alexos had to bite back a squeak as he hurried out of the room, moving so fast he couldn't even mumble out a thank you. He took a few moments in the corridor, leaning one shoulder against the wall and doing his best to collect himself before he inflicted the stairs on his aching knees.

He wouldn't go back to the library after all, he didn't think – he would retire to his bedroom for an hour and rest.

"I do hope I did nothing to offend your son, Mr Fox," he heard Sutton say.

"He doesn't mean anything by it," his father replied. "Your uncle didn't speak in detail about his condition, I suppose?"

"I wouldn't presume to ask, Mr Fox," said the butler.

"No, no," said Father. "We make no secret of it, Sutton. Alexos was quite sick with polio, as a young boy – we were very lucky, and he's mostly recovered, but he's prone to sudden fits of fatigue, and his joints are weak, particularly on the left side. He's a little embarrassed of it at times, that's all – please don't take it as some personal slight when he needs a moment to himself."

"Not at all, Mr Fox," said Sutton.

It was better than when his mother talked about it, Alexos thought disconsolately, and descended the stairs one by one.

The warmth of his bedroom was a welcome relief from the draught in the corridor, and even more wonderfully, his mother's dog, a Basset Hound by the name of Aristaeus, was waiting for him on the bed, and wagged his tail lazily.

"Hullo, Aristaeus," said Alexos, falling onto his back on the bed, and immediately Aristaeus wriggled closer, clambering onto his knees to warm them and laying his chin on Alexos' ankles. The animal had a great fondness for laying on Alexos like this, as though Alexos' straightened legs were a log and he was some sort of jungle cat lying upon it with his legs hanging down.

Alexos had made attempts, over the years, to explain to Aristaeus that he was, in fact, a dog, but the creature had cheese and honey for brains, perhaps owing to his namesake, and never seemed to understand.

"I think this new butler shall be the death of me, you know," Alexos said, ashamed of the wistful note that eked its way into his own voice.

Aristaeus wagged his tail, so that it tickled Alexos' belly, and he laughed, absently scratching the dog's lower back. They dozed together for a time, two classicists as they were, each with their own aching joints.

"Do you ever think about men, Aristaeus?" asked Alexos.

The dog raised his head, turning to glance at him, and hopefully wagged his tail.

"No, I thought not," he said. "You're a wiser man than me."

There was no relief for pained knees quite like a hot water bottle made of dog.

* * *

That evening, Harry sat down at the desk in his bedroom with a page laid out before him. On the other side of the paper were a few lines of vague, rather generalized text bidding his uncle well, and advising that he was installed at the Foxes' safe and sound, and happy indeed to be there.

On this side, in neat and easy code written in invisible ink of his own brewing, he wrote something of actual substance.

Dear Uncle Reg,

I know your feelings toward the young man, being as they are of that paternal lilt, but I think I would be remiss if I didn't point out that you'd rather underestimated – or at least, underdescribed – precisely how handsome young Mr Fox is.

You described him as doe-eyed, as I recall, but I don't believe you noted precisely how wide his eyes are, nor imparted the deep brown of their colour; his lips are far more defined than ever I expected, and although the whole of him seems to be made up of points and sharp angles, particularly in his chin and cheekbones, there is a charming delicacy to his features I should never have expected, as though some dollmaker or similar artist of repute had carved them for the purposes of aesthetic alone.

As you warned me he might be, he was skittish from the very outset, but I don't believe I imagined the fire of interest in his eyes, nor the hungry way he took in the sight of me. It seemed to me in the moment we met that there was a spark of mutual interest, of attraction, and in touching his hand there was a rightness I don't know that I have ever felt before.

Perhaps I am being overly romantic – I know that is a flaw of mine – but he is lovely.

Even as I write this, I think of how lonely he must be, how he isolates himself, bricking himself in with his books and his paperwork, and I think...

Well.

You know what I think, Uncle.

I shall, of course, keep you abreast of some developments – I know that this is no guarantee, that I might well be entirely imagining that he likes the look of me as much as I do of him, but I do hope that is not the case.

He's so lovely, after all. I know it would be my loss.

I shall sign off here and put myself to bed. A bright and exciting morning beckons, I think.

Affectionately,

Harry

Setting the letter down to dry, he turned out the lamp, and crawled into the warmth of his bed.

On the other side of the wall beside him, he knew – unless he was still in the library – Alexos Fox was probably lying in his own bed.

The happy thought led to easy and pleasant dreams.

Chapter Two

Alexos would never get married.

He had resigned himself to this fact quite a long time ago, the first time he was eleven or twelve and sitting on the bench as the other boys played cricket, the summer heat making him feel sweaty and uncomfortable. The leather of his braces stuck and shifted against his skin, and the metal just felt so heavy, and his legs felt even sorer than usual.

Sitting there in a white shirt and shorts that did little to hide the frame holding him upright, he'd watched Mr Wickers, one of their schoolmasters, in his full cricket whites, and the way the sweat made his shirt cling tight to his body and go almost transparent so that you could see his chest hair through the cloth—

He'd been aware even then, before then, even, that he felt the certain way about Mr Wickers that most of the young men playing cricket felt about young ladies, and knew, too, that he felt nothing about young ladies at all.

Well, that wasn't entirely true.

He quite liked Audrey Jones, who used to regularly come around to the house when she'd still lived nearby – the two of them had learned to play Bridge, and had set themselves to compete against her aunts, who'd been delighted.

But he did not kid himself that his enjoyment at playing cards with a young lady was the same as more masculine desires – in his case, very masculine desires indeed.

He wasn't handsome, he didn't think, or at least, not handsome enough to draw undue attention. He had examined his face in the mirror, from time to time, and although he felt he had been drawn with a cartoonist's proportions, God's own precursor to the funny pages, he did not feel he was ugly. He was fine, he thought, and drew no especial attention one way or the other.

Many was the time that he had come along to a luncheon or a party where a pretty girl had laid eyes on him and he had seen the look in her eyes as she glanced around at all the very handsome men already speaking with other girls. Many was the time he had seen that moment of consideration, of careful thought as they looked at his face, thinking as to whether they found him handsome or the opposite – which never offended him, because he looked at men in much the same way, from time to time. It brought him great comfort, the moment where such women nodded to themselves or smiled, thinking to approach him, took one or two steps, and then their gazes flitted down to the cane he leaned on, and their cautious interest evaporated like mist.

And perhaps, perhaps, he exaggerated the extent to which he relied on his cane from time to time.

Certainly, he needed an aid and needed it quite keenly, even walking the corridors of his own house, but he had caught himself hunching his shoulders or making it appear that he was leaning more heavily upon it when someone looked at him for too long.

Perhaps he restrained himself from bobbing along to the music, even when it was a nice song, in order to dissuade anyone from asking him to dance. Perhaps he sat down a great deal, and always hovered off to the side...

But there weren't so many dances these days, even with the war having finished – or at least, not so many that Alexos accepted invitations to.

He missed, at times, the bustle of university. He'd liked living on the campus, had enjoyed taking up with other young men even with all the temptations this came with, seeing the young Austrian gentleman across the hall who had a habit of playing his cello almost undressed, for example, sweat glistening on his flesh in an enticing way that made one want to lean in and *lick*.

Alexos opened his eyes, staring up at the ceiling, and shifted uncomfortably, pressing the heel of his palm down between his legs in a useless attempt to stave off his erection.

He'd laid for a long time in a sort of dreamy daze, and his mind had strayed to the figure of Henry Sutton, his great breast, his shoulders, his arse, his thighs. He was a big man. Alexos wondered what his skin was like, under his clothes, if he was a bear of a man thick with hair all over or if it was about his body in patches, at his chest and his navel or on sections of his arms.

He wondered if he had a big cock.

Probably.

This was not, in any way whatsoever, convincing his own cock it was best to calm down, but before he could weaken and wrap his hand around himself, there was a crisp, quiet knock at the door, and Brydon walked in.

"You're awake, Mr Fox," he remarked as he went to pull open the curtains, letting bright sunshine into the room. "I've a bath run for you, but it might be a little hot – there's space enough to pour some cold in if you want to get in right away."

Brydon was his father's valet, but he had made it his habit to assist Alexos in the mornings – Alexos woke an hour or so earlier than his father, most days, and he tried not to take too much of the man's busy schedule. It wasn't as though he really needed assistance dressing himself or picking out his clothes – the most difficult thing was carrying things about with his limp.

He always laid out the next morning's clothes in the evening himself, and Brydon took the pile from on top of his dresser.

"I'll set this on the bathroom table, sir. Any particular requests for breakfast?"

"Not at all," said Alexos softly. "I trust Mrs Perry's judgement."

Brydon gave him a small smile – they had this conversation, in some form or other, every morning.

"Has our new Mr Sutton been barking orders at you?" Alexos asked, rubbing at his eye as he sat clumsily up in bed and felt the sun on his face.

"He's remarkably well-scheduled," Brydon said thoughtfully, considering the question. "A regimented man – your father mentioned he was a lieutenant in the army, but it seems to be he schedules his day to the minute. Military *is* the word for it."

"He's demanding the same of you?"

"No, not demand – he hasn't been unpleasant about it at all. I rather get the impression, Mr Fox, that he is trying to capture the best spirit of our schedules to see where they might intersect with his own. Do you need anything from him?"

"No, no," said Alexos, rolling his shoulders and beginning his morning stretches before he got out of bed. "Not at all. Thank you, Brydon."

He stepped into the bath with the water still a little too hot, feeling the scalding heat against his legs, the sudden stinging pain on his skin being replaced with utter bliss as the hot water seeped further into his flesh, into his *bones*, and soothed the ache in them.

Closing his eyes, he rested his head back, sinking into the salted water and sighing blissfully.

He stewed for some time in the relaxing heat before he washed his hair and scrubbed himself clean, and then stood up to get himself dry, pulling his clothes on and making to comb his hair. His hair was still somewhat damp when he descended the stairs to breakfast and found, as ever, that his father had yet to rise. They always set two place settings, but inevitably, Alexos' was taken away before his father even sat down to his.

He ate his breakfast in silence whilst idly paging through the newspaper, and when the door opened, he glanced toward the clock on the mantel, surprised that his father should already be awake, but it was Mr Sutton who made his way in.

"Oh," said Alexos chewing and swallowing a little bit harder than he meant to. "Good morning, Sutton."

"Good morning, Mr Fox," said Sutton pleasantly, his hands folded in front of his belly. He was dressed in a very fine morning suit, and Alexos distantly wondered if the tight white waistcoat was new, if he'd gotten it for his new position as butler, or if he'd already had it, and it was simply once reserved for special occasions until now. "Does breakfast meet with your approval?"

"Oh, yes, of course, always," said Alexos, feeling himself sit up a little straighter. "I know it's a little odd, but with just me and Father in the house, it's just easier if Mrs Perry serves us a plate each rather than bother with all the serving platter palaver. We normally only take out the service if we've guests."

"Mr Brydon advised me of that," said Sutton. "And Mrs Perry told me that yourself and your father each trust her judgement in filling a breakfast plate for you, that neither of you have any particular preferences except for a hot breakfast."

"That's right," Alexos said. "Mrs Perry rather knows us inside out."

"Do forgive me for inquiring, Mr Fox – I am merely doing my best to accurately make my surmise of the routines and schedules of the household, that I not interrupt happy processes in a push for efficiency. I confess myself to be a far more rigid man than my uncle, and I'm afraid I greatly crave predictability in my day to day."

"Don't we all," Alexos said weakly, trying not to dwell overmuch on the word "rigid" pronounced in Sutton's rich voice.

"I'm disturbing you," said Sutton softly, tilting his head slightly and raising his perfectly kept eyebrows. "Perhaps I ought make my inquiries of you later today?"

"No, no, now is— now is quite alright, Sutton," said Alexos, cutting a piece of bacon on his plate.

"I merely wished to know if you would want to oversee my work in the cellar, sir. I understand that your father has no interest in wine, and in the absence of Mrs Fox, I should think that in organising the cellar I ought tailor my curation to your tastes. You are a young gentleman, no doubt with a sophisticated tongue, and I would like to keep your pleasure in mind."

Alexos swallowed again, despite having nothing in his mouth to swallow but spit.

The idea of being down in the cool air of the cellar with Sutton, where the racks were very tightly packed in very thin corridors a man like Sutton would have to go down sideways, even without Alexos beside him, was an exercise in imagination in itself.

"Oh," he demurred hurriedly, "I shouldn't worry about me, Mr Sutton, I'm sure you're very knowledgeable about— about wine, I should happily trust you to distinguish what will make the best addition and investment to the cellar."

"Wine is to be drunk, Mr Fox, not merely collected," Sutton said wisely. Alexos was trying not to look at his face. "After all, the bottles are quite handsome in their neat racks, but are not truly appreciated until the lip of a glass kisses our own, that the wine might flow between them. What sort of wines do you like most?"

"I'm sure I like all sorts, Sutton," Alexos said, aware that he sounded slightly weak. "As I said, I should trust your judgement to put good wine in front of me as I trust Mrs Perry to deliver good food."

"But Mrs Perry has had years to ascertain what pleases you best, Mr Fox," said Sutton reasonably, as Alexos pressed his knees together under the table. "I should like very much to learn how to please you best."

Alexos inhaled very slowly through his nose, doing his very best not to be too obvious about it, and he finally looked to Sutton's face instead of his plate. There was no hint of innuendo or implication drawing on the butler's expression, no hidden smirk, no raised eyebrow: Sutton's face was entirely polite and respectable, as befitting a man of his station, and merely exuded a sort of attentiveness.

Because Sutton *was* polite and respectable, and *was* paying keen attention.

He wanted to do well in his new position without being ogled by the young man of the house, and if he had the slightest idea what thoughts were currently running through Alexos' mind, like the Olympians naked and glistening with olive oil, he would probably beat him senseless.

Before him in the paper were a few articles about recent sodomy trials, each of which he had done his best to page past without letting himself read through them. Sometimes, his horror manifested in a sort of helpless, masochistic curiosity, and he let himself read every word of the little articles to their completion. With that done, the words would linger with him as though he had carved them into his skin – and smart as if he had, too.

He'd never been beaten.

He'd never so much as kissed another man, although certainly he'd wanted to – a handful of times at university, he'd ventured out with some of the more obvious young men on the circuit, allowed himself to be swept along to certain secreted little places, in backrooms or down alleyways. He never really involved himself in the action of everything, often just sat aside and watched, too cowardly to attempt a seduction of anyone, and—

Well.

Once or twice, someone his age would sit on his knee and play with his hair and be terribly, *terribly* nice, and it—

It never seemed to go anywhere. He never knew how to make it go anywhere, or if he even wanted to risk it. It was bad enough he was always bristling with anxiety just dipping into one of those speakeasies, fully aware that if it was raided, as they apparently were from time to time, he'd never have a chance at outrunning the police.

"Sir?" asked Sutton, and Alexos looked up from his plate. Sutton's polite attentiveness had morphed into something more concentrated – concern.

"I do beg your pardon, Sutton," said Alexos hurriedly, wiping his hands and pushing his plate aside. "I'm rather in my own head this morning. I've a lot of work to be getting on with."

"Very good, sir," said Sutton, and as Alexos put his fork and knife on top of his plate, ready to hold the whole of it in one hand to carry into the other room, Sutton interrupted him, and swept the plate out from his grip. His fingers brushed Alexos', warm even through his gloves, and Alexos let out a tiny exhalation.

"Thank you," said Alexos briskly, and picked up his cane to go upstairs.

He wrote in blissful silence, buried in his work, for some hours afterward, and tuned out the world the best he could.

* * *

It was a nice house, Harry thought.

The Bisphams' home was not so much a house and more a manor, with some dozens of rooms. Complicated corridors with servants' walkways to accommodate a servant moving out of sight ran through the different wings, and whilst he had appreciated the shortcuts from side to side, he'd always struggled somewhat with them, the side corridors being built so narrowly they scarcely accommodated a wide dinner tray, let alone a wide valet.

The Fox House was far less hyperbolic in its size: the three floors were neatly laid out, sensibly and efficiently designed, and while there was one back stairway that led into the servants' bedrooms upstairs, it wasn't so narrow one had to sidle down it with one's elbows forward.

Harry's room was right beside Alexos', although they were accessed from entirely different corridors and directions. It was a comfortable room with a strong, plush bed, a good writing desk, space to move within the room, and the window gave a neat view of the grounds, much the same view Alexos had, when he woke up.

Harry rather liked the symmetry in that.

Breakfast was a strange affair indeed – his uncle had advised him that Alexos was a repressed young man, that he was unlikely to flirt without hesitation, but Harry hadn't realised he wouldn't even recognise it for what it was. Harry had rather thickly layered double entendre into his words, and how interesting it had been to see Alexos shift and squirm in his seat, to press his knees together, for his hands to tremble, for his ears to turn pink.

Would he be so shy, so retiring, when Harry had him undressed and bent him over the nearest hard surface, when he had Harry's cock buried in him, Harry fucking him hard enough that he could taste it? Would he blush when Harry fingered him open, when Harry swallowed his cock into his mouth?

It was arrogant of him, to think of *when* instead of *if*, but a man had to have some hopes in life, and watching Alexos walk away from him, his grip tight on his cane, the back of his neck ruddy with rushing blood—

How could Harry think of anything but fucking the young master senseless?

That morning, Harry sat down with the whole silver service a to inventory and polish it all. It was kept in good order, of course, but as soon as Mrs Perry had advised they didn't often use the full service he had wanted to inspect the whole of it, and as he had worried, the larger serving dishes had a little tarnish on them, though nothing extreme.

This was a house of certain binary extremes – Mrs Fox demanded a great deal; the two Messrs Fox requested a certain modesty of service. When Mrs Fox was home, the house was continuously entertaining, the guest bedrooms full, using the larger dinner and tea services, laying out a tight schedule of luncheons, dinners, walks, picnics, and parties; when she was abroad and it was just the two gentlemen, they received almost no visitors whatsoever, and rarely received so much as an aunt as an overnight guest on her way up to London.

It took him a few hours to finish his work, and then he set all the everyday silver away in its cabinet, making a note in his diary to add it to his schedule on a regular basis, as the plates in the back weren't to be inspected as regularly as the others. It would do no huge damage to the silver, of course – it was a hardwearing substance, and tarnish was primarily an aesthetic flaw, so long as it wasn't allowed to deepen, but in the event they had sudden and unexpected guests, he hardly wanted for anyone to have to sit down and spend twice as much time as expected on the platters.

He liked for time to be accounted for.

Already, moving through the house, he was making his own quiet calculations as to how quickly certain journeys might be made, from his bedroom down to the entrance hall, from the servants' quarters to the servants' hall, from the kitchen to the dining room, and so on and so forth.

His pocket watch was an ever present comfort against his heart, had been since his uncle had given it to him years ago, and his affection for his timepiece had only deepened with the years, although there was glancing damage to its side, where a piece of shell had glanced off its edge, though luckily done the mechanism no damage.

"Hullo, Mr Sutton," said young Betty politely as he entered the kitchen, apparently finished with her maid's work and now here to learn more of Mrs Perry's craft.

"Good morning, Betty," said Harry pleasantly. "I am told Mr Fox takes his tea at ten-thirty, Mrs Perry."

"I don't know what he notices when he has it, Mr Sutton," was the cook's reply, flour clouding the air in front of her as she continued to knead tomorrow's bread under strong fingers. "He'll have his head in them books and won't even know the time unless the gong sounds or someone pats him on the shoulder. There's a pastry in the cold cabinet for him, or biscuits in the larder."

"Has he a preference?" Harry asked, taking the hot water off the stove and filling a pot.

"He doesn't really notice that either," said Betty sheepishly when Mrs Perry scoffed and didn't turn around to answer him. "He just sort of eats while working, Mr Sutton, a bit mechanically. I don't know that the modern world exists for him when he's wrapped up with Homer and his friends."

"Mr Fox has been known to say he yearns for a time before timepieces, Mr Sutton," said Brydon as he entered, and Harry handed him the rest of the hot water, watching him pour tea for Fox Senior.

"That does disturb me," Harry admitted, and Brydon laughed, nodding his head. The two of them worked in neat parallel to one another, setting tea trays for a Fox each, although Harry saw that Fox Snr *did* have a preference for what he took with his tea, as Brydon put together a cucumber sandwich and cut it diagonally in two, placing it on a plate with a napkin.

"We have to keep on top of him if he has an appointment and gets to working," said Brydon quietly, with a rueful smile. "But he doesn't do it on purpose – he and his father share a tendency to singular purpose, when left to their work. I will say, the son isn't quite so scatterbrained as his father, once you rouse him to the modern day."

"My uncle did warn me of Fox Senior's absent-minded nature," said Harry. "And he doesn't have any preferences for wine, so he tells me."

"Mr Fox takes what he's given," Brydon said, a little more quietly now, and his tone was almost solemn when he said, "Young Mr Fox is a very kind gentleman, Mr Sutton, but he's not like many men his age. He's very keenly aware of other people and their needs, but I fear he has a bad habit of ignoring his own."

"He's insular is what he is," grunted Mrs Perry. "What he needs is friends."

"Hasn't he got any?" asked Harry.

"He has a few pen pals from university," said Brydon. "But he tends to keep to himself."

"Hardly becoming of a young heir," said Harry, and Brydon laughed.

"You've a job convincing him of what he should become, Mr Sutton," said Brydon, not without affection. "I don't envy you the task."

Harry picked up his tray and made the ascent to the library, where the junior Mr Fox was at work.

True to what Mr Brydon had told him, Alexos didn't even look up from his papers as Harry leaned on the door with his shoulders to push it open, making his way inside. The library dominated the first floor, a great, sprawling room with floor-to-ceiling shelves, a few sofas to the edge about the fire.

Mr Fox had said that they entertained in here from time to time, that it was a comfortable place to settle with guests when not downstairs in the dining room or the parlour, but that most of the time, it was Alexos' space as Mr Fox's office was his.

In the centre of the room was a long table with a few chairs around it, the sort of thing he would expect of a public library rather than installed in a private home, but Alexos' studies were spread out along it, several books and manuscripts open with different pages marked.

Alexos' cane was resting in a little hook that stood out from one corner of the desk – Uncle Reggie had advised that there were a lot of little flourishes throughout the house for purposes like this – and the man himself was leaning forward, a frown pulling at his mouth, his brow deeply furrowed. His eyes flitted back and forth over the page in front of him, and his notes, Harry noticed, were not in English but in an easy and sweeping Greek, his wrist lifted from the page and his elbow at an odd angle.

He was nervous of staining his sleeves, Harry suspected – Alexos had stripped off his jacket, laying it over the back of another chair, and thus down to his shirt sleeves, he had carefully rolled his cuffs up to his elbows, pinning them there to ensure he didn't get any ink on the white fabric.

He had fine, delicate wrists, though Harry was glad to see he wasn't quite so thin as he looked at a glance – Alexos had a habit of somewhat shrinking into his clothes, making himself appear smaller than he truly was, but although he was thin, he didn't seem unhealthily so.

Harry set the tea tray down on a side table and stepped forward: even when he stood directly beside the young master, he didn't stir or look up from his work until Harry cleared his throat.

He expected the other man to jump or startle, but he did no such thing: the way he suddenly lifted his head and peered around was reminiscent of a rabbit or a deer, his body and shoulders still, and when his gaze landed on Harry, he straightened up, leaning away from his notes.

"I've tea for you, sir," said Harry mildly. "Where do you prefer to take it?"

"Oh," said Alexos quietly, setting his pen aside and leaning back in his chair. "There's a folding table against the fireplace there, do you see it?"

"Of course," Harry said, and took up the folding table, his palm sliding over the leather surface, feeling the neat clasps for the purposes of holding the tea tray in place.

His brother, John Edmund, a smith, had made this. There were a few of them dotted around the house – they made it easier on the young master, Uncle Reggie had said when he'd paid John to make them, when he couldn't move well on hard days and he needed a table close by.

"On my right, please," said Alexos.

"You write with your left hand, sir," observed Harry as he pulled the lever on the table and set it down, and he watched the sweet flush that began to gather in Alexos' cheeks, like reddening clouds with the sunrise.

"Yes, well," Alexos said quietly. "My mother harboured doubts as to my learning to hold a pen at all, and certain allowances were made. My schoolmasters were frightened to beat me."

"I've never heard of a schoolmaster frightened to beat his charge," said Harry with an easy smile laying the tray down and clipping it into place, and Alexos laughed quietly.

"I think they were frightened of the result that came of it, Sutton – that is to say, my mother's wrath."

"There are few things quite so frightening, sir."

"Quite right, Sutton," said Alexos softly, and he drew his hands neatly into his lap, watching as Harry poured tea for him. "Thank you."

"Does this time suit you well for tea, Mr Fox?" asked Harry.

Quite delightfully, quite wonderfully, for all he disliked the reason, Alexos blinked. "What time is it?" he asked, and looked to the clock on the wall. He didn't wear a watch of his own, Harry noted. "Oh. Yes, that's quite alright, Sutton. Thank you. The dog didn't follow you up?"

"I haven't seen him, sir."

"You couldn't call him as you go, could you?"

"If the pastry does not meet with your approval, Mr Fox, I would bring you another," said Harry teasingly, daringly. "You needn't give it to the dog."

"The pastry...?" Alexos glanced to the plate, and then laughed breathlessly: once more, he was shy and sweet, avoiding Harry's gaze, and the blush in his cheeks deepened. "I assure you Aristaeus will receive not a crumb, Sutton," he said softly. "My feet are cold, that's all."

"I'll put more wood on the fire, sir."

"It's not the room, Sutton, it's my blood," said Alexos, more quietly now, with a subdued resignation. "The dog will help."

"Very well, sir," said Harry, noting the sobriety in the young master's tone, and he pushed open the door, whistling for the dog.

The tubby little hound's claws skittered on the stairs as he rushed upstairs, and he stopped to allow Harry to scratch his ears before he wandered in, dropping onto his belly at Alexos' feet, which slipped from his shoes and rested on his back.

There was something uniquely endearing in it.

"Do ring if you require anything, Mr Fox," said Harry.

Alexos had already returned to his work, teacup held in his free hand, and didn't seem to hear him.

Chapter Three

Alexos was breathing heavily, his shoulders pressed back so hard against the wall that he almost felt as though their blades would pierce his own skin. All of his weight was on his back and his good leg, his cane lost somewhere else, because Alexos couldn't keep hold of his cane at a time like this: his hands were splayed on Sutton's great breast, his fingers sliding over the sweat-slick skin there – Mr Sutton's hair grew in patches after all – and doing their best to hold him back.

Sutton's hands were braced either side of Alexos' head, and Sutton was leaning in, his lips curled into the smallest of easy smiles, his eyes gleaming with desire.

"May I, sir?" he was asking softly, the sound of his port-rich voice soaking into Alexos' ears and rendering him even more drunk in feeling than he already was. "Won't you allow me, sir, to kiss you? To embrace you?"

"You mustn't, you mustn't, Sutton, you mustn—"

"I must *kiss* you," said Sutton. "I feel it will be terrible for my health if I don't, Mr Fox."

Alexos' cheeks were burning, every inch of his skin flushed, and there was a heat pooling between his legs that filled him to the brim and over with shame, made all his hair stand on end, made him feel as though he would tremble completely to pieces.

"Mr Sutton," he begged again, "Mr Sutton, please—"

And before he could finish his sentence, Sutton's mouth was crushing into his, and Alexos was whining from low in his throat, whining sharply and desperately, so much that it felt like a keen.

It was the sound of this noise, he suspected later, that woke him from his dreams and made him sit up straight in his bed, soaked to the skin and *sticky*, and he put his head in his hands, exhaling hard.

Limping from his bed, he dropped his stained pyjama trousers directly into a basin of water to soak, and then he leaned awkwardly on the edge of his bed, wrestling with the bedclothes and stripping off their sheets, leaving it all in a messy pile before he went into the bathroom to start running hot water into his bath.

He jarred his leg twice in his haste, each time sending a painful bolt of juddering heat up his leg and right up his body, such that it chattered his teeth and made him grunt in pain, but he set the bath running nonetheless, and then went into the other room again. He scrubbed at his pyjama bottoms with a nail brush before he tossed them into the pile with his sheets, and dragged off his pyjama shirt to join them.

It was an awkward, clumsy carry-on, and he hated how embarrassed he felt even knowing there was no one to witness his fumbling – and hopefully never would be, given as he had no intentions to marry, and had never seen fit to have a valet of his own. His skin was heated with shame and lingering arousal and humiliation, and he tossed the heavy outer blanket to the side of the bed, so that when the maid came into the room later, she would see that the bed had been stripped and needed new clothes.

"The young master," he imagined Brydon telling Sutton quietly, in that subtle and quiet way Brydon had, "is prone to sudden fevers and night sweats, especially when it's cold and his pain is at its worst. Now and then, he experiences bouts of somnambulism – these aren't in themselves dangerous, of course, but in young Mr Fox's case, he often sleepwalks without the use of his cane, and wakes when he falls."

Sutton already knew about the somnambulism, of course – or so Alexos thought, anyway. He'd had a bout last week and had come to on the stairs, luckily with his cane in hand, and Sutton had stopped on the landing underneath him, looking his way. He hadn't come up to find him, and Alexos didn't think he'd made a great deal of noise – it was simply dumb luck, or the lack thereof.

"Are you well, sir?" he'd asked, candle in hand, looking as though he were about to turn in for bed himself. "Walking in your sleep?"

Alexos had been too groggy to string sufficient words together to answer him, had simply nodded and gone back to his bed, but that didn't mean Sutton knew that he was so stupid in his dreams sometimes, he forgot his legs couldn't carry his weight.

Shaking his head now, he drained the basin of the dirtied water and went into the bathroom, running the cold tap alongside the hot to cool down the liquid steam filling the tub. Clouds of it were thick in the room, leaving condensation on the floor, and the tile was slippery: it was on this that he fell hard, and couldn't contain his shout of shock and pain.

It was only a little past five in the morning, and he swore profusely, cursing every inch of the tile he was stood on and slapping his palm hard against it – swore so profusely, in fact, that instead of coming directly in, he was fairly certain Sutton paused at the bathroom door, because when he knocked, it was hesitant, and didn't come until Alexos paused in his outpouring of profanity to catch his breath.

"Sir?" he called. "Have you need of assistance?"

Alexos dragged himself to the bathroom mat, which someone always laid down for him in the evenings in case he took an early morning bath like this one, and tried to push himself to his feet. He managed to get his good knee bent under him, but when he tried to pull himself to his feet his left leg spasmed under his weight, and he collapsed onto the floor again.

"I'm afraid so, Mr Sutton," he called back, and the door opened with a neat turn of the knob. "I'm quite undressed," said Alexos miserably, more to the white side of the bath than to Sutton himself, his arms hooked over its edge. "Could you just support me into the tub? The hot water will set me to rights."

"Is it cool enough?" asked Sutton, coming from the clouds of white steam toward him like some hero from the fog, and Alexos stared up at him from the other side of the bath, watching as he bent neatly at the portly waist to put his fingers in the water. "*Sir*," he said, almost as scaldingly as the water he'd tested, whipping his hand back. "I will not assist you of a morning by setting you to broil."

"It will help," said Alexos powerlessly.

Sutton turned up the cold tap and turned off the hot, and as Alexos watched powerlessly from his place on the floor, he poured some salts into the water. "Sleepwalking again?" he asked quietly.

Sutton's time thus far in the Fox household had given him a little more understanding of their eccentricities, Alexos knew – he had not delved with great interest into the new scheduling of the household's processes, but at such a time as he noticed the chiming of the hour, immediately after came a sudden bustle and surge of new activity, as everyone moved precisely with the time. He had overheard the gardener, Tom, speaking with some approval to the footman, a clumsy but affable young lad named Felix, that Felix had been coming on in leaps and bounds, and Felix had said Mr Sutton scheduled an hour to work with him every day, and that he was very grateful.

They did all seem to like Sutton for the most part – he'd heard Mrs Perry complain about Sutton reorganising the larder, even though part of this had been putting in more shelves suited to Mrs Perry's height, and Sutton had quarrelled with Tom about coming into the house in his mud-stained trousers, although Alexos didn't know the precise nature of that disagreement, nor its resolution.

He *did* know that Sutton had wrought a lot of changes in his time thus far, and that he seemed to be well-suited to his position, as much as his uncle had been.

He hadn't yet, of course, had to assist Alexos like this – Reginald Sutton had had to help him not irregularly, but ordinarily, it was

Brydon, and whenever it was Felix or one of the maids that knocked when he fell, regardless of his state of dress, Alexos asked that they fetch him.

It wasn't about modesty or care for being seen in his bedclothes – it was more the shame of it, and the nasty mood it put him in. It was bad enough that the rest of the house sometimes saw him fall on the stairs or stumble elsewhere, but he looked at his most pathetic in the mornings, and when he fell on the stairs, at least it looked suitably dramatic. When he fell in the bathroom or the bedroom and needed help, it was normally a bad fall, and when he didn't feel as pitiable as he did right now, he just tended to an unpleasant and off-putting anger.

"I slipped," said Alexos. He felt like drowning in shame – he'd wiped off the stains from his thighs and his cock when he'd stripped off his nightclothes, so at least he wasn't wet with his own emissions like he was fresh from some brothel, but this was no great comfort when one was sat on one's arse, wearing not a stitch, and being tended to by one's new butler. "You're a month in, Mr Sutton. Do you find yourself suited to a household made up of one gentleman and his defective son?"

"I couldn't say, sir, belonging to no such household," replied Sutton immediately, with not even the mildest of hesitation, and giving him quite a stern look. "Unless the defect you refer to is self-pity."

Alexos, despite himself, laughed. It was a soft, defeated sound, but to his surprise, just laughing made him feel better, and he watched Sutton's handsome hands dip through the water again, swirling the bubble bath and the salts in the water and spurring the froth to multiply.

"You are your uncle's nephew, Sutton," said Alexos softly. "You scold a man in much the same manner he does." He sighed, pressing his face to the bath's side and trying to ignore the tremors of pain juddering up his side – his bad leg was awkwardly laid at his side, because he hadn't been able to force himself to bend the knee and get it beneath him, but that was not to say that this position was comfortable.

"Shall I fetch you something for the pain?" asked Sutton cautiously.

Sutton didn't have the script for this situation, was feeling out his way – evidently, none of his previous households had featured the presence of infirm, crippled old men, let alone young ones.

"I've no interest in being dashed out of my skull on the codeine all day," muttered Alexos, aware that he was speaking irritably and feeling a distant guilt about it, "and the aspirin won't do much, I'm afraid. The hot water will soothe pain, relax the strained muscle, and hasten the healing process. I just landed badly on already scarred tissue, that's all, Mr Sutton. No sense going to pieces over it."

"You will forgive me, I hope, for not wishing to see my employer in pain," said Sutton slightly coolly.

"You are quite forgiven," said Alexos, breathing in the sweet-smelling steam as it rose from the bath, "but also instructed, without meaning to impugn your good wishes, to buck yourself up. I'm not yet forty, Sutton. I'm only going to get worse. Would you help me to stand?"

"Of course," said Sutton, coming around the edge of the bath.

"Don't put your hands on me, if you don't mind," said Alexos quietly, fighting the urge to turn and suddenly beg Sutton to call for Brydon instead, that he not learn to debase himself for a new assistant. "Just crouch with your arm out, let me put my weight on you. Is that alright?"

Sutton's arm was so strong and solid that Alexos felt as though twenty of him could hang off it whilst being pulled to stand, and Alexos carefully lifted his bad leg into the bath before he sank the rest of his body after it.

The relief was immediate, and he let out a low noise of bliss as the pain faded, his eyes falling closed, even as Sutton turned off the tap.

"I am sorry," said Alexos. "For my poor mood. You've not yet had to see me in this state."

"Why, sir?" asked Sutton, looking down at him with his eyebrows raised, and for the first time this morning Alexos looked properly at his face, at his expression. He didn't look as disgusted or distressed as Alexos had thought he might – but nor was he wearing a butler's mask of neutrality. His gaze was quite active, not shying away from meeting Alexos' own, and his lips were shifted into a small, casual smile. "You forget my uncle advised me precisely as to the household I was entering. You think he forgot to mention my employer's impairments?"

"Having it mentioned that your employer is sickly and frail is one thing," said Alexos. "Peeling him nude and shaking from the bathroom tile and having to drop him into his bath is another – particularly when he is, theoretically, a healthy young man."

"You seem more than healthy to me," said Sutton, with such rich intonation that Alexos was reminded of last night's dreams, and he sank further into his water, feeling his sore knee and hip twinge before soothing further as Sutton moved about the room, picking up towels for him. "Will you take your breakfast in bed, sir?" he asked.

"No, Sutton, I shall take it in the parlour, as I always do."

Sutton hesitated before he started, "But—"

"Yes, yes, I have a sore leg," Alexos said irritably, unable to stop himself, "but I have a cane, too."

Sutton closed his mouth, inclined his head, and went into the other room to fetch Alexos' clothes. Alexos watched his back when he paused in the bedroom doorway, surveying the scene of chaos within, before he went forward.

"I could, of course," he said slowly as he re-entered, setting Alexos' clothes down, "remake your bed with fresh sheets, that you might return to bed nonetheless."

"Mr Sutton," said Alexos.

"Mr Fox," replied Sutton.

"Do you know what would happen if I spent all the day resting in bed and taking my medicine *every* time I took a fall?"

"Why is it, Mr Fox, that I feel some greatly exaggerated imagery of the young master adrift in an opium den is forthcoming?" asked Sutton, arching one eyebrow, and Alexos laughed, picking up a sponge.

"It's not exaggerated," he said. "If I took as much of the codeine as my doctor prescribed me I'd be dead. I've always felt it was a casual ploy at euthanasia on his part, that he might finish the job the polio didn't."

"*Sir?*" asked Sutton, frozen, angry, and abruptly severe, and Alexos waved him down. There was something quite hypnotising in the anger on Sutton's face, not at all like his uncle's was – there was a commanding power in it, the spirit of Ares' own, and Alexos exhaled. He was already red and flushed, and he was spent with his dreams, but nonetheless, there was an allure in Sutton's expression now that made him nauseous with dislike for himself.

"At ease, Lieutenant," he said. "Just a joke."

Sutton adjusted his waistcoat, standing straighter to attention, and Alexos watched him school his expressions into something somewhat less severe, but disapproval still poured from the steep downward curve of his lip and the slight narrow of his eyes. "You don't think that a somewhat dark thing to joke about, sir?"

"I was writing about Thyestes' banquet last night, Mr Sutton, I've no measure for dark," said Alexos, and when Sutton frowned slightly, but didn't seem to immediately understand, he occupied himself with scrubbing down his arms, bruised elbows included, as he explained. "Thyestes and Atreus returned to Pisa following the death of their father, who had banished them for their part in the death of their half-brother, Chrysippus. They quarrelled upon their return – Thyestes stole from his brother a golden ram, the command of which the right to rule was predicated, not to mention seduced his wife. Atreus invited Thyestes to a banquet in his honour, supposedly as a precursor to inviting his brother to rule alongside him, but at this feast served him a meal of his own sons, and wine made rich with their blood."

Sutton stared at him, his lips parted, but then he went slowly to folding Alexos' clothes. "That is very dark," he agreed. "I don't recall the inclusion of that particular tale in Homer."

"It's Seneca," said Alexos. "Euripides, originally, but we don't have the original play, only the fabula cothurnata."

"I don't know much about your work," said Sutton, and Alexos watched the way his own skin turned red at how hard he scrubbed it, dreading getting to his legs – once he'd scrubbed them hard, it would soothe the pain some more in the aftermath, but that didn't make the scrubbing more pleasant. "I am given to understand you are an essayist of some repute, and contribute to various academic publications."

"That's the long and short of it," said Alexos quietly. "I'm a philologist, Mr Sutton. My studies at university were broadly in deciphering one script or other, but most of my work now is in reconstructing text as best we can, comparing different manuscripts and interpretations and seeing what threads remain the same. Euripides is my white whale – or at least, his lost body of work is."

"You mourn the loss of Alexandria every day, I expect," said Sutton, and Alexos sighed, tipping his head back against the bath's curved edge.

"Every day, indeed. There are and were a great many other libraries, but those lost to us are the most painful – Alexandria,

Antioch, Nishapur." Mournfully, he sank further into his waters, and said, "Constantinople."

Sutton chuckled, and Alexos watched him as he poured water and made up shaving cream for him.

"Do you think me very ridiculous, Sutton?" asked Alexos.

"Perhaps somewhat, sir," said Sutton, "but I hope you don't feel it amounts to disapproval."

"If you didn't think me at least a little ridiculous I couldn't trust you," Alexos said. "Even Brydon admits to it, although Felix doesn't."

"Young Felix is a man possessed of immense respect for his betters, Mr Fox," said Sutton after a moment's consideration. "He worries that he will offend."

"As if he could," said Alexos. "I'm sure Brydon has told him that he could call myself or my father a slur to our faces and we'd be like as not to forget it within the hour." Sutton said nothing for a moment, taking great care not to let his expression change, and Alexos asked, "Do I shock you with my plain speaking this morning, Sutton?"

"Only because I have not heard you speak this way before, sir," said Sutton evenly.

"Well, when one needs to be lifted naked from one's bathroom floor one doesn't see the point in holding one's tongue, Sutton," said Alexos. "I am without dignity already."

"Without meaning to impugn your self-pity, sir," said Sutton, making Alexos laugh, "all men are undignified in the privacy of their rooms, whilst bathing and performing their ablutions particularly. You are no less dignified than anyone else I have served."

"You say that now," said Alexos. "What will you do when I fall down the stairs in front of company, or collapse unexpectedly when I stand from the dinner table?"

"I'm sure I'll think of something, sir," said Sutton.

He wasn't like his uncle, but the patter was similar – in its tone, in its comfort, if not in its precise phrasing. "I shouldn't worry, Mr

Sutton," said Alexos quietly. "I'll have calmed down again by later on."

"Mr Brydon informs me you prefer not to be assisted as you dress."

"Mr Brydon informs you correctly."

"Is there no other act of service I might provide you with, sir, before I take my leave?" Mr Sutton asked the question whilst standing directly beside the bath, one of his strong, wonderful hands resting on its curved edge, and Alexos' mouth was dry as he looked from Sutton's calloused fingers and defined knuckles and robust wrist up to Sutton's face. Alexos' spent cock, hidden under the white foam of his bath, gave a valiant twitch, and he allowed himself a moment to imagine drowning himself in the water.

He coughed as he tried to answer, clearing his throat, and said, "Not at all, Mr Sutton, you have serviced me more than enough – that is, I mean to say, you've been quite the, quite the help, I..." He closed his eyes. "Thank you, Sutton. For your words of mild impatience and severity, and lacking in grating sympathy."

"I shall make note of your preference, sir, as I have for your preferred strength of tea."

"You are a star amongst men, Sutton."

"Ring the bell for service if you change your mind about breakfast, sir," said Sutton, and took his leave.

After the door closed, Alexos slipped his hand between his legs, wrapping his hand around his mostly soft cock – and when he stiffened, his hips shifting forward, he immediately regretted it, because his bad leg twinged horribly, and he let himself go.

"Hubris," he said to his bathwater, and sank his head down under the surface.

* * *

"I was about to attend to young Mr Fox and run his bath," said Brydon two hours later, as Harry was straining the wine for dinner into their decanters. "But I see he's already at work in the library."

"His night sweats woke him early," said Sutton, "and he fell in his bathroom. I attended to him at around five o'clock. Does he do that often?"

"Fall? Yes, quite regularly," said Brydon. "He stumbles and falls often – he rights himself if he can, but when he's moving about without his cane, he can fall worse. He fell on the tile?"

"He slipped on the condensation, I think. I felt quite badly for him," said Harry. "He was shame-faced, asking me to help him up, and he seemed quite bitter about it. I didn't want to embarrass him by insisting, but—"

"He ordinarily has the others call for me," said Brydon quietly, leaning on the door with his arms crossed over his chest. In his time at the Fox house thus far, Harry had a growing affection for Brydon – he was an easygoing man, utterly unflappable regardless of what was said to him, and took even apparent insults with calculated good humour. He played for the local darts team and was involved in several card games and gambling dens, and was very popular at several public houses in the area.

Harry knew to treat this with a certain level of caution – Brydon never returned from his nights off in any state of inebriation, and nor had he actually heard rumours of his being particularly *good* at cards, only that he played often and at several tables, but whether it was a vice of alcoholism, gambling, or con artistry, one or any of the others could cause trouble if they applied. Uncle Reg mentioned that from time to time, someone would come around owing Brydon money, and rarely the reverse, but Harry didn't know that he liked that.

"It's a sign of some trust, I think," Brydon went on, "that he let you assist him. I think some part of his honour only allows the house butler and valets to see him so undone – he doesn't even like for his parents to come into his rooms without warning so that they shouldn't see him unwell."

Harry thought of Alexos Fox on his bathroom floor, slumped against the side of his bath in utter defeat. He had found it almost curious, that Alexos made no attempt to hide his body from Harry, not to ask for his banyan or a towel – he was used, as Harry supposed some men of one infirmity or another were, to being seen undressed.

Harry hadn't looked tremendously lasciviously, but of course he had looked: Alexos had had a lovely body, thin but not emaciated, rounder at the middle and the chest. There were scars on the back of his neck, and particularly at his hips and his knees – these were from the braces he'd worn as a child, worn so tightly they bore in places into the flesh, Harry presumed.

He hadn't gotten a glimpse of his cock, but that hadn't mattered. What he had seen were Alexos' flushed cheeks and chest as he sank into his bathwater, heard his quiet moan of pleasure, his soft sighs of satisfaction, seen his eyes close, seen his face go slack. He'd heard him curse from the other side of the door as he'd been passing in the corridor, heard him release a slew of curse words and profanity in English, Latin, and Greek.

Once Harry had spoken to him in the bathroom, all that sharp anger had faded, and he'd seen a sign of Alexos he hadn't before thus far.

Alexos, whilst working or while at breakfast, even at dinner with his father, Harry had observed, was often somewhat out of himself – scatterbrained and distracted, he and his father often dipped in and out of conversation, even with one another, spoke past one another and got excited about their subjects. It wasn't that they didn't listen, Harry didn't think, observing them in conversation with one another. They were simply somewhat chaotic in their natures, and their respective chaoses weren't well combined.

This morning, he had been... *lucid.*

Lucid and focused, yes, but more than that, he had been quite sharp. Brittle, in a vulnerable way, but more than that, he had been rather delightfully cold – each time he had corrected Harry or disagreed with him, a part of Harry had grown only more interested, more curious.

This was part of Alexos' private infirmity, it seemed to him: as he hid his scars and his clumsiness and his injury, like a cat who secreted himself to lick its wounds, he hid this, his sharper attitude, his self-awareness, his... What could one call it?

"Is it the pain that makes him that way?" asked Harry, and Brydon tilted his head slightly to the side, arching one eyebrow in expectation. "This morning, whilst I tended to Mr Fox in his bath, he was... different. Keener, perhaps."

"Nastier?" asked Brydon, and Harry chuckled, but nodded his head. "He thinks it's ungentlemanly – he was scolded for it, as a boy, for being too ungrateful for people's care of him, for being too brutal in conversation. It isn't a lack of tact – he knows precisely what he says, and when he cuts, he knows where he's cutting and how deeply. He gets frustrated with people's pity, but he has been advised this frustration is improper."

"I found I rather liked it," said Harry softly, watching the red wine strain through the muslin cloth and into the decanter as he continued to pour, thick red dripping into the crystal. He thought of Alexos, with his impatient, distracted passion, talking so easily of wine made thick with children's blood, speaking on such a gory story as though anyone should know it, as though it were nothing, as he scrubbed at his arms.

"I do too," said Brydon. "He says very funny things, behind closed doors with one of us, I must say. Nasty things, but funny ones, and true ones, too. Your uncle knew him best, but I do often get the impression there are depths to him that other people aren't privy to – that no one is privy to."

"I'll get those depths out of him yet," said Harry, and Brydon laughed.

"I wish you luck," he said, and Harry smiled to himself, and set the cloth aside.

Chapter Four

In the weeks he had been working for the Foxes, Harry had been watching Alexos more and more closely. He recalled when his uncle had first suggested that he take over the position, that Harry come to the Foxes in Reggie's stead, at such a time as he retired.

Uncle Reg had wanted for him to receive a good promotion, of course, had wanted Harry to have command over a household of his own, to be able to move forward in his career with more experience, but he had wanted also to entrust his position to someone who would understand the family and appreciate them for who they were – who might carry on his work as butler to the same standard for the family he'd served so long, maintaining the wine cellar, well-engaging the other servants.

And might care for Alexos Fox, of course.

Harry remembered when they had first discussed it, the two of them sitting together with a bottle of whiskey between them, when Uncle Reg had said, "You've no young man of your own, have you?"

"I have yet to go out and lasso one," Harry had said, sitting back in his seat with his hands loosely rested over his belly. "Why, you want me to mount one on my wall?"

"You know other men your age who have marriages of one sort or other to one another, who serve in the same household or share lodgings. What I'm suggesting is not so different to your friend Ulysses and that artist he serves, is it?"

"The two of them met by chance – it was fate that introduced them."

"You would trust fate better than your own flesh and blood?"

Harry had laughed, and he'd looked at the other man with care and affection – had listened keenly, carefully, as he'd gone on.

Uncle Reg had laughed, fondly shaking his head. "You oughtn't be alone," he'd said, his voice quiet and thoughtful. Introspective, in its way, although Harry hadn't said so, didn't like to point it out. "It oughtn't be the case that you come to be an old man, with no marriage or connection to a wife, but not to another man either, no intimacy. Even for men such as us, dear boy, there remains a human need for love and affection."

"Love and affection isn't as expensive as you might worry, Uncle."

"Tch, don't be crass, Harry," Reg had said, clucking his tongue. "A marriage you pay for is no marriage at all."

"Something there falls flat, in between what you say," said Harry, "and the Bible, kings and queens, dowries—"

"You'll like him," had said Reg confidently. "He'll like you."

Harry did like him.

Now and then, these past few weeks, he found himself watching Alexos Fox while he was at work – he would linger in doorways and watch Alexos concentrate on his essays, see the frown of his lips and the furrow of his handsome brows, see his careful hand movements, his grip very tight upon his pen; he would watch Alexos walk with his cane in his hand, his chin high and his gait smooth, his gaze far away and his mind elsewhere; he would occasionally witness Alexos half-undressed for bath or bed, his hair wet, some of his skin bared.

Harry had believed his Uncle Reg, when he'd said he thought that he and Alexos would get on – he'd believed him when he said he was handsome, that Alexos was kind, that Alexos was funny. Alexos Fox was all of those things – he was also cool and frosty, was prone to poor moods and self-pity, particularly, so it emerged, when he had not slept.

The night previous, Harry had been advised that Alexos had already risen with a bout of somnambulism at some time in the earlier evening, at a little past ten. Felix had found him and guided him back to his rooms, which was all well and good – it was midnight when Harry was approaching the stairs and heard a scream of pain.

Mr Fox, without the use of his cane, had limped to the top of the stairs, and tipped downward.

Outside, the rain was thundering down so loudly that it sounded like distant gunfire, and Harry's skin had been prickling with recollection and heat and roiling tension since it had begun: the scream kicked him into action and primed his body for the fight, although he knew he wouldn't find one.

Alexos was sprawled on the landing, swearing in such smooth, unerring Greek that one might have thought him a true Spartan, and there was blood down the side of his face where he'd caught himself on the edge of the banister on his way down. Clutching at his bad leg, he had his eyes tightly shut, spitting out words as though they'd shut out the world, and Harry did not hesitate.

He put his arms under the backs of Alexos' knees and his shoulders, and lifted him bodily from the floor.

"*Ungh*, fuck," growled Alexos, his voice husky from sleep and pain, and his eyes were wild as they searched around, but Harry said nothing as he brought him back to his room and set him down upon the bed, moving promptly to turn the taps upon the bath and put out hot water. "*No*, Sutton," said Alexos. "I'm not having a bath at this time."

"Then, sir, will you be convinced to take the codei—"

"No, I will not," snapped Alexos, and stripped off the shirt of his pyjamas rapidly, so much so that Harry heard the pop and tear of its seams.

He returned with the little first aid tin from Alexos' bathroom, and gently pushed the young master to tip back his head.

"Let it bleed," Alexos muttered, dropping the blood-soaked shirt to the ground. "Let it kill me."

"Very good that would look upon my next application to a place of employment too, Mr Fox," said Harry coolly. "Yes, I watched my last employer die of a head wound, at his instruction. After a poor night's sleep, he chose to commit himself to death, being as the inconvenience of it put him in ill mood."

"It's as good a reason to kill oneself as any," said Alexos listlessly.

"Suicide rarely has a good reason, sir," replied Harry, swiping iodine over the cut – which, he was glad to see, was more a nasty graze that a deep wound – and making the other man grit his teeth and muffle his shout. "Unless one's greatest desire is to make a mess for others to clean up."

"You have just described the essence of my existence, Mr Sutton," said Alexos.

Harry tugged on a lock of his hair, making him gasp in surprised pain, and then despite his scowling mood and exhausted irritation, Alexos laughed, and the sound was so beautiful, so unexpectedly joyful, that Harry's very heart surged in his chest.

"You treat me so cruelly, Mr Sutton," said Alexos, softer now, with sweetness and warmth folded into his words like sugar folded into dough. "I shall write this on your reference, if ever you decide to leave us, that you see fit to discipline the young master as if he's still a child."

"Will this be before or after your death, sir?"

"I will decide closer to the time," said Alexos, and closed his eyes as Harry put a bandage against his head. "I'm going to ask you to do something you don't want to do, now."

"Very well."

"I want you to tie my wrist to the bedpost."

"You're quite correct, sir: I do not want to do that."

"Oh, Sutton, please," said Alexos, as if Harry was being somehow unreasonable at refusing him this act of bondage. "Your uncle has done it a hundred times before. You needn't do it tight to my wrist –

leave a two-finger gap, that I not cut off the circulation, and it'll just wake me up if I try to get off, a tug out of the shoulder joint instead of my face planting against the landing."

"Why not just latch the door?"

"I can unlock the door without waking," said Alexos. "I do, frequently, quite automatically. Please, Sutton, won't you? I just want to sleep."

Alexos' eyes were rimmed red with a lack thereof.

Harry wanted nothing more than to tie him up – tie him up by both wrists, and bend between his legs, watch him arch and beg and try to struggle free, desperate for more than what Harry would give him.

Tonight was not the night for that.

Alexos had a pair of ties bound together for this purpose, and after he had folded himself back into his bedclothes, lying on his side, Harry leaned over him and looped the tie around the central post of the bed. He was aware, leaning over the young master, of the way Alexos' gaze went from Harry's belly to his crotch and then away from both.

Harry's lip twitched, and when he came to tie the loop around Alexos' wrist instead, he did so in a neat, careful motion, and leaned much of his body over Alexos'. He could feel the heat that radiated from the younger man, and more than anything he wanted to climb on top of him, straddle him and pin him in his place.

Would he curse in Latin, swear in Greek, when Harry finally fucked inside him, or mounted him upon his cock?

Alexos was looking up at him, his lips parted, his eyes half-lidded, as Harry drew away his hands. He smelt faintly of laundry soap and sweat, and like this, Harry was aware of how easy it would be to kiss him, to lean in and close the gap between them. Alexos' fingers flexed, his bound wrist shifting in its silk bondage, and he broke eye contact, as he so often did, looking away. All this did was give Harry a better view of the column of his neck.

In the dim light of the room, most of it filtering in from the hall, it looked beautifully unmarred, the sort of expanse a man would delight to bring to bloom with bites and bruises.

"Thank you, Sutton," said Alexos, his head turned on the pillow, his hair a halo about his head, so fine that in the light, the pale brown looked almost blond. "I know that your uncle coached you as to what to expect, but I'm sure this is far from the position you dreamed of, when first you entered service."

"I don't remember what I dreamed about, sir, when first I entered service," said Harry. In the quiet of the room, he kept his voice low, and the sound came from low in his chest. "I'm sure I must have dreamt of something, but I no longer recall."

"Was it truly so long ago?" asked Alexos softly, in barely more than a whisper. He was looking not at Harry's face, but at his chest. He had made no mention of the way Harry was leaning over him, had not even stiffened, and that, Harry thought, was a good sign.

"A little more than twenty years, sir," said Harry in the same soft voice. "But with the war in the middle, it feels like fifty."

Alexos tipped his head back into the pillow, shifting himself in his place – as Harry stood up straight, he was very aware, looking down at him, that Alexos had slept like this before, that he was used, in a way, to sleeping bound. Something about that very thought thrummed beneath his skin, made him feel like a plucked cello string, although he held back the sound he felt compelled to make.

"Of course," said Alexos. "How old were you, when you went?"

"Twenty-four," said Harry. "I served in the trenches throughout the war, and then stayed on, a little while after the ceasefire. I lingered on the Western Front for some while, until the last of us were recalled, and following this I volunteered in a veterans' hospital, sir.

I did advise your father of these details when first I joined your staff, but he seemed to think they were of no great import."

"I hope he didn't offend you," said Alexos. "He forgets details, that's all – my father is a man quite attached to the now, for the past soon becomes a very distant friend."

"I did not take offence at all," said Harry. He did not say that he had noticed this trait in Alexos himself – he thought, judging by the way his expression froze a moment, that he was considering saying it himself, but he held his tongue.

"I thought you seemed rather confident in your application of first aid," muttered Alexos, and Harry gave him a very small smile in the darkness.

"Without meaning to embarrass you, sir," he said, "I believe it was a factor that influenced my uncle's recommending me for the position."

"My being so accident prone, you mean?"

"I don't recall saying that, sir," said Harry, and Alexos laughed in a sleepy, soporific way, stretching out upon his bed. Harry saw the slight stiffness on his one side, the way his expression froze a moment for the pain, but then his face slackened again, and he let his head drop further into the weight of his pillow.

"A lot of my friends went to war," said Alexos. "Directly from university or just after. I recall going into an office one morning, and finding myself the only man there, but for my tutor, where I ought have been one of six."

"May I ask you a question of a very personal lilt, sir?"

"Of course."

"Do many of your friends live some ways away, in London, or elsewhere in the country?"

Alexos said nothing, but shifted his wrist in the silk bond, wrapping his hands loosely around the tie that connected him to the bed post.

"You work every day, sir, without fail," said Harry, "and your correspondence, I have noticed, is addressed either to academic institutions or presses."

"You're asking me in quite a roundabout and polite way, Mr Sutton, if all my friends are dead."

"Yes, sir," said Harry. "If you would prefer me to be frank, then yes, that is what I'm asking."

"I never really had good friends even before a good many of my peers died, Sutton," said Alexos. "I do apologise if you feel your talents are underutilised, with my lacking any particular adherence to a social calendar, but when my mother is home, she does like to put herself to things like that."

"I would never expect an employer to make appointments that I might have the pleasure of planning for them, Mr Fox," said Harry. "I ask merely that you know this matter is in my thoughts, that I have not neglected the consideration."

"It is not you that neglects my friendships, Mr Sutton, it is I," said Alexos. "Don't waste your time wondering if I might be lonely – it's not a matter I concern myself with. I care that the staff are well-treated and compensated, and that you can each take your time off, as allotted you. That is the most I think about other people, outside of myself and my parents."

Uncle Reg had said that Alexos was a lonely man, that he had few friends, few intimate connections, but there was something profoundly tragic in Alexos' low and muted tones, not particularly weighted with tristesse so much as resignation.

"I'll come to wake you in the morning," said Harry softly. "Good night, sir."

"Yes," said Alexos, his eyes already closed. "Good night, Mr Sutton."

Harry took his leave, and Alexos spent the rest of the evening in his bed, where he belonged. He made his decision, somewhere in between tying Alexos' wrist in place and leaving for the evening, to dispense with subtlety, and to mount his seduction in earnest.

* * *

Alexos' sleep had been very poor, these past few weeks, and the lack of rest had made him anxious, irritable, and even more prone to accidents and clumsiness than usual. He dropped papers, books, plates, pens, cutlery, and anything else one could think of quite frequently; he not irregularly stumbled and had to take haste to right himself, particularly on the stairs; every day, he jarred his bad leg badly, or some other part of himself.

His temper was quite short, and he felt very badly when he swore profusely under his breath – in English – after falling against his door when trying to pull it closed, and he realised that young Betty was standing behind him, looking up at him with her eyes quite wide with horror, before she rushed past and away.

It was the turn of the season that did it, the cool spring days giving more and more over to the summer, and the brightness and length of the days was beginning to wear on him, not to mention the fact that soon enough, his rooms would no longer need a fire lit, and after that, there would be days where he should want to sleep in the cellar because his rooms were too hot and balmy.

The warmth soothed his sore limbs, at least, the muscle and the joints, but that didn't count for much when he felt like peeling his skin off when he woke in the night, or tore off his clothes in a fit of overheated somnambulism and strained the aforementioned sore limbs in the process.

Were any of the Titans to be put to death, he would put forward Chronos' name before the rest – was there any torture on this earth so painful as the passage of time?

The summer heat did more than soothe, at that: already, his blood was hotter, his skin ever prickling to life in want of touch, and he took cold baths some days just to quieten his body's plaintive, wanting demands, found himself infuriated by the burning passion of his own desires.

Mr Sutton didn't help, of course.

In Alexos' dreams, of late, he had been making one appearance after the next, each time in some state of undress – he dreamed of Henry Sutton coming in wet from the rain, his shirt stuck fast and wet and tight to the rounded edges of his belly and chest, his heaving shoulders; he dreamed of Henry Sutton lounging in just his shirt sleeves, a cigarette hanging from his lips, which would be curved in a smug and superior smile; he dreamed of Henry Sutton naked of every stitch of clothing, and dreamt of his weight over Alexos, crushing him down.

The week before, he'd asked Sutton to tie him to the bedpost, as Brydon had done before, as Reginald had done so many times before – but had Brydon or Reginald ever leaned over him, as Sutton had that night? Had either of them ever leaned close to him, so much so that Alexos could smell their subtle cologne or the grease in their hair or the starch in their shirts, could feel the warmth radiate from their bodies?

Reginald had done as Sutton had last nihgt, more than once, had lingered at his bedside and spoken to him in the darkness, but—

Not like Sutton had.

It had been for the best, in the end, that Alexos had been bound, and unable to reach for him – not that he would have, not that he ever could have, but he wanted to. He had thought about it, considered it, what it might be like to reach out and touch, squeeze, hold – be held in return.

Held by the throat, Alexos supposed, until Sutton had him suitably overpowered or thrown away from him. What would be worse, that Sutton should hate the pathetic, lonely cripple for his perversion, or pity him for it, take it for another sign of the infirmity of Alexos' mind, his spirit?

He somewhat avoided Sutton, from then on.

He'd spoken too freely, on the verge of sleep, been too bolstered by how freely it had seemed Sutton spoke to him – Sutton was his butler, not his friend, and Alexos did know that, *ought* know that, but he turned it over and over in his mind, the thought of Sutton in his uniform and his great coat on the Western Front, his rifle in his hand, perhaps – or his aid kit, more accurately, if he was a medic. Both, perhaps: he didn't know.

Alexos hadn't lied, when he'd told Sutton he'd never had many friends – he'd had a few contacts, men with whom he was casually friendly, men who seemed like they might be of a kind with him. Alexos was always on the outside of everything, no matter who he took up with – it wasn't wholly his cane or his tendency to exhaustion, nor wholly his scattered personality or his impatience, nor again his shyness and uncertainty of new people, but these factors in combination.

He had never been good at making friends, and never any good at keeping them either, and his loneliness was an easier state to maintain than the opposite.

Men he'd written to had died, in the war. He was aware that quite a few young men he'd gone to school with had died themselves – upperclassmen, mostly, those a year or two older than him, or as old as Sutton himself.

He'd have been sent off to war himself, he supposed, were it not for the fact that he were unfit. He'd never even received a letter or some notification that he needed to be examined – the family doctor had written him off for him in advance, he thought.

People thought it was a war wound, at time – he never knew how to respond, when people made those assumptions, thought him a veteran, thought he'd done something somehow noble, when what he'd done is managed to wrestle his way out of the fatal vice grip of polio.

He'd let his letters taper off to the one or two casual friends that had made it out of the war alive, and come home, and never left again. It was for the best, really.

"After you, sir," he heard a voice from behind him, actually managing to disturb him from his reverie, his concentration was so shot for lack of sleep, and when he turned to look at Mr Sutton, he saw that Sutton had stood back to allow Aristaeus to walk ahead of him into the room.

The dog approached Alexos with his customary chubby, speedy trot, and Alexos smiled down at him and slipped off his shoes, resting them immediately upon the hound's belly as soon as he dropped onto his side underneath the desk.

He tried not to look at Sutton directly, but when the butler walked away from him to fetch the side table, Alexos' gaze dropped to the curve of Sutton's hefty arse, and he wondered—

No.

He'd spent the whole of the week dragging his mind through one gutter to the next, and he was distracted enough already.

"You needn't bring up my tea of a morning, you know, Sutton," said Alexos. "I'm sure there are better uses of your time – please, do delegate the task to Felix, in future."

"I'm sure it is no great sink of my time, sir," said Sutton as he set out the table, "but I can of course arrange to dispatch Felix with your morning tea." Sutton's strong hands were steady and handsome, pouring from the pot, and there were a pair of biscuits upon the plate. "How proceeds your work this morning?"

"I'm afraid it doesn't," said Alexos quietly. "This last essay is nearly finished, but not yet – and I'll redraft again once I've typed it up."

"Typed it, sir?"

"My typewriter is in a case on top of my wardrobe, Sutton," said Alexos. "It has been neglected some while as I've drafted, but it's soon to come down again."

"Is it not impersonal, sir, a typewriter?" asked Sutton, although he sounded interested more than he looked disapproving, and there was surprise in his features, as though it were quite unusual that a man should use a typewriter in the year 1926. "Do you not crave the pen in your hand, its flow upon the page? The typewriter, mechanical as it is, seems so... distant."

Sutton had a wonderful mouth. He was a plump man, so it only followed that he had plump lips, and when he spoke in his calm, measured, collected way, Alexos felt like swallowing every word, drinking them from his tongue, capitulating at his feet that Sutton should just keep talking, that Alexos should just be able to observe the smooth movement of his plump lips and his fine teeth and his tongue, and hear, *hear*, that rich, plummy voice, that deep rumble, that came from a man with a barrel chest like Sutton's own.

"One needs distance at times, Mr Sutton," said Alexos, scratching Aristaeus' chest with his better foot and smiling when he snorted, his tail wagging. "But there is a reason I write it out first, and type it up after. I can't type directly onto the machine, as some men do."

"Do you play piano, sir?" asked Sutton in his rich, wonderful voice. Alexos felt like burying himself in the earth, if not against his chest.

"I do. Or— I have, in the past. I don't often."

"Your hands seem primed for it – beautiful instruments, with such long fingers, such graceful presentation of the hands. It seems apt, sir, that you should play the piano, but I suppose hands like yours are as-suited to the keys of a typewriter as they may be the instrument."

Alexos knew not how to reply to that, knew not what he could say, he was so flattered and so embarrassed and so surprised, and by the time he had halfway collected his thoughts, Sutton had departed, the door closing behind him.

Aristaeus gave a low and plaintive "roo!" at being neglected, and Alexos looked down at him, meeting his drooping, red-brown eyes as he went back to rubbing his belly, rocking Aristaeus back and forth as a nanny might rock a baby with her foot upon the cradle, and picked up his tea.

He almost regretted it when the morning after, it was Felix that brought in his tea, but it was for the best, he thought. Felix was a nice young man, handsome insofar as he was full of youthful potential – he held no dangerous appeal as Sutton did.

And yet, as the days went on after this instance, Alexos still saw Sutton.

Of course he still saw him. Sutton was the fucking butler, the leader of the household below stairs, and he oversaw all their mealtimes, but there was a distance there when Alexos was eating with his father, or when he read while he ate, which he took to doing, that Sutton not speak with him.

He asked for Brydon, always Brydon, if he stumbled or fell and Felix or Betty asked who they ought fetch to help him, if they couldn't help him themselves, and Alexos did quietly ask Brydon if he might be the one to come in the morning, as before, which Brydon agreed to quite readily.

Alexos made no great spectacle of it – if anything, he was somewhat shrewd and rather manipulative about it, feigning vulnerability with his father's valet, as if his reasons for desiring Brydon's care were out of nervousness and shyness and insecurity in his infirmity and his body, and not in his being unable to swallow down fantasies of Sutton taking his body quite apart.

It came to the point where, for some two weeks, he had not spoken to Sutton one-on-one at all – the only words that had passed between them had been a polite good morning as Sutton served him breakfast or handed him the newspaper, or asking Sutton to pour him another glass of wine.

He was sleeping even worse, the dreams just as vivid, just as often wet, and he knew from experience that practising any sort of maintenance, tugging himself off too often, would only spur his body to action even more, make him want *more*. Twenty years of erections that went nowhere except his own bathwater or bedsheets, and one would think his body would come to understand the unfortunate fact that he would never be anybody's husband nor anyone's lover, and it had best give up the fight.

"Felix," he called into the hall as the steps went by, sitting as he was on the bed and massaging a pattern into his bad leg, but it was not the footman who appeared in the doorway, but the butler himself. "Ah," said Alexos. "Mr Sutton."

"Mr Fox," said Sutton, "I can summon Felix for you, but I'm afraid he's currently polishing silver below stairs. If you'll give me just—"

"Oh, no, Sutton," interrupted Alexos, and gestured to the top of the wardrobe. "I just wonder if you might get my typewriter down, that's all, and put it into the library for me?"

"Of course, sir," said Sutton, moving across the room to fetch it down. "Your draft is completed, then?"

"As completed as they ever get," said Alexos, looking away from Sutton's arse, his strong, round thighs, his muscled calves.

"About Seneca?"

Alexos almost asked how he knew, but they must have discussed it, he knew, he must have told him. "Yes," he said. "Yes, about Thyestes and Atreus, who after the death of their brot— Have I told you this before?"

"You have, sir," said Sutton as he came down.

"I do beg your pardon," said Alexos. "I forget, you know. What I tell people."

Sutton was standing right ahead of him, the typewriter's leather case held in his hands, and he was looking down at Alexos where he sat upon the edge of the bed, and he was so tall, and so beautiful, and Alexos wondered if he would already be dead, if he'd never had the polio. If the polio hadn't killed him, if it had never gotten him to begin with – would he have died in the Great War? Would he have been arrested, caught in some police raid?

"You speak well upon your subjects, sir, with erudition and passion, and I'm sure you know that the cadence of your voice is pleasing," said Sutton. "I would be quite content to listen to any anecdote of yours thrice over, if you felt compelled to reiterate it."

Alexos, stunned, stared up at him. "Are you mocking me, Sutton?" he asked, aware that his voice was quiet and severe and very cold, that his cheeks were burning with humiliation, even as he stood to his feet and his cane.

He tried to take a step forward, that they be toe to toe, but although there were scarce two inches between their heights, Sutton's girth was twice or three times around as Alexos' own, and stood like this, Alexos felt incredibly small indeed. Were it not for the typewriter Sutton was holding, Alexos might step closer – were it not for the typewriter, their chests might brush against one another.

How would that feel?

Sutton's expression seemed genuine, but Alexos had never been any judge of all that.

"I am not mocking you, sir," said Sutton seriously. "I'm speaking quite truly. You are an academic – you know your subject, and you know your voice. Does it truly surprise you that I should enjoy to hear you speak?"

Alexos was breathing heavier now, was aware of the hard beat of his heart in his chest, and he stared at, studied Sutton's face. He stared at the neat curve of his plump lips, at Sutton's green eyes, the part of his hair. He looked... cool. Collected. Calm.

"You needn't say these things to flatter me," muttered Alexos.

"Why not, sir?"

"Why not?"

"You object to a butler flattering his employer, sir?"

"I do not..." Alexos stumbled, leaning slightly back to better look at Sutton's face, but in the other man's features there was scarcely the smallest falter, no sign of anger or mockery, not that he could see. He sounded earnest – he seemed earnest. Alexos felt like swimming in lava. "I do not object," he said, "but I don't see why you... why you would."

"Why indeed?" asked Sutton, and leaned in closer.

Alexos gasped as Sutton's face came closer to his, their mouths not brushing, their noses not even touching, but he almost expected the kiss, and it didn't come – Sutton plucked a piece of lint from his collar, and stepped away.

Alexos stared at his back.

"At another place setting on the long table in the library, sir?" asked Sutton.

"Yes," said Alexos numbly, reaching up and touching his own mouth, assuring himself that it had not been kissed. "Yes, precisely." Watching Sutton take his leave, Alexos felt quite unsteady, and frowned to himself as he tried to think on the words that had just passed between them, tried to make sense of them.

He didn't know that there was sense to be found – all that was there was want, and want could not be trusted.

Chapter Five

Harry placed the typewriter on the table before he pulled back the chair for Alexos, and he eased the chair back under the table as Alexos slipped his cane into its hook. Alexos kept his distance as they came back into the library, and there was a flatness to his features, as though he were struggling to control his expression.

He had removed his blazer before taking his seat, leaving him in his shirt sleeves only, and as Harry fetched the small table and folded it out at the other side of him, ready for tea in a few moments, Alexos took the links out of his cuffs and set them aside. He was very careful, very particular, about the way that he rolled up his sleeves – Harry hated to do that himself, to put them all the way up to the elbow the way that Alexos did, and would instead clip them with a band at his mid forearm, but Alexos folded them crisply, over and over, so that they were rolled almost flat to the skin.

"May I have a sandwich as well as my tea, please, Sutton?"

"Of course, sir – if I may ask, would it be possible for me to stay before I fetch it for you?"

Alexos glanced up at him.

His shirt sleeves rolled up, he had removed the typewriter from its case, removing a small roll of tools from a pocket, and a pair of rounded discs. It was partly an excuse, that much was true, but another part of Harry was genuinely interested to observe the process of readying the typewriter for use – he had never closely observed the use of a typewriter, and foolish as it might have been, he found himself inquisitive, wondering if the mechanism was as loud as he had heard, if it was so easy as it was made to look, in the advertisements.

"Oh," said Alexos, after a few moments had passed. "You want to watch me put in the new ribbon?"

"The ribbon?" Harry repeated, and Alexos' lips twitched, but there was no unkindness in his smile. If anything, he seemed almost shy of his expertise, looking Harry up and down – Harry had set him off-balance earlier, feigning as if almost to kiss him, simply to see how he would react, and Alexos seemed to be determined to forget the moment entirely, to convince himself that it had been but an accident, a misinterpretation. This was the strange balance that Alexos seemed to go through, whenever they did talk, these past weeks: Alexos avoided him, for in his presence he went from suspicion to uncertainty to fear to desire to embarrassment...

And always back to desire.

Alexos did want him, and would come around to embracing that want.

Harry wanted to believe it, wanted to be certain of it, but one could never be certain until one tread unto the breach whether desire would be enough. Alexos did desire him – did he desire him enough not to panic when the gap was broached between them? Did he desire him enough not to flee from him, to call for his resignation if not his arrest?

All he could do was observe the many signs pointing in the direction he wanted them to point, and draw Alexos closer. Alexos either looked at his body with hunger in his eyes, or he studiously looked elsewhere: did he ache to touch Harry as badly as Harry wanted to touch him? More so? Had he ever been touched before, by a man, by a woman? What did he like, to be tied up, to tie another in bondage? To submit, to rule? To be beaten, to have his hair pulled, to be caressed, threatened, bitten, kissed?

"Of course," said Alexos softly. "I suppose no one at the Bisphams was a typist."

"No, sir," said Harry, stepping closer and standing to Alexos' side and just beside him, looking over his shoulder. "I'm sure I know typists by extension – one or two of my brothers work in offices – but I have never closely observed the use of the machine."

"Your missives during the war weren't typed?"

"They were, sir, but not the notes we used within the infirmary. None of us had time to learn to type, given all the chaos all about us – it would have sunk more time than it might have saved."

"Here," said Alexos. He seemed more confident, more comfortable with Harry, with some task to occupy his hands – the biggest clue as to his shared desire, as Harry saw it, was the way he had been avoiding Harry's presence of recent. It had been subtle, so much so that Brydon had even gone out of his way to assure Harry it was likely to do with the young master's embarrassment around his infirmity, that it was unlikely to do with Harry himself.

Harry believed otherwise.

Alexos unclipped the upper lid of the typewriter, pulling it aside, and Harry peered at its inner workings with interest – at the front of the machine was the array of keys, but now revealed, he saw a disc of carefully arranged hammers and pins, and standing either side of this disc were a pair of small prongs.

"You can use a sewing machine, can't you, Sutton?"

"Yes, sir, of course."

"Ribbon spools aren't so different to one's bobbin – they just hold an ink ribbon instead of thread."

Harry observed very keenly as Alexos carefully pulled two spools of dark metal apart, and Harry inhaled the heavy, familiar smell of ink as the ribbon soaked in the stuff was bared to the air. Neatly, Alexos laid the spools on the prongs, clipping them into place, and Harry listened to the click, wondered if it felt the same as the click of a bobbin into place, as Alexos went on.

"You see these hammers, they're not dissimilar to the hammers that strike a piano's strings," said Alexos, gesturing to the disc of pins. "Each of them, in much the same way as a piano, falls with the press of a key. Instead of the hammer striking a string, however, it hits the ribbon held taut just here, by the ribbon vibrator, so we feed it into place..." Alexos manipulated the ribbon with tweezers, that he not touch the black ink with his bare hands, and Harry watched the neat and easy way he fed the ribbon between the tiny metal clips, turning one of the spools to pull the ribbon tight. "With that, it's as simple as pressing a key." He pushed down very gently on the Q key, and Harry watched the hammer move forward, not yet touching the ribbon – when it did, he saw it would press the ribbon against the paper from the other side.

His hand splayed over the keys with each of his fingertips resting on letters, Alexos looked very much at home, as though his hand had been trained to a starting position: his pale fingers, long and graceful, looked just as right and correct laid upon this instrument as they might against the ivory keys of a piano. Delicate flesh stood in stark contrast to the polished dark metal of the mechanism beneath it.

There was something deeply appealing, more so than Harry expected, in the sight of Alexos at his typewriter – he enjoyed very much to observe the other man writing his notes, whether they be in Latin, Ancient Greek, English, or whatever arcane languages he had committed to memory, because Alexos had a very square and particular hand. It was not neat, exactly, and it was perhaps not handsome, but it was supremely legible, no matter that it was rather cramped and small upon the page. The appeal in the typewriter was a different one – Alexos conducted himself at the machine's keys with ease and a great deal of visible experience, competence.

Harry had always found a certain appeal in those men with skills different than his own.

"Thank you, sir," said Harry as Alexos removed a sheaf of paper sized to the typewriter, and fed a page through the machine to work from, tightening it into place. He set his margins with deft, simple movements of levers and keys, and Harry wondered when it was he had learned, if he had been compelled to – did his mother use a typewriter? Had his university requested it of him? "What sort of sandwich would you like, sir?"

"Sandwich, Sutton?" repeated Alexos distractedly, frowning deeply as he tightened a wheel on the side of the typewriter, pressing experimentally down on a key to check the machine was properly calibrated.

When Harry returned twenty minutes later, sandwich in hand – cheese, lettuce, and ham – he found Alexos frowning very deeply in concentration at a page of handwritten notes. His fingers moved at such a pace over the mechanical keys, creating a great chattering of metallic noise, that Harry could scarcely believe his eyes: with each key hammered home the page would move to the right a tiny increment, and when a bell chimed, Alexos would release a lever and pull the paper back across and continue typing almost uninterrupted, as smoothly as if he was part of the machine himself.

Harry really did not know for how long he stood there, mesmerised by the perfect rhythm of Alexos' work as he typed, his focus narrowed down to the world he was creating with his words, that terrible banquet set down in printed type.

"Oh," he said when he took a moment, moving the page with a turn of a dial, manually pushing up the page. "How long have you been there, Sutton?"

Harry really didn't know. There was a warmth under his suit, observing Alexos focused and impassioned and with such unexpected mechanical skill – Uncle Reg had never mentioned this particular quality in Alexos Fox, but he had known of Harry's affection, his delight, with such things.

The first man Harry had ever gone to bed with had been a chauffeur.

"I didn't wish to interrupt your focus, sir," he said simply, and set the tray at Alexos' side. "Might I ask you a question, Mr Fox, about your typewriter?"

"Hm? Oh, yes, Sutton, of course," said Alexos as he picked up his tea and sipped at it.

"Is the device often serviced? Sent away for the purpose, I mean?"

"Oh, no, no," he said dismissively. "I can rather take this machine apart and put it back together, Sutton – I had another until two years ago, 'til I dropped it on the stairs, and I might have put that one back together, but these new models are a good deal lighter and more compact, so I just traded it in. I clean and maintain the machine myself."

Harry's lips shifted without his permission at the same time that Alexos looked up at his face, and Alexos smiled.

"Don't tell me you disapprove, Sutton. Were I a man besotted with a bicycle, you wouldn't bat an eye at my caring for that myself."

"On the contrary, sir," said Harry, "I would think that work best left to the chauffeur."

"The sky will not fall, Sutton, if I brush and clean my typewriter myself."

"The sky notwithstanding, sir, the cleaning and maintenance of tools and devices is not a responsibility due the young master of any household."

"Do you know how to clean a typewriter, Sutton?" asked Alexos, arching an eyebrow. For all they were on differing sides of the field, Harry rather wanted to kiss him in this moment, and wipe that challenge and superiority from his face – Harry did not smile at being teased, but that did not mean he did not inwardly surge to be met with it.

"I would readily commence to learn, sir."

"But you don't at this moment?"

"... No, sir."

"Then I'll take the *responsibility*," said Alexos, tone warm and wry, his large eyes sparkling with a sort of enticing mischief, "all for my own."

Harry leaned over him to reach for the typewriter case, his chest brushing against the back of Alexos' shoulders, and he heard Alexos' soft gasp, felt the way he stiffened. Harry leaned forward, putting just the slightest bit more of his weight on Alexos' back before he drew away and set the leather case down on a side table, making more space for Alexos' usual spread of papers and notes.

Alexos' cheeks were flushed pink, when Harry looked back to him.

"Are you quite alright, sir?" asked Harry.

Alexos' expression was at first one of embarrassed uncertainty, but as Sutton remained in place, keeping his gaze, Alexos' brow furrowed, his lip curling fractionally. "I sometimes feel, Mr Sutton," he said, in very measured tones, "that you are playing some joke on me to which I am not privy."

"What joke would I play, sir?" asked Harry: at the same time, he drew himself up to his full height, pulling on the hem of his waistcoat that it settle more tightly against his breast. Alexos, as he had expected him to, glanced down at his chest, and then looked away. "Would I be correct in presuming, sir, that this apparent jape on my part is the reason you have avoided my presence, of late?"

"I hardly fail to see, Mr Sutton, how it's any of your business," said Alexos, so coldly and so cleanly that Harry almost smiled, and had to stop himself. "If I choose to dislike you, I will do so – there is no clause in your contract of employment that I should take pleasure in your company, nor seek it out."

"I endeavour only to please, sir," said Harry smoothly. "Might I ask what error on my part has fostered this dislike?"

"You may ask," said Alexos, "but I am not compelled to answer."

"Ought I guess the answer?" asked Harry, stepping closer, that he stood directly over the chair in which Alexos was sitting, and now in line with Harry's belly, forced to look up at him, Alexos faltered. He shrank slightly back, his lips parted, and Harry began to see his cheeks flush pink. First, it was two tiny pinpricks of redness, but as Harry stood his ground, breathing evenly, his shoulders squared, the flush widened, the colour blooming.

"Mr Sutton," said Alexos, "I believe you have severely overestimated where lies the limit of your bounds."

"I endeavour only to please, sir," said Harry for a second time, and leaned over him. Alexos drew in a shuttered gasp. "I believe I am correct in estimating, sir," he went on in a low voice, drenching it in all the syrup he could muster, "that there are bounds between us you would like for me to cross."

"Get out," said Alexos sharply. "Out, Sutton, now."

Harry straightened, kept the movement slow and deliberate, and finally allowed himself a small smile.

Alexos clenched his beautiful hands tightly into fists.

He did not shout. He did not tell Harry to hand in his resignation, nor advise he was being given his notice. He did not call Harry disgusting, or perverted, or even attempt to say he was wrong.

He said, "Leave me be," and for the time being, Harry did.

He carried his victory with him as he went.

* * *

For some time, following this, Harry allowed Alexos the distance he desired.

He allowed Brydon or Felix to take up the vast majority of the young master's service, as far as it was needed; at breakfast and at dinner, he made no attempts at conversation or even at eye contact when Alexos came in alone; when he did come up to the library where Alexos was working, he would silently set down his tea and something to eat and take his leave.

Alexos would not acknowledge him in these moments, would not even look in his direction.

This was all well and good: Harry was more than content to let his desire simmer, and a watched pot would not come to boil.

I hope you are not being too cruel to him, nor too impatient, Uncle Reg had written to him recently. *He is stubborn, and he will be cold, when first you begin to lean on him – I don't know that he has ever allowed himself to be shown affection, and as an animal cornered, he will bare his teeth and swipe with his claws. But if you can only get close, Harry, I do think he will soften. I think if you get close, he will come to pieces, in the way anything must come to pieces before you can make the proper repairs.*

Harry swept out the whole of the cellar: with the summer heat so increasingly oppressive, there was a great deal of relief to be found in the cool, dank rooms beneath the Fox household, and Harry liked the work. By the time the cellar was entirely in order, every bottle of wine and spirit newly catalogued and organised, the whole of the space cleaner and tidier than it had been in some decades, Alexos – according to Betty and Felix – had finished typing up his manuscript.

It had been three weeks or so since their toe-to-toe in the library – it had been months since this silent treatment first began.

When Harry went up to the library in the afternoon, he found that Alexos' manuscript was neatly bound in string and resting on the edge of the table. Alexos himself was on his feet, favouring his right leg as he bent over the table and scrubbed carefully and painstakingly at the segment of his typewriter.

It had seemed to Harry that the typewriter had been incredibly clean when first he had seen it unveiled earlier in the month, but now its metallic pieces gleamed under the light. Alexos moved his hand, gripping so tightly at a small brush that his knuckles whitened and the tendons showed in his hands, quite briskly, but with an astounding delicacy and precision, never straying from the piece he meant to scrub.

Felix or Betty were scarcely known to shirk their duties, but if they had even a fraction of his dedication to cleaning or polishing, Harry might be able to see his reflection on every surface in the house.

"Send that to my editor, please," Alexos said, by way of greeting. They were the first words he had spoken to Harry in some time, intoned very crisply, and Harry inclined his head, setting the lunch tray down on the side table. Felix was late, but not very – it was only two minutes past the hour.

"Is there anything else I can do for you, sir?" asked Harry.

"Yes, Sutton," said Alexos, "you can go away, and go away quickly. Leave me to work in peace."

Harry was in a good mood. He said, "Something tells me, sir, that I am capable of disturbing your peace even in my absence."

Alexos' foul look was terrific in its makeup: defiant, furious, vulnerable, a cocktail of handsome emotions on a handsome face. Alexos' hands twitched against the bared undercarriage of his machine.

"Does it please you?" he asked. "To be so— so *improper* with your employer? Do you want that I should give you your notice?"

"No, sir," said Harry. "Of the things I want from you, my notice is not among them."

"I am not what you think I am. I have nothing against your— your sort, Sutton, but I am not as you are. That you think I might entertain or indulge these unnatural urges is..." Alexos was sweating. Harry could see the glisten of moisture on his skin, around his temples, dripping down his jaw, and he could see, too, the way he trembled, the way his beautiful fingers twitched, resisting the urge to clench into fists. There was a tragedy in it, seeing a man so full with desire, and yet feeling he ought restrain it to himself, let himself fill up and over with it. Harry had never much cared for tragedies. "I could have you arrested, I'm sure you know."

Harry considered his answer, wondering what phrasing precisely might be most effective, and then made his decision: "I *am* arrested, sir."

He did not linger, having said this – it would only reduce his impact – but he committed Alexos' shocked expression, his mouth ajar, his eyes wide, to memory.

Alexos would look at his cock in precisely that manner, before the year was out. Harry would ensure that this was so.

* * *

Alexos was losing his mind.

In the aftermath of Sutton leaving, he scrubbed frenetically at the segment of his typewriter, so frenetically in fact that he almost cut his fingers on the hard brush – his hands were already aching from the way he'd been holding them, his fingers the whole day through gripped tight upon one brush or other, desperate to keep it stable as he worked.

His typewriter was the cleanest it had ever been. He'd finished the manuscript at a little past eight o'clock, and then commenced working on the typewriter, and time had sort of narrowed down to a very fine point, and that point had been facing the other direction.

He struggled to unclench his hands as he finally set the brush down, and he wrapped both of his sore palms around the warm pot of tea, feeling its heat against his stiff fingers and clenching his eyes tightly shut.

He hadn't slept in weeks.

Every time he tried to sleep, he woke from heated and vivid dreams, the blood in his veins boiling with want, and all the cold baths in the world wouldn't stop him waking up soaked through with his own emissions – and Christ knew that if he allowed himself too much space to, too much time to, he'd end up rubbing himself fucking raw.

He felt like tearing off his skin – he *would* tear off his skin soon, or at least tear the skin off his cock, he felt so frantic and feral with want, felt like a hound beset with the rut, and what could he do to work out that pointless energy?

Run? Lift weights? Fuck?

Ha.

When he stood to his feet, forcing his palms flat against the table so that his fingers *had* to straighten, he heard and felt the knuckles pop in all of his fingers at once. He stood too fast, jarring his hip in the process, and he cursed sharply, slamming his hand down hard against the table.

The slap on his palm burned, and he'd brought his hand down with enough force that it made all the nerves up his arm, right up to his shoulder, jangle like silent sleigh bells. It distracted from the aching, desperate ache in his bad knee, if only for a few moments, and it was enough to collect himself.

Felix must have cleared his throat or moved or something, because somehow Alexos knew he'd been stood in the doorway even though he hadn't seen him, and as Alexos turned to regard him, he tried to rack his brain to remember what he'd said a moment ago, when he'd cursed aloud.

He so hated to curse in front of the staff – he wasn't intrinsically an intimidating man, but it frightened them, all of them except Brydon, and he so hated the idea that they should think him ready to abuse them, that he might curse at them, and not at his situation. If they had to hear him swear, the least he could hope for was that it not be in English – he couldn't remember.

His brains were awash.

"Do apologise, sir," said Felix hurriedly. "I see Mr Sutton's already brought you some lunch, sir."

"What time is it?"

"A little past noon, sir."

"You weren't here on the hour."

"Sir?"

"Sutton has you all running like soldiers on a cuckoo clock's dial, doesn't he?" asked Alexos, more coldly than was right, because poor Felix didn't know a thing about it, and was looking at him with a sort of dismayed bafflement. "Ready to move at the chime of the clock?"

Felix actually looked rather guilty, and Alexos' chest clenched with shame, as though someone were squeezing his heart in their hand.

"I'm sorry, sir, I lost track of time, sir, I was only ironing the—"

"Felix, please," said Alexos hurriedly, and tried to force his tone to soften, but he couldn't tell if he was doing it right, couldn't tell if he sounded genuine or wooden. He couldn't feel his teeth. "I wasn't... I wasn't scolding you. I do apologise for my tone, and I can assure you, I am in no way dissatisfied with your work – nor would I even have known you were late, had Mr Sutton not already been through. I don't keep track of the clock, and do not carry a watch – I note the change of the hour only because of the butler's march."

Felix seemed, Alexos thought, somewhat comforted by this, although he wasn't entirely sure – he did seem to straighten up, no longer seeming so small, although Alexos wasn't sure if he was just imagining it. Hoping it.

"And I wasn't swearing at you," he added. "Only at my own stiff joints."

Felix hesitated. "Can I, ah, can I get you something for the pain, sir?"

"Do you know where Tom is?"

"Mr Lloyd, sir?" asked Felix, then nodded.

"Go tell him I want something to take apart. Bring whatever it is to me here, and my tool box, and the white sheet. Mr Lloyd will give those to you as well."

Felix stared at him.

Alexos shifted his jaw, felt his temper rising, and he pressed both palms harder against the table top. It took the weight off his legs, and at the same time the pressure against the flat surface made his fingers stretch out again where they'd begun to curl. He could feel the build-up of stiffness in the muscles burn slightly at the pressure, feel the ache turn to something in the bones, the nerves, instead of just the flesh.

"Was something about my request unclear, Felix?" he asked.

He tried his best to make it as gentle as possible – he obviously failed, because Felix looked at him as though Alexos had just pronounced his intention to slit his throat directly.

"Yessir," he blurted out, and went away so quickly that Alexos could actually hear him jog in the corridor.

He reached slowly back for the case of the typewriter, putting the lid on and clipping it into place to protect the segment from dust, and then set it into its leather bag. It gleamed with how clean it was, every piece of chrome and steel shining like the paint on a new car, but there was no satisfaction in it – there was only a sort of numb frustration that he'd finished the job, but didn't *feel* finished yet.

Sutton had brought him a sandwich, and he ate it with a dry mouth and no real head for what it tasted like. Once the plate was empty, which seemed to take about sixty thousand years, he realised he hadn't noticed what had been in it. Bread, certainly. Butter, he expected.

His legs hurt, and he wanted a hot bath, and he wanted codeine – fuck the codeine, he wanted the *morphine*, which he never wanted, because the aftermath always made him feel like he was dying. He had to feel like he was dying in the first place, to want to touch the stuff, and that was fucking stupid, because he didn't feel anything at all, except for want and pain.

He wanted a wank.

He wanted to lie in the hot bath and fuck into his hand until he brought himself off, and then do it again, do it a third time, wanted to spread his legs apart and slide two fingers inside himself, wanted to curl his fingers and rub against the knot of nerves there until his bollocks were so empty that it was agony to touch himself anymore, and then he wanted to keep going.

Sutton.

Henry Sutton – Henry Reginald Sutton.

An invert, a *pervert*. A queer. And it was one thing, thinking about it, imagining it, knowing it was just a stupid and unwholesome fantasy, just dirty dreams that had a new, precise target, but were not in themselves a new activity.

It was another, if Sutton was there, Sutton who was tall and fat and strong and commanding and had that rich, wonderful voice, Sutton with his plump lips and his strong hands, Sutton whose thighs were almost as wide each as Alexos' waist, Sutton who could kill him with a fucking look, let alone his fingers – his *cock*!

He couldn't get him arrested. It was an empty threat, and Sutton had to know that, probably saw it on Alexos' face. He couldn't do that to someone like him – and even were he not the way that he was, even were he not inclined the way he was, he couldn't.

He didn't think he could report another man for murder, let alone buggery – he'd met men who'd been put to hard labour, and he couldn't see anyone put to that, not in all his life. He'd kill himself before he'd testify to have another man arrested for anything. He'd kill a policeman before he did.

Perhaps that wasn't true.

Policemen scared him to his bones.

He was gripping so tightly at the wooden edge of the table that his thumb felt like it would break. He released it, making blood suddenly start to exist in his hands again, although he wished it would have the good graces to stay there, and stop flowing down to his cock at every available opportunity.

He couldn't have Sutton arrested – he couldn't even end his employment, even if he gave him a glowing reference. How would he explain it to Reginald, to his father, his mother, without drawing some suspicion, without everyone knowing, suspecting, then despising him?

He didn't know if Sutton would resign – why should he? He evidently thought he was onto a terribly good thing: driving the young master out of the library and into the nearest sanatorium.

"Erm," said Felix, and Alexos turned to look at him, and breathed a desperate sigh of relief. "Where do you want it, sir?"

"Pass me that sheet, Felix," said Alexos. "And put my typewriter on top of the wardrobe in my room."

Chapter Six

That evening, Alexos did not come down for dinner, and Harry attended Mr Fox Senior alone.

This did not trouble Mr Fox unduly – Harry had already observed that not irregularly, father and son would come to dinner and eat whilst buried in the depths of their own thoughts or sit across from one another each with a book or a page of notes, and eat with the hand with which they were not consumed; likewise, now and then one or the other would miss the meal entirely, and remain buried in their work.

It was not an antisocial act, he didn't think, and as much as father and son did talk past one another, the both of them often speaking on their own pursuits and asking little about the other's, it never seemed to Harry that this was done with any desire to be rude, nor even showed a lack of engagement on either of their parts.

The Foxes seemed to be quite affable in making conversation, happy and satisfied with one another's company, whether they were sitting in silence or speaking together. In some months at the Foxes' home, Harry had not once witnessed so much as a moment of tension between the two of them, let alone an argument – his uncle had often mentioned how peaceful the Fox household was, how quiet it was for nine months out of the year, but Harry had never realised precisely *how* peaceful, nor the nature of that peace.

Patrick and Alexos Fox were very similar to one another, each of them lanky and sandy-haired, with strong cheekbones and exaggerated features, the two of them each with large eyes and long lashes. The both of them too, at a glance, looked to be innocent and tended quickly to confusion – in the father, Harry felt that this affable naivety was precisely what it appeared to be, but in the son...

Well.

He had discovered already, upon fine manipulation, that Alexos had depths hidden within him. Harry's uncle had never made mention of Patrick Fox being lonely, and it was somewhat clear that he wasn't – he liked his numbers, liked his work, and at no point did Harry get the impression he disliked or was frightened of people. The older man seemed quite content in his isolation; perhaps it was this contentment of his father's that made Alexos so determined to go through his life alone, no matter how he wore his ache and desire for company in every plane and wrinkle in his face.

"Brydon told me my son has been sleeping poorly of late, Sutton," said Mr Fox over his meal, and Harry watched him as he continued to eat, cutting his lamb into extremely small, bite-sized pieces before he ate them.

(Once or twice, on nights he was dining alone, Harry had observed him cut his food into very small pieces and then arrange the pieces into columns, precise gaps between them, that he might stare down at the arrangement upon his plate. Harry suspected, though he had no way of knowing without asking, that he employed the exercise to somehow assist him with more mystifying equations.)

"I'm afraid that is so, sir," said Harry.

"Don't worry too much about it," said Mr Fox mildly, with a small smile – it was comforting, but there was a distant sadness in it. "He often struggles more in the summer, sleeps less, walks about more. He dreams so vividly, you know. When he was a little boy, he used to drive the nanny quite mad – she had to sleep in a room adjoining his down on the ground floor, and we had to put a bell over his door, like the sort in a shop, you know, so that she knew when it opened. Before that, she'd go into his room of a morning and panic, not knowing where he'd gone, and all of us would have to search the house through, and find him on a sofa or sat at the dining table. Once, rather memorably, we found him down in the pantry on top of a sack of potatoes, and another time curled up under Mr Lloyd's rosebushes outside." The smile widened, warm and full of affection, Mr Fox's wide eyes even more distant than usual. "When he started to wear the braces for his legs, we put the bells on those at night – at university, he avoided rooming with any of the other boys, and I believe he had a very complicated lock put on his door. These days he rarely gets very far."

"Yes, sir," said Harry. "I only wish I could assist further, sir. I knew whilst working as a medic a great many men afflicted with sleep troubles, particularly nightmares or sudden starts that left them leaping from their beds, but I am quite unfamiliar with somnambulism – or I was, ere now."

"I'm afflicted with the same condition, you know," said Mr Fox casually, and Harry regarded his employer with interest, such that Mr Fox laughed. "I suppose it is very queer, that it should be so obvious in him but not in me. Now and then Brydon comes to wake me and finds me asleep at my desk instead of in my bed, that's all – I don't go far. Even as a little boy, when it started, I think the most unusual place I was ever found was in the library, half in the cat's basket with her kittens all over me, and that was only a little ways down the hall from my bedroom. My son has a more adventurous soul than I – he used to be quite fiercely obsessed with the journeys of Odysseus, that endless wanderer, a natural explorer. He declared he would be an archaeologist, a sailor, a cartographer. Anything that would take him from one end of this world to the other."

Harry had not ever heard Mr Fox speak at such length on a subject that was not their business' accounts or mathematical theory, heard him use so many words and so few numbers. Both men of the Fox household shared, it seemed to Harry, a certain quality where they seemed at first to be very shy, but turned out to possess a surprising confidence – Mr Fox Snr was laconic only when he had nothing to say, and when he did, he would speak at length.

"He lost this spirit for adventure after his illness, sir?"

"Not at first," said Mr Fox. "He was incorrigible in his sickbed, whilst recovering, even through the pain – he wanted more books, more newspapers, asked if he might be taken about the grounds in his wheelchair, wanted always to be in someone's company. Fiercely exhausted and in constant pain, and yet he was ever consumed with restless energy. Your uncle had a second desk in his bedroom, the latter half of that year, and would do his paperwork in Alex's company whenever the nurse was out. He cried with relief when he was finally allowed to walk about again, no matter that he stumbled, was so clumsy before they started to straighten his legs out, especially his bad knee. The frames on his legs were quite painful, I think, which slowed his enthusiasm, and then, once he went back to school, he... Ah, Mr Sutton. You know, of course, that children can be terribly cruel."

"I do, sir," said Harry.

"He lost his spirit a little. Became a good deal more reserved. Categorically refused to go to boarding school when it was suggested, but really, Georgie didn't want to send him, and honestly, I didn't either. When he went to university, we thought he might stay, you know, he insisted so strongly he would go, that he'd be out in the world, but he came back to us. Does it make me sound terribly cold, that I say to you I wish I might see the back of my son, and not have him home with us?"

"No, sir," said Harry quietly, digesting all that he had been told. Mr Fox spoke without making a great deal of eye contact and spoke somewhat softly and with strange tones at times, as though talking to himself, but he was looking at Harry now – or, kept glancing at him, at least. "It sounds only as if you have a great deal of love for your son, and wish him happiness."

"I do," said Mr Fox. "Your uncle did his best, you know – I've tried myself, but I was never, ah. I'm not very good with words. Not very good with... advice, encouragement, and Alex is so curious, so intelligent. He's like his mother that way – I really can't keep up with either of them, much as I try. Your uncle understood it much better than I did. I don't know that there's anything your uncle doesn't understand, seems to me that the man is a veritable genius, but you're not so different. Most butlers seem to be geniuses about everything."

"It's kind of you to say, sir," said Harry.

"Except wine," said Mr Fox, suddenly stern and rather angry, his brow furrowing, his nose wrinkled in disgust. "It's terrible to taste – so strong! I hate very much the taste of alcohol, but wine is the most abhorrent of all."

Something must have shown in Harry's face, no matter that he attempted to retain a neutral mask, because Mr Fox suddenly looked at him with something akin to panic, and raised a comforting hand.

"Oh, Mr Sutton, please," he said hurriedly, "I'm... I'm teasing, of course. I don't mean to disparage your work – you're very good at it, and Georgie adores the stuff, knows all about it, and Alex, he does." He chuckled to himself, somewhat nervously, and then exhaled. "I'm not good at teasing, either," he said defeatedly. "Alex is. Your uncle taught him that – Georgie taught him to be quite cutting, I think, to, to talk and to stand up for himself, but he was severe, like I am. Too... mathematical. Cold. Your uncle warmed him up."

"If I may say, sir," said Harry quietly, "you have never struck me as cold at all."

"That's the trouble with butlers," said Mr Fox, "all of you being so intelligent, I mean. You see what's underneath, you know, for the most part. The most of us are quite simple – we just add up whatever we see. We never think to ask if there's any variables in the equation that are out of sight."

"I think you are giving my profession far too much credit, sir," said Harry. "That, or making me quite nervous about living up to the standards set by my uncle."

Mr Fox laughed.

For all Alexos' tightness, he often laughed in quite an open way – his laughter was open-mouthed, and he often leaned back or opened outward, when something amused him; his father tightened, shoulders hunching, and he laughed almost without opening his lips.

"I think you've been quite tremendous so far," he said. "The real test of your mettle will be when Georgie – Mrs Fox, Georgina – when she comes home. She'll be here a month or two at Christmas time, and then go off again, and then be back a month or two again in the late spring." He sighed. "I do miss her when she's not here, but she fills up my life, when she's about, so that I almost don't miss her when she's gone again, I carry so much of her with me – and she writes me, of course, even though I'm so terrible at writing back. She'll have meetings and lunches and parties and fetes and all of that twice or thrice a week, when she's home."

Mr Fox received letters from his wife twice a week, and wrote her back every month or two – Harry was aware that Mrs Fox was constantly in motion, travelling across and between countries, sailing or taking trains or cars hither and thither, and she was quite a prominent novelist, with a dozen or so mysteries under her belt. She was an essayist of great repute, too. Her prose was tightly written, had a cutting wit to it, and Harry had read some of her books before and found himself laughing out loud at the cold, rapier-sharp humour of her heroes, and the dark tone of the comedy itself.

He couldn't help but wonder how much this would translate to the figure of the actual woman when he finally met her, no longer knowing her as the shadow over the lives of her husband and son, or the rest of the staff.

"I don't mind parties," said Mr Fox. "I quite like them, as it happens, now and then, so long as I'm able to keep on top of my work in between, and be left alone to rest. Alex, on the other hand, can be... prickly."

"Prickly, sir?" Harry repeated, keeping his voice even and polite, and Mr Fox leaned back in his seat, setting his knife and fork neatly down on his empty plate and folding his hands over his belly.

"He has a habit of excusing himself from dinner parties as soon as the last course is finished, having already waited until the absolute last moment to come down for dinner. Georgie chastises him for it – he's really quite transparent, and she says people do notice – but there's no dissuading him. He abhors having guests in the house, declines party invitations from all his friends, won't come with us if we visit my brother, Lord Henley, or any of the rest of the family." Mr Fox glanced up to Harry's face again, once more meeting his eye before looking away, as though he needed to look away to concentrate on what he was saying. "You must be surprised by that. He's so— so good-natured, after all. Friendly."

Harry thought of Alexos saying that what he wanted was for him to go away and leave him to work, resisting the instinct to smile.

"Yes, sir," said Harry. "Since my joining your household, he has been nothing but welcoming."

"Well, I suppose that's because you've never sat down to dinner with him," said Mr Fox. "The boy clams up like a... Well, like a..." He trailed off, going silent for some few moments.

"Like a clam, sir?"

"Oh, yes, Sutton. Exactly the thing. Sorry, I suppose I'm keeping you from getting off, all this rambling of mine. Would you take this plate away?"

"Of course, sir," said Harry, and as Mr Fox Snr ambled back upstairs, he cleared everything from dinner away.

* * *

"Um, Mr Sutton," said Felix some hours later, just as Harry was closing his office behind him, ready to do his final rounds of the evening.

"Felix," said Harry, arching an eyebrow. "I thought I told you to close the library for the evening and retire to bed."

"Well, that's just it, sir," said Felix. "Mr Fox is still in the library, sir."

It was unusual that Alexos should make any kind of complaint where Felix was concerned. It was true, certainly, that he didn't like Felix to see him undressed or in distress, but he was as gentle with Felix as he was with Betty, as a rule, or any of the young maids. "He complained when you made to close the curtains?"

Felix hesitated, biting his lip and glancing back to the stairwell. He was only fifteen, but he was tall and would soon be strapping, and even looking so nervous, he did cut a good figure, would be really quite good as a footman, once he learned to stop showing his emotion so freely on his face. Harry had to wonder if he would be one of the last young men to join the profession, and more than that, he had to wonder if he even expected he would stay in service the whole of his life, as Harry had thought to do at his age, as he still hoped to do, after a fashion.

Brydon, Mrs Perry, and Mr Lloyd had all casually mentioned that the Fox house had never had a great many staff – after Mrs Ainsley, their previous housekeeper, had retired in 1918 to help care for her nephew returned from France a triple amputee, they hadn't hired on another housekeeper, and while one of the maids, Becca, did still live in the house, the other walked in each morning from the village. Even before the war, they only hired in additional maids and footmen from the village during the busy seasons of the year.

The Fox house was a relatively modest one, neither embroiled in the midst of the city's cosmopolitan rush, nor situated on sprawling fields in the way of the manor houses. It was a good place, Harry thought, for a young man like Felix to learn his trade, even if it didn't turn out to be his lifelong vocation.

"He didn't complain, Mr Sutton," said Felix. "He's— Well, he's asleep, sir, but I think he is drunk, or maybe he's had some codeine, I'm not sure. Not that it's my place to say," he added hurriedly, "just that Mr Brydon says you can tell what he's been at, when he's been at something, only I can't, just yet." He swallowed, his Adam's apple bobbing in his throat – he'd only recently begun to regularly shave, and there was a little cut on the side of it, the scab still healing.

"Not to worry," said Harry quietly, with a small smile, once Felix glanced up from the floor and met his gaze again. "I'll attend to Mr Fox, Felix."

"Should I have woken him? Or, or closed the curtains anyway? Or done something? I'm not trying to fob him off on you or get out of the work, Mr Sutton, because I know he's left a big mess on the table, but I can come and help with it, it's just—"

"No, no," said Harry. "Best to leave it to me or Mr Brydon when you're uncertain of Mr Fox, Felix. Does he really intimidate you so?"

"It's not that he intimidates me, Mr Sutton, I just never feel as though I can get a footing with him. He's never said a bad word to me and he does apologise when he feels he's been harsh, but he really does almost explode, sometimes, whether he's been drinking or not, and it just... It sets my teeth on edge, is all."

"Your father is a veteran, isn't he?" asked Harry. "He has outbursts of shouting himself, an uneven temperament?"

Felix, who had squared his shoulders and set his jaw, as though trying to show he wasn't frightened of his employer, suddenly stared at Harry with his mouth agape. He blinked, once, and then a few more times. "Well," he said, "yes, but he's... he's not..."

"Mr Fox hasn't seen war himself, lad, but he is a man in pain. Pain makes a man unpredictable, and try as we might, it's only natural to be unsure of that which is unpredictable."

"I don't speak ill of him, sir," said Felix. "Or my dad – or, or soldiers, you know."

"I know," said Harry, with a neat nod of his head. "Get yourself off to bed, and we can talk a little more about this later in the week, if you like."

Felix nodded, mumbling a thank you, and Harry moved past him, beginning to ascend the stairs.

Brydon had served in the war, but he'd been struck with appendicitis after barely two months in France, and had apparently had some ensuing medical issue that left him in a hospital for nearly six months, after which he was declared unfit for return to service; as for Mr Fox Snr, Harry had vaguely understood that he'd been honourably discharged for some reason before, had guessed that perhaps that he was just too old for the draft, but if he was a regular sleepwalker, he supposed it only made sense that his doctor would have recommended against his serving.

Nightmares were one thing; a soldier placidly walking along whilst asleep on his feet was another entirely.

The library was bathed in red-tinged, late evening light, and Harry came to stand at the head of the long table, surveying the tableau with interest. A white sheet dappled with paint and varnish stains had been laid out over the table like a tablecloth, and spread out on its surface were piles of various pieces of metal. Some were panelled sheets of shining brass, but it was mostly screws, cogs, and axels, as well as what appeared to be keys, and for a baffling moment, Harry thought that Alexos had taken his typewriter apart in some sort of rage, before he saw the object's main carapace and drawer – a cash register, it looked like.

Written out on some paper was a list of pieces, and as ever, the notes were in Alexos' scrawled-out Greek, but Harry could read the numbers and see the tiny illustrations of each piece, enough to see that it was some kind of inventory.

Alexos himself was slumped in his chair, his head tipped forward in a way that made Harry's neck twinge just to look at, but while

Harry could see a glass at his side still with half a measure of golden liquid in it, he couldn't smell the drink at all even when he came closer.

"Mr Fox?" asked Harry in a clear, but not very loud voice. He didn't even stir, and Harry touched his shoulder. "Sir?"

Harry hid his wince as Alexos jolted, knowing what would come even as he jumped: Alexos hissed in pain after he suddenly straightened, both hands going to his bad knee, and at the same time he awkwardly straightened his neck, casting his gaze around the room. His teeth were gritted, his lips pulled back, and Harry felt a pang of genuine sympathy, seeing the pain writ all over his expression, and more than that, in the tension of his shoulders and chest.

"I do apologise for waking you, sir," said Harry.

"Time's it?" Alexos asked, teeth remaining clenched as he awkwardly rolled his shoulders, moving his neck back and forth. His hands were stained with oil and grime, which meant he'd cleaned the cash register pieces, Harry supposed, and that they'd been filthy when he'd started. It didn't look to Harry as though he were drunk, and without Brydon or Harry to bring it, he couldn't have had any of his stronger palliatives.

Harry had not yet seen Alexos Fox drunk, nor made to slur his words and come apart at his seams with codeine, but others on the staff had spoken about it. Felix had mentioned helping carry a drunken Mr Fox down the corridor in his very first week at the house, and while Mrs Perry rarely commented on it directly, instead making a great variety of "harrumph" and "hah" sounds when the subject was broached, Brydon had mentioned it.

Brydon had said, in relatively gentle, understanding tones, that Alexos' mood could be understood by what bottle he asked for, that he drank whiskey to soothe or to rest, gin or vodka to be drunk, cognac to be very drunk.

Uncle Reg hadn't phrased it like that. Uncle Reg said he drank cognac when he wanted to numb his mind. Codeine to numb his aching limbs.

Morphine to numb his soul.

"Past ten, sir."

"Fuck," muttered Alexos, rubbing at his head and leaving a smear of brown grease on the skin. He didn't appear to notice, didn't even glance down at his hand, and Harry saw there were a few stains on his rolled-up sleeves, the front of his waistcoat.

"Shall I run you a bath, sir?" asked Harry as he began to pull the curtains shut.

"Oh, yes, why don't you run me a bath, Sutton?" retorted Alexos sarcastically, shoving back his seat from the table. "Anything to get me undressed."

"I wasn't suggesting I chaperone the bath itself, sir, but I am of course happy to offer my assistance, if you find you desire it. Being as the subject appears to be on your mind."

This earned Harry a loud scoff.

"I don't desire it. I don't desire *you*, or your perversions," Alexos grumbled, voice hoarse with sleep, and then grunted. Harry, pulling the last of the curtains closed, turned to look at him, and saw the way he was leaning back against the table, rubbing at his leg while gripping his cane tightly in the other hand. He was leaning heavily back on the table, seemed not quite balanced as he tried to lean to rub just above his bad knee without tipping too far forwards.

"As you say, sir," said Harry, so pleasantly that Alexos turned a foul look on him. Harry stepped closer. "Ought I do anything with this disassembly, sir?"

"Leave it for now," muttered Alexos, rubbing at one eye with the heel of one hand, and mercifully it was clean enough not to stain the skin or, apparently, to sting, although he looked so exhausted and so focused on the pain elsewhere in his body that Harry wasn't certain that he'd feel it in any case. "I'm sorry if it offsets the maid, but I'll pack it all up to return to Mr Lloyd tomorrow." When Harry didn't say anything, Alexos said, more to the floor between them than to Harry himself, "I take things apart, sometimes. Devices, machines. I make use of some parts, and Mr Lloyd sells the scrap."

"Where does he get the machines?"

"Here and there. I don't tend to ask."

"How do you make use of the parts?"

"You're too close."

Harry, who'd come closer with each word passed between them, came to a stop. Standing directly in front of Alexos now, he kept his feet rooted to the floor but leaned closer, and Alexos' breath caught in his throat, his head tipping back and away. Harry wondered what his skin would feel like, if he slid his hands under his shirt, gripped his hips, wondered how Alexos would whimper if Harry straddled him and forcibly massaged the new crick out of his neck, turned his sleep-stiffened shoulders to jelly in his hands.

He was a more than adequate masseuse, and as soon as he could fuck him, he thought to massage Alexos too, soothe his pain as best he could. When Reg had first mentioned Alexos' drinking, some years ago, Harry had thought he meant he was a lush, but it was plain that wasn't true, and he took every other palliative very sparingly, feared to become reliant on any of it. He'd never truly internalised what that meant, before coming to the house, never fully understood quite why his uncle favoured Alexos so much, got a certain pinched expression when talking about him, at times.

Uncle Reg had never said he'd *prefer* it if Alexos were a drunk or an addict, but Harry had thought, at times, that perhaps he would. Seeing Alexos now, desperately leaning away from Harry but unable to move too far back because of the pain in his legs, his back, his shoulders, Harry understood.

"Am I?" asked Harry, keeping his voice low and warm, sultry in a way he knew made other men shiver, but Alexos didn't even flinch. "You don't want me this close, sir?"

He didn't lean even closer, not just yet. He stood his ground, and with Alexos' head turned dramatically away from him, he admired the column of his long neck, thought about how nice it would be to drag his tongue over the skin, bite at it, suck a bruise into place at its base.

"I will have your employment terminated, Mr Sutton," said Alexos, staring across the room instead of at Harry.

"Really? And how will you do so, Mr Fox? Tell your father, your mother? My uncle?"

Alexos' head whipped around to meet his gaze, and Harry saw the twinge in his expression at moving his neck so quickly, watched the careful way he brought up his hand to rub at its side, his elbow angled so that it didn't brush against Harry's chest.

"Your uncle," said Alexos, "does he know what a foul and despicable thing you are?"

"I'm his favourite nephew," said Harry. "He might have seen me as a son, were it not that you rank higher in his estimations."

Alexos' eyes narrowed, his lips drawing slightly back and his nose wrinkling. "Is that what this is?" he asked. "Jealousy?"

"No," said Harry. "Felix was uncertain of waking you, that's all. He saw your whiskey, thought you might be drunk."

Alexos glanced down at the glass, his face crumpling slightly. "My hands were shaking," he said. "I drank a measure, maybe two, to steady them. It made me tired, too, that's all – and I've been... rather involved, all day."

"Where did Mr Lloyd get a cash register? It looks as though it were filthy."

"This one, out of a demolition," said Alexos softly. "It was only slightly dented, the mechanism mostly intact, but it was filthy with smut from the fire beforehand, and that's before being relegated to the back of Mr Lloyd's shed, covered with dust and cobwebs." For the first time, he looked down at his hands, seeming to realise only now that his fingers were caked with filth, his clothes stained, and he reached up to his face again, but didn't actually touch it.

"Shall I run you a bath, sir?" Harry asked again.

"What do you think, Sutton?" asked Alexos, and met his gaze. His eyes, which carried the same naïve look his father's did at first glance, showed no naivety at all, up close like this, no matter that they remained large and brown and shone with the light in the room. There was a severity in them that Harry wanted to taste. "That if you carry this on often enough that I'll let you bend me over and bugger me? Am I the easiest target about, crippled as I am? You think I'm stupid as well, powerless, think you can blackmail me?"

"I don't want to blackmail you," said Harry plainly. "I have no intention of forcing you into anything, Mr Fox, nor strongarming you, nor taking you by surprise or coming up on you without your knowledge. I approach you face-on, Mr Fox, that you might see my intentions in their entirety, and comprehend them."

Alexos, lip curled, said mildly, "You've not denied wanting to bugger me, I notice."

"I do want to bugger you," said Harry. "I have every intention of doing so, Mr Fox – perhaps I will bend you over, over this desk or perhaps the end of your bed, your arms pinned at the small of your back, or perhaps my hand around your throat, pulling you against my breast, that you feel the full weight of my body against yours, and understand yourself overpowered. Perhaps I'll have you on your back, me between your legs, one of my hands holding your wrists in place as my other tugs at your cock, our gazes locked – in a position like that, perhaps I'd kiss you, too, feel your lips against mine. Lying back, I might bring you to straddle me, that your weight should best drive you down on my cock, or the reverse, perhaps. I'm not ordinarily one to take cock, but I'd be happy to sample yours, and I can assure you I'm capable of doing so without putting too much weight on your hips. I'm afraid I can't make any particular promises yet, Mr Fox, how I intend to sodomise you, or indeed, be sodomised – I rather plan to tailor our activities to your capabilities, what with your ailing joints. Were I to fuck you in such a way as to give you injury, we might not be able to fuck again."

Alexos hadn't interrupted him.

He looked almost too stunned to breathe, his eyes wide as dinnerplates now, his lips parted and showing the pink tip of his tongue and the order of his teeth. His face had whitened, took on a pallor, but as he'd gone on talking, his cheeks had taken up colour again, and they were blooming with red now.

"Why would I let you?" asked Alexos, breathing out the words. "You say you won't force me, Mr Sutton, and yet repeatedly I have refused you, each refusal falling on deaf ears."

"I'm going to run you a bath, Mr Fox," said Harry. "That you might wash off that grease before bed. Your cock is hard, I notice. Might I assist you with that, as well?"

He caught the fist before it landed, cupping Alexos' clenched fist between his hands and absorbing its momentum, bringing Alexos' hand against his chest instead. He had a good stance for fighting – imbalanced, more weight on the good leg than the bad one, but he kept his shoulders squared and let his hips move, and the punch had a surprising amount of power in it.

If it had landed, it would have been a solid strike across the jaw, would have been such a surprise it might even have knocked him for six. Alexos' hand, clutched against his breast, felt warm and slightly sweaty.

Alexos was looking at him, staring at him with his eyes wide and the snarl slowly falling from his lips, and Harry realised he was smiling. It was a genuine smile, felt warm where it curved his lips, was too much, and he schooled his expression back to something more professional.

"If I may say, sir, you don't appear as a man who throws a lot of punches," said Harry softly, "but your technique is impeccable."

Alexos swallowed, the gulp audible, and the muscles in his jaw moved at the same time. His hand clenched slightly tighter where it was cupped in Harry's hands, and Harry very carefully pushed his thumbs into the ball of his fist, prying his fingers open.

Alexos let out a gasping grunt of pain as he went to wrench back his hand, and Harry said, "Shh, shh, let me," and pressed down. Alexos whimpered, his eyes clenching shut, and Harry released another hushing sound as he carefully took the first knuckles of each of his fingers and massaged them between his thumbs and forefingers. He could feel the slick stickiness of the grease and dirt still clinging to Alexos' skin, felt it stick to his own instead, and as he worked to the next knuckles, he watched Alexos' face slacken further, jaw open. Alexos' face was unspeakably expressive, and he leaned all of his weight back against the table as Harry continued, to the middle knuckle, the first, pressing down on the tips of each of his fingers. His knees were pressed together, thighs rubbing against one another and the rest of his body stiff, even as Harry forced his hand to relax as much as he could.

"After exercise, particularly intense or vigorous exercise," said Harry, "small tears can occur in our muscle fibres. The stiffness and the tightness in your hands is because you've been clenching them so tightly, and the fibre is now repairing itself, knitting itself back together. The massage is forcing the stiff muscle tissue to relax, and it will help your blood flow, too, reduce inflammation. That soothes the pain in itself, but there are a lot of nerves in your fingers, and when they're as tight and stiff as they are now," Alexos gasped as Harry pressed his thumb hard into the meat of his palm, and began to rub a circle into it, "the nerves are contracted too, can easily be pinched or strained. Massage therapy is common for polio sufferers now, you know. I could help with your legs, too."

"Ye-*es*," Alexos grunted, breathing heavily, his cheeks a burning red and his eyes clenched tightly shut as Harry went on. "Because you'd, fuck, like that, wouldn't you? Lay me down so you can put your ha-*ands, ands*, on my thighs and reach higher while you're *at* it." Every other word jumped up in intonation, almost squeaking, and when Harry turned his hand over and slid his thumbs under the base of Alexos' own, the sound he released was unmistakably a moan. Harry kept going, didn't let up for a moment as he felt Alexos' tight muscles turn to butter under his ministrations, watched his thighs press tighter together. Alexos' cane fell to the floor beside them.

When Alexos suddenly leaned forward, Harry pressed harder, and Alexos' sobbing sound was something Harry wanted to clutch in his hands just like he was clutching Alexos' palm, wanted to hold forever as he watched Alexos' knees clench and his hips jump, his eyes clenching tightly shut even as a tear eked out of one of them.

"There," said Harry, gently coaxing Alexos' fingers to straighten and then bend again as his breathing began to even out, as he stopped rocking in his place. Alexos was trembling, and Harry cupped his hand, squeezing it between his palms.

Alexos took in a shuddering breath.

"Would you like for me to run you a bath first," asked Harry, "or attend to your other hand?"

"Bath," Alexos whispered.

Harry brought Alexos' hand up to his mouth, brushed his lips against the back of his knuckles and took care not to lick his lips afterwards, knowing he'd taste smut and oil instead of Alexos' skin. Alexos' intake of breath was hitched and beautiful and really quite tragic, in that it told Harry without words that no one had ever kissed his hand that way before.

He bent to pick up Alexos' cane, handing it over, and walked ahead of him to start running the hot water.

Alone in the corridor, he let himself smile again.

Chapter Seven

Alexos didn't know for how long he stood in his place, his feet frozen to the floor, his cane loosely clasped in his left hand. His right hand still ached, was still sore and hard to unclench from the natural fist it had been forced into, and he was trying to focus on it, focus on the pain, the discomfort, the tension.

It was hard to do that, when his left hand felt so loose and relaxed, when he was disgustedly aware of the wetness under the surface of his trousers, his cock soft and slick with it. He'd been sweating in his clothes all day, but not like this, not—

Sutton had smiled at him.

Not smirked at him. There had been nothing snarky, smug, or superior in the curve of his lips – it had been a gentle bow of their shape, his eyes soft, and when his lips had brushed over the backs of Alexos' well-massaged knuckles, they'd been so warm, and softer than he could have imagined.

Alexos slowly inhaled, carefully filling his lungs.

When he stepped into his bedroom, he could hear the water running next door, and he unbuttoned his waistcoat, his shirt, hesitated at the fastenings of his trousers. Where did he go from here?

He didn't have to wonder, in the end, had no time to think. Sutton stepped in from the bathroom and reached for him as though this were quite ordinary, pushing his shirt and vest from his shoulders before he dropped into a crouch at Alexos' feet. Alexos' cheeks experienced such a sudden flush of blood that he actually felt light-headed, although he preferred that the blood should rush upward than downward.

He couldn't breathe. Couldn't think. All he could do was step out of his shoes and socks when Sutton removed them, and although he gulped on nothing more than air and phlegm, he stepped out of his trousers and took off his under things, too.

Sutton's gaze lingered on parts of Alexos' body – the scarring from his leg braces worn too tight for too many years, minor at his ankles, more significant around his waist and his knees; another few scars at the back and sides of his neck; the way his left knee twisted slightly inward, the joint off-centre, the muscle of the thigh subtly lighter than that on his other leg; the light hair that dusted his belly, his chest.

Alexos' cock was soft, stained with its own slick and spend, but at Sutton's gaze on his naked body, it stirred to attention.

His grip was so tight on his cane that he thought it might crumble in his palm.

Sutton met his gaze. There was no smile, nor a smirk, on his plump lips. His expression was neutral, betrayed no emotion at all except perhaps for expectation, and it occurred to Alexos that in all his life, he had never been naked in front of another man as he was naked in front of Sutton now – had Sutton been naked in front of men? Many of them?

Had he fucked them, been fucked? He'd named half a dozen ways to fuck Alexos, easily, off the top of his head, each time with the tone of one who knew precisely how to action that position, who had actioned it a hundred times before, for whom sex with men was not merely a salacious fantasy, a dark secret, but was—

Fact.

Experience.

Alexos swallowed to keep from licking his lips as Sutton moved to fold his clothes, setting his soiled underclothes and his trousers by the basin to scrub out – Alexos' cheeks and the back of his neck burned hot with embarrassment, and he dropped his cane aside, limping into the bathroom where he could hide himself in the heavy mists made by the steam.

He said nothing as Sutton came back into the room, turning off the taps, and Alexos watched as he drew his fingers through the water, making the salts swirl in the mixture.

A part of Alexos almost dreamed, almost hoped, that Sutton would reach for him, that he would bend Alexos over the edge of the bath or shove him back onto the floor, fuck him against his will, by force. Would Alexos be forgiven by the world at large if he came with Sutton's cock piercing him open so long as he protested in the process?

"Do you require assistance, sir, climbing in?" asked Sutton softly. He could speak in such a warm and gentle voice, so rich as it was, and Alexos wanted to drink it like wine. "I might steady your arm."

"No," said Alexos, and braced his hands on the edge of the bath before easing his bad leg over the side and following after it.

He couldn't help the pained – and relieved – groan that escaped him as he sank into the hot water, falling in a little more clumsily than he intended and sending some of the water splashing against his chest, although he was lucky not to jar either of his legs in the process.

The water was hot, and the high temperature was a soothing but stinging balm. It bit at his skin and sank into his flesh, and he felt the ache in his muscles deepen before it let off somewhat. When he lowered his hands into the water, his left hand felt as though it were almost ready to become just as liquid; his right hand was soothed only a little, and his fingers remained stiff. He sank a little lower, feeling the water lap around his neck, and the momentary relief it offered the cricked and tired muscle there made him close his eyes and sigh.

"When I took my first leave from the war," said Sutton, holding out soap and a flannel, that Alexos would take them, "I had been abroad eleven months. In all that time I had not truly experienced a hot bath – the closest I had come was lukewarm water left over from some dented and abused kettle, and that only very rarely. This was not to say I or most of us were ever truly *dry*, for when it rained the rain stayed and settled, and even rotating between the trenches on the frontlines and further back, to the reserves or any of the support lines, even if for a moment I felt dry, I never felt clean, and I knew it would never be for long. When I came home my family hugged and kissed me, then dispatched me immediately to the bath waiting for me. I sank into it as best I could – being a large man, Mr Fox, I'm sure you understand I rarely sink into a bath as easily as others might – and felt the water on my every side. I felt it on the raw and blistered flesh of feet, where the skin peeled in places from my soles and between my toes, where I was always battling one infection or other, felt it kiss and bite at my grazes and small wounds, all my bruises, all my tired aches. For some few minutes I sank as deeply into that water as I could, like a newt or a frog with only his eyes peeking out, though for me it was my knees and my head. I wept with relief – cried until my eyes were dry, before I started scrubbing myself clean. I felt purified by it, and when I finally climbed out of the water, stained red and brown with the muck I'd carried with me, I felt born anew."

Alexos, still holding the flannel and soap in his hands, stared at the way his own knees almost peeked out from the water, listening, before he slowly began to scrub at his arms. He scrubbed his left side first, the bits he couldn't well reach with his dominant hand, although it hurt even to hold the flannel, different as it was to the brushes he'd been cleaning with. The hand Sutton hadn't massaged still wanted to return to that tight fist, scarcely able to stand the looser grasp the flannel demanded instead.

"You have a great many wounds from the war?" he heard himself ask, his voice coming out as little more than a whisper. Sutton was making himself busy, folding things about the room, setting his pyjamas close at hand – Alexos had seen he'd put his towels to hang over the hot water pipe, that they be warm when they touched his skin.

"Nothing terribly extreme," said Sutton. "A cut across my side, here, from a German bayonet, and above my elbow, here," he gestured to the bottom half of his left forearm, "a bullet glanced off me. Not enough to really pierce me through, but enough to create a mess and a scar. I'm dappled all over with little wounds from shrapnel or grazes and what have you, but nothing that you'd think of as a war wound to look at them, I'm sure. Most of my lasting injuries, Mr Fox, were mental more than physical – I'm sure the same might be said of us all. Even men missing limbs, I've heard state that to be the case."

"You were a medic."

"Yes, sir."

"Why?"

"Sir?"

"You volunteered? To be a medic?"

"I did, sir."

"I ask again, then: why?"

If Sutton was deterred by the way that Alexos was looking at him, keeping his gaze on Sutton and only Sutton as he filled the sink basin with water, he made no display of it, did not seem willing to admit to discomfort. He glanced back, meeting Alexos' eyes, and simply answered.

"I already knew how to set a broken bone, how to dress and bandage a wound, how to break a fever. It was my belief that I might be of more use, training in nursing and basic field medicine before I enlisted, and I believe this was so."

"But you were still on the frontlines?"

"Of course," said Sutton. "What place on earth would be better to dress an open wound than a trench, drenched in mud and smelling the ghost of mustard gas, your hands stained with the blood and gore of three comrades just disassembled by a grenade blast, gunfire over your head, more explosions sounding in the distance?" Alexos felt slightly sick at the cool, distant tone that Sutton used, but when Sutton saw his face, he gave him a small smile. "Some men do assume that I approached field medicine in an attempt to shirk my duty, and flee any scene of active battle. I did not mean to imply you were one of them, Mr Fox."

"I didn't feel that you did," said Alexos, and washed the flannel between his thighs, ran it over his cock, his belly, until he felt clean – until he stained the water with filth, no matter that he couldn't see it. There was something about the idea of Sutton with a rifle in his hands, a bayonet ready, holding a pistol, holding a gun, that made inner parts of him clench and twist and coil. Sutton, rippling as he did with muscle, was a strong man, and there was something mouth-wateringly enticing at the idea only of the strength in his hands, but the idea of his holding a blade, a firearm, some other weapon? Alexos focused on the rough scrub of the flannel gripped in his hand. "People think I'm a veteran at times, assume it must be so, when they meet me. Ask me what regiment I was in, or make some reference to my service."

He didn't know why he was speaking so casually, why he was letting Sutton talk about the war – certainly didn't understand why Sutton was talking about the war in the first place, but it meant they weren't talking about sex, or Alexos' cock, or the fact that Sutton had brought him off just by massaging his hand.

Sutton had said he'd do the other one. When?

"That bothers you?"

"Of course," said Alexos. "They imagine they're speaking to a hero, a gentleman who served in the heat of battle, was wounded by some German weapon in the service of his nation. It disappoints them to learn I'm merely an invalid scholar – assuming I am allotted the opportunity to correct them, that the conversation does not move on too quickly before I can."

"Do you wish you had?" asked Sutton.

"I beg your pardon?"

"Do you wish you had served?" asked Sutton a second time, and Alexos stared after him as he dipped into the bedroom, retrieving Alexos' trousers and setting them into the sink. "Do you wish you had had the opportunity – would you trade your polio and your somnambulism, if it meant you would have had to go to war?"

"No," said Alexos, without hesitation. He liked the way his answer seemed to give Sutton pause, the way Sutton's brow furrowed just slightly, the way that Sutton gave him a sideways look that showed his surprise.

"No?" Sutton repeated.

"I am not disparaging your service, Sutton," said Alexos. "Merely that I see no honour in war, and do not believe I would have felt proud to be a soldier. To be reduced to a pawn on Britain's chessboard, and just as easily sacrificed."

The rage that flashed in Sutton's eyes made Alexos' cock give a dangerous stir, and he set his jaw, setting himself to scrubbing at his shoulders with greater focus.

"I suppose it is quite easy, Mr Fox," said Sutton coolly, "to make your measures of honour and sacrifice, when you were never made to serve on those battlefields yourself."

"I expect that's the case, Mr Sutton," replied Alexos. "Mr Asquith and Mr Lloyd George were quite adept at doing so, in any case."

"You aren't a Liberal, I take it?"

"I'm not anything, Mr Sutton," said Alexos. "Not a soldier, not a Liberal, not a Conservative. I give nothing in service to this country, and nor do I betray it. I'm not so much as a feather on either side of the scale."

"Does that satisfy you?" was the response to that, a sort of bite to Sutton's voice, and Alexos shrugged his shoulders.

"I don't know, Mr Sutton. Do you think that it ought?"

"I think I might offer you a different kind of satisfaction," said Sutton. His expression changed, becoming keener, and Alexos didn't break his gaze.

"Masterfully played," muttered Alexos, though still jumped when Sutton came to kneel at the side of his bath. Alexos' mouth was dry, but he did not protest, did not pull away, as Sutton took his right hand from the water and held it in his own. "Did you do this at the Bisphams?"

"Massage the young master's hand?"

"Seduce him."

"Are you seduced, sir?" asked Sutton softly.

Alexos held his tongue then moaned as Sutton slid his thumbs hard against his four fingers, gently forcing them to straighten out. His bathwater sloshed about him as he stiffened, knees drawing up, his other elbow pressing against the bath's edge. His eyes closed tightly because he couldn't bear to look at Sutton as he worked over his hand, rubbing hard and pressing at every line of muscle and flesh just as he had on the other side, and mercifully, his cock was too recently spent to work itself fully to arousal again – it was half-hard in the water, the sensation *sublime*, but got no further.

"Do you like women, Mr Fox?" asked Sutton softly as his thumb slid over the heel of Alexos' palm, and Alexos whimpered, the sound breathless and airy to his own ears. "Are you a bachelor because you could not stand to marry?"

Alexos squeezed his eyes more tightly shut, gasping, and Sutton kept working and how, *how*, could he be so merciless, so unwavering, so constant? Was this the way that Sutton fucked? Even after Alexos had come, would he keep fucking him, use him as though he were but a toy, until he sobbed and begged for mercy?

It hurt.

It hurt, felt tight, felt pressured and hard and painful, and then it felt like his own muscle and flesh were being turned to heated, fluid wonder, felt like bread kneaded into softness and warm from the baker's own hand, and the relief was unbearable and like nothing he had ever known before. He was trying not to moan too loudly, trying not to cry out loudly enough that it should be heard in the corridor or in any of the other rooms, and Sutton kept going—

Until he stopped.

Alexos heaved in a gasp, feeling the tears that had been squeezed out once again fall onto his cheeks, and went limp in the water, shuddering, shaking. His cock was aching because it *wanted* to be hard, his bollocks drawn up tight in the water, though he couldn't quite reach a real erection, not just yet. He felt raw and ripped open, like all of his flesh had been peeled back to reveal what was underneath.

"I could do that," said Sutton in a slow, quiet voice that promised of things to come, "to every muscle in your body. Piece by piece, Mr Fox, I could work the tension out of your every line and fibre of flesh until you feel that relief, that sense of sudden jelly-like painlessness, almost all over."

"Almost all over?" repeated Alexos, opening his eyes, and Sutton smiled at him with heavily lidded eyes, his green eyes intent and aglow with a quiet passion.

"I can massage your muscles, sir, but not your bones and your scars – I have no doubt that I might palpate the painful flesh at your knees, your thighs, might relieve some pain, but there is a limit to what I might do. If my hands could cure polio, I would remain a medic today – and a popular one, I have no doubt."

Alexos laughed, and felt another tear on his cheek, to his surprise: he wiped it away quite hard.

"Do you dislike women?" asked Sutton quietly. "Do you find you lack attraction to them, as you find you have to men?"

"It used to be," said Alexos, "that at a function or party, women would see my cane and my retiring nature, and look past me to someone else. I'm not particularly handsome, after all – my features are exaggerated, I am thin and gangling, even before they notice my cane and signs of pain. But now, there are fewer men to choose from – and of those left of marriageable age, rather a few have worse scars and worse disabling injuries than I do. I might still be presentable, after all, if I might be subtly supported in a photograph, my cane hidden."

Sutton considered this, looking thoughtful, his lips shifted pressed together and his expression focused, concentrated. It was a professional look, really quite appropriate to and quite desirable in one's butler – stern and solid, with an unshakable air to it. Alexos wondered if this was the sort of expression Sutton wore when fucking men, pinning them beneath him, and he swallowed around the thickness in his throat.

"What is it you fear?" asked Sutton, still serious.

"I beg your pardon?" asked Alexos in immediate reply, and Sutton leaned slightly back upon his heels, his wrists resting upon the edge of the bath. He hadn't rolled up his sleeves to touch Alexos' hand, and a few droplets of moisture were dampening the white cuffs of his shirt beneath his jacket, and the skin of his hands shone with the wetness where it hadn't been entirely dried off, too. Alexos was struck, very quickly, with the wonder of what Sutton's fingers would taste like, if he had them in his mouth, and he swallowed hard to keep from coughing or letting out a noise, the water shifting as he pressed his knees together.

"You fear your desire of men, or fear that they should desire you," said Sutton. "What is it that scares you about this desire? You say you aren't particularly handsome – is that it? That you think yourself unattractive, undesirable, because of the proportions of your eyes, your nose, your mouth, because of the scars on your body, because of the weakness in your legs?"

Alexos stared at him, struck dumb, unable to answer.

"Do you fear arrest, reprisal? To be discovered for what you are, and condemned to public humiliation, if not hard labour? Do you fear the intensity of your desires, that they should consume you, were you only to indulge them? Or, perhaps..." Sutton's strong, meaty fingers curled around the edge of the bath, and Alexos stared at their shift and bend, at each of the knuckles, at the thickness of Sutton's thumb, the muscles that twitched in his hands. "Is it other men that you fear, Mr Fox?" he asked this in a quieter voice, a dangerous note to its tenor that made Alexos want to squirm. His gaze bored into Alexos' soul. "Do you fear the strength of other men, and the strength of their desire? Do you fear, perhaps, how easily a man such as me could unman you, if it struck me to do so? How I might throw your cane aside and pin you as it pleases me, move and position you like a ragdoll and bounce you upon the thickness of my cock? Do you secretly desire, Mr Fox, to be impaled and fucked by a man who ignores your cries of pain and powerlessness, until you are made quite mad by the pleasure and the pain alike?"

Alexos barely felt able to breathe, and after a few moments of silence ticked by, Sutton looked demonstrably down to his cock in the water, his erection finally stirring back to life in the face of such painfully arousing threats.

"Mm," hummed Sutton, and stood to his feet.

Alexos closed his eyes, thinking Sutton would draw away, but instead Sutton's hands landed on his naked shoulders, his palms resting heavily on the naked part of Alexos' upper back, and before Alexos could say a word, he squeezed.

Alexos' whine was muted by the grit of his teeth, his hands striking out to grip on the edges of the bath and squeeze as Sutton's strong thumbs traced lines down either side of his spine, as his fingers pressed into the muscle at the base of his neck. He felt Sutton's fingers slide smoothly over the textured scar tissue at his nape and the centre of his upper shoulders, felt the way he traced it. It was experimental, the way that Sutton moved his thumbs and his fingers, testing how thickly the scar tissue was laid, how deeply it went, and Alexos couldn't help but be aware, even as Sutton took hold of every tangled knot under his flesh and untangled it with agonising ease, that Sutton was doing this wherever he moved his hands.

He sensed, he traced and explored and searched, beneath Alexos' flesh and muscle to find where it was weak, to find where it was strong, to find where it was scarred and where it was healthy, and Alexos could feel the pressure change on his second and third passes over his shoulders, feel Sutton's movements change.

He mapped Alexos' body, not only based on its shape from the outside, but how it worked underneath. Sutton's hands pressed and pushed and massaged, and found where Alexos' bones were, how his muscles and fat and flesh were laid, all the better to work him over.

Alexos had to force his own thumb into his mouth, against his gritted teeth, to muffle the whines and moans he was letting out without actually biting down on his hand, and he felt it was merciful that Sutton didn't speak as he kneaded his shoulders into the same perfect, painless wonder.

His hips twitched, jumping forward in the water against his will, the water sloshing about when he couldn't control himself and moved too violently, some of it spattering over the side, no doubt dampening Sutton, too.

He couldn't tell exactly, this time, when it was that he came – there was a sudden release of pressure, but he felt as though that release happened twice or three times in the same few minutes, because Sutton's hands just kept working, so much so that Alexos felt a few pops and movements in his back as pieces out of alignment were put into their rightful place as the stiff muscle relaxed enough to allow them to, and it *hurt*, but it was ecstasy.

When Sutton finally finished, Alexos was limp, and Sutton curled his fingers in Alexos' hair, lowering him back against the bath's back, positioning him with his face upwards, his throat exposed.

"You're not frightened of anything," said Alexos softly, as Sutton's fingers now massaged his scalp, not pressing very deeply or very hard, but just running patterns over the flesh, under his hair.

"Do you think so?" asked Sutton.

"I must assume that to be the case," said Alexos. "Either you fear nothing, or there is something in me so desirable you would weight it against any sensible fear – fear of arrest, of lost employment, of humiliation, of reprisal. That stretches the bounds of my imagination."

"Don't you find me desirable?" Alexos opened his eyes, but couldn't turn his head to look at Sutton, to make out the expression on his face, with Sutton's hands holding his head in place. Not by gripping him by his neck or his ears or his hair, but simply by making such waves of gentle pleasure radiate out from his scalp he could not stand to move it. "Is it so unthinkable, that a man should desire another?"

"It's not unthinkable in the least that someone should desire *you*," said Alexos. "But if you haven't noticed, Sutton, you and I are made up of very different facets."

"I should like to combine our facets," said Sutton, curling his hand casually around the shape of Alexos' throat, making him shudder, although he applied no pressure, didn't even tease at choking. "Or at least, insert one of my facets into one of yours."

Alexos didn't mean to laugh. It tumbled out of his lips before he could even think about it.

"Let me get a jug," said Sutton, withdrawing his hands. "I'll wash your hair."

That night, Alexos laid in the middle of his bed, his shoulders so loose and relaxed it almost didn't feel believable, didn't feel in line with reality, let alone the rest of his body – Sutton had worked the tension from the upper part of his neck and shoulders, battled the tension and pain through his lower back, his waist, his legs, his arms, until it all came to looseness under his hands.

He couldn't decide whether he wanted Sutton to fuck him or massage his every inch – given a choice between one and the other, he didn't know that he would ever be able to decide.

His sleep that night, mercifully, was quite dreamless, and yet when he woke, Sutton's hands were what came first and foremost to his mind. He laid in bed, lax and impossibly rested, and thought of them for quite some time before he made to rise.

Chapter Eight

Harry's sleep that night was easy, somewhat dreamless, and quite restful.

His sleep the night after, on the other hand, was uneasy, fevered, and frequently interrupted by sudden fits and starts.

It was not for any reason in particular – he ordinarily had nightmares and did not consider them in themselves to be remarkable, but on nights where there was a certain wet, balmy heat to the evening's air, making it sticky, or on nights where fresh rain let the smell of mud filter into the house and settle in his nostrils, or on nights where his body remembered for some other reason what was behind it, in short, as viscerally as his mind did...

On nights like these, the dreams were worse. Such was a veteran's lot, and Harry knew very well that he was to be very grateful for how small his burden was in contrast to that of so many others.

The first time he woke, he was certain he was wet with sticky blood, and only when he had dropped two matches from trembling, clammy fingers and finally lit his candle again with the third was he convinced it was simply his own sweat; the second time he woke, he was sure the falling rain was the rattle of gunfire; the third time, it was with a hard, sudden start, and he was convinced for no reason whatsoever that he was eminently to perish in some horrible way.

The fourth time, he didn't try to go back to sleep, and stumbled down the servants' staircase in a distant haze after getting himself dressed.

It was a little past three with still an hour or two before Betty and Mrs Perry were due to rise, and so he sat for some time in the cool of the kitchen's stone walls, sipping at coffee. His breathing was even, his heart beating slow: his nightmares did not ordinarily trouble him overmuch, and although the nights like these were more visceral than others, they were not so visceral that they would interrupt or impact his capacity to perform his duties.

He thought of Alexos Fox in his bath, and that was a balm for the soul against all others, the way that the young gentleman responded to Harry's voice, to his idle thoughts and threads and flirtations, and most of all how he responded to Harry's hands...

Yes, Harry thought. He had made some progress with Alexos the night previous, making him come as he had, and he knew the skill of his own hands, knew that Alexos would crave their touch even more than he had before now that he had a taste of Harry's skill, but it wasn't only massage that Harry thought of.

He had had his suspicions spending time as he did with Alexos and observing that which made him free and easy and of good humour, and that which made him stiffen and harden his skin, and last night... Alexos wanted to play, and what was more, he wanted to play with what frightened him – Harry's strength, Harry's size, Harry's power over him, Harry's ability to ruin him, if he so chose.

Just at the thought, Harry felt the pleasant heat of the blood rushing between his legs, felt the slight flare to life of his cock, and he sighed, thinking of the day when he would finally work it into the tight channel of Alexos' arse – would Alexos moan? Scream? Cry, even, tears wet and shining on his cheeks even as he begged that Harry feed him more?

Harry hadn't been touching himself, of late.

He was not a man to deny himself pleasures, as a rule – he liked food, he liked good wine and whiskey, and most of all he liked to slide his hand over his cock, strum over the barbels it was pierced with, sink back into his blankets and enjoy the sensation. No, to touch himself was not quite so satisfying as when he speared another man open with his cock, broke them to pieces and rebuilt them in a more pleasing arrangement, worked them over until they begged for release, for Harry's touch, but it was not something he habitually denied himself—

Unless, in times like this, there was a further satisfaction to come, one that self-denial would only make all the keener, all the more pleasing. If he held off for a few days, he had no doubt that his orgasm would be all the more powerful when it came time to bury himself in Alexos – and he might spend more too, and leave even more than he otherwise would leaking out of his hole, which would wink so prettily, unable to clench itself fully closed again after Harry's passage.

Harry pressed the heel of his hand over his hardening cock, humming his satisfaction at the dull pleasure the motion offered him.

Yes.

Oh, yes, it would be *nice*, when he finally had Alexos wrapped around him.

It had been curious indeed to observe his reactions last night, to see the different ways in which Alexos showed his reaction to one thing or another, the twitch of his lips, the widening or the narrowing of his eyes, the things he said, and more prominently, of course, the things he didn't say.

He was everything Harry's uncle had described him as being, and yet he was so much more than that, so much more intriguing.

He had known him to be an academic. He had known him to be scarred and with a tendency to injury, known him to be disabled by his illness. His uncle had told him that Alexos was *quiet*, but that underneath that apparent retiring nature was a biting wit and a cool, cold sharpness, and yet when first Uncle Reg had described it, Harry hadn't thought as to what might make it up.

That icy nature was not merely bitterness at his invalidity – if anything, it seemed to Harry, Alexos was more irritable about people's responses to his cane and his limp than he was the muscle weakness itself. No, there was something deeper than that, a complexity and depth of thought and consideration that Harry had not expected to see in a young man of decent means, for all he was no prominent aristocrat.

There was something *more* under his skin, something that Harry had yet to unearth.

He'd taken it for cowardice, when Alexos had bluntly and immediately answered he preferred his polio to experience of a battlefield, but the other man had spoken with certainty and assuredness when he'd made his quips about the prime ministers. Alexos Fox might not have any friends, and no regular conversational partners that Harry knew of, but for all that it was plain this was an argument he'd had many times before, even if it was in the comfort of his own head.

And all this work he translated, the cannibalism, the Greek stories, the way he spoke about them so easily, with so much careful thought and consideration, such focus, and yet, there was no starry-eyed innocence in his eyes. For a man who, by all accounts, spent his every day and night ensconced within the walls of his home if not those of his library, he had a surprising weariness about him, and more than that, an awareness of the world at large.

It was very easy to be tired of the world and one's place in it – anybody could do that, even knowing nothing at all.

Alexos read the newspaper, rarely the headlines, and rarely the financial sections either – Alexos Fox paged idly through, almost casually, to the pages about local by-elections, minor fracas within the House of Commons or on the mainland, in France, Germany, Austria, or in the United States.

It amused Harry not that he did this, but that when his father asked him if he'd looked in the newspaper, Alexos would shrug and say he'd only glanced at the crossword, and that was all.

(The crossword, as it happened, that he could do as easily as breathing, and scarcely ever took him longer than five or ten minutes to fill out with a pen.)

Alexos, who pretended he had nothing to say so often, but would speak so keenly and so clearly; Alexos, who was fascinated by violence and his own fears; Alexos, who hated war and told a soldier so, and was unflinching even as he politely gave his apologies.

Harry left the kitchens just as Betty made her way inside, and it was as he came into the hall that he heard the sudden shout, and sprinted up the stairs to find Alexos sprawled on the landing, groaning in pain.

* * *

"How are we feeling?" asked Sutton.

"*We* are, on average, doing quite alright, I'm sure," muttered Alexos irritably, leaning heavily on the banister and breathing in a laboured fashion, his head forward against the varnished wood surface. "I, on the other hand, am fucking furious, and pretty Christ-damned tired, to boot."

Felix, who had been walking underneath the stairwell, flinched, and Alexos closed his eyes tighter and didn't look at the boy's face as he hurried away. Most of his body ached, obviously, which wasn't new, but the aches were in new and unusual places – having woken up just as he went over the barrier on the upper landing, he had at least managed to roll when he hit the floor instead of landing on his neck or spine.

His shoulder had been dislocated, which had been easy enough to fix, and from what the doctor had been able to ascertain, his side was primarily bruised, with no breaks or cracks to his ribs. He'd injured his hip, although before the doctor had even had a look, Alexos had known it was just the joint being jarred out of place enough to bruise the soft tissues, that there were no breaks or sprains to anything around the area.

The break in his arm had been clean, at least, and the doctor and Sutton had set it together, pinning it in place. It would be set for at least six or eight weeks, assuming the fracture healed well.

His right arm, mercifully. He could still write, still use his cane to pull things closer, still have a fucking wank – and not much else, because he'd sprained his fucking ankle, too.

"Do you still have your service revolver, Sutton?" Alexos asked the banister he was wrapped around, the varnished wood not soothing his sweaty forehead as much as he would prefer.

"Yes, sir," said Sutton.

"Will you shoot me with it?"

"No, sir, I will not."

"Teach me how to shoot myself?"

"If you don't continue your way up the stairs, Mr Fox," said Sutton pleasantly, "I will be forced to carry you."

Alexos, gripping tight to the banister, slid upward.

He'd slept the night downstairs on one of the more plush sofas, nursing his various new injuries and the ache in his head, and when he had stated his intention to do the same again tonight, Sutton had looked at him quite coolly, and replied, "No, sir."

It had made Alexos bark out a laugh, but he'd let himself be herded upstairs nonetheless.

"Will you help me shave?" asked Alexos two thirds of the way up the stairwell, taking another break and *aching*, all of his weight on his left arm and shoulder, taking as much weight as possible off of his useless left leg, even more useless than usual today. "I hate the stubble."

"Yes, sir," said Sutton. "Gladly."

They hadn't been alone together, since the other night, and at the top of the stairs, he clung tight to the banister even as Sutton loosely gripped his cane in his hand, offering it out. Alexos was soaked with sweat, trembling slightly, and his lungs ached from the effort of breathing whilst dragging himself up the stairs.

"I'll carry you next time," said Sutton in an undertone.

"You want there to be a next time," Alexos retorted in the same low voice, "you'll have to shoulder me down the stairs."

"I needn't do that," replied Sutton. "Blowing out a lungful of air to unbalance you would probably do the trick."

Alexos laughed. It made his bruised ribs hurt – it made everything hurt, naturally. He almost wished he *had* broken his neck in the fall.

There was a bowl of hot water and foam waiting for them in the bathroom, and Sutton set a stool down for him, letting Alexos sink down against it before he helped Alexos off with his clothes, and Alexos didn't argue, didn't struggle. He savoured, although he didn't want to admit to it, the brush of Sutton's warm fingers over his skin as he loosened the sling and held Alexos' arm steady, letting him remove his clothes.

"No complaints," said Sutton softly. "Ought I take this to mean you're no longer to make token resistance to my seduction of you?"

"Do you use the phrase *token resistance* with all your victims, Sutton?" asked Alexos.

"Only the most satisfied ones," replied Sutton breezily, and Alexos stared at him as he took the straight razor, flicked the blade out, and began to sharpen it on a belt. Alexos didn't much like the new safety razors, didn't like their shape or the way they felt in his hand – he liked the precision of a real straight blade.

Sutton had looked him over before the doctor had arrived, and Alexos had found him capable and assured in his administration of first aid; the past day, Sutton had mostly kept in Alexos' presence, had brought his notes and his books downstairs for him to work from, although it had been almost impossible to concentrate.

"I want to take the codeine tomorrow, Sutton," Alexos said quietly, shivering at the slight cool of the room and awkwardly leaning forward, trying to take some of the weight off of his injured hip.

"The morphine might be better," said Sutton.

"Shut the fuck up," he muttered. "The codeine will more than do."

"And will you be drinking as much gin with your codeine as you've drunk this evening?"

"Only time will tell," said Alexos, "but for all Brydon might have implied to you I'm an addict and a lush, Sutton, I don't tend to mix my poisons unless I'm drinking a cocktail."

"Mr Brydon has never said anything of the sort, sir," said Sutton, with too much wry humour to be diplomatic. "Though in future, if you would take my recommendation, I should rather a night like this be spent with vodka than gin. Your mild inebriation is not nearly so strong a deterrent as the smell."

"Your objection is duly noted, Lieutenant," said Alexos, rolling back his shoulders. The gin had settled as a pleasant warmth in his extremities, dimly distracting from although not nullifying the pain, and perhaps it was that pleasant heat that made him so uncaring of his shirtlessness, or perhaps it was simply the fact that Sutton had seen him shirtless enough that it almost didn't matter.

It did matter, of course.

He watched Sutton's hands as he ran a brush through a bowl of shaving foam, and distantly wondered what they'd feel like if Sutton tugged at his nipples. His skin was hot, wanting. His gaze dipped down to Sutton's crotch, and although he looked away almost immediately after, Sutton chuckled.

"What *are* you frightened of?" asked Sutton.

"According to you, cock and murder," Alexos murmured, sighing with pleasure as Sutton started daubing the cool, frothed scream over his stubbled cheeks. "Isn't that what everyone's afraid of?"

"I used to be frightened of mustard gas," said Sutton casually.

"You astonish me, Sutton," said Alexos. "All that time in the trenches gave you no affection for the stuff?"

"I'm still frightened of horses," said Sutton.

"Really?"

"Not ponies or riding horses," was the answer as Sutton pushed his head gently to the side, putting more foam into place. Alexos grunted quietly, shifting the position of his sling. "Cart and plough horses, though – the big ones."

"Draft horses," Alexos said. "Clydesdales, Shires, Suffolks. You're still frightened of them?"

"I wouldn't run and hide from them," said Sutton. "But I'm on edge with them, and I flinch easily, which as I'm sure you can imagine, they don't much like."

"I'm frightened of birds," said Alexos. "Not like you and horses – I'm actually frightened of them. They don't bother me when they're where they belong – outside, in trees, but not... not inside. I can't move properly away from them, and I don't like how fast they move, how erratic they are."

"They don't mean any harm," said Sutton softly. "Any bird that's trapped inside just wants to make its way out again."

"I know they don't mean any harm," said Alexos. "I know it's not their fault. No more than it's my fault I can't move fast enough to get away from them."

Sutton's look was wry and distantly hungry.

"Have you fucked a lot of men like me?" asked Alexos. "Invalids, cripples?"

"Imagining me bouncing a quadruple amputee on my cock, are you?" asked Sutton, and Alexos stared at him, his jaw dropped open, which made Sutton hum, amused. "Not so easy to shock a man that can shock you back, is it?"

"No," Alexos murmured, hypnotised by the forest green and verdant colour of Sutton's eyes, and the delicate shine of his thick eyelashes. They were thicker than any lashes he'd ever seen on a man, but they didn't make him look unmasculine at all, somehow, what with how heavily lidded his eyes were.

When Sutton lifted the razor, the blade glinted under the shine of the light, and Alexos' heart was thumping heart in his chest.

"It would be very easy for me to kill you like this," said Sutton softly.

Alexos gulped, feeling more heat on his skin, more sweat, the exertion of the stairs, the pain, the gin, all combining with the sudden arousal that came at Sutton holding a sharpened blade in his hand and talking about his murder.

"I'm sorry," Sutton said, not sounding at all like he meant it, and he chuckled very quietly. "I only mean, sir... Am I more or less frightening than a bird?"

"Less, I should think," said Alexos, feeling pink and flushed, the shaving foam strangely heavy on his cheeks and the underside of his neck. "You won't hurt me. A bird might without meaning to."

"Isn't it worse if I mean to?"

"Do you?" asked Alexos.

The butler slid the razor up the side of his jaw, rendering the skin underneath hairless and utterly smooth, and Alexos released an embarrassing squeak of sound, his free hand gripping the base of the stool beneath him, his injured arm still against his chest as he squeezed his palm into a fist, all in aid of not fidgeting under the blade.

"Not today," said Sutton mildly. "Apparently."

Alexos pressed his knees together. "You shouldn't say such dark things with me, Sutton," he said. "People might misconstrue your intentions, and then where will you be?"

"What intentions do you think I have toward you?" asked Sutton, and gripped him by the hair, tilting his head to the side and adjusting the angle at which he was working. Alexos' eyes fluttered closed as Sutton slid the blade up over his skin, the movement too smooth, the blade too sharp, for it to be called a scrape.

"I believe you've made your intentions quite clear, one way or another."

"Mm, maybe so," said Sutton. "But between the gentleman who throws out more fucks than he does thank yous, curses like a sailor, and the butler, honourable veteran than he is, who makes a few occasional teases of violence, I believe we'd be hard-pressed to find an easy winner between us in a dispute of public opinion."

"You needn't spare my feelings, Sutton," Alexos murmured. "My bourgeois position aside, I'm a funny-looking creature with no friends, no wife, and a cane to keep me company, and my filthy mouth is only icing on that cake. You'll win every time."

"Best we stay on the same side, then," whispered Sutton in his ear, and Alexos moaned out an exhalation at the delicate graze of his teeth over where the foam had just been shaved away, the skin sensitive from the slide of the blade.

Sutton rinsed the blade in hot water, and Alexos shivered at the sight of his eyes, their colour a little darker – his pupils were bigger, his skin slightly flushed.

"My uncle always sang your praises, you know," said Sutton.

"I'm sorry," said Alexos, and Sutton laughed.

It was a wonderful laugh, deep and rich and all-encompassing, and Alexos ached to know what it felt like, that laugh, if you were touching Sutton's chest, his belly, as he let it out.

"What ever are you sorry for?"

"I don't know."

"He says you do that," said Sutton. "Apologise for nothing. But of course, you're not apologising for nothing – you're apologising because you're worried about being the favourite nephew of a man who isn't even your uncle."

"Second favourite," said Alexos. "You come first, as far as I can tell."

"Oh, but it's hotly contested," said Sutton, and slid the blade once more up the side of Alexos' jaw.

"I'd hate to have you angry with me," muttered Alexos. "Seems a dangerous thing, one's butler being angry with one."

"I'm not angry with you."

"You're threatening to kill me out of love and affection, then?"

"Something like that," purred Sutton, and delicately slid the base of the blade up underneath Alexos' throat and jaw, and Alexos resisted the urge to swallow and make the skin jump or hop under the sharp cut. "If you and I are ever to get along, Mr Fox, you really must learn to determine when I am *really* threatening, and when I am teasing."

"Do you always tease with a blade in hand?"

"Sometimes I tease with a gun."

Alexos shivered, and Sutton smirked down at him.

The razor scraped delicately over the underside of his jaw. Sutton's hands were impossibly strong and steady, and the movements of his hand were pleasant and rhythmic – slower than they needed to be, too, because he was taking his time.

"My uncle said you used to go out," said Sutton. "When you were still in university, and for a few years afterward. He said you stopped."

Alexos thought of the little speakeasies he'd once gone into from time to time – the friends he distantly knew, casual as they'd been, were most of them gone now, the ones that hadn't died, and he didn't talk to anyone any longer. "I had no idea Reginald spoke about me so much."

"He liked you," said Sutton. "Still does, in fact."

"What *are* your intentions toward me?"

"To be your butler," said Sutton.

"That's not all."

"You'd like to be more?"

"*You'd* like to be more," Alexos retorted. "Fuck me, fuck my throat, make use of my body, take me to pieces and examine what's left in the middle."

"That's hardly fair," said Sutton. "You don't think I'd like for you to fuck *my* throat?"

"I can't move my hips like you can move yours."

"Luckily, I can still move my head."

"Were you a whore before you joined the army?"

"I was, but I got a good deal of practice there," Sutton replied smoothly.

Alexos had never talked like this with anybody. Not with another man, a woman, a stranger or a friend, not with anybody – he'd never dare or want to dare, but now he wanted to dare and desire and feel Sutton's hands on his cock. It was invigorating, liberating.

Arousing. His cock was hard.

"I don't go out anymore," said Alexos, "because even as a young man, I wasn't well-equipped to flee if an establishment I was in was raided. I'm not *old* by any means, but I can't run as well as I used to."

"Perhaps a policeman would take pity on you," said Sutton idly.

"I'm not rich or titled enough for a policeman's pity, Sutton," said Alexos. "Unless you mean a policeman's *compassion*, which I'm not of the opinion they're in possession of."

Sutton stared down at him, his lips shifting into a slight smirk, seeming pleased, his gaze focused and hungry and wanting.

"I thought about pursuing medicine after the war," said Sutton, beginning to shave away the little edges and corners of Alexos' jaw and chin, shaving away the last of the hair that clung to his skin. Sutton's hand was wonderful in his hair too, and Alexos almost wanted to melt between its grip and the sharp blade occasionally threatening to slit his throat.

This situation was somewhat more precarious than being in the backroom of a clandestine establishment for like-minded men.

"Why didn't you?"

"I couldn't be a doctor," said Sutton. "I didn't go to a particularly fine school, and nor did I go for long enough... But I might have been a nurse."

"Why weren't you?"

"My uncle said he wanted me here," said Sutton. "That he should like for me to take his position."

Alexos stared at him in horror, feeling his stomach give an uncomfortable flip as Sutton went away for a towel to wash off his face. Alexos was dry-mouthed and couldn't believe it, couldn't *believe* it, as he demanded, "You meant to tell me you could have left service, and you didn't, because your uncle insisted?"

"He didn't insist," said Sutton. "He suggested. More than that – he offered."

"Offered?"

"You read a lot of books, Mr Fox," said Sutton mildly. "A lot of books, and all those ancient stories. Isn't that so?"

"Yes?"

Sutton leaned in close again, dangerously close, so close that he could smell Sutton's spiced cologne, and feel the whisper of Sutton's breath against his lips.

A sound, quiet and desperate, eked out of his throat.

"My uncle," said the butler, as their noses touched, as Alexos looked so deeply into his eyes he felt like he might drown in their forest green colour, "told me you were quite a handsome man, for being flat-footed, clumsy, and a pain in the arse."

Alexos laughed, surprised. "Is that so?"

"Yes," said the butler. This was teasing, Alexos thought, because he was holding the blade once again, cleaning the lingering foam off of the blade. "In all those books and ancient tales, Mr Fox, haven't you ever heard of an arranged marriage?"

"Marriage?" Alexos repeated in a whisper, his horror fading into something warmer and indescribably pleasant, so much so that he felt like he'd taken the codeine already. He felt *giddy*. "Sutton, what the fuck are you *talking* about?"

"You and I are made of the same unspeakable material," said Sutton simply, and stroked two fingers down the side of Alexos' jaw, and the touch was so impossibly tender, making the newly shaved skin tingle, that Alexos slowly inhaled. "You are to be the master of this house, Mr Fox, and my uncle did not want you isolated and alone; with me as your butler, you will be neither, and I will command your household, be permitted not only the employment security that even a *butler* is guaranteed as we move away from traditional service and traditional domestic staff in these changing times, but the power and status that accompanies it. Apart from that, my uncle thought we might... complement one another."

"But we can't," said Alexos, trying not to laugh with his breathless enthusiasm, the burn in his cheeks, his arousal forgotten in the place of a far more overwhelming emotion, "I can't, *you* can't, it's... Sutton, we couldn't possibly—"

"Why not?" asked Sutton. "Don't you want to?"

Sutton had set the shaving blade aside, and his hands were sliding up Alexos' knees, his thighs, touching his good hip and avoiding his bruised one, and Alexos thought he might burst into flames, it was so overwhelming a sensation.

"Don't you see that I can help you, Mr Fox?" asked Sutton. "And suffice it to say, I do feel I've made clear how this particular union might be mutually beneficial even if you never let me touch your cock. However—" One of his thumbs hooked in the loop of Alexos' belt, and Alexos gasped and grabbed his wrist with his good hand.

"It's wrong," he said.

"How can it be?" asked Sutton. "Who will bat an eyelid at a gentleman performing his duties and the butler who manages his household?"

"This is your intention?" asked Alexos. "This was your intention all along?"

"It is," said Sutton. "I suppose it might be more appropriate at this juncture to call it a proposal. My uncle views you already as something like a favourite nephew – why not affiance us, and take you as a nephew in uncommon law?" Sutton sighed with apparent pleasure, then dropped to his knees on the bathmat. "But I can see you need further convincing. Or threatening – you seem to respond rather positively to that."

"Didn't you just assure me you were teasing?"

"It gets you hotter under the collar to imagine I was threatening, doesn't it?"

"I don't see how that's any of your business."

"Were we to be married, I would make it my business." Resting on the floor, he said softly, "You needn't say yes right away."

"How could I possibly say yes?" asked Alexos.

Sitting up on his knees but remaining on the floor, Sutton unbuttoned the front of his jacket, and slid it off his shoulders, passing it up to Alexos. Obediently, his mouth dry and his throat spasming against his will, Alexos set the jacket aside and stared down at the way Sutton filled out the white press of his shirt and of course, his waistcoat. He was very... Large. Rounded. Heavy. *Strong*.

"Looking at me," purred Sutton, "how could you possibly say no?"

"Arrogant," said Alexos.

"Realistic," replied Sutton, and when he undid the front of Alexos' trousers, Alexos shivered, but he didn't pull away. He carefully spread his legs a little further apart, and bit the inside of his lip.

"My father—"

"Your father need never know, nor your mother," said Sutton. "You are, as you are fond of telling me in your infuriatingly self-pitying terms, invalid and infirm. Who in this house will bat an eyelid at the time we spend together in private like this, knowing you to be in pain and disabled, and me to carry medical training and your trust?"

"Mr Sutton, I've always tried very hard," said Alexos in a strained voice, feeling his cock strain just as much in his trousers, "to resist temptation."

"Then I shall simply endeavour to try harder in tempting you," said Sutton, sliding his fingers over the shaft of Alexos' cock through his underwear, his head soaking the fabric with pre-slick, and Alexos whined.

"I shall die if you tease me like this, Sutton."

"I plan to bring you to a thousand little deaths," said Sutton softy. "If you will only consent to let me."

He should have said no. He should have told Sutton no, told him he was a degenerate, a pervert, that he would never consent as Sutton wanted him to, that it was insane beyond measure to suggest a—

A *marriage*, and yet...

A marriage.

Alexos Fox, married. To a man, yes – to Sutton. Pre-arranged.

"We would not be spouses right away," said Alexos. "We need to— If you change your mind, Sutton, you must tell me. I can give you a glowing recommendation that you might take a similar position in another house, or lean on my father. You could work in medicine yet, if I didn't meet with your expectations."

"And if I don't meet with yours?" asked Sutton.

"Mr Sutton, a cynic I might be, but even I'm not in the habit of making complaints because I've won the lottery."

To Alexos' surprise and impossible, flustered delight, Sutton actually averted his gaze, and a fresh heat came into his plum-red cheeks. What with the beautiful thickness of his eyelashes, he looked almost—

Demure.

"Flattery will not get you everywhere, Mr Fox," said Sutton, "but it will get you somewhere."

He leaned in toward Alexos' crotch, mouth open, and Alexos grabbed his shoulder. "Wait. Wait."

"Wait?"

"I can't— Not here. The stool, I'll fall."

"Ah," said Sutton, standing to his feet, and he gave Alexos no warning before he lifted him, laughing breathlessly, head spinning, mouth dry, giddy and feeling like he had to be dreaming with a blush burning to the roots of his hair, and carried him bridal-style over the threshold of the bathroom toward the bed.

Chapter Nine

Alexos wasn't sure quite how he came to be naked on the bed. Certainly, he understood the typical process, the removal of socks, of his trousers and underwear, all that usual wherewithal, but for all he knew, Sutton had vaporised what he'd been wearing with some sort of sorcerous power, because it was all lost to him.

All he was aware of now was himself back on the bed, Sutton on top of him with his hands either side of his waist, his mouth dragging down the side of Alexos' neck, his tongue slipping down to dip and curl around the rim of his collarbones' hollow. Sutton's tongue was hot, dexterous, and skilful, leaving a streak of heat down Alexos' chest as he mouthed further down, and Alexos couldn't help the noise that eked out of his throat, breathless and full of want.

Alexos' cock was so hard it *ached*, and Sutton gently pushed his thighs apart. His hands on Alexos' skin were strong, full of weight, and his fingers played delicately over the muscle of his flesh, careful not to touch or press on scar or injured muscle. His hands were unspeakably warm, but far hotter than his touch was the weight of his gaze: Sutton was looking at Alexos' cock as though he saw in its shaft's curve and the wetness of its head a reflection of the divine, his lips open, his eyes focused in worshipful attendance.

Sutton was still fully dressed, his shirt cuffs still buttoned even, his collar, but Alexos was more than naked; his foreskin was drawn back, such that his cock was bared and brightly pink, glistening with a wet shine, and Alexos couldn't help but clench his muscles so that his prick jumped and bobbed.

Alexos' heart was pounding so heart he felt as though it were going to jump right out of his chest, perhaps that his veins would burst and that his whole body would be wrenched apart by the strain of it.

Harry leaned forward, tilted his head to the side and looked over the side of his cock, tracing the curve of his shift with his eyes. He wasn't touching him just yet, pressing his hands a little harder against Alexos' thighs, sliding further, up into the inner crease of his thighs. A little pearl of liquid came up from his cockhead, sliding down the shaft of his cock and over his balls, and he hissed.

"Sutton," he whispered, "Sutton, Sutton, Sutton—"

"I believe you can probably call me Harry at this juncture, sir," said Sutton.

Alexos opened his mouth to reply, but he didn't get the chance to: Sutton opened his mouth and swallowed Alexos' cock down whole, taking him right into his mouth, his throat, his lips encircling the base of Alexos' cock, and Alexos almost screamed. It was sublime beyond measure, so overwhelming he thought it might kill him, the wet heat of Sutton's mouth, the slide of his tongue against Alexos' cock, and he didn't mean to, didn't *want* to, but he was coming.

Sutton swallowed it down, swallowed *him* down, and Alexos could feel the clench and pull of Sutton's muscles around him, the tightening of the muscles at his throat, the push and press of his tongue, the tightening of his lips, and all of it, all of it so wet, so hot—

"Shh," Sutton hushed him when he pulled away, and Alexos realised there were tears streaking his cheeks, dripping down off his jaw on each side, and Sutton wiped his cheeks with his handkerchief, the movement gentle and easy, and Alexos gasped in his next breaths, dizzy with sensation.

His cock was softening, spend stained on the sheets between them, but Sutton was laying kisses against the side of his neck, his hand curled around his other hip, and then he pulled delicately away from him.

"Harry?"

Sutton was already halfway across the room when the knock sounded on the door, and Alexos flinched, dragging at the sheets to cover himself, but Sutton had already opened the door a crack, and was saying, "He's alright – I'm afraid he just fell getting out of his bath."

"It was a hell of a shout," said Felix, out-of-breath. "They heard it down in the kitchens."

Alexos put his head in his hands, mortified, and called, "Sorry!"

"It's alright, sir, I'm glad you're not hurt!" Felix called back, and Sutton closed the door, turned to look at him, his hands and shoulders back against the wood, his eyebrows raised.

He looked playful, dangerously so, and Alexos stared at him, almost imagined a sort of halo around his dark hair, imagined that he was some angel – or perhaps, delectably, a demon – come to do him in.

"Your responsiveness is quite the enticement," said Sutton mildly as he came forward, undoing the links of his shirt cuffs and setting them on the dresser. "Although we might want to work on your vocalisations – or at least, how loud you are about making them."

"I've never had a mouth on my cock before," said Alexos. "Apologies for enjoying it."

"Your apology is accepted," said Sutton, sitting on the edge of the bed, and Alexos leaned forward, leaning on his good hand as his other remained against his chest. He didn't know if Sutton would make him put it back in the sling before bed. "I plan to inure you to some effects of my mouth, though not entirely."

"Oh, really?" asked Alexos, and then felt his mouth fall open.

Quite delicately, Sutton was folding up the fabric of his shirt sleeves, folding them back bit by bit until he settled them up to his elbow. This was all well and good, and would have been painfully attractive in itself – with Sutton being such a big and muscular man, this showed in the fat, strong meat of his forearms, the thick hair dusting them, the dangerous strength of his wrists, even the slight pulse and movement of his tendons under the skin. They were hands that could kill a man quite easily, squeeze his neck, and it was impossible not to consider what he might do with them to a man's cock, but—

Alexos wasn't really thinking of any of that, in the moment.

Sutton's arms, both of them, were covered in tattoos.

Alexos awkwardly shifted forward on the bed, taking Sutton's great hand in his own, and he almost reverently pulled Sutton's hand forward, examining his left arm. He'd seen tattoos before, of course – he remembered one older man laughing and scandalously showing a friend the hot air balloon tattooed on his ankle at a bar years ago in Oxford; naturally, he'd seen labourers and sailors in the city or in towns, but what Sutton had wasn't a hastily tattooed name in a banner, nor the more elaborate but relatively simple sparrows and compasses that were usually tattooed on the visible parts of a sailing man, on his hands or lower arms.

Sutton's arm was wrapped all around with beautiful etchings: flowers of all kinds, growing out of what appeared to be a hedge behind them, and the tattoo artist had even made little holes and gaps in the hedge to show tiny bits of his flesh underneath, almost as if the hedge was a sleeve with its own tears.

He recognised a lily, an orchid, a carnation, a pansy, an African daisy. Each one of them was inked in such vibrant black ink, with delicate shadows and highlights inked underneath their petals and the upper part of their stems, that they seemed to pop up off the skin.

Even as Alexos touched them with his thumb, sliding his fingers up Sutton's wrist, he almost couldn't believe they weren't all *real*, no matter that he was brushing past and underneath the hair on Sutton's arm to do so.

"Would you like to see the other arm?" asked Sutton.

"You have more?"

Sutton pulled up his other sleeve, and Alexos laughed breathlessly, reaching out to touch these tattoos too – on this side, there was another hedge, but it was tattooed all over with criss-crossing brambles, showing blackberries in glistening black bundles, ready to pick; there were rosehips, plump sloe berries, and as if they'd landed on one of the leaves, some elderflower petals that looked so phenomenally real he almost couldn't believe they didn't come away when he brushed over them with his thumb. Everything was tattooed in shades of dark blue and black, but somehow, he almost imagined he could see the colour in them.

"Oh," whispered Alexos, and shoved Sutton's sleeve up further, making him laugh. Sutton put his hand out, palm up, and straightened his arm slightly to give Alexos the space to push up his sleeve. Tattooed on the inside of his elbow was a little dormouse, curled up with his paws and tail shifted up to clutch the fat, shiny rosehip against its chest. Sutton put out his other arm, pushing up his sleeve, and Alexos laughed at the way it was designed, like a head poking out from between the bushes. "A polecat?"

"A weasel," said Sutton, and Alexos touched the weasel's delicately inked muzzle and its shiny black nose, its beady black eyes, the strange rounded edges of its little ears.

Alexos looked from where he was holding Sutton's wrist, his long fingers wrapped around the wonderful heat of him, up his shoulders, his chest, down to his belly. Sutton was a big man, fat, broad, tall – there was a lot of canvas on him for a tattoo artist to work with, and he could never have imagined he would find *tattoos* on his body.

He'd never seen a man with tattoos like this except in etchings for the circus or some other manner of freakshow.

"You have more?" he asked.

"Yes," said Sutton.

"Where?"

"All over," murmured Sutton. "I had no idea you'd be so entranced."

"Well, I don't get out much," said Alexos. "When you reveal I can see more art than in a museum from the comfort of my own bed, and touch the canvas with my fingers, no less, a man is going to be entranced. I've never seen tattoos up close before – and never any so, so *real*-looking, so vibrant! Did they hurt?"

"Yes," said Sutton, chuckling. "Don't you know how a man is tattooed, Mr Fox?"

"Alex," he said.

"Alexos," said Sutton, and Alexos was surprised by the relief it gave him, chuckling, glancing down a moment.

"It used to be that tattoos were used to mark criminals and prisoners of war," said Alexos. "A tattoo was a punishment, you see, a permanent mark of shame – or used for bureaucratic purposes elsewhere, for example, to mark if a slave had paid his taxes, or that a criminal had served his sentence, or to mark a gladiator in service to the colosseum. These are just the various Greeks and Romans, of course – the Celts, the Picts, the Britons, they all had tattoos themselves apart from body paint with woad, and the Thracians..."

Sutton was looking at him with an expression Alexos didn't know what to make of, and he faltered, uncertain. Sutton smiled, his handsome cheeks warmly red.

"Please," he said. "The Thracians?"

"Nobles wore tattoos," said Alexos softly. "People of noble birth, rich people. Priests and priestesses, even. According to Herodotus, anyway, as much as the old bastard can be trusted."

"They're made with a machine nowadays," said Sutton. "Most of mine were, anyway – it's almost like the needle on a sewing machine, one primed with ink instead of thread, operated by a small engine. The needle pierces the flesh, deposits ink beneath it, where it settles, insoluble, permanent."

"All over?"

"My sleeves are completed," said Sutton quietly. "My back. A good deal of my chest, some of my belly. My left leg is more finished than my right."

"You got them in the army?"

"I started in the army," said Sutton. "A lot of us got tattoos as a passing curiosity, when meeting circuses or travelling artists, but I became rather fascinated with the art, and I'm in contact with a few artists in London, in Manchester. An old friend who lives in Paris. I enjoy the challenge and focus the pain brings, not to mention the art itself – and the response it gets from other men."

"They're beautiful," said Alexos. "I never... I never imagined..."

"Did you imagine much of me?"

Alexos nodded dumbly.

Sutton kissed him.

It was a tender kiss, slow and very gentle, Sutton's lips warm against his own, and Alexos kissed him back. He expected Sutton to break away, for this to be a precursor, but it was no such thing. Sutton moved slowly on the bed, only breaking away from the kissing to scatter a few pecks and nibbles on Alexos' jaw, his cheek, before beginning to kiss him again.

Sutton's weight was a wonderful impression on the bed beside him, and with the softness of Alexos' mattress, one that he'd picked out specifically so that he'd sink into it and wouldn't move around too much in the night, assuming he didn't sleepwalk, Sutton made a well in the surface and Alexos was naturally pulled in toward him. Alexos fell against Sutton's chest, overwhelmed by the plushness of it, its heat under his hands and the lean of his body.

One of Sutton's legs slid against his, but didn't push between his thighs or hard against him: he let Alexos control that, so he could do it in a way that wouldn't too much pressure on the joint of his knee, or put his newly sprained ankle in a difficult position.

Sutton was still kissing him, and Alexos' head was spinning.

How long had they been kissing now? Five minutes? Ten?

Every moment made his lips more sensitive, blood filling them fat and full and bruised with kisses – he'd only ever read that in stolen romance novels, had never thought what it might really mean, to be kiss-bruised, and he didn't think he ever wanted his lips to be unbruised again. Sutton's tongue slid against his and Alexos whimpered into his mouth: Sutton's laugh was rich and resonant, and Alexos wriggled at the way it vibrated through his mouth, made his lips tingle.

Sutton traced the tip of his tongue over Alexos' lower lip, leaving a lighting trail of sensitivity in its wake, and then he mouthed over the side of Alexos' jaw, down the side of his neck. He nipped and nibbled, catching his skin and tugging at it, and Alexos gasped, grabbed at him.

"Is this what Achilles did to Patroclus, do you think? When he bandaged his arm, as I've bandaged yours tonight, do you think he crossed his body with kisses as I plan to yours?"

"It's hotly debated," said Alexos breathlessly, moaning as Sutton kissed sloppily down the line of his sternum, making him arch his back no matter how it made his neck ache slightly. He couldn't easily move his broken arm out of the way, pinned as it was, but Sutton was careful not to jostle or jar it.

The thought almost made him want to sob. His cock was *aching*, blood flushing down between his legs and throbbing there, but as much as he strained, his cock wasn't quite ready to work itself up to an erection again yet.

What might it have been like, meeting Sutton at nineteen, at twenty?

"Why should it be debated?" asked Sutton.

"Oh, well, some scholars think it was— it was Patroclus who took the, ah, the dominant role, so to speak. Most of the Athenians assumed it had to be a, *ah, fuck, fuck,* a pederastic relationship, but then they'd bicker over who was the erastes and eromenos, I can, can show you the different arguments, but you'll have to make do with my translation, publishers hate to make the important parts readable in Eng— *ah!*"

Sutton had swiped his tongue over Alexos' nipple and then sucked at it with his mouth, tugged on it with his teeth. It was an electrifying sensation, sent thrills through the whole of Alexos' body that almost made him dizzy, but then, Sutton pulled back and put his lips into a little O, blowing cool air over it and making it stiffen like a fucking meringue, and crumbling Alexos' ability to speak intelligently rather like a meringue as well.

He was meringue all over, which was excellent, as Sutton seemed keen to devour him.

"I can't get, I can't get hard again, you know, not for— for a while—"

"I've got a while," said Sutton, and commenced on mouthing at the other nipple, making Alexos choke on air.

"Oughtn't I... Oughtn't I be, be reciprocating?"

"Mmm, no, I'm having a marvellous time like this," said Sutton, taking the other nipple between his teeth and tugging hard, and Alexos went cross-eyed, heaving in a pained gasp.

"Is this ecstasy?"

"Not yet," said Sutton confidently, and patted his chest. "But we'll get you there."

Helpless to do anything else, Alexos submitted himself to Sutton's attentions, and it was some time before he slept.

* * *

Alexos slept that night all the way through, but that was no great surprise – Harry fetched him some codeine before he quite managed to fall asleep on top of wringing another orgasm out of him. It turned out that for periods of being bed-ridden, Alexos had a few standing trays for working and eating from his bed, including a broad tray desk.

Harry brought in his working materials from downstairs and the library, the books he'd been reading and the notes and papers he'd been drafting of recent, but the codeine made it difficult to concentrate on his work.

By the early afternoon, Alexos was picking at a sandwich, not really eating it properly, and sitting back against the headboard and the stacked pillows there.

He had expected Alexos to be scandalised by the tattoos on his arms, had expected him to act upset or nervous about them, to think that to see tattoos on a man meant he was even more dangerous, but instead, *instead*... He had been enraptured. He had been almost worshipful as he'd pushed up Harry's sleeves to better see the ink embedded in the skin, his fingers impossibly gentle as he'd traced each and every design.

He'd do that for the whole of Harry's body, Harry had no doubt, with that same near-religious focus. He had seen men delighted by his tattoos before, even impressed by them, but never had he known another man to be so entirely awed.

Would he respond that way when he saw the rest of the tattoos on Harry's body, on his chest, his back, the tattoos at the base of his crotch? Would he respond with the same sense of mystified wonder when he saw the rings pierced through Harry's nipples, the two more at the head of his cock, the third at his cock's base?

Men were often surprised by the sensation of the piercings, the weight and texture of the barbels where they pulled past the tight ring of their arses, moaned and came apart beneath him. Would Alexos be like that? Would Alexos beg for more, be utterly ruined by the foreign touch of metal and skin at once – better than that, would he respond as he had thus far to Harry's tattoos, and grab and tug at

Harry's cock to examine it as though it were the finest and rarest art he'd ever laid eyes on?

The thought held a certain erotic quality.

Most thoughts did, where Alexos was concerned, the more Harry dwelled on them.

"Your uncle used to sit with me when I was sick with polio," said Alexos.

"He was sick with it as a boy," said Harry. He was tidying Alexos' bedroom, picking up books, dusting behind and under them, and then setting them back into place. "He had an immunity, after – he looked after my youngest brothers when they were ill with it, too."

"He put his desk in my sickroom," said Alexos. "I was really quite pathetic – cried when I was left alone, and I really did prefer him to the poor nanny. He took such good care of me."

"Do I remind you of my uncle?"

"Not particularly," said Alexos. When drunk, he became rather less restrained, and more forthcoming, more openly chatty – he tended to speak more at length about his favourite subjects, to share a great deal of information or enthuse, or rant. It was all quite charming to observe and to listen to, and Harry enjoyed it.

He had yet to observe Alexos' general responses to the morphine, although Brydon had said he only took it when pain was proving near impossible to manage, and that his sour mood was only ever soured further by the morphine's heavy effects, that he tended to take his morphine and then retire immediately to bed for some days.

On the codeine, he was not of a very poor mood, and somewhat less talkative than his usual, but he was blunt, and quite direct. He was having difficulty concentrating, and it made him quick to get to the point.

"You're quite a lot fatter than Reginald," said Alexos. "More attractive, of course, and I'd never given it a great deal of thought, but I would wager your cock is a good deal bigger than his – not to mention, Reginald has only ever treated me with a paternal affection that I have returned in kind. I've not gathered that your intentions toward me are paternal."

"By no means," agreed Harry. "Although there's many the young man who's treated me as a stand-in for his father as I fuck him mindless."

"Really?" asked Alexos, raising his eyebrows, and looking quite bemused. The dilation of his pupils made his eyes look very dark. "What a curious thought. A treatment for men with fathers rather unlike mine, I suppose."

"You're not wrong," said Harry idly.

"Have you ever been on codeine, Henry?"

"No."

"Do you prefer Harry or Henry?"

"Harry."

"Harry. Drowsiness is amongst the effects – difficulty concentrating. I don't normally take enough to feel nauseous, but the morphine does that to me something awful.

"Constipation?"

"*You*," said Alexos, pointing an accusing finger, "just want to give me an enema."

Harry's lips twitched. "Would you like an enema, sir?"

"Don't call me sir unless you're flirting, Harry."

"Flirting or threatening?"

"Either. Both."

"An enema can't be either or both?"

"I don't need an enema," said Alexos. "No constipation on the codeine, usually – when I'm on morphine, I might need the enema *then*, but I won't be in any position to enjoy it."

"Noted. Before you ask, I've not experienced morphine, either."

"Good God, man," said Alexos. "Have you experienced fucking anything?"

Harry started laughing, unable not to. "A few things, here and there – I gather there's not a great overlap between our spheres of experience."

"Oh, don't flatter me," muttered Alexos, and Harry watched the way his handsome head tipped back against the pillows. "Most of my experience amounts to staring at various walls and ceilings, getting angry with men a few thousand years dead, and wanking miserably."

"I've wanked miserably," said Harry.

"Not as miserably as me," said Alexos. "Not that it's a competition, Harry, but it *is*, and as it is, it's one of the few competitions I'm a winner of. Won't you come and embrace me?"

"Alright," said Harry, and when he sat on the bed, Alexos laughed giddily, flushed pink, looked down at the mattress.

"I'm only being obnoxious," he said softly. "For my sake, you really needn't..."

Henry brushed their lips against one another, not deepening the kiss, and Alexos said softly, "A most uncommon betrothal, this is."

"You're due your next dose in a little while," murmured Henry. "Would you like me to read to you for a while first?"

"That would be wonderful," said Alexos breathlessly. "Will you stay with me, when I fall asleep?"

"Do you sleepwalk on the codeine? Can you, I mean?"

"Mmm," said Alexos. "Not usually on the morphine, but on the codeine, I can. It's certainly rarer, though. Harry?"

"Alexos."

"I really won't be this... this easy," said Alexos softly. "Once I'm under no outside influences. Does that not trouble you? I can hardly promise I'll become a man with no chemical dependencies a week from now – I have far too many agonies to promise you that. I'll always be... inconsistent. Drunk, drugged, bitter, manic. I'm a man of unexpected extremes – I'm quite unlikable."

"I've sat for some dozens of hours while needles have pierced my skin," Harry pointed out softly, "and yet all of them are hidden in the course of my day. Do you really think yourself the only man of extremes between us?"

"Yours are charming. Mine are... undesirable."

"Speak for yourself," said Harry, and moved to sit beside him in the bed, taking up a book. Alexos was almost nervous to insinuate himself against Harry's side, didn't lean fully into him, but he did do so slightly, and Harry smiled at the shy, careful way he leaned in as Harry began to read.

"You must be mad," Alexos mumbled drowsily when he took his next dose.

"Yes," Harry agreed. "But no more than you."

"Oh, much less than me," said Alexos, waving his hand idly. "But mad, nonetheless."

"As you say, sir," said Harry, and smiled slightly as he came away.

Chapter Ten

A strange levee had broken in the weeks following that night.

Alexos' arm healed bit by bit, and Harry had been warned a hundred times, a thousand times, by the other household staff that during periods of being bedridden, the young Mr Fox became incredibly difficult to manage.

He would be even colder than usual, even more so than he had been in the previous weeks; he became prone not only to fits of profanity and loudly telegraphed self-loathing, but would also become cruel – if not abusive – on a personal level; he would ordinarily deaden himself more with morphine than codeine, and some weeks would drink himself through whole bottles of spirits in the course of just a few days.

Brydon had mildly advised him that he tended to take responsibility for the majority of Alexos' care during these periods, except for that which Uncle Reg hadn't taken over.

Reg had never mentioned *that,* or at least, he hadn't described it in detail – Harry remembered significant periods where he would advise that the young master was bedridden with some illness or other, that he was spending more time with him.

"It's not that he insults us, so much as he rather aims to eviscerate at times like this, or does so almost without aiming," Brydon had said over a quiet breakfast the two of them shared the morning after Harry had first taken Alexos to bed. "The young Mr Fox is a remarkably observant man, and he knows more about me and my sins than I've ever admitted to anybody out loud, least of all confessed to *him* – and he has a certain ability to feel for one's most vulnerable parts, the better to create a deep and long-lasting wound. The things he said to your uncle at times, sir, were spellbindingly cruel – comments about his being unmarried and alone, implying he was on bad terms with the rest of your family, about his lack of education, his..."

Brydon had trailed off as Harry had looked at him, and then glanced down at the table, took a sip of his tea.

"And me, too, of course. He says the most dreadful things to me – I won't let Felix in the room, when he's in one of his states, let alone one of the girls, not that Mr Fox wants them there."

"Why ever do you let him?" Harry had asked, and Brydon had laughed, seeming to think the question through, his lips pressing together. "You've been telling me since I've come here what a kind man the young master is, despite his brittle nature."

"He is," said Brydon softly. "Perhaps it's because he's such a kind man that I always ignore him when he tells me to leave his drugs with him and let him be. I followed Reginald's wake in that respect, but it is... worth it. Worth doing."

"You think it's alright what he says," said Harry, "in these states, because he doesn't really *mean* it?"

"What he says about me has never been as cruel as the things he says about himself," admitted Brydon, with a delicate shrug of his shoulder. "And more than once he's begged me not to put myself in front of him, when he's like that. Told me I ought let him stew alone in his misery, that he not lash out and draw me in."

"You said you liked his frank speaking before," said Harry.

Brydon's lips had twitched. "Mmm," he'd said. "I do, actually."

"Even when he insults you?"

"Weathering the insults of the young master has made me far better at poker," he admitted with a wry smile.

The funny thing was, as much as these warnings were given to him, by Brydon, by Felix, even by Mrs Perry and the other young women serving in the household, that Alexos would be in a very foul mood, crueller than ever, in the weeks to come, he wasn't.

He was blunted by the codeine when he took it, yes, but he drank surprisingly little, and he worked so prodigiously that one of them not irregularly had to bring him more paper or change the ink cartridge in his pen. When he was not working, he talked, and it was the most open that Harry had ever found him to be – the most open, he rather got the impression, that he had ever been, perhaps with anyone.

It wasn't that he shared a great deal about his life or his personal feelings, his experiences – in fact, he avoided these almost pathologically – but he enthused about the work he was doing, his reading. Whenever Harry entered his room throughout the course of the day, Alexos would read or recite to him a passage hastily translated from Greek or Latin, and would speak at length about the different ways it was translated – Harry had laughed for some time when he had recited a piece from Aristophanes' *The Clouds* and insulted a good many translators for their work in approaching it, but had enthused about what the passage taught the modern reader about standards of attractiveness in the minds of Aristophanes and his contemporaries.

"So," said Harry, "I have a fat arse, strong shoulders, a gleaming chest, good skin... Is my tongue small?"

"No," said Alexos mildly. "And nor is your cock, I'd wager."

"Do you think Aristophanes might have deigned to sleep with me nonetheless?"

Alexos laughed. "I think he might have lowered himself," he murmured quietly, a smile tugging at his lips. He'd been sleeping extremely poorly, and there were heavy bags showing under his eyes. "Do many men admire your arse?"

"Certainly they do," said Harry pleasantly, and as he turned away to pour Alexos more tea from the pot he'd brought up, he felt the heat of the young master's gaze on his backside.

This was where Alexos was fundamentally quite open – he asked questions, genuine, real questions about Harry, engaged with him. The questions weren't only about sex or his relationships with men – he'd asked about the war, too, asked about his work.

He had come alive, held himself with a certain vivacity that Harry had never witnessed from him even on his most cheerful and pain-free days, let alone days when he was confined to his bedchamber. He expected it to be commented on by Brydon or Felix, but no such comments were forthcoming, and Harry was interested to note, as the days passed by, that Alexos retained his ordinary politeness, his delicate propriety, with them.

He retained a good mood, yes, but not this new verbal liberty – Harry was an exception.

The reason why was simple enough, obvious even, but Harry brought it up anyway: "You've been speaking to me very freely, these past weeks."

Alexos stopped short on the bed, where he'd been making copious annotations on a medieval transcript of a Latin text that he'd recently been complaining about, his gaze settling on Harry's face before it flitted to the door. It seemed to Harry that Alexos stiffened, his body seeming smaller in the bed, his healing arm clutched a little tighter to his chest.

"You want me to stop?" he asked.

"By no means," said Harry, moving forward.

The door was locked, but this raised no eyebrows – Brydon had accepted that however it had come to pass, Alexos had gotten over his nervousness of Harry seeing him disabled and exhausted by his condition, and that for whatever reason, Alexos was content to have Harry serve as his primary assistant. If anyone wanted to come in, they'd knock on the bedroom door, and Harry was always careful not to put himself into any state of undress unless everyone else had gone to bed, for now.

Once Alexos' arm was healed, and they had further run of the house, then—

Well.

Then, they might experiment a little more.

"Why comment on it, then?" asked Alexos.

"You don't speak so freely with Brydon or Felix."

Alexos arched one eyebrow, and gave Harry a delightfully cold look. "Neither Brydon nor Felix," he said scathingly, "have been putting their mouths between my legs – and I don't expect them to."

"Surely other men have wanted to put their mouths between your legs," said Harry, and Alexos set down his pen, placing its lid on. Harry moved forward, sliding onto the bed as he had done several times the past few weeks, and Alexos went square and stiff until Harry's hands alighted on his back and his thumbs pressed into the hard, knotted muscle of his shoulders.

Alexos grunted, his eyes squeezing shut – his body rather reminded Harry, in many ways, of a spring. No matter that he could convince the muscle to temporarily relax and uncoil, as you might stretch a spring, it would inevitably tighten up against as soon as you drew away, and this was the Sisyphean journey he'd been experiencing in his attempt to massage Alexos' body into a state of genuine relaxation.

Any small progress he made on the other man's shoulders, his back, his upper arms, his thighs, was undone within what seemed like hours, let alone a night's fitful lack of sleep, but Harry was *determined.*

As tightly coiled and bound as Alexos' shoulders were at first touch, Harry firmly kneaded them into something more resembling relaxation, delighting in the way Alexos squirmed and hissed underneath him.

"Why would they?"

"You really had no friends of the same bent as you?"

"Here and there," muttered Alexos. "But none that found *me* attractive – the cripple with his cane is not as hotly in demand as you might believe."

Harry kissed the side of Alexos' neck, feeling the way he shuddered and gasped under the touch, and shyly, his hands moved up to touch Harry back, one hand cupping his shoulder, the other sliding to nervously touch his cheek. He didn't know how to touch Harry back – increasingly, Harry was of the impression he thought he needed to ask permission to do so, to even *think* of doing so.

How long would it take before he felt confident in grasping for him, moving him here and there, taking from Harry what he wanted, or *asking* for Harry to give it to him?

"I don't believe the cripple is as unlovable as you seem keen to telegraph," Harry agreed, pressing fingers either side of Alexos' spine and feeling him straighten like a wooden toy, muscles popping under his fingers. "Quite fuckable the cripple is, in fact – or he will be, once I see fit to bounce him on my cock."

Alexos shuddered. "A horrible word," he scolded. "You oughtn't use it."

"What will you do if I continue?" asked Harry, taking Alexos' earlobe in his mouth and delicately nibbling at it, almost laughing at the gasping whimper he got in response. "Give me a swift smack on the backside?"

"I might deny you the privilege of massaging me."

"*Might* you? Oh, don't do that. I might just die, so deprived." He slid his hand down over the fabric of Alexos' pyjamas, cupping his cock, and Alexos gasped, his head tipping back against Harry's chest. "You've turned men down. Don't lie."

"And if I have?"

"You've accepted me. Gone from denying your desire for men to letting me touch you in a heartbeat. Why—"

Alexos grabbed hard at his wrist, and Harry's smile froze on his lips at the cold, serious look Alexos was giving him, the twist of his lips, the heaviness in the world.

"You really wish I hadn't?"

"Of course not," Harry murmured. "But you've softened so entirely in so short a time – and yet, only with me."

"Of course, only with you," replied Alexos.

"Because of our arrangement."

"If you like."

"And your friends?"

Alexos' cold gaze grew colder. "I told you, Sutton, I—"

"Harry," he corrected him gently, and twisting the arm that Alexos was holding, he pressed a kiss to the side of Alexos' hand.

"Does it truly bother you to see me of a good mood?" asked Alexos. "You wish to put a stop to it?"

Harry, an idea coming to mind, shook his head. "No, Alexos, I don't. Will you object to *my* having friends, even as you don't?"

"Why would I?"

"We *will* have to have a serious conversation about this," murmured Harry, "but I'm not in a terribly serious mood."

"Aren't you?"

Harry licked a swipe up the side of Alexos' neck, feeling the way the other man shuddered, and then submitted himself to Harry's attentions, still nervous and uncertain of touching him, but he would learn.

Harry would teach him.

* * *

The pain had been a near continuous hum the past few weeks, as much as he tried his best to soothe it – true, Alexos was almost always in pain, always experiencing some level of distant, dull ache in his thighs and hips and knees, if not his shoulders too, but the pain had been worse of recent, which was only natural. He attempted to do some small exercises from his bed, straightening and bending his legs so that he wasn't experiencing stiffness of the muscle and flesh as well as the deeper ache of the bones underneath, but it was difficult to do with one ankle sprained and the rest of his legs never much in good commission anyway.

That aside, his arm was really very awful, and it ached horribly as the bone worked to knit itself back together, regular twinges of nastier, sharper pain burning up his upper arm and into his shoulder apart from the continuous gentle agony that made up the ache. He tried to open and close his hand, to move the wrist a little, his elbow, because he knew it had to be done, and yet, what difference did it make?

The pain continued.

The codeine never really numbed the pain away entirely, but spread a layer of unawareness and unsensation across the top, the same way you might spread jam over a slice of burnt toast – it wasn't that you couldn't taste that it was burnt, or that the burntness went away, merely that the jam obfuscated the flavour and the texture, so that it wasn't quite as noticeable.

Work helped.

He couldn't always concentrate when working from his bed – he preferred to sit properly at the table in the library, without so much softness underneath him, and although he had a desk in his bedroom, he disliked the small space the desk offered him in comparison to the broader spread of the library table, constantly felt cramped and confused whenever he had to place one paper beneath another so that it would fit, instead of simply broadening the space he took up. This week, though, he retained a certain energy that allowed him to focus, and Sutton—

It was possible, of course, that this remained an elaborate scheme the better to blackmail him, or that it was something worse, but something had snapped in Alexos Fox.

He found that it almost didn't matter any longer, so long as Sutton kept touching him, put his hands on Alexos' body, and more than that, looked at him the way that he did with his plump-lipped handsome smiles and his dazzlingly green eyes and his rounded, bright cheeks.

He didn't know that he could ever remember feeling quite so little weight on his shoulders, feeling so entirely at liberty to speak with another man – he had never known well the men who'd engaged him as a like-minded fellow at university, or at least, never permitted them to know *him* well. They would ask too many questions about his polio, his cane, the status of his legs or the rest of him; they would look at him in discomfiting, unpleasant ways, as though measuring his coffin for him in their heads; they would invite him and disinvite him from somewhere in the same breath, recalling the stairs he would struggle to clamber up, or the steep incline that would give him trouble.

Sutton was—

Here.

At *home*.

And he knew already the state of Alexos' body, had seen it before he'd seen anything else, and seemed utterly undeterred and unbothered by it, and he *talked* about it, and it was...

Perhaps it wasn't easy. Perhaps it was all an act, and if it was, Alexos would act along.

"Your post, sir," said Sutton.

It had been a little over five weeks since his fall on the stairs, and Doctor Logan would be coming over before lunch time to examine his broken arm. With his ankle healed, he was at least able to move about his room and to the bathroom more freely, and he had taken to pacing clumsily with his cane in hand some evenings.

When they'd thought him asleep, he'd heard Felix asking as he'd helped Sutton take out tea things and just-changed bedsheets, "Why's he still on bed-rest if his legs are alright?"

"If he trips on the stairs with the hand not on his cane still out of service, how does he break his fall?" Sutton had replied. He hadn't taken on a sarcastic tone, and nor had he responded as Alexos might have, blustering and defensive and uncertain. His voice had been quiet but full of a pleasant kindness, not for Alexos but for the young man taking instruction, and Felix had replied with an "Ah," of understanding, and the matter had been left at that.

In the sheaf of letters brought him, two were expected – one being a colleague's notes on a recent publication on Aristotle's politics, another a rather amusingly angry response to a footnote in one of Alexos' books, disliking the tone he had employed to refer to the destructive legacy of Heinrich Schliemann – and one was a pleasant surprise – a missive from Reginald Sutton about the state of his garden and his home in retirement, chattering on about this and that.

The fourth, however, was an unknown, and Alexos examined the flourished, exaggerated handwriting of a stranger on the envelope, glancing then at the return address, which was for an address in Cambridgeshire.

"Dear Mr Fox,

I beg your pardon for penning what I expect is rather an unexpected missive – my name is Lawrence Kidd, and I'm a novelist. I'm well-acquainted with your mother, and whilst I know she is currently out of the country..."

Alexos felt his heart sink as he read onward, his lips twisting, and Sutton, who had been throwing open the curtains to allow in some of the uncomfortably bright morning light – Alexos ached to go out and sit under the kiss of it, and rather thought he might brave the stairs this morning, so long as someone was there to catch him as he descended – looked his way.

"Is all well, sir?" he asked.

"Do you know Lawrence Kidd?" asked Alexos quietly.

"The author, sir? His most recent book was a romance between a watchmaker and a pickpocket – he has a certain capacity for novel ideas in his work, but I often find his execution is too saccharine for my liking."

"He isn't one of your heroes, then?"

Sutton's expression was so very innocent that Alexos could almost see the mechanisms whirring underneath it, and Alexos looked at him very flatly as he said, "No, sir. Ought he be?"

"Stop calling me *sir*, Harry," Alexos muttered. "You've met him, haven't you?"

Sutton actually looked surprised, but he didn't deny it, turning about and standing at the foot of his bed, looking at him seriously. Sutton had complained, idly, about Alexos' lack of footboard – it was a favourite pastime of his, he'd said, to lean on the footboard to speak to whomever was in bed, but Alexos preferred his bed to be accessible on three sides than two – earlier in the week, and Alexos almost wanted to see him with his hands resting on it, his chest forward, his gaze focused on Alexos and Alexos alone.

"He's an author," Sutton said, the innocence polished out of his tone, and replaced with a sort of familiarity. "I wouldn't call him a close confidant, but we are acquainted and on friendly terms – we have some friends in common, and his valet, Riggs, was a student of mine whilst I was serving Lord Loxley at the Bisphams' as underbutler."

"What do you make of him?"

"He's a very friendly man," said Sutton. "Self-centred and arrogant, as many authors are, and the sort that can only be tricked into discussing craft so long as he's first plied with drink, good food, and good company, but he's funny, flirtatious, a skilled raconteur."

Alexos stared at Sutton's face, taking it in, examining it as carefully as he could. "He's like us," he said – a statement, not a question.

"He is," said Sutton slowly, and he narrowed his eyes as he looked back at Alexos, so that the two of them were studying one another now. "Riggs, too."

"They're involved?"

Sutton shook his head. "I doubt it, Alexos. Riggs is... Well, he's a peculiar young man, not very keen on being touched, and Kidd isn't keen on being *un*touched. Why's he written you?"

"He wants to stay here," said Alexos. "Apparently there's a play adapted from one of his books here in Brighton, and he wants to stay a few weeks as he oversees the production."

"You don't like guests."

"No, I bloody *don't* like guests," said Alexos, sighing. "When my mother's here, the house is always full up with guests – when she's not, there's a bit of respite, at least."

Sutton took this in, his head tilting to the side. "You plan to refuse him?"

"Well, I can't do that," muttered Alexos, sighing, setting the letter down against his thigh.

"Your father warned me when I joined the household," said Sutton, and Alexos' gaze whipped up to his face, seeing Sutton's small smile, the playfulness showing in his eyes, "that you dislike houseguests. That you tend to avoid them."

"And if I do?" asked Alexos coolly.

"Lawrence Kidd is the sort of man who'll get up from the table and follow you if he's still interested in talking."

"Alexos Fox," replied Alexos, "is the sort of man to trip another with his cane if he finds he's being followed."

"And if you like him?"

"Like him?" repeated Alexos, uncomprehending.

Sutton shrugged his shoulders. "He's handsome, charming. A whore."

Alexos stared at Sutton's face, his raised eyebrows, his handsome lips and cheeks. "You want me to *fuck* him?"

"No, not particularly," said Sutton. "But he's going to flirt with you – he'll compliment you, I expect, ask about your work, tell you about his. None of your friends, from what I have gathered in my time here, ever come to visit you. Your correspondence is entirely made up of academic commentary and the exchange of notes – you receive not irregular social invitations by other academics, literary commentators, archaeologists, archivists, translators, authors, and you refuse them all."

"And so you've employed a charming and whorish novelist to be my friend?" asked Alexos, and leaned forward, his lips pressing together. "Did you *tell* him to do this?"

Sutton laughed. "You overestimate my influence, I'm afraid," he said smoothly, "but I think you might like him. I think he'll like you, so long as he's permitted a glimpse at your personality."

"My personality is best kept behind closed doors," muttered Alexos, looking down at Kidd's widely-looping – fruity – handwriting on the page.

"As you say, sir," said Sutton.

"Sir," Alexos repeated.

"I might give you my advice," said Sutton mildly. "It's your choice as to whether you take it from me as your butler or as a friend."

"*Is* he handsome?"

"No," admitted Sutton, making Alexos laugh. "Not particularly. He's a man of exaggerated proportions – his ears and nose are larger than the rest of his face, his eyes are a little small and sunken in. His smile has a bend in the lip, so while it isn't imbalanced to one side or the other, it retains a crookedness in the middle. He's got a handful of acne scars on his forehead and around one eye – but he's got a phenomenal head of hair, dull in colour but thick and handsome. His voice is smooth and easy, strong – he sings wonderfully, and he's impossibly charming. It's rather difficult to remember how bland his features are when he gives you his full attention – or so I'm told, in any case. He's not exactly my type."

"Your type is wide-eyed men with limps and drinking problems."

"It is, it is," said Sutton. "But to be more specific about what my type *isn't*, it's men who are a little too keen to display how friendly they are to all and sundry."

"You've enough arrogance without anyone else's being involved, I suppose."

"Precisely."

Alexos set the letter aside in a pile with the rest, pushing aside the little standing desk he'd been working from.

"Harry," he said quietly.

"Alexos?"

"Eat with me."

"I've already eaten."

"Eat some more."

"If you agree to speak with Kidd," said Sutton. "One meal together once he's here, Alexos, just the two of you, without your father's supervision to worry about. Let him talk to you – and try talking back."

"Why do you care?"

Reginald had tried this, once or twice. He'd ensured certain people were invited to the house, or arranged seating so that Alexos was sitting across from those Reginald thought he'd like best – communists, artists, a sitting Labour MP, an antiquities specialist. A dancer, once.

He was certainly better at picking potential friends for Alexos than Alexos' mother was, because she picked anyone she thought might be *proper* or *appropriate* rather than those he might like, but it wasn't about propriety or liking anyone, at the end of the day.

What Alexos didn't like was people in his life – he liked *work*, liked to read, liked to be left to attend to it in peace. It was good enough for his father – why shouldn't it be good enough for him?

"If you don't like him," said Sutton, "you can still watch me fuck him."

Alexos' lips parted, and he stared at Sutton's face, at the completely honest and genuine look on his features. He was unrelenting, confident, and spellbindingly, quite frighteningly beautiful.

"Watch you...?" he repeated, and Sutton showed his teeth as his smile widened further. "I thought he wasn't your type."

"Does it make your cock hard, Alexos, to think of me fucking another man in front of you?"

Alexos swallowed, feeling heat burn in his cheeks, feeling more heat pool between his legs. After a short inhalation, he said, "One meal with him, Harry. I'll have one meal with him."

"That's all I ask," said Sutton pleasantly, and Alexos watched him go before he pulled his desk back over his lap, and started penning a curt but polite response to Kidd, inviting him to stay in the Foxes' home for as long as he needed.

Outside, the sun grew a little brighter, and Alexos moved to the side of the bed so he could feel the rays on his face.

He was smiling as he took his codeine, but he didn't know why.

Chapter Eleven

It was mid-morning, and although the full heat of the day hadn't yet arrived, there was enough warmth in the air that Alexos walked without a full jacket on, only wearing a loose, comfortable cardigan over his shirt, buttoned up over his belly. He didn't move too quickly, and he leaned very heavily on his cane, stopping every thirty or forty steps to stretch out each leg, testing his joints, how much weight he could put on the limbs.

He had managed to creep out unaccompanied, but evidently Brydon or Sutton had spied him from the window, because Felix came running out from the house to keep pace with him, skidding to a stop when Alexos leaned on his cane to carefully straighten out his leg.

"How is your arm feeling, sir?" asked Felix, out of breath.

"Quite well, Felix, thank you," said Alexos mildly. "My legs too."

"They don't hurt? Your ankle?"

"Oh, everything hurts, Felix," said Alexos. "But I've taken my codeine like a good little soldier, and the unfortunate fact of my life is that pain continues regardless. Which of our gallant commanders sent you after me?"

Felix bit his lip, and Alexos gave him as warm a smile as he could, aware that he was uncomfortable, aware that Alexos *made* him uncomfortable, and he did feel guilty, felt a painful stab in his gut as he often did when he and Felix contended with one another after Alexos had been deeply embroiled in an episode of illness.

"I'm not angry with you," said Alexos, "nor with either of them. They don't want to see me plant my face into the paving stones, that's all – but for all I know that, I don't always like to be attended."

"Do you want me to go back inside?" asked Felix uncertainly, and Alexos shook his head.

"Not if you don't mind walking with me," said Alexos quietly, although he'd rather be alone. "Best you and I both escape the scolding we'll each receive if I send you back inside. If it's any consolation, Felix, I'll do my best not to fall over."

Felix gave him a small, shy smile, and Alexos wondered how long the both of them would do this together, Felix liking him and fearing him in turns, taking a little while to soften with him and trust him again, then clamming up once Alexos showed himself for what he was: a lush with a sailor's mouth.

He and Betty were so alike in age, but Betty liked and trusted Alexos to pieces – Alexos was certain she must have heard him curse once or twice, but only in Greek, and never as loudly or as sharply as Felix had heard him. Betty never went upstairs except to change bedsheets with Rebecca when she came in from the village a few days a week, and Alexos never went downstairs unless he was sober and serious – with those two facts borne together, Betty only ever saw him at his best.

Felix, naturally, saw him at his worst often enough, and would continue to.

"It must be difficult," said Felix. "I'm sorry that you... You know, being the young gentleman of the house, I'm sorry if it feels like you can't be independent."

Alexos chuckled, beginning to walk again, Felix beside him. "You and Mr Sutton have been having words, I see. Was it him that sent you out here this morning?"

"Yes, sir," said Felix quietly. "Does it— I shouldn't say..."

"You're worried I'm offended that Sutton talks about me the way he does, are you?" asked Alexos evenly, leaning heavily on his cane as they moved forward, and he watched the careful way Felix measured his steps to match him. Reginald had always been tremendously good at matching his gait without making it obvious that that was what he was doing, almost gliding beside him, and naturally, Sutton was tremendously good at doing the same thing, just as he was good at everything else. Felix was still learning, of course. "You know his predecessor spoke of me in the same way."

"Yes, sir," said Felix. "But I..."

"Felix," said Alexos, "one day, assuming you stay in service, assuming that Sutton trains you up as a butler and you go elsewhere to serve another household, you will take with you the lessons you learned here. The biggest of those lessons, I think, will be that you can and will and do inhabit a caretaking role for your employers. I only resist it so much because I cannot deny the truth as many of my counterparts do – that I'm reliant on you. Most of our ilk rely on our servants because we are rich and stupid and inexperienced of the ways of the world – I am all of those things, and crippled to boot."

Felix was staring down at the floor, not meeting his gaze, and Alexos kept moving.

"Sutton's an expert at it," said Alexos. "You can learn from him."

"I'm sorry," said Felix again.

Alexos didn't say anything, and for a while they kept walking, until Alexos needed a break and came to ease himself down onto a bench, leaning back against it with a low grunt of sound.

"You needn't stay if you don't like, Felix," said Alexos softly. "I'm just going to sit and rest here a while."

He expected to have to argue with him, for Felix to linger, but he did no such thing, rushing back toward the house for the time being, and Alexos sighed quietly, his eyes falling closed, one of his arms over the back of the bench and his cane loosely gripped in his hand.

He must have fallen asleep for a little while, perhaps forty minutes or an hour – when he woke, Sutton had brought over one of the folding tables and set a pot of tea out for him, underneath a cosy so that it didn't go cold. His shoulders ached a little, but they weren't nearly as bad as he expected.

The sun was wonderful on his skin – he looked around for Sutton, saw him from behind, which was a wonderful view. Sutton's arse all but threatened to burst out of its neatly tailored trousers, big and wide and looking splendidly soft, and his hands twitched in his lap with the urge to grasp at it and squeeze it under his hands, feel Sutton's hips thrust a little forward, hear Sutton's pleasured sigh.

He was talking with Mr Lloyd, listening to Lloyd talk as he gestured down the garden toward the old shed where he kept the scrap. Alexos wondered in an idle way exactly how honest Mr Lloyd was being with him about who he sold the scrap to and what it was used for, or how Alexos used it himself.

It had been some time since Alexos had managed to go down to his own worktable in the shed, and he wasn't yet in a state where he'd be able to walk quickly enough without Sutton following him or noticing where he'd gone.

When Sutton realised Alexos was awake and came back toward him, Alexos met Lloyd's gaze over his shoulder, and Lloyd winked at him.

"Mr Riggs telephoned a few minutes ago, sir," said Sutton, taking the cosy off of the teapot and pouring him a cup of tea, and Alexos shifted in his seat, pulling his arse back onto the bench properly. "Mr Kidd will be arriving from the train station just in time for lunch."

"What did you say to Felix earlier?" asked Alexos, and Sutton looked at him thoughtfully, arching an eyebrow. "He seemed more nervous than usual – or more self-conscious, in any case."

"Do you want me to actually tell you?" asked Sutton, and Alexos frowned slightly, furrowing his brows as he looked at Sutton, thinking carefully about his answer.

"Will I be that offended if you do?"

"Not offended, but perhaps raw."

"Tell me."

"His father has a strong case of shellshock," said Sutton. "You remind him of the man, and he struggles with that."

"Oh," said Alexos, pressing his lips together. He didn't feel offended, but Sutton was right – he did feel raw and slightly sensitive about it, remembering every time Felix had come over uncomfortable and nervous with him, brittle and uncertain. He wasn't angry. "I remind him of his father?"

"You make him nervous the way his father does."

"I don't suppose you can recommend him for a position somewhere else?"

"Don't be ridiculous, sir," said Sutton coolly, his expression stern, as he pushed the cup of tea into Alexos' hands. "He needs to inure himself to that sensitivity in one way or another if he's to remain in service."

"I'd write him a letter of recommendation if he wanted to leave service," said Alexos.

"My uncle said you had an unfortunate habit of attempting to fix the world's problems," said Sutton in a gentle, tremendously cutting way. "It's quite the endearing trait, as impotent as it may be."

"Calling a helpless cripple impotent," said Alexos. "Very original." When Sutton chuckled, Alexos went on, "I don't want to fix the world's problems. I'd just rather not be one of them."

Sutton stepped closer, ostensibly to drop a cube of sugar in his tea, and used the proximity to gently squeeze his hand, his body disguising the action from Mr Lloyd's view. "You aren't, you know," he said, though Alexos didn't believe him.

Sighing as Sutton drew away, Alexos drank his tea.

* * *

Alexos stood out on the doorstep, leaning heavily on his cane as the car pulled up. The cabman they'd hired jumped out to let out

Lawrence Kidd as the other fellow – his valet, Riggs – went to unbuckle his trunk from the luggage rack, setting it aside.

"Good afternoon," said Alexos with a tight smile, putting out his hand. He could barely breathe.

Lawrence Kidd was a plain-looking man with dappled acne scars and protuberant ears, as Sutton had informed him, but he had a sort of bright energy as he came forward, his shoulders back, his hips swinging a little. He moved *jauntily*, he *sauntered*, and he wore a very light summer suit, the colour such a light tan it was very nearly pink.

"Hullo!" said Kidd brightly – his voice *was* very nice, richer than one might have expected of a man of his stature, which was quite average. "Alexos Fox, I take it – you don't look much like your mother."

"Sorry to disappoint you," said Alexos, shaking his hand and keeping his grip a little tighter than he needed to.

"Strong handshake!" remarked Kidd, and tugged Alexos' hand closer to him. Alexos grunted as he was forced to shift on his feet, adjusting the weight he was putting on his cane to keep from being pulled over, and he stared, his lips parted, as Kidd turned his hand over and examined his palm, stroking it. "Strong hands. Do you play piano?"

"I do not," said Alexos curtly, and dragged back his hand. "This is my butler, Mr Sutton, and this is our footman, Felix. My father sends his apologies that he can't be with us this afternoon, he's visiting my uncle, but he'll return tomorrow."

"You're the master of the house in his absence, I suppose," said Kidd dazzlingly, and Alexos inclined his head.

"Lunch has been laid out for us in the dining room," said Alexos, and Kidd jumped ahead of him to the door, pulling it open before Sutton could move to do it in what Alexos supposed was meant to be a display of chivalry, and he pressed his lips together, moving slowly inside and directing him toward the dining room.

Kidd rushed to take out his chair for him, and Alexos turned to look at Sutton over his shoulder.

"*He's being considerate*," mouthed Sutton as he followed after them.

"He's going to be beaten if he carries on," Alexos retorted in a whisper, and Sutton pulled out the chair for Kidd as he followed after them, pouring a glass of wine for each of them before he stepped out to fetch their plates.

"I've known your mother for a few years," said Kidd, pulling his seat forward and coming in closer to the table, taking a slice of bread and buttering it. "She's really quite a wonderful woman – she's very strong, isn't she? It delights me when a woman conducts herself like a battalion commander."

"I wasn't aware she bore such similarity," said Alexos, taking a sip of his wine, which was a pleasant white burgundy.

"She always schedules things to a T, gets everybody in order," said Kidd, taking a mouthful of his bread and chewing, swallowing. "But I'm told she's not the only author in the house! You're an author yourself, are you not?"

"Not of fiction."

"No, no, you write scholarly sorts of things, yes, notes on ancient plays and all of that, and translations?"

"Precisely."

"I rather struggled with all that at school," said Kidd. "Not enough romance in the *Iliad* for me – I've an open heart, you see. I crave to read about people's love and affection for one another."

"I see."

"You don't like romances, I suppose?"

"I don't read novels."

"Oh, what a shame," said Kidd. "Not even your mother's?"

"I'm afraid not," said Alexos quietly, feeling rather as though he were being baited. "I have limited hours in my day, and a great many texts to work through."

"What do you do for fun, if not read novels?"

"I'm not a man who especially craves leisure," said Alexos slowly. "My work satisfies me."

"Oh, I'm not like that at all," said Kidd, setting his bread down. He really did have an animated face, and his mouth was just as crooked as Sutton had said, with a strange dip in the middle so that his mouth didn't quite close all the way, but his mouth was strangely handsome nonetheless. "Me, I work like a dog most hours of the week, but I like to play just as passionately. I read quite a bit, I enjoy music, the theatre, boardgames, you know – I like to go out dancing, to the theatre, the opera, to bars and such forth. I'm not any good at any of it, but I enjoy football, shooting, rugby, you know, all of that. How about you?"

"You're asking if I like to play rugby?" asked Alexos coolly.

"I'd tackle you," said Kidd immediately, and Alexos arched an eyebrow.

"You seem to think I'm not even capable of pulling out my own chair," he said mildly. "You'd really be that confident in throwing me to the ground?"

Kidd, for the first time, faltered. His mouth fell open, and he looked down at the table, then up at Alexos' face. "Well," he said. "Maybe that... I'd not like to hurt you."

"I'm sure you wouldn't," replied Alexos.

"Have I offended very grievously?"

"I'm not in the habit of being offended."

"You can tell me if I'm insulting you, you know," said Kidd confidently. "Or rap me across the knuckles with your cane, smack me around. Call me names."

"You seem to have an unorthodox idea as to how a man typically treats his guests," said Alexos.

"Well, I shouldn't worry about that, I'm no typical guest," said Kidd, and Alexos looked to Sutton as he brought in plates and set them down, swiftly followed by Felix who filled their glasses.

"If you would leave us a moment, Felix, I have one or two items to discuss with the gentlemen."

Sutton closed the door to the dining room, and he waited a moment, appearing to listen as Felix retreated down the corridor.

"Harry," said Kidd, and Alexos felt his mouth fall open, but he immediately closed it again. Kidd sprawled back in his seat, putting his chin on his hand, and he looked up at Sutton with his eyes wide and his lips pouted out. "Won't you tell Mr Fox here that he can smack me across the face if I get on his nerves?"

"Mr Fox is your host, Mr Kidd," said Sutton, although his lips were smiling slightly as he poured wine. "He is not your schoolmaster."

"I don't want him to be my schoolmaster," said Kidd. "I want him to be my friend."

Alexos clenched his teeth slightly, and focused on eating from his plate.

"I've met Harry a few times," said Kidd. "He's a good friend of the valet of Vincent Samuels, who does my book covers. He's a splendid illustrator. Do you know him?"

"No," said Alexos.

"Kit Sanders?"

"No."

"What about Donald Howard? You must know the Howards, there's dozens of them."

"Mr Kidd, I can assure you that I don't know anybody."

"We'll fix that," said Kidd, and Alexos looked to Sutton, who met his gaze.

"*One meal*," mouthed Sutton.

Alexos knew his nostrils were flaring as he inhaled, and he took a sip of his wine. "Mr Sutton tells me you're quite the social butterfly," said Alexos.

"I'm a whore," Kidd pronounced with pride, and Alexos blinked.

"Are your rates reasonable?" he asked sharply, and Kidd's face lit up as though he'd been connected to the mains, his head tipping forward as he looked over the table, his crooked mouth beaming.

"Why, what do you think I'm worth?" he asked.

"I'm sure I don't know the going rate," said Alexos. "Let alone the market rate for a below-average product."

Kidd blinked at him, and then looked at Sutton. "Did he just imply I'd be a very poor prostitute, Harry?"

"You set him up for it, Mr Kidd, I shouldn't complain."

"Between the two of you, a man rather feels skewered from both ends," said Kidd, wagging his eyebrows and looking at Alexos across the table.

"I hope that doesn't mean I should expect an invoice," Alexos replied, and tried not to show his surprise as Kidd laughed, clapping his hands together. "I do hope you'll forgive me, Mr Kidd, but I'm afraid that I am not a particularly social man, and this house will not host soirées or the like whilst you're here."

"What do you do?" asked Kidd.

"I told you, Mr Kidd, I am satisfied by my work."

"You must have some hobbies," said Kidd, tilting his head to the side. "Don't you like music, to sing? Do you play any instruments?"

"No."

"The piano, sir," Sutton said in the tone of one reminding him, and Alexos pressed his lips together at the glint in Kidd's eyes. He was eating with a sort of dangerous relish.

"I asked if you played piano a few minutes ago," he said, softer now. "You told me you didn't."

"I haven't for some years," said Alexos, glaring at Sutton.

"But you do know how," said Kidd. "You've been educated in its playing. Me, I play the guitar, but I'm mostly a singer. I rather love music – modern music, you know. I'm always playing something from a show or whatever that I've been to."

"How nice," said Alexos insincerely.

"There must be something you're passionate about," said Kidd. "Are you passionate about Harry, perhaps? He's got the most marvellous arse – it's difficult not to be passionate about a man who looks the way he does."

Sutton barely even reacted, standing up straight with his hands behind his back, his head up – he was already smirking, and that didn't change at being complimented so openly.

"With respect, Mr Kidd, I could do without filth at my dinner table."

"I'll make you a deal," said Kidd. "You call me Larry – or Lawrence, even – and I'll stop flirting with your butler."

"I'm not in the habit of bartering over table manners."

"You must be passionate about something," said Kidd, seeming to change tact. "I'd be passionate about Harry's arse were I you, but that aside, there must be something. Do you like cocaine?"

The stem of the glass snapped in Alexos' hand, and he immediately stood to his feet to keep from spilling it.

"Sir—" said Sutton, but Alexos twisted free of his hand as he leaned on his cane with his other hand. The stem had cut his pam as it had snapped, but it wasn't a deep cut, and would be easy enough to dress himself: to prevent Sutton from grasping at him again, he pushed the bowl of his glass into Sutton's reaching hands.

"Do *excuse* me," said Alexos as venomously as he could manage, and he left the room, ignoring the way that Kidd stood up from his seat but just stood there, his mouth agape, his eyes wide.

Felix met him in the corridor.

"Fetch me the first aid kit and bring it up to the library, please," he said, and Felix stared at the way he was holding his hand higher to keep it from bleeding too badly, gripping a napkin tightly in his palm.

"Did you... Did you finish eating, sir?" he asked as Alexos moved past him. "Shall I bring you your plate?"

"That would be appreciated, Felix, thank you," said Alexos, and began his way up the stairs.

Sutton had the good sense, at least, to leave him be.

Chapter Twelve

"Oh, dear," said Larry Kidd once Alexos had left the room, and Harry focused on picking up the pieces of the glass that had broken in the young master's hand, resisting the urge to run right after him. He had been prepared for this eventuality, and his Uncle Reg had told him in no short order that it was a likely possibility even if a houseguest he brought in *did* behave themselves. "I *am* sorry, Harry," Larry went on, visibly aghast and dismayed, wilting like a piece of cooked spinach. "He hates me."

"For now," Harry agreed, wrapping the broken glass in paper. "Do you recall that I asked you not to drink or take any stimulants before you arrived here?"

"I... do," said Larry hesitantly.

"Did you, in fact, take my advice?"

"I did not," admitted Larry, and when Harry put out his hand and gave him a rather stern look, he produced a compact from the inside pocket of his jacket and handed it over. "I was quite drunk last night, so all I did was take a bit to spruce me up, you know."

"You took more than enough to spruce you up," said Harry, opening the little metal case and examining the white powder inside, hidden in a puzzle compartment that Harry was more adept at opening than he might admit to. "You've been conducting yourself like quite the lunatic."

"Have I?"

"A bit, sir," said Harry, and closed the compact up. It had a cigarette case on one side and a mirrored compact on the other, the hatch for the cocaine within the latter, and it was far nicer than anything he would expect Larry Kidd to own, even having received it as a gift. "Is this yours?"

"No, no, it's Cherry Flintman's," said Larry, and Harry raised an eyebrow, surprised.

Cherry Flintman – whose actual name, Harry was fully aware, was Gareth Solihull – was wonderful for a party, and was well-versed in all manners of erotic dance, modern music, dirty poetry and, of course, an array of highs and stimulants, but he was typically too hard a party master for the likes of Larry, who was frightened of crowds and became ill upon exposure to very loud music.

"Is he expecting it back?"

"On Monday," said Larry. "When I go down into Brighton, you know."

"Ah, he's acting in the play, I suppose," said Harry, beginning to understand, and Larry nodded his head. He looked quite miserable, and Harry touched his shoulder just before the knock came at the door.

Felix entered upon Harry's invitation, and Harry picked up Alexos' plate, setting the knife and fork on it before pouring a fresh glass of accompanying wine for Alexos, setting it all on a tray.

"His hand is alright?"

"Yes, sir, I brought the antiseptic up to him, and his hands aren't trembling too badly today, so he bandaged it himself," said Felix, although he glanced over to Larry uncertainly, who at least had the good grace to look very chagrined.

"Bring him whatever he needs, Felix."

"You aren't going to go up, sir?"

"I believe Mr Fox would prefer he be permitted to eat and then work in peace for a while, Felix," said Harry quietly, putting the tray in his hands. "Bring him his tray, ask if he would like anything else, and if he says no, just leave him to his own devices. I'll close the library this evening."

Once Felix left, he cleared away Alexos' side of the table as Larry ate – he seemed, at least, to have a significant appetite despite the lingering drunkenness and the current high, his knees shifting under the table and bouncing in their place.

"I am sorry to make him hate me so," said Larry. "I know you said he's rather cat-like and needs a light touch, but I'm not tremendously good at that sort of thing."

"I was aware this might happen, Mr Kidd," said Harry quietly. "As I told you, Mr Fox is a man of particular tastes who is very keenly attached to his privacy. I did advise you *also*, if you recall, not to make any mention of inversion unless he broached the topic first."

"Did I broach it?"

"When you asked him how well he liked my arse? Yes, Larry, you did."

"Oh, yes," said Larry, making a slight face. "I suppose I rather did. Will he warm to me?"

"When you're sober and better controlled, perhaps."

"I wish you'd say you had no doubt."

"I have significant doubts, Mr Kidd, but I also have hopes. It's my intention to introduce Mr Fox to a great many men of like-minded interest, bring him into as varied a series of friendships as I have myself, but he is not social by nature, and our tastes run to different directions. I do genuinely believe that the two of you will get on, once certain obstacles are overcome."

"Perhaps I should go up and apologise," said Larry suddenly, getting to his feet, and Harry put his hand on his shoulder, nudging him to sit again.

"By no means, sir," said Harry quietly. "It would be my suggestion that you not attempt to enter the library whilst Mr Fox lies therein – it is his domain, and he guards the territory fiercely. He'll react poorly if he finds it encroached upon."

Larry sighed, leaning back in his seat. "He'll like me better sober," he said – promised. "I'll not say a word next time. I won't even ask him a question."

Harry doubted this immensely, but Larry's eagerness to please and his crushing desperation for other people to like him, even if that person was an ornery, angry gentleman with no friends, was encouraging and really quite useful for Harry's purposes. It would have been kind to say that he wanted to introduce Larry and Alexos knowing that if Alexos could learn to like Larry, he could learn to like a great many more inoffensive men – while this was a motivator, it was not his primary one.

Larry was desperate for everyone to like him, and avoided conflict almost pathologically, bending over backwards to keep people happy, changing his apparent values from one party to the next – quite annoying, and in Harry's own opinion an indicator of spinelessness, but a people-pleaser like Larry would mould himself to Alexos' preferences as much as he could.

"He's very handsome, isn't he?" asked Larry, taking a mouthful of his food, swallowing. "I can't believe nobody knows him."

Harry had told Larry very little about Alexos when they'd met some weeks ago on Harry's day off – he had told him that Alexos wasn't already involved in any of their communities, that he ventured out very little on account of his disability, and had confirmed it when Larry had asked if Alexos were of the same bent as them, but said nothing more. He'd intentionally held back too much information, knowing that Larry often gossiped and asked questions about anybody he learned of.

"Nobody?" Harry repeated.

"Well, I suppose he is a bit old," said Larry. "What is he, forty?"

"Thirty-three."

"Oh," said Larry, seeming slightly surprised. "He's younger than I thought, then. But older than me, certainly, and most of my friends – I don't actually know many people older than thirty, you know."

"Aren't you thirty, yet?"

"Twenty-nine!" said Larry sharply, and Harry hid his smile as he turned away. "A decade younger than you, remember. The closest to Mr Fox that I can think of is Donald Howard, have you tried him?"

"I haven't tried anybody except you, Mr Kidd," said Harry – this was true, and saying it had the benefit of making Larry look up at him with his lips parted and his eyes slightly wide, his expression almost wondering.

"I— You don't mean that," said Larry. "You've tried other people."

"No, sir," said Harry, and Larry fidgeted in his seat, looking down at his plate. "I thought you the best introduction to a broader social calendar, sir, being as kind, gregarious, and charming as you are. Even Mr Fox is not immune to charm."

"Nor am I, judging by the way you have me blushing," muttered Larry, reaching up and awkwardly brushing his own cheek. He looked more anxious than he did pleased, but it was an anxiety *to* please.

"You are a man who greatly excels at connecting like-minded men with one another, sir, even if you don't connect with them yourself," said Harry. "I did consider your expertise in this area, as well."

"Well, I don't know that he'd like a lot of my friends," said Larry. "Except Donald."

"Howard, sir?"

"He's a solitary sort of man," said Larry. "Very romantic, you know – sort of Byronic, in his way of being. Well, he's a terrible slut, everybody's had a piece of him, and he's quite lovely, but it's all a smokescreen for what lies beneath. He refuses nearly every party invitation, and even when he comes, he's oh-so-quiet, and not only because he's got his mouth full. He doesn't brood, exactly, but he has an aura of loneliness that rather makes one ache to touch him, the same way you want to touch the very still surface of calm water." There was a sort of quiet, painful yearning in Larry's voice as he spoke, which didn't necessarily mean he was aching for some sort of romantic connection with the man – the handful of occasions Harry had met him, he'd known Larry to slip into these reveries about one person or another at least twice.

"I've never met him," said Harry – but then, there was no reason he should.

Harry had first been acquainted with Larry through Gregson Carmichael, who was a glazier, because Larry tended to frequent a wide variety of little bars and cafés and speakeasies depending on wherever had the least crowding, and while he was comfortably well-off now, he had gone to school on a scholarship, and had always known work even though he had never known labour. Many of his friends were rich or aristocrats, but Larry himself was not, and mingled happily with various social classes.

Larry was not a close friend of Harry's, but knowing Ulysses Valentine, who he liked very well, he did see him regularly at the home or in the sphere of Vincent Lucas Samuels, and of course, Harry had already met Riggs, who was now Larry's valet.

"Do you know the names of any of his household?"

"His butler's name is Mead, Victor Mead," said Larry, thinking. "His father's valet is a Jones... I think there's a McNair somewhere in there, maybe he's a footman. I'm afraid I've not often had cause to visit since I was a boy, all the way up in the Yorkshire Dales – Donald and I were in the same year at school, you see, and our beds were next to one another's, what with there being no boys with I- or J-names between us in the dormitory. Howard, then Kidd, you know. I'd like very much to see him be a bit happier – perhaps he and Fox might be well-suited to one another."

"We shall see," said Harry – none of the names particularly rang a bell, but perhaps, perhaps...

"Could I have the compact back?" asked Larry.

"Of course, sir," said Harry, and smiled. "On Monday morning."

Larry opened his mouth, but then he sighed – he showed no surprise whatsoever, though, and went back to his meal. He really could be very good-natured – he was *obedient*, given the correct pressure, and for this situation, that was best.

* * *

Alexos ate in silence upstairs, drank his wine, and then went back to work. He had buried himself in it for some time, reading and making copious notes without, he was pleased to note, being interrupted except for when Felix let in the dog, who was now asleep at his feet.

His bad leg was aching quite terribly, making him think perhaps he'd strained himself when he suddenly got to his feet, but he didn't feel any desire to ring for service and take something for it.

He felt oversensitive and indignant and *humiliated*, wanting to stew in his own misery for a bit, and when the door quietly opened some little while after he'd been working, Alexos scowled down at his page.

"I do hope you're pleased with yourself," he said coldly, but the man in the doorway was not, as he had expected, Sutton – instead, he found himself faced with Riggs, Kidd's valet. Riggs was a plain young man, pale, dark-haired, and unremarkable, and now he looked at Alexos quite uncertainly.

"My apologies, sir, I didn't mean to interrupt," he said quietly. "I thought that you were still sat down to lunch with Mr Kidd. Mr Brydon said I was welcome to come up and borrow a book, if I wanted."

He moved to go, but Alexos stood to his feet, ignoring Aristaeus' grunt of complaint, saying, "No, no, Riggs, please."

He'd already been made to feel unreasonable and really quite awful – and a part of him, a spiteful part perhaps, wanted to be kind to Kidd's valet in a way he had no intention of being kind to Kidd himself.

"The library is at your disposal, if anything here suits your fancy. What is it you're looking for?"

"I've been reading Hugo of late, sir," said Riggs. "I just finished *Toilers of the Sea*."

"Oh, of course, Hugo is over here," said Alexos, gesturing for Riggs to follow him past the long desk and between two of the tall shelves, gesturing. "Here, in the original French—"

Riggs looked uncertain, and Alexos pivoted to the other shelf. "Here, in translation. You've read *Les Misérables*?"

"And *Notre-Dame*," said Riggs. "And some of his poetry."

"You like his social commentary?" asked Alexos, and Riggs' expression froze. It was a terribly loaded question to ask of a servant, even of a valet for a young bachelor, and he didn't press on it or provoke as he might someone else. "Sorry, Riggs, I'm not asking you to confess yourself a communist. What I mean to ask is, are you more interested in what Mr Hugo has to say about hunger for power, about class conflict, about being an outcast? Or did you appreciate the break from Mr Hugo's tendency to lecture in *Toilers*?"

"I don't know that he stopped lecturing, sir," said Riggs, and looked surprised when Alexos laughed, but Alexos was surprised himself.

"*The Man Who Laughs* is my favourite of Hugo's," said Alexos, touching his fingers to the spine of the volume. "Gwynplaine is a tragic figure, but is at the same time quite detestable. Nonetheless, the text is as others of his – it's about the cancerous quality of those most power-hungry people, the venom of polity, and quite particularly the ways in which the aristocracy consume and feed upon the suffering of the lower classes. There's *Ninety-Three*, which is about la Terreur, or at least, revolts there against, but he has plays—"

"*The Man Who Laughs* sounds good, sir," said Riggs, almost shyly, and Alexos smiled at him, hooking his finger against the binding and tugging it free from the shelf, handing it over. "Is Hugo a favourite author of yours?"

"Not particularly," said Alexos, shifting his grip on his cane and moving his other hand about, opening and closing it and feeling the stiffness of the healing wound underneath the gauze. "I think he had a great deal of value to say, and I agree most heartily with many of the campaigns to which he gave his life, especially his fierce opposition to capital punishment – he was also rather a repulsive man, self-indulgent, hedonistic, and a hypocrite."

Riggs was blinking at him, not seeming quite to comprehend, and he stepped after Alexos as he limped back to his seat.

"He was an adulterer and a whoremonger," said Alexos quietly. "He is quite renowned for his depiction of women's tragedy, considering characters like Esmerelda or Fantine and Éponine, and yet he himself made a tragedy of one woman or another numerous times – a mistress of his, Léonie d'Aunet, spent some months imprisoned, in a gaol and then a convent, for the crime of their being caught in bed together, whereas he escaped punishment. Women to him were either tragic children, equally tragic old women, or receptacles for his sexuality, and it is said he spied on his guests through illicit peepholes."

Bad enough to think about the people in one's home, or who crossed one's path, than to actually—

But then, Alexos had often been quite disgusted with tales of Hugo's engagement with servants, taking advantage of the differences in their positions, and he was really no better, was he? He just was more interested in men than women.

"I had no idea, sir," said Riggs as Alexos sank into his chair again and felt with his foot for Aristaeus, who rolled over onto his back that Alexos would rub his belly with his foot. He smiled down at the sleepy old hound, who looked up at him with his eyes rheumy and his ears flopping. "I've been reading Mr Hugo of late having been recommended him."

"By your employer, I suppose?"

"Oh, no, sir," said Riggs. "Mr Valentine, he's the valet of Mr Kidd's illustrator, recommended him, he recommends me a lot of books he thinks will be improving or helpful, or just that I will enjoy. He takes a great deal of time with me – your Mr Sutton gave me tutelage when I was initially coming up as a footman in his household, and I believe Mr Valentine did the same for him, though I suppose you would know better than I who Mr Sutton likes to read. Mr Kidd has no particular fondness for Hugo, nor of similarly... protractive authors."

Alexos found himself laughing again, although it made his leg sore, and he looked over at Riggs, arching his eyebrow. "Long-winded, you mean?" he asked. "He has no care for Hugo, nor Dostoyevsky, nor Dickens?"

"No, sir," said Riggs. "But Mr Kidd is a passionate reader – he reads quite voraciously, and very fast too, reads a lot of contemporary authors and more classic ones. I'm far slower than he is, but I do enjoy to read."

"Have you read my mother's books?"

"Of course, sir, some of them," said Riggs, nodding. "I'm not passionate about mysteries myself – I asked Mr Kidd to recommend me the ones that had very little gory depiction, you know. I come over rather faint at times, reading some of the modern crime novels Mr Kidd likes."

"Well, I'm not particularly au fait with many contemporary novels, but if you want much from the last century or two, I might be able to give you some recommendations here and there," said Alexos quietly. He was surprised, genuinely, at how calm and easy Riggs was in contrast to his master – and indeed, how polite.

"I read a few Victorian crime novels thinking they'd be of a similar lilt but less, you know, ones that are fifty, sixty years old, thinking they'd be less, erm, graphic, but..."

"They used to call then penny dreadfuls or penny bloods," Alexos said sympathetically, trying not to laugh, and Riggs laughed a little himself, his hand twitching as though he were going to reach up and rub the back of his neck, but of course, he was too well-trained to actually do so.

"Yes, Mr Kidd did tell me," he said. "He doesn't constrain himself only to crime novels, he reads a lot of other romances, of course, and even a little of scientifiction, which I like a bit better – you know, H.G. Wells and Jules Verne, I have a subscription to this magazine, *The Electrical Experimenter,* it comes in from America each month, and it has stories as well as real articles about radio and wireless technology."

Mr Riggs seemed embarrassed at having talked so long, bringing the book in against his breast, and Alexos smiled at him, genuinely rather interested in this little nugget of information, and indeed, the magazine. He didn't know much about radio himself, bar what he did occasionally read in a copy of *English Mechanic* or *Everyday Engineering.*

"As a rule," he said now, "I would ask that if you duck your head into the library and see me at work, that you not bother to knock or get my attention – just go and browse the shelves as you like."

"Yes, sir, of course," said Riggs. "Thank you very much for your recommendation."

"It's nothing," said Alexos. "Are you going back down to the servant's hall?"

"Yes, sir, are you in need of anything?"

Only the butler's attention, Alexos didn't say. "No, no, Riggs, not at all. Enjoy the book."

He itched not to write or read, for now – he wanted to go out to the shed, or ask that something be brought into the house for him to take apart, but he didn't particularly want Mr Kidd to see evidence of his being so eccentric right away, not when he was so... chatty.

In the evening, he took his dinner in the library, and he didn't see Sutton until it was time for him to retire to bed.

* * *

Harry was waiting for Alexos when he retired to his bedroom. He'd heard him on the stair and had slipped inside, the lamps already dimmed, his bath just run and awaiting him. As soon as Alexos entered, Harry grabbed him by the throat at the same time he pushed the door closed, pinning him against it.

Alexos' cane clattered against the side table and he grunted quietly in pain, his bandaged hand coming up to grip at Harry's wrist as the other splayed against the door behind him to keep him steady. His eyes were wide, pink showing in his cheeks, and his breathing was heavier.

"Is this the method by which you plan to apologise for today's fiasco?" he asked coldly, but when Harry moved deliberately to press a knee between his thighs, careful not to put undue pressure on his bad leg as he nudged against Alexos' crotch, Alexos' eyes fluttered shut and his defiance faltered.

"Perhaps it is," said Harry. "Has a man ever apologised to you with buggery before?"

Alexos' eyes reopened, his gasp audible, his pulse speeding under Harry's hand. The beat of it was really quite powerful, a palpable thumb underneath his palm.

Harry turned the key in the lock.

"Who's to say I'm in the mood to permit buggery?" asked Alexos, and Harry grinned down at him, squeezing his throat tighter.

"Who's to say I'm in the mood to ask for your permission?" he replied, making his voice rumble as much as he could, although when Alexos took in a reedy breath and blushed further, he couldn't help but laugh.

"Does that amuse you?" demanded Alexos, seeming indignant and a little embarrassed as Harry drew away from him to pick up his cane and hand it back to him. "Threatening to assault me?"

"It's not making the threat that amuses me so much as your enthusiastic reaction. I have a bath already run for us."

"For *us*?"

"I told Felix that barring particular crisis, he is to leave me be for the evening, that I have certain delicate exercises to go through with the young master in order to alleviate the day's pain. To spare Mr Kidd's reputation, I did imply that your pain was your reason for so immediately excusing yourself from luncheon."

"Imply whatever you like," said Alexos grimly, sitting down on the bed and sighing in relief when Harry knelt to slip off his shoes and socks for him, helping him off with his trousers as Alexos shrugged off his jacket. "He'll soon be disabused of any attempt to rehabilitate said reputation."

"I have no doubt Mr Kidd will extend his own apologies at breakfast tomorrow," said Harry, and when Alexos gave him a cool look, Harry looked up at him. "You don't mean you'll avoid him at breakfast, too?"

"I don't even take every meal with my father, Harry."

"Kidd was quite out of sorts this afternoon," said Harry, folding his trousers over a rail before taking up his vest and setting it aside with his jacket. "He was still drunk from the night before, and in an attempt to remove the edge from his drunkenness, he'd taken quite a bit of cocaine. You must have noticed he was unusually manic."

"For all I knew, that level of mania *was* his usual," muttered Alexos, although Harry was gratified indeed to see his stiff features soften slightly as he unbuttoned his shirt. His fingers were moving well today, without stiffness or tremble, and Harry hoped he'd be able to remove the bandage without resetting it once they'd bathed together – the glass had only appeared to cut shallowly, after all, and so long as Alexos had no plans to commence his engineering focus tomorrow, it ought heal well enough unwrapped. "Cocaine? Really?"

"Mr Kidd is not typically one to partake – he drinks often, but other indulgences are not to his taste. I'm given to understand he was at a party the night before with some of the cast members for this production in Brighton, and I expect he was advised the powder, with the assumption being that it would be better for him to be manic than sodden from the night previous."

"You realise little of what you're saying is improving the figure of Lawrence Kidd in my mind's eye," said Alexos.

"You say that, Alexos, and yet your voice is softened, and your posture is not quite as stiff."

"What has that got to do with Kidd?" Alexos was raising his eyebrows as he handed Harry his shirt, and didn't wait for him as he stood and limped toward the bathroom in just his underwear. "You've promised me buggery – isn't that reason enough to relax?"

"One likes to think so, but one can never assume," said Harry in his soupiest voice, and laughed when it earned him a very foul hand signal.

He helped Alexos into his bath, and as he sank beneath the steaming hot water, his whole body went slack – his bad leg twitched and shifted, pained and uncomfortable, but it did seem to give way to relief as he sank back against the bath's wall. His left arm was weeks now removed from its pin and rod, but he did occasionally feel odd twinges on the inside of the bone at a sudden change in temperature, and Harry believed he was experiencing one of them now, wrinkling his nose and adjusting his position in the bathwater, wiggling his fingers.

Seeing Harry looking, he muttered, "One would think, already ravaged as it has been by polio, that going over balconies or bannisters, my body would see fit to land on the right side, rather than allow new scars and injuries to my already weaker left."

"Which side should I ravage you from?"

"Behave a *moment*, would you? Incorrigible bastard that you are. Pass me my flannel."

"Mr Riggs, if it means anything to you," said Harry as he assented, "seems to like you very much."

"Oh, yes," said Alexos vaguely. "He came into the library thinking I was still downstairs. I was a bit distracted, I'm afraid. I wasn't drunk, and I forewent the analgesic I was perhaps in need of – I seem to recall being somewhat distracted by the pain, and it's possible I gave him a speech on the sins of Victor Hugo."

"He came away quite impressed," said Harry, hanging up his own jacket and setting his pocket watch inside, smiling to himself as he recalled the quiet praise that Riggs had laid on the back of *Mr Fox*.

Riggs was quite reserved by nature, wasn't tremendously social and was one of life's natural observers, not out of loneliness or even social awkwardness, but instead due to a sort of contented spirit. He was an affable young man, good-natured and content to follow the flow of life around him, and while it wouldn't be true to say he enthused about Alexos – Harry had only ever heard Riggs enthuse on such joys as an empty train compartment or a good book on a sunny day, or a particularly entrancing radio play – he had spoken well of him, and had seemed pleased to make his acquaintance.

"He advised me that he knew little of Hugo except that he was a politician and very erudite, and said he had no idea Hugo so ill-treated the women in his life, and that he had never thought of Hugo as a real man with a real life at all. He may well ask you for a biographical recommendation later this month."

Alexos didn't appear to be listening – Harry had taken off his waistcoat and was in the process of unbuttoning his shirt, bearing more of his chest to Alexos' sight. Alexos, who had been idly scrubbing at his back with the flannel he'd asked for, was now simply holding it loosely against his chest, and was observing with rapt attention as Harry fully undid his shirt and set it aside, then removed his vest.

"Good God," Alexos whispered, his tone almost devout in its fervour.

"I take that to mean I meet with your approval?"

"Your ego is quite swollen enough without hearing my treatise on the glory of your body," whispered Alexos softly, staring at him as Harry slid off now his trousers. "Suffice it to say it's quite fucking nice, Harry."

Across three quarters of Harry's chest, the right-side of his hedgerow tattoos extended across – a hawk was tattooed over the centre of his chest, its wings outstretched, and while underneath the right side of his breast was a salmon upon which the hawk's eyes were fixed, the left side was as yet bare. His belly was a work in progress: apart from the salmon was depicted a pike curling about his left-hand side and a chunky carp a little over his navel. Jack Limby, the tattooist responsible for this foray into the nation's waterways, had enthused over the space available on his belly for more, and as Harry recalled, his next intended was a roach.

Limby had done his left leg, which was mostly completed, and it depicted a great many other coastal creatures – an eel, a jellyfish, several other fish and sea creatures, all peeked out from between different sorts of corals and sea grasses up the leg. Limby was a Welshman who had grown up free-diving at his childhood home in Anglesey, and upon seeing the Harry's sleeves and backpiece, he had jumped at the chance to respond to the woodland creatures and flowers with some of what which might be found beneath the waves. He'd even gone to some effort to match the style of the water and bubbles he etched to that about the mermaid on his other thigh, the only tattoo on the front of his right leg thus far, barring the upper edges of the pocket watch tattooed on his foot.

"Goodness, you're like a canvas mostly filled in," said Alexos eagerly, and Harry turned to face away from him as he slid off his underthings: he heard Alexos gasp in delight at Harry's back, which was something of a wonder. His sleeves had been mostly completed by John Jacob Manford, an Englishman who rippled with muscle, and a very petite German woman named Eckhart, with a few of the smaller details added in by other artists in between, but his backpiece was all by one man. Nikhil Adhikari travelled with a circus, and Harry had done favours for a little over two dozen people in exchange for favours they'd do for Mr Adhikari in exchange for his time – the man was a master of the art, and Harry had bade him do whatever pleased him.

His sleeves already completed, Mr Adhikari had been inspired, and had knitted the hedgerows on each side in a huge scene quite unlike the usual bejewelled and geometric patterns he favoured in his body of work, or the dancing goddesses and standing warriors: instead, he'd inked in a mighty stag with a forest behind him, putting such incredible detail into its antlers, the shine of its eyes, even the dappled pattern on some of its coat that it really did look as though you could reach out and touch it.

"Nothing on your arse," said Alexos, but his fingers brushed the back of his thigh – Jack had done a seal peeking out from kelp there, and across his calf a spiny crab surrounded by small fish and anemones; on the other leg were a medley of more traditional bits and pieces that he'd picked up: a treasure chest, a ship's wheel... "Oh, is this the Argo?" he asked, touching the back of his calf on the other side.

"It was tattooed by a Greek, it might be," said Harry, smirking to himself as he stepped back into Alexos' space, feeling his hands on the backs of his legs, stroking with delight over the ink there. "He just said it was done in the ancient style. Is it your favourite?"

"They're all my favourite," said Alexos, and Harry chose this moment to turn around.

Alexos first looked up at his face, his smile quite indulgent, and then dropped lower, back to waist-height. His lips parted. His eyes did not widen incredibly, but Harry could see his pupils dilate. He looked at Harry's cock not merely with arousal or admiration, but with the same sudden, almost scientific, passionate fervour with which he had responded to the first view of Harry's tattoos – he took Harry's cock in hand with fascination writ on his features, almost seeming to forget what it was he was holding, although to Harry's relief he did tilt his head instead of forgetting himself so much that he twisted Harry's penis in search of a better angle for examination.

"Is this *metal*?" he asked, delighted and quite intrigued, as though discovering an exciting new invention.

"It is," said Harry affectionately.

"How remarkable," said Alexos in much the same tone Harry imagined the first admirers had responded to the advent of the steam train.

It occurred to Harry that this was the first time Alexos had ever held another man's cock in his hand, by his own admission was likely the closest he'd ever been to another man's cock, and yet he had no doubt that this fact couldn't be furthest from his mind. He was distracted, in his wonderful way, and had greater novelties on his mind.

"May I?" asked Harry, his hand hovering over Alexos', and suppressed his laughter as Alexos politely handed his penis back.

"Please, by all means," he said, and there was a hot flush on the back of Harry's neck and rippling on his skin – he was trying not to get overexcited too quickly, not to let himself get too close to a peak, but it was surprisingly evocative to be so admired as a piece of art and an example of great innovation, for Alexos to look at him in a way that was simultaneously so forgetfully asexual and yet still so passionate.

"I've a hafada here, this is a piercing of the scrotum," said Harry, pulling the shaft of his cock against his belly and leaning back, feeling for his bollocks and then pressing against the curved barbell he had a little under the base of his cock. He might not be able to look down and peer at his cock piercings the way some men could, but he knew very well where each of his piercings were without looking directly – and if he had been remotely insecure about the large swell of his belly, which he was not and never particularly had been, he had no doubt it would have been difficult to hold onto that insecurity when Alexos reached out and touched the skin so worshipfully as he did now. "And here I've a piercing of the frenulum down here, but if I pull back my foreskin..."

Alexos' gasp was wonderful. It was mildly aroused, but mostly delighted – "Another!" he said, and touched his thumb to the edge of one of the barbels as it glinted visibly, his foreskin pulled back. "Is this a Prince Albert?"

"No, it's another frenulum piercing," said Harry. "I like having one within and one without – I could probably call it a ladder, what with there being three barbels in parallel, but it seems to be it would be a very unsensible ladder to climb indeed."

"The metal's so warm," said Alexos wonderingly, carefully nudging the two piercings at the head of his cock and shifting with delight, making the water splash, at their slight mobility in their places. "Do they feel good?"

"For me," asked Harry, exhaling in quiet pleasure at the undirected and thoughtless touches of Alexos' hand on his cock, "or for you?"

Alexos seemed to remember very abruptly what Harry's cock was *for*, and his jaw dropped, his eyes widening. "*Oh*," he said breathlessly, and his tongue darted out to wet his lips. "Oh, of course." He looked up at Sutton's chest, and suddenly saw the rings through his nipples, and then said, "*Oh!*"

"Alexos, I'm becoming cold," said Harry, catching his hands before they could grab greedily for his chest, and Alexos laughed, embarrassed, but shifted back in the bath. "I was going to get in behind you."

"Why? I want to face you."

"So I can attend your back."

"Well, I'm attending your tits, you can attend my back later."

Harry's cock gave a significant twitch at that, something he might have found embarrassing were Alexos aware enough to notice, but he didn't: when Harry stepped into the bath, sinking into it, the water level rose up to Alexos' neck, making him let out a breathless noise.

"How should I sit?"

"I couldn't give a toss."

"You say that now, you won't say it if I crush your bad leg."

"Oh, right," said Alexos, realising the way that Harry was awkwardly crumpled to one side of the bed, and he laughed, leaning forward and cupping his hands around the back of Harry's calf. His fingers were warm and strong as he pulled Harry to relax slightly, carefully setting his foot at the side of Alexos' thigh. "I can't bend it like you can bend yours, not bend it and keep it there."

"I don't think that should be a problem," murmured Harry, sliding forward, his legs over Alexos', feet either side of his hips. It was awkward, but the bath was large enough that there was space enough for it to be possible and for his thighs to remain spread, and Alexos immediately put his hands on Harry's chest. He cupped his chest as though they were breasts, thumbs pressing and pushing at the metal pierced through each of his nipples, and Harry moaned quietly at the pleasant, rushing pleasure of it, his cock perking up against his stomach.

"Fuck me," whispered Alexos, pulling at one of Harry's nipples very delicately by the ring, and Harry groaned.

"I intend to," he muttered.

"Can I do it harder?"

"As hard as you dare," said Harry – Alexos responded by tugging *hard*, and Harry had to clench his teeth to keep from moaning too loudly at the sting and pleasure of it, his head tipping back and his hand coming to grip at Alexos' good knee, although he did his best not to do so too roughly.

"That's really very good," said Alexos, pulling at the other side before realising he could move the piercing in its hole and doing so, making a gentler, tingling tug rush through his chest. "It feels good?"

"Very," said Harry, and reached to tug on one of Alexos' nipples, having noted already that they were sensitive, and Alexos shivered, his hips bucking and making the water slosh, although he immediately grunted in pain and shifted his leg slightly against Harry's body. "Need me to move?"

"By no means," said Alexos, and reached underneath Harry's belly, tickling the hair dusted over the skin before he grasped hold of Harry's cock, and pulled. "God, this is— Fuck. Your cock is really quite big, isn't it?"

"Did you expect something smaller, given the size of me?"

"It's all very well talking about proportion," muttered Alexos, squeezing the shaft of Harry's cock and tugging up the length of it until his hand met the piercings around his cockhead, and then he shifted his grip slightly, moving and tugging at the flesh around the piercings with his fingertips as his thumb slid over the top of his shaft. It was unspeakably good, making him moan again. "If your cock is as big as the rest of your body, it might well follow my arse is in line with the rest of mine, and too small to take it."

"Oh, my cock will fit, I'll make sure of it," Harry promised him. "It might well be so that you're so tight around it we can see the barbels of my cock through the flesh of your belly, but nonetheless, it *will* fit."

Alexos let out a noise so wheezed it almost sounded pained, and squirmed in his place as he kept pulling and shifting his hand around Harry's cock. Harry was fully hard now, his bollocks shifting, his cock pulsing gently, but he gripped Alexos' wrist before he could work him up any further.

"I've been intending on savouring getting my cock into you, Alexos," he said, aware his voice was low. "I have no intention of letting you pop my cork before I have it buried in your arse."

"Fuck," said Alexos, and tipped his body forward.

He was eager as he fell against Harry's chest, one of his arms wrapping loosely around his neck and the other about his belly: his whole body shocked when Harry carefully moved closer, ensuring he wasn't putting too much weight on Alexos but closing the gap so that Alexos didn't have to move too far forward.

"More," said Alexos against his lips, sliding his palm down to one of Harry's thighs and gripping the flesh there, pressing his fingers into it hard enough that Harry sighed at the pressure.

"I can't sit in your lap, I weigh a great deal more than the dog, Alexos."

"You needn't put all your weight on me, but you don't need to balance yourself on your heels quite like that, I'm not going to turn to dust," said Alexos, and Harry carefully eased himself down somewhat, sitting back on Alexos' thighs. He was very careful about it, keeping his legs tense, and he watched Alexos' face carefully for signs of pain, which lingered for a moment, but then relaxed. "*Fuck.* I wish you could sit on me properly."

"At some point, when I take your cock in me, perhaps," said Harry, sliding his hand up Alexos' back before he hooked his middle finger against Alexos' arse, and Alexos heaved in a gasp, tipping forward and burying his face against Harry's neck, hot water sloshing between them. "Do you like my body more than Aristophanes might have?"

"I think I like your body better than any other man could," Alexos said – or, more accurately, he almost whimpered, because as Harry curled his fingers and managed to press his finger further into Alexos' arse, the muscle slack and open in the warm water despite the lack of lubrication, he was rubbing his cock eagerly against the underside of Harry's belly, clumsily letting it slide against Harry's own. "God, you're built like a warrior."

"A warrior?" repeated Harry, and laughed not because it wasn't true but because it was, no matter that he hadn't fought in years and preferred being a medic to the man with the rifle in his hands. "Is that what you've dreamed of, reading those ancient texts of yours? Being beset by big, fat warriors all rippling muscle and strongman's weight?"

"The nipple piercings were unexpected," said Alexos, and his moan was open-mouthed against Harry's neck as Harry pressed another finger inside him. "That's— that's *queer*—"

"I thought that was what we were up to."

"Oh, fuck off," said Alexos, pinching his side and making him laugh. "I meant the feeling of the hot water on the inside of my arse, thank you."

"You've never had an enema before?"

"I was a very sickly little boy and I'm a sickly adult, I've had more enemas than you'd know what to do with."

"I expect I could deliver a far more enjoyable enema than your average nurse, as I've threatened before," said Harry huskily, and scissored his fingers as best he could, feeling Alexos' hips stutter and his legs stiffen, sighing when Alexos began to mouth with more intention at his neck.

"I hope you mean with your cock and balls, and not with an enema bag."

"Even with an actual enema, I've no doubt I could make you come from it," said Harry.

"Let's not make future medical appointments more difficult for me than they already are by adding inconvenient erections to the mix," grunted Alexos, and Harry shifted position to capture his mouth again. It wasn't the best position to finger him by, bending as he was to reach and with Alexos sitting upright. He couldn't press deeply and couldn't easily feel for his prostate, but it was still nice to feel Alexos open, feel Alexos press between his hand and thrusting against his belly.

"Is the pain terrible?"

"The pain's fine," grunted Alexos. "But for my inexperience, not to mention my disability and the size of this bath, I'd be riding you right here."

Harry laughed at that, and grazed his teeth down Alexos' neck, making him groan – and then he withdrew his fingers, making Alexos groan for a different reason, the sound quite plaintive.

"Don't you want to be clean?" asked Harry.

"I want to be *fucked*," growled Alexos, and Harry thrilled at the way he said it, the way he pronounced the f- and so emphasised the -ck, and he thought too of the way Alexos had eagerly pulled and tugged at his nipple piercings, how Alexos kept touching his body – clumsy, unpractised, but *eager*. Even if he'd never fucked before, he'd certainly thought of it, and he was wanting for it, and he was *Harry's*.

Harry's to deflower, to play with, to fuck open and fuck full.

"I have every intention, Mr Fox, of ruining you this evening."

"You can't bring to ruin what is ruined already," said Alexos, but reluctantly allowed himself to be manipulated in place, Harry scrubbing over his shoulder. "Are you going to choke me again?"

"I didn't choke you badly, did I?"

"Not in the least – it was really quite exciting. I don't know that I'm a passionate convert to asphyxiation, but it's... Your hand on my throat, being pinned in that way, it has a certain appeal."

Harry smirked. This he had noticed already, of course, Alexos' delight in his own peril, his own bondage, but it was pleasing indeed to hear it repeated and stated so explicitly, especially with so much tension in Alexos' voice.

"Am I forgiven yet?" he asked, and Alexos scowled at him.

"Don't push your luck, Mr Sutton," he said, and Harry laughed.

* * *

Alexos' skin was mostly dry, his hair a little damp, as he limped into the bedroom. His leg was just a little bit stiff from the position in the bath – it was a large bath, but it was large because Alexos himself was tall and lanky, not because it was made to accommodate *two* tall men, and while Sutton had done very well to spread his legs as best he could either side of Alexos' body, the bath didn't quite have the breadth sufficient for him to spread out as easily as Alexos himself. Alexos hadn't been able to subtly bend and shift his leg in the water as he ordinarily would, and there was a lingering numbness from being held in one position, but it was worth it, more than worth it.

His cock *ached*, he was so hard, wetness gathered at its head, and his head was still whirling, almost rushing, with the wonder of Sutton's body – all those many tattoos, what seemed to be hundreds of them, and the *piercings*, that wonderful shining silver through his cock thrice over, and through his nipples too!

It was incredible, pulling on the rings or rubbing over the bars and feeling them move in their places, feeling the *weight* of them against Sutton's flesh, warmed by his skin but cooler than his body, and there was a prickling heat under his flesh when he considered the tattoos, the piercings, those *needles*—

He had thought about a piercing, once or twice, not through his nipples or his cock, but thought distantly about piercing his ears. He'd never actually have done it, he didn't think – it was far too flashy for someone like him, he thought, would draw more attention than he'd really enjoy with his ears already on the larger side, but had always appealed, the idea of wearing gold rings through his earlobes.

Through his *nipples*? Through the head of his cock, or the shaft of it, that before now had never so much as entered his mind, but despite the fear and trepidation the idea naturally came with, there was an agonising heat to it, too.

"Are you very keen to face me when we do this?" asked Harry. "I think it might be easiest to begin with if I take you from behind, but if you'd prefer to face me—"

"Can you fuck me as hard, facing me? As you can from behind?" Alexos asked, and Harry faltered, his lips parting. There was a darkening in his cheeks and his lips and most of all in his eyes, the green in them very dark and surprisingly intense, as he looked at Alexos hungrily.

"I can fuck you hardest from behind," he said slowly, and Alexos nodded, watching Harry gather pillows from the bed and more from the side of the room, where he'd apparently stacked them ready. Alexos felt quite ridiculous, laying himself on his belly over the stacked up pillows, the most of them under his hips and keeping his arse in the air – his good knee he bent properly, able to bend it without putting too much pressure on it, and his left he let bend slightly, but kept it somewhat straighter. It meant he was leaning more into his right side, his weight on that part of his body, and that would mean he was better braced, once Harry fucked him.

"Fuck," he said breathlessly as the mattress depressed behind him, Harry a warm and heavy presence on the bed, and Harry's laugh was quiet and tremendously appealing as he brought his fingers, now slick with paraffin wax, between Alexos' legs. Harry had fucking teased him, scrubbing at his arse and between his thighs with the sponge, and Alexos was fully aware of the way his cock was dripping even before Harry slid two slick fingers into his arse like it was *nothing*.

The fullness was wonderful, making the muscle stretch slightly, and he moaned into his forearm, spreading his legs a little further apart as best he could without moving his right leg too much.

Harry pushed a third finger into him, and Alexos heaved in a breathless gasp. "Just— just *fuck* me, you needn't tease."

"I'm not teasing, I'm preparing," said Harry smoothly, thrusting his fingers into him at a slow, easy rhythm, pushing and putting pressure on the muscle. "You don't want me to tear you open, do you?"

Alexos' cock gave an embarrassing twitch underneath him, and Harry laughed a rich, plummy chuckle that Alexos' stomach do flips. His fingers were sliding deeper in this position than they'd been able to earlier, and Alexos gripped and pulled at the pillows underneath him, his hips stuttering.

The stretch when Harry pushed his fingers was really quite sublime, a heated pressure, and then Harry was leaning over him, slick cock pressed up against Alexos' hole, and Alexos heaved in a breath and filled his lungs at the pressure. Harry's cock, huge, fat thing that it was, was quite a bit thicker than his fingers, and hotter to the touch, too, and slicker. Harry pushed forward very slowly, the pressure burning in a spectacular way, not dissimilar to when Harry was shoving his hands into whatever the tightest muscles were that he could find in Alexos' back, but somehow so much more overwhelming—

And then Harry's cock popped past the ring of muscle, and Alexos was struck with the incredible sensation not only of Harry's ridiculous, mushroom-like cockhead in his arse, but also the sensation of the four little tips of the two barbels in him, sandwiched either side of his ring. He was letting out the most humiliating sounds, desperate sobs at the incredible, electric pressure of the little bits of metal pressed tight against the muscle, rolling and shifting against it as Harry adjusted himself, and his cock was spurting pre and leaving a wet spot underneath him on the stacked pillows.

"That was a great many words you just blurted out," said Harry, sliding his hands over Alexos' hips. "Were they all very filthy?"

"Filthy or profane," Alexos said breathlessly, tongue stopping before the next curse could fall out of his mouth. "Eurúproktos, you know that one? It means you've got a wide—"

He expected Harry to slowly inch his way forward, but he didn't: quite abruptly, he slammed his hips forward, burying his cock in Alexos' body and making him feel as though all of his organs were suddenly rushing out of its way, the piercings dragging at his inner walls in a way that made him feel like his head would explode – the last barbel tugged and rolled against his hole, the piercing *just* at the very end of where Harry could press his cock inside, and Alexos sobbed at the intensity of the sensation.

He was blurting out nonsense words, couldn't stop his mouth running as Harry pulled back his cock and then thrust into him again, thrust again and again, his superlatively large bollocks knocking against Alexos' own, his thighs smacking against Alexos' arse. He couldn't string two thoughts together at it, the thunderclap of their bodies together – his legs ached, even as he put more of his weight on his left side to compensate for it, but that pain faded into the background in response to the sheer intensity of *this*. There was pleasure, yes, of course there was, keen and electric and ready to make him fucking burst, but the intensity wasn't just from the pleasure: there was satisfaction from the sudden fill of his arse, satisfaction and just pure *feeling*.

His orgasm hit him like a sudden blow, his cock pulsing underneath him, and Harry didn't stop for a moment, kept slamming their hips together and yes, *yes*, it hurt, but the pain was a distant concern that he couldn't quite grasp hold of through the hot, dazzling thrill of his orgasm, the way it rocked through his body. Harry was hot and heavy on top of him, and when Harry leaned forward, his belly a weight on Alexos' back, his body framing Alexos' and shadowing him, Alexos *whined*.

"You like this?" Harry asked, voice hot and rumbling in his ear, and Alexos sobbed out an indiscriminate noise, unable to string together the words in any language to answer him; he reached back with the hand not fisted in the pillows underneath him and grasped clumsily for Harry's hand, squeezing his fingers and then bringing his hand up to grip at his shoulder, then—

"Oh, *fuck*, yeah, yes—"

"On the back of your neck?" asked Harry, and didn't wait for an answer: he shoved down with the full weight of his hand, shoving Alexos' face down into the pillows and pinning him there so that he couldn't raise his head even if he wanted to. The angle like this was sublime, dragging again and again over the most sensitive bits of him, and he was oversensitive from just coming, some of the thrusts making a sort of brilliant pleasure-pain burst through him and make his vision go white, but he was pretty sure he'd kill Harry before he let him stop.

Harry's breathing was heavy, and Alexos could hear him letting out the most magnificent fucking noises, breathy grunts that came from low in his throat as though he were really having trouble controlling himself, holding himself back, even as every thrust of his hips made Alexos' whole body thrum.

"Go on," he managed to say between moans. "All this teasing, and you're not even going to give it to me? All this effort putting that— that *obscene* length of prick inside me, and you're not even going to come? To leave yourself leaking out of me like a— *Mngh*—"

Harry pulled his hair so hard that Alexos whined, grabbing a fistful of it and shoving him down with all his weight on top of his body, hips snapping into him and forcing him to just take it, to just *withstand* it. He was hot all over, soaked with sweat and slippery with it, and he felt not just Harry's cock pulse, feeling the strange twitch and thickening and movement of his actual shaft buried in his arse, but also the additional wetness, strangely – and more than that, the way the piercings shifted through that extra wetness, the sensation making him sob.

He felt like a dishrag wrung dry when Harry finally stilled on top of him, most of his weight on Alexos' back, his breathing heavy. Alexos could feel the pound of Harry's heart where they were touching, from Harry's thighs, his belly, his palm.

"Good God," whispered Alexos as Harry released his hair and Alexos was able to lift his head. "Fuck."

"Fuck," Harry agreed, leaning back from him, and Alexos let out a surprised noise at the strange sensation of his arse, fucked-open, now left to gape – he could feel the coolness of the air on his skin, around his opened-up rim, slick with paraffin wax and sweat and Harry's *come*.

He reached back, sliding his own fingers inside himself – he flinched at the sudden sensitivity, grunting, but touched at the wetness, fell on his left side and looked blearily at the white, slick mixture sticking to his fingertips.

"Harry," said Alexos.

"Mm?"

"I think perhaps you should run another bath."

He said this before he turned further onto his side, looking back at Harry, and his mouth dropped open: Harry was drenched in sweat, his chest heaving slightly with his breaths, and his hair was a furious mess, all about his head.

Alexos' cock, brave and tireless warrior as it apparently was, twitched manfully despite being twice-spent and *aching* with it, his balls aching too, not to mention his leg, which was beginning to call out its soreness quite a bit louder than it had a moment ago.

"Jesus," said Harry, and Alexos looked at where he was gesturing, then pulled a face – it was one thing to have semen dripping out of his arse, which was surprisingly arousing and really quite wonderful: it was another to have a whole mess of it, swiftly drying and turning uncomfortably sticky, under his belly and clinging to his still-leaking cock. "If I milked you, I could fill a pint bottle."

"What an alarming suggestion," said Alexos. "I hope you don't mind if we forego that one." He swallowed, pushing himself up to sit, and Harry gently tugged him forward by his arm, letting him sit forward. One of Harry's hands touched the side of his face, the other coming down to almost dance over Alexos' bad right thigh. Grunting, Alexos pushed his hand away.

"I hurt you?"

"Polio *hurt* me," muttered Alexos. "You've made me a bit sore, but it was more than worth it on my end, I can assure you."

He'd just had sex. Just been buggered, in fact. Just fucked a man – a very handsome man, taller than him, and whipsmart with a biting wit, one who was cupping the side of his cheek as though he were... *something*. Something desirable, someone worth wanting.

Alexos suddenly felt like bursting into tears.

"Was I, uh," he started, and hesitated. "Was it alright? I know I'm not as mobile as most of the men you've likely fucked but—"

"Are you mad?" demanded Harry, voice hoarse, and Alexos looked at his face, at the wildness in his eyes, the redness in his cheeks, the wetness and bitten marks on his own lips, his hair all over. "Alexos, that was..." He inhaled, then kissed Alexos hard and hungrily, biting into his mouth and leaving Alexos dizzy with it before he said, "It was very good. It was superb. It was— I have no fucking *words*."

Alexos' cheeks were burning – his whole body was burning on the inside, although on the outside he felt suddenly cold as his sweat cooled.

"Another bath," agreed Harry before Alexos could lend voice to the thought a second time, and Alexos watched his arse admiringly as he strode away to start running more hot water, which Alexos prayed there'd be enough of.

"I have no choice but to forgive you," said Alexos, shifting forward on the bed and wincing at the sudden, awful pain that wrenched up the whole of his right side, abruptly reminding him he wasn't exactly meant to be having that sort of vigorous exercise. "Against my better judgement."

"I'm glad to hear I've an escape clause if I ever badly provoke your temper," said Harry, and Alexos laughed, pushing himself to his feet and gritting his teeth at the pain as he limped into the bathroom, putting all of his weight onto the nearest furniture. "I— Oh, I really did hurt you," he said regretfully, looking at Alexos as he struggled into the bathroom, dropping down onto the stool beside the bath.

"I believe I'll need the codeine tonight, Mr Sutton," said Alexos lowly. "But I should note that avoiding severe injury, I will actually accustom to this. I just don't know how to hold myself, that's all."

"You should have told me I was hurting you," said Harry, and Alexos laughed.

"You *weren't*. It faded into the background – I was a bit distracted, couldn't focus on it. Wrung out as I now am, I don't have anything else to focus on. Do you think I'd look very ridiculous if I pierced my ears?"

Harry stared at him, naked and glorious as he was, tattooed all over with the sweat on his body shining and the rings through his nipples glinting, and when he laughed, Alexos saw the movement of his chest and belly and wondered what it would feel like to be sat on Harry's cock while he laughed like that, what it might be like to straddle him – how the fuck would he hold his leg? He didn't know, but he wanted to try it.

He wanted to do everything.

"I think you'd look quite dashing," said Harry.

"I'd look ridiculous," said Alexos. "My ears are already overlarge – earrings would draw attention to it. And people would think I was a bohemian."

"No one will ever think you're a bohemian," Harry said damningly. "And perhaps they'd distract from the size of your ears."

"I feel like I should be angry with you for that comment."

"Be as angry as you like. Pass the bath salts."

Alexos passed him the bottle, shifting in his position, and he was really quite astounded by the feeling of warmth settled in his chest, a sort of overwhelming wonder, a delight, a real affection. He was aware, distantly, that perhaps he ought feel guilty or embarrassed or something, and instead, he just felt on top of the world.

"I really don't think I'll be able to eat breakfast with Mr Kidd tomorrow morning," said Alexos.

"Alexos," said Harry. "You've still not gone one full meal with him."

"That may be so," said Alexos, "but I can tell you now I won't be able to walk downstairs tomorrow morning."

Harry opened his mouth, then closed it. A bit of the plummy blush had come back into his cheeks, and Alexos could tell from the way he pressed his lips together that he was trying not to smile.

"Proud of yourself, are you?" he asked, arching an eyebrow.

"Somewhat."

"I don't know that it has quite the same impressive edge when I can't very well walk in the first place."

“I don’t have to mention that bit when I brag about it in pubs,” said Harry, and Alexos laughed, then reached out. Harry’s arm was warm under his touch, even though his sweat was cooling, and Alexos slid his palm over the flowers there, then tipped his head forward, leaning his forehead into his upper arm.

For a moment the two of them stood there, Alexos leaning into him, Harry stood there, the bath running, and then Harry slid an arm around his shoulder, squeezed him closer.

Alexos closed his eyes, staying leaned into Harry’s body, and he lingered there as the bath ran.

(It was a bit colder than they’d like, in the end, but warm enough to be bearable.

The real cold came later, when Alexos got into bed alone, and wished that Harry could get in beside him.)

Chapter Thirteen

For several days following that night, Alexos didn't really leave his room – his body was utterly wrecked, his hips and knees so full of new aches and pains that he almost thought he was really ruined by it. Sutton kept coming to help him and looking at him guiltily, which did make him laugh even as he hobbled miserably to and from the other room to bathe and see to his ablutions.

"Stop fussing over me," he said on the second morning, resting heavily on the dresser just inside the bathroom, letting it hold him up. "I did tell you, I'll get used to it."

"You're in agony with every step," replied Harry, and Alexos laughed.

"This isn't agony," he said dryly, shifting his weight on his good leg, which today was not a very good leg at all. "If you want to see me in agony, you should see me when I have the flu and all my joints are aching, I'm coughing out my lungs, and my guts are eviscerated with every unsuccessful attempt to hurry to the bathroom because they're already shot."

"Very evocative imagery," said Harry. "Very sexually appealing, I'm sure."

"It's not my fault polio lacks the sexual appeal of tuberculosis, Harry," said Alexos. "Take it up with God."

Harry sniggered, shaking his head, but he only relaxed once Alexos had sunk into the heat of the bath and fully relaxed with it, his head tipping back against the back. He didn't move immediately, just stayed there for a few minutes and let the hot water sink into him, soothing his exhausted joints, his muscles, seep right into his bones. There were only a few bruises on him, but they were light, lighter than he'd thought they'd be, and in future, he wanted Harry to bruise him more, bruise him harder.

He wanted to bruise him back.

Only Brydon had come into the room the past few days other than Harry, and ordinarily only when Alexos was asleep or when he was so buried in his work that he didn't notice he'd been until he'd done again.

"What have you told them is wrong with me?"

"Oh, I made a formal announcement at supper the night after," said Harry. "Said I'd fucked the young master silly."

"Men have lost their positions for lesser insolences than that," said Alexos.

"What, fucking the master silly?"

Alexos chuckled, wincing as he reached for a sponge and it sent a painful throb through his body, rippling down his legs and up his back. It was settled heavy in his body like a penetrating cold, only at least cold had a numbing effect – this just made him very aware of the way that his body was put together, and precisely how poor the construction was.

"Are you going to make a habit of threatening to render me unemployed?"

"Only until I'm used to all this exercise," said Alexos. "There's a good deal I had to learn to do once again after I was ill, you know. Walk and play piano – and whenever I've gotten into new things over the years, there's been a process of adjustment. To typing, to long walks, to working on machinery. I have to work up muscle and stamina like any other man, you know – it's just a slower and more painful process for me."

"While I take a great deal of pleasure in causing you pain, a good deal of the appeal is in my control over it," said Harry, and Alexos sighed, running the sponge over his bad knee even though it hurt, and making a face.

"As soon as I have the slightest control over my body, Harry, you can be sure I'll be ceding it directly to you."

Harry came over to the bath, and when Alexos saw that his sleeves were rolled up and that he'd put aside his jacket, he handed him the sponge, bracing himself for the touch when Harry brought it down his side. He was just the right balance of tense and gentle, and although it ached, there was no rawness in it, so he only sighed instead of crying out in response.

"You knew what I was," said Alexos, more quietly now, with more vulnerability in his voice than he intended, and Harry gripped him so suddenly by the hair, forcing his head back, that he choked on his moan, staring up at him.

"I know what you are," said Harry quietly, his expression severe, his gaze focused, his lips pressed hard together. There was a sort of pained look on his face, his jaw squarely held, and his grip was so tight on the back of Alexos' neck with his fistful of curls. "Alexos, I promise you, I'm not trying to... disrespect you. I don't mean to..." He looked down at the bathwater. The hand not gripping the back of Alexos' hair was still holding the sponge, and water dripped from it into the bath proper. "I'm sorry."

"I won't get better," Alexos told him quietly, leaning his head slightly back into Harry's hand, the pull at his scalp distracting from all the rest of the pain, and the novelty was wonderful, was a relief he wanted to latch onto and hold onto forever. "I'll get worse, by and by. We can joke about you ravaging me, but polio really did ravage my body – it's not just the muscle wasting, it's on my insides too, and my body will weaken at a faster rate than another man's. I told you that – I have told you that."

"Yes."

"But I'm not lying about the exercise, Harry. I will get used to it. Believe it or not, I've learned to wank off and finger myself without hurting myself too badly – I'll learn to be fucked and to fuck without hurting myself either."

Harry stared at him, and then he relaxed the grip he had on Alexos' hair, sliding his palm around the back of his head, his fingers scratching over the scalp, making him sigh and close his eyes.

"I'll learn too, I hope," Harry murmured, and Alexos laughed.

"No, I'll keep it secret," he said. "It amuses me that you should strain my muscles without meaning to."

Harry smacked him upside the head, and Alexos laughed again, grabbing him by the wrist and pressing a kiss to the inside of his palm. For a second, Harry was completely frozen, his green eyes wide, his lips parting, and then his cheeks darkened and he wrenched his hand back, and tried to hide his smile as he went back to washing over Alexos' sides.

"That flusters you," Alexos remarked, not bothering to hide his feelings of pleasure and superiority. Harry pressed his lips harder together as if he could flatten the smile out of them. "Aren't you used to tenderness?"

"Not delivered so earnestly," said Harry mildly. "Men don't often act like they're in love with me."

"I'm afraid that when you propose marriage, Mr Sutton, someone acting like they're in love with you is one of the attendant risks," said Alexos, and his tone was playful, but he didn't quite know what Harry meant by it. Was he being too much? Was kissing him on the palm too much, too queer, even for this dynamic between them? "You don't like it?"

"Being engaged?" asked Harry.

"Being kissed on the palm."

"Oh," said Harry lowly, not meeting his gaze. "No, I think I quite like that. I've been kissed on the hands before, but never like that."

"How have you been kissed on the hands?"

"Theatrically," said Harry. "Performatively. Exaggeratedly."

"I suppose I should learn to exaggerate better."

"You're exaggerated enough," said Harry. "I like the ways that you're exaggerated."

"I'm too much for most people."

"Not for me," said Harry.

Alexos' cheeks burned hot, and his next sigh was shuddered as Harry leaned over on the side of the bath, and maybe it was the way his hand moved over Alexos' body, scrubbing over his skin and taking care as he worked him over. He'd already mapped so much of Alexos' body under his hands, learned where the sensitive spots were, where the most pain was, and if Alexos stared at his face he could see him recalculate as he worked, finding the parts of Alexos' skin where he still felt the strain, and then he'd be gentler, or change his angle, or lighten his touch. Harry's chest was in front of him, tantalisingly big and strong, and he could smell Harry's skin, smell his sweat, wanted to reach out and touch him, but he didn't want to get his clothes wet.

"How many men have you been with?" asked Alexos. "Or— had sex with, I mean."

"More than you," said Harry, and Alexos huffed out a low laugh.

"Well, that could mean anything. That could mean anything between two men and a thousand."

"It's between two and a thousand," Harry agreed, and Alexos flicked water onto his face: the laugh that came out of him was rich and dark, plummy as his voice but with a deeper hoarseness to it, because that laugh was from low in his chest, from his very gut, and it made him shiver with anticipation. "Does that really make your cock hard?"

"It's you that makes my cock hard," said Alexos. "A dozen? Two dozen?"

"At least," said Harry.

"And no cripples among them?"

Harry thinned his lips, looking disapprovingly at him before gently tipping Alexos' head forward, not forcing him but nudging him to move, and Alexos readjusted himself, resting his forehead on the perfect cushion of his belly while spreading his legs a little to keep from putting too much pressure on his hips or his knees. Harry squeezed the sponge over the back of his neck, letting water drip down his back and making Alexos exhale, but then he washed over it, and Alexos went limp and lax, feeling as though he could melt into the other man.

"You must have fucked a few," said Alexos. "Given a few handjobs in the medical tents."

"Believe it or not, that's not in the guidebook of army medical protocol," said Harry. "There's an old army mate of mine with one leg, we've had sex a few times, and another man I was with once, he was missing an arm and a few chunks out of his side."

"What's the difference between them and me?"

"Other than the fact that I like you better?"

"I mean— You never worry about hurting them, do you?"

"I flatter myself, but I can't do quite the same damage to a man with my cock as I might with artillery fire or a shell blast."

"It's less impressive to say, Harry, but you can't do the same damage as polio, either."

Harry leaned back, and Alexos sat back on his arse in the bath and looked up at him, at the serious expression on his face. "You will tell me?" he asked quietly. "If I'm hurting you?"

"I told you the other night, didn't I? Said what position I wanted to be in, said when I was strained?"

"You enjoy it when I hurt you," said Harry, and his expression was so serious, so grave, that Alexos rather felt like he was being stood up in front of his schoolmaster. There was a sternness in it, and as Alexos stared up at him and tried not to squirm, Harry smirked, because he was evidently quite aware of the effect said sternness was having on Alexos' libido. "You like it when I take command, take control of you. It excites you, arouses you. And I don't imagine I have to convince you that I'm just as invigorated by the inverse."

"I'm quite convinced," agreed Alexos, his mouth slightly dry.

"With any man at all," said Harry quietly, "I'd discuss... the importance of being told his limits. Beating someone over the backside is easy enough – tying a man up, on the other hand, or choking him, or teasing him with a knife, I've done all that, but not without first discussing... Not without knowing first that he will tell me, in no uncertain terms, when we reach a limit of his. When we reach something that frightens him too much, or hurts him too much – any point that turns arousal and excitement to something else."

"Why are you telling me this?"

"Because I don't want you to think these are requirements of mine I've invented purely because of your legs, or the state of your joints," said Harry. "It's a tenet of the practice."

"Well, it's only common sense," said Alexos. "You can't go around choking men and having them expect them to read your mind and know when you're about to kill them dead."

"You have far too low an opinion of other people to actually believe in common sense," said Harry dryly, and Alexos laughed, leaning back in the water and looking up at him. "But a lot of people don't know their limits until they reach them, that's all. I've been with men before, and... I knew a man who liked to be called names, and one day I called him the wrong thing, I don't even remember exactly what – this was ten years ago, and I haven't seen him in about seven – but it broke something in him, and he just started sobbing his eyes out. Completely forgot about fucking him – I ended up bundling him in a blanket and holding him in my lap until he was halfway alright again, made him drink a cup of cocoa and stroked his back until he fell asleep."

"You didn't fuck him again?"

"Oh, I did, of course," said Harry. "Called him names again, just not that one, or didn't say whatever I'd said – I think it was about his weight, or how he looked, something along those lines, but it was a step too far. Not a step I made again."

"Just about anything from you could do it for me, I'm beginning to think," murmured Alexos. "I'm curious as to whether you were as excited by other men's disabilities as you are by mine."

"I'm not excited by your—"

"Posh," said Alexos immediately, interrupting Harry before he could keep talking. "You can take away my cane and virtually pin me in place, no ropes required. You can't tell me that doesn't excite you."

"You're exaggerating the extent to which you're handicapped by your condition."

"Perhaps so," Alexos agreed. "But you enjoy the extent to which I'm reliant on you."

"Yes," said Harry quietly. "I like for people to rely on me – those who are richer or stronger or more powerful than me most of all, as a rule."

"As a rule," repeated Alexos. "Does that appendation mean I don't count?"

"You're certainly richer than I am," said Harry. "For all your disability and your lack of friends, I still wouldn't gamble going up against you in the courts, or even in gossip circles."

It was astoundingly, brutally honest, and it made Alexos' lips shift into a small smile, full of relief full of ease.

"Will you be getting dressed today?"

"Mmm," said Alexos. "I'll work in the library today."

"Breakfast with Mr Kidd?"

"No."

"Alexos."

"I said one meal," said Alexos. "I did not say when."

Harry sighed, looking down at him coolly, but then he got to his feet and picked up a towel.

"You haven't fucked him before, have you?" asked Alexos.

"Kidd? No."

"You've never wanted to?"

"Not particularly," said Harry. "I would for your entertainment, if you'd like to see him fucked."

"I'd rather see him fucked than listen to him talk."

Harry laughed. "He's really not so awful," he said quietly. "When not drugged to the gills."

"Resounding praise," said Alexos, and grunted as he pulled himself up from the bath, but Harry didn't push the matter any further.

* * *

Over the next week, Alexos went primarily between the bedroom and the library, and didn't come downstairs at all. Harry initially thought this was purely to do with his desire to avoid Larry, but he soon came to suspect that it was actually to do with his avoiding the stairs, because his knees really did seem particularly bad, and took time to relax again.

Harry massaged his legs the first day after he'd finally begun to leave the bedroom again, and Alexos had ended up sobbing by the time he was done, but when Harry offered to stop, Alexos shook his head, asked him to keep going, said it did help.

"Wouldn't you rather pursue medicine than this?" he'd asked, and Harry had laughed.

"Being a nurse wouldn't give me as much comfort or luxury as I have here."

"The work is harder."

"No," disagreed Harry. "Not for me."

"It's less respected."

"By whom? By you?"

"What? No, of course I respect you."

"Name someone who respects me less that might matter to me," he'd retorted, and Alexos had stared at him, then laughed and rubbed at his own cheeks, shaking his head and putting himself to whatever it was he'd been doing.

Mr Fox Senior, when he came home, was quite pleasant to Mr Kidd, and attending to them both at meals, Harry was relieved to find that Larry wasn't nearly as manic as he was capable of being, and that he held back the clumsier and more shocking aspects of his personality.

Much of his chaos with Alexos, Harry was certain, was because he already knew that Alexos was involved with Harry and that they were of a similar lilt – his reservations with Alexos' father, for being reserved, were by no means unnatural or stunted, and if anything, were smoother for his holding back the full force of his personality.

He still chattered near constantly, of course, but this went down well with Mr Fox, who was more than comfortable listening to other people speak as he settled placidly to listen, and on the occasion that Larry asked him questions, he was nonetheless pleased enough to answer them. He stumbled when he tried to explain his maths to Larry, not adept at concentrating his knowledge for the benefit of a layman, but he did try his best, and Larry was a concentrated listener.

"Alexos despises me," he said miserably to Harry after he'd been in the house for a week.

"He does no such thing," replied Harry. "He's in pain, that's all – I compared him to a cat before, and the comparison stands now. When a cat is injured, he doesn't want anybody looking at him or observing him, and just wants to be left alone."

"Perhaps I should go up to the library," he said, anxiously pacing the floor, and Harry clucked his tongue, shaking his head.

"Under no circumstances."

"I could just go up for a book," Larry suggested almost feverishly, rubbing at the back of his neck. "I wouldn't even talk to him, I'd just… just go and pick out some books. Let him talk to me."

"He wouldn't talk to you," said Harry. "If he noticed you were there at all, Mr Kidd, he would pretend not to, and you would be so overwhelmed with your desire for his attention that you would say something, whereupon he would, and I can assure you of this, eviscerate you verbally if not physically."

"He couldn't eviscerate me physically," said Larry anxiously. "I'd keep my distance."

"He moves faster than you might expect," said Harry, more for the way that it made Larry look abruptly concerned and a little frightened than because he thought Alexos really would lunge for him. Harry was increasingly convinced that Alexos could and would do Larry some moderate injury were he significantly provoked, and while he didn't think that simply entering his domain without warning would be sufficient, he thought it best to instil some caution now lest Larry continue to underestimate him.

Larry threw himself down in front of his desk, but sitting down didn't stop his constant frenetic motion: he began to bounce his knee and tap his fingers against the desk surface, his lips twisted. The desk itself was absolutely covered in stacks of pages, each and every one of them printed on one side in Larry's tight, looping handwriting. His anxiety over his host not liking him did not seem to have impacted his ability to work in any way – if anything, he was working really very feverishly, and writing far more, far quicker, than was ordinarily his habit.

And that was even having returned his cocaine compact to Cherry Flintman.

"Harry," he said quietly, "are you really sure he will come to like me?"

"I do," said Harry honestly. "So long as you're patient with him, and don't try quite so hard to force it, Mr Kidd."

"Please call me Larry when we're alone," said Larry in a low voice, and Harry glanced at him. Perhaps he might have felt a pang of sympathy, were he not that he'd heard so many of these nervous outbursts over the past few days, and were he not aware that these expressions of anxiety were so integral to Larry Kidd's nature, particularly when expressed to one servant or other. "Won't you, Harry? I'd like to fool myself I have one friend in this house."

"Larry," said Harry quietly, and looked at the other man very seriously. "He'll warm to you. He will."

Larry nodded, though he didn't seem to have much faith in it. He picked up his pen and commenced to work, seeming to forget Harry was even there after a minute or two, and Harry left him be to write.

Later that evening, Alexos came down to dinner late, but Larry was so excited that he was coming to join him and his father for dinner that he almost shot up out of his chair. Alexos certainly seemed to notice this sudden burst of excitement, but he made no comment on it and avoided making eye contact with Larry, pressing his lips together and focusing on his plate as he took his seat.

"Have you been working much, Alex?" he asked, and Alexos didn't look up as he unfolded a napkin over his lap and concentrated primarily on his food. When Harry came forward to pour his wine, Alexos made meaningful (and strikingly violent) eye contact with Harry only, and Harry's lips twitched, although he didn't allow himself to smile.

"Yes, Mr Kidd," he said, putting a great deal of weight on Larry's surname, which made him falter, although he worked quite desperately to keep the rictus smile on his face. "I typically do."

Harry didn't kick him under the table, but used his knee to put pressure on his hip just before he turned away, and Alexos let out an aborted hiss of pain, looking up at him with fierce indignation, but he smoothed the pain away as soon as his father looked at him askance.

"And yourself?" he asked, the words so polite that Harry could almost taste the venom in them.

"Oh, God, yes, absolutely," said Larry, sounding positively giddy to be asked a question in return. "I've been writing pages upon pages – my wrist was cramped last night, and Riggs was good enough to make up a hot water bottle for me to soothe it. I've got a bundle of pages tied up, a draft for a new novella, and I'll be dispatching that by post back home when I go into Brighton on Monday, I think, for it to be typed up."

"Well," said Alexos, stiffly, but not entirely unpleasantly. "There's no need for all that, Mr Kidd. I'm currently typing up a draft myself and have need of my machine, but this is an unusual house, and we've always one or two typewriters spare. I can take one out for you to use."

"Oh," said Larry, blinking. "Well, that's very kind of you, Mr Fox, but I don't type."

Harry looked with interest at the expression on Alexos' face, at the conflicting emotions there – indignation, irritation, genuine surprise, bafflement. He really did crave to get Alexos introduced to a few different men, because he did want to see that expression in a group setting, or just see Alexos shut down more confident men the way he shot down Larry.

"I beg your pardon, Mr Kidd?"

"I don't type," Larry said again. "I've got a girl to type for me – it's really very good, actually, because she was a typist and was so upset about having to stop working when she married and had her baby, her husband is my second cousin, and this way she can keep working and keep up her experience, you know, so that when her daughter goes off to school, she can go back into the workforce."

"How unusual," remarked Mr Fox Senior, looking amused. "She sounds the sort that George would love."

"George?" Larry repeated.

"Georgina," said Alexos. "My mother. Mr Kidd, has it not occurred to you that you might learn to type?"

"Oh, well, no," said Larry. "It's so messy, you know, and complicated, all that hectic little machinery, it's not really my sort of thing at all. I'm more for nature than industry, you see."

Alexos stared at him for some long moments, and Harry held his breath, waiting for him to say something, to further express his disapproval, but then he turned back to his meal. "I do see," he said tersely.

He said very little for the rest of the evening, but it had been a conversation, and for all he had experienced such resounding disapproval, Larry looked very relieved to have made any progress at all.

And—

In truth, Harry thought, he really almost had.

Because when Larry asked Alexos over a slice of lemon pound cake, "Do you like dessert very much, A— Mr Fox?" Alexos looked at him in utter bafflement for a moment, and then exhaled.

"Not *very* much, Mr Kidd," he said, with a sort of forced placidity. "But yes, I do like them."

"I don't understand how they do it," said Larry.

"... Mr Kidd?"

"Oh, well, it just seems like witchcraft, you know," said Larry. "Throwing an egg together and flour and— and whatever else, and it comes out like this. You'd never imagine it was possible, looking at the ingredients."

"Eggs, flour, sugar, butter, vegetable shortening, whipped cream, milk, lemon zest," said Alexos after a few moments. "There are a variety of processes going on in the baking of a cake like this, Mr

Kidd, but foremost would be the function of the leavening agent, in this case, the baking powder. As it's heated during baking, it releases carbon dioxide, which makes all those tiny little bubbles within the cake, gives the sponge that texture. The eggs contribute to that – when the cake mixture is whipped, which of course puts more air bubbles in, the protein from the egg white helps protect those bubbles, gives them a little skin, which is why a cake sinks if the mixture is not sufficiently beaten. That same protein also contributes to the sponge's structure, keeps it solid and standing. For this, the cream and milk keep it from drying out – it's fairly easy to dry out pound cake, if you've not sufficient moisture put in."

Alexos hadn't looked up from his cake as he spoke, cutting it into smaller pieces, albeit not as meticulously as his father, who had been cutting up his into evenly sized cubes and cutting up a slice of candied lemon with the same focus, so that it might be split evenly between every cube he made.

Larry was looking at Alexos with something akin to awe writ on his features.

"Oh," he said. "Wow. I had no idea it was so... That there as quite so much, ah... You're a chef, Mr Fox."

"I'm an amateur baker," said Alexos. "And not a particularly skilled one."

"You sound very skilled," said Larry enthusiastically.

"Knowledge of chemistry doesn't follow onto practical application, Mr Kidd," said Alexos. "Not by default."

"Sounds like my love life," said Larry breezily, and Alexos looked at him seriously, but didn't laugh – he didn't insult him either.

"Are you involved with a great many chemists?" asked Mr Fox Senior seriously.

Alexos' lips twitched into something that was almost a smile, and as Larry blustered to explain his joke, Harry saw that Mr Fox wasn't looking at him – he was looking at his son, his expression warm and really quite indulgent, until he glanced up at Harry, and smiled himself.

* * *

When Alexos had woken up this morning, Brydon had come in to help him up and dressed, as it was Harry's day off, which was something of a relief. Not because Alexos particularly wanted to avoid his company, of course, but simply because the absence of Harry on the same day there was an absence of Larry Kidd meant that Alexos had an opportunity.

His legs twinged a little from having come down the stairs, but it wasn't anything like the ache he'd been nursing the past few days, and it was really a relief to settle down for breakfast with his father, one of his feet resting on the dog's belly, without pain – or Larry Kidd, who was a sort of pain in himself – distracting him too badly.

"Do you like that Larry Kidd?" asked his father.

"Not particularly," said Alexos.

"Ah well," said his father quietly, smiling to himself. "I like him."

"Good," said Alexos, and got himself to his feet.

He put on his coat, although it was a fine enough day and he hoped he wouldn't need it, and said in an undertone to Brydon, "I'm going out to the shed."

Brydon looked at him a moment, then nodded his head. "Need help carrying anything, sir?"

"Oh, no," said Alexos. "If I need anything, I'll ask Mr Lloyd. Thank you, Brydon."

Alexos had not been out to the shed, he didn't think, since Harry had taken over the position as butler, perhaps a while before then – he went through periods of wanting to work out there quite feverishly, and periods where he left it be. It was reliant, of course, on how good he felt about walking, how bad the pain was. When Mr Lloyd saw him coming down the path, he went into the shed before him, and by the time Alexos had limped inside, he had the furnace going, heat radiating out from it.

"I put all them new bits aside," said Mr Lloyd, gesturing to the metal drawers where he stored typewriter pieces.

"What's this?" asked Alexos, gesturing to the unfamiliar item on the big wooden worktable that he liked to work at – he had a big metal table that was more solid, but he didn't much like to work at it until the furnace had been on for a while, because the cold bit into his forearms.

The shed was a stone and wood building, and three walls were covered in floor-to-ceiling shelves that Mr Lloyd had put in for him, with a lot of wood crates keeping the bigger scrap pieces. A few metal drawers and cabinets were arranged against one wall, in which were meticulously arranged smaller pieces – scrapped cogs, screws, nails, springs, and all other manner of small ephemera – and the majority of his tools, the ones that weren't in the tool box Mr Lloyd brought into the house for him when he asked.

In a few stacked crates were some of Mr Lloyd's reclaimed and stolen objects, the ones that Alexos normally took to disassembling to sell or reuse himself for scrap, but the clock on his worktable looked far too shiny and well-kept to be one of these items – none of the glass pieces were cracked, and it really looked in very good condition, except for how it didn't work properly, the minute hand continuously moving back and forth instead of moving through its proper cycle.

"It's a clock," said Mr Lloyd.

"Astonishing, the secrets you enable me to be privy to, Tom," said Alexos dryly, and Mr Lloyd laughed, putting his hands on his hips.

"It's Mrs Glover's," he said. "You know, from the village?"

"No," said Alexos blankly.

Mr Lloyd scowled at him. "She's the cobbler's wife."

"I'm not acquainted with Mrs or Mr Glover, Mr Lloyd."

"Well, the wind knocked the clock off the mantel the other day, and she asked if I could have a look at it, and I figured you could. D'I figure wrong?"

"No," said Alexos quietly. "Thank you. Has it been waiting long?"

"Two weeks," said Mr Lloyd as he moved toward the door. "Want a cup of tea, lad?"

"Have I ever told you I'd die for you, Mr Lloyd?"

"That don't mean much," said Mr Lloyd. "Stiff wind'd kill you."

Alexos sniggered, shooting the old man a foul hand signal, and Mr Lloyd laughed to himself as he went outside again, going over to the little house he kept nearby, the door shutting behind him. Alexos opened up the back of the clock, setting it aside, and he looked at the cog work stutter in its place before he started to delicately disassemble it.

He hadn't been working for five minutes before the door opened again – he was far more aware of comings and goings in here than he ever was in the library, what with the heavy draft whenever the door opened or closed – and he said, "Could you put it just here? My hands are busy."

"Put what where?" asked Larry Kidd, and Alexos whipped around to glare at him.

"Get out," he growled, but Kidd was already all the way inside, and was looking around with wide-eyed fascination.

"What a treasure trove," said Kidd, and Alexos stood to his feet, clenching his hands into fists. "What is this? A sort of— a workshop? Are you fixing something – can you fix things? Al— Mr Fox! You never said you did things like this! Can you fix cars, too?"

"No, Mr Kidd, seeing as I can't exactly drive one," said Alexos darkly. "I was given to understand you were in Brighton."

"Oh, I came back last night – or, er, this morning. I only just woke up. What are you fixing?"

"Mr Kidd, I like to work in peace and quiet," said Alexos sharply.

"I'll be quiet," Kidd promised, desperately, fervently, putting his hands together in a motion akin to prayer. "Oh, please, Mr Fox, I love nothing more than to watch a craftsman at work, and all this is so interesting – do you make typewriters?"

"I've taken apart more typewriters than I've repaired," said Alexos hurriedly, trying to think of what answer would suitably push him to leave. "Look, just—"

"What's this?" asked Kidd, picking up a mechanical puzzle box Alexos had made last year, and Alexos' hands twitched at his hands, powerless to do anything to stop him, until the door opened again and Mr Lloyd stood there with a cup of tea in his hand.

"Hullo," he said, looking askance at Alexos.

"Mr Lloyd," said Alexos, taking the mug from him with a murmur of thanks, "this is Mr Kidd, he's our guest, an author. Mr Kidd, this is Tom Lloyd, he's our gardener and our groundskeeper."

"Oh, hallo, Mr Lloyd, how do you do?"

Mr Lloyd looked far too entertained by the situation as he asked, "Shall I get Mr Kidd a chair, sir?"

Alexos pressed his lips together, looking at the other man foully, but before he could say a word, Kidd said, "Oh, would you? Mr Lloyd, what a darling man you are."

"Oh, aye," said Lloyd ironically, chuckling to himself as he left again. "Darling is right."

Kidd barely seemed to notice the old man's humour, focused as he was on pressing and twisting at the sides of the box, and Alexos sighed to himself, dropping resignedly back into his seat.

"What is it?" asked Kidd.

"It's a box," said Alexos. "There's nothing inside it."

"What's it for?"

"It's a puzzle."

"Oh," said Kidd enthusiastically, and pulled himself up to sit on the metal desk, his legs hanging down as he put his focus to it, and Alexos stared at him, his lips parted. He sipped at his tea, watching Kidd as he slid at one of the dials with his thumb, then twisting the other.

It wasn't a very good design – it had just been an experiment of his, wasn't nearly as sophisticated as other mechanisms he liked to play about with, wasn't nearly so smoothly designed.

Kidd was looking at it like it really was treasure – but to his credit, he genuinely was quiet as Alexos turned back to the clock and kept working.

Chapter Fourteen

It had been a difficult night.

Nightmares were not uncommon for Harry, were something he'd been very used to even before he'd been shipped off to the frontlines to have the peaceful nights shelled out of him, but there were nights when he simply had uneasy dreams, and there were other nights when his dreams were vivid and his sleep unrestful, and there were nights like this, when he hadn't slept so much as lain awake for long periods with small windows of unconsciousness in between.

Every fall of rain on the roof had made him think of rifle fire, and the night through he'd been plagued by ghosts – he'd fall asleep for barely ten minutes, just finally manage to doze off, and then half open his eyes to the silhouette of a man standing over him with a knife, a sniper standing at his window, a wounded man bloodied and sobbing for want of a medic, and as soon as he jolted out of bed to work, to help, to fight...

Well.

Naturally, there'd been no one there at all.

At one point, he'd even thought that Alexos was in the room with him, that the young master had somehow materialised directly through the wall between their two bedrooms for all they existed in different sections of the house. In that strange, dream logic way, it had made sense to him before he'd really been awake, and he recalled sleepily holding back the sheet, feeling the other man crawl into bed beside him before he remembered that Alexos Fox struggled to walk down the corridor unaided, let alone materialise through walls, and awoke suddenly in a cold sweat, alone and disoriented.

He tried to work properly when his sleep was poor, didn't like to use such a thing as an excuse not to put himself to work with discipline and focus, but he was unbelievably grateful for his luck, that last night had fallen before a day he had off.

It had been a long, painful day, all in all – he'd gone about the errands he had on his list to get on with, gotten a pair of shoes repaired, sent off a parcel with a birthday gift for one of his nephews, attended a few orders for wine and similar household necessities while he was in town. Each and every task had proved slow, laborious, taxing his exhausted mind, and although no one showed the slightest bit of impatience with him, everyone relatively intimidated by his stature and his status at the Fox House, he disliked to be seen at his slowest or most stupid, which today he very much was.

"Tea, Mr Sutton?" asked Felix when he came into the kitchen, having already changed his clothes, and Harry shook his head.

"Thank you, but no," said Harry, turning his head so that Felix wouldn't see when he wiped at one tired eye. "Is Mr Fox in the library?"

"No, sir," said Felix "I went up to bring him his tea, but he's not there, nor in his bedroom."

Harry slowly turned to examine Felix, his lips pressed loosely together. "Where is he, then?"

"I don't know, sir," admitted Felix. He stood stiffly, his lips pressed together and his eyes not quite meeting Harry's. "I thought he might come down here, and be cooking or something, because he does sometimes with Betty, but I've not seen hide nor hair of him."

"And Mr Kidd?" asked Harry.

Felix looked at him blankly a moment, and Harry inhaled, but then turned around and commenced moving through the servants' rooms one by one, checking the kitchen, the pantry, even ducking his head down into the cellar before he ascended the stairs.

There was no sign of Larry or Alexos on the ground floor, either in the rooms that Larry might frequent – the dining room, one of the front-facing sitting rooms, even the storage rooms, before he ascended the stairs and checked the library in its entirety, Alexos' bedroom and bathroom, then Larry's.

Larry's bedroom was a last resort, a sort of vain and maddening hope that somehow Larry had seduced Alexos into bed, but his room was empty, and nor was there any sign of them upstairs.

"Mr Brydon," he said as he came up to the second floor, and Brydon looked at him as he came out from Mr Fox Senior's bedroom, looking at him in consternation. "Did Mr Kidd call for a taxi, or the use of a car?"

"No," said Brydon. "Not that I know of – and I would doubt it, as Riggs has been working with me all afternoon, he's only just gone downstairs to work on a tear in Mr Kidd's trousers. Why, is he gone?"

"He is," said Harry, feeling a painful tightness in his chest, his body stiff. "As is Mr Fox."

Brydon stared at him, then looked behind him at the other rooms. Harry could see the calculation on his face as he stepped back and ducked his head into another room, one of the spare bedrooms, Harry supposed.

"And they're not outside?" he asked. "Mr Fox did say—"

"Both of them?" Harry asked rhetorically, but he went down the stairs regardless, almost running down the steps to go out into the garden. He couldn't quite envisage any situation wherein Alexos, who virtually said how much he despised Larry every moment of the day, would go off into Brighton with him or anyone else, couldn't quite imagine—

"Mr Fox!" he called out, striding out from the house and scanning the grounds. His skin felt hot, and he was aware he was sweating, and he knew full well that were he properly rested he wouldn't be the mess of nerves he was now, wouldn't feel the fear quite so keenly – and what fear, precisely? What harm could Larry do Alexos, even if he wanted?

And yet—

"Hullo, Mr Sutton," said Tom Lloyd, the gardener. "Trouble?"

"I'm looking for Messrs Fox and Kidd," said Harry.

"Oh, them," said Tom dismissively. "They're in the shed, so."

"Shed?" Harry repeated.

Tom gestured, easy as you please, to a shack that stood beside the potting shed, and Harry looked at him askance, but then moved past him, striding over. It was a simple building, stone with a slate roof and thick glazed windows, but he grabbed hold of the metal door and slammed it against the inner wall as he pushed it open.

Alexos, who was sitting at a wooden desk right in front of the door, looked up from the work he was doing; despite the loud bang, Larry, who was fast asleep in a rocking chair beside a roaring furnace with a magazine in his lap, didn't so much as stir.

"Hullo, Harry," said Alexos, looking the calmest and most relaxed Harry had ever seen him, although he was looking at Harry now with a sort of gentle concern, apparently baffled by Harry's state of barely concealed distress. "Are you alright?"

"I didn't know where either of you were," Harry muttered, closing the door behind him. "I had no idea that this was... here." He trailed off, looking about the room from his position near to the door: on the shelves were different machines in varying states of disrepair – typewriters and a cash register, a box of watches, several clocks that weren't ticking, a few wind-up machines and different utensils that used a crank. Up against a wall was even a mechanical clothes wringer, the cogs rusted and the mechanism itself looking very stiff.

In front of Alexos was a clock intended for a mantelpiece, and on several pages on the desk Harry saw several sketches of the internal mechanism of the piece. To one side was a crate of periodicals with notes and labels in Alexos' familiar Greek handwriting – magazines about engineering and industry, it seemed.

"May I?" Harry asked, and Alexos waved him off, not even looking at Harry as he kept working with his tweezers, putting cogs into place on small pins. Alexos had labelled each layer of cog work as he'd worked further into the mechanism, sketching each layer before he took it apart apparently to make his repairs, and Harry saw a tray of several hundred little cogs on the desk before him, arranged by shape and size and material in the little troughs.

"This was a broken one?" Harry asked, picking up a cog no bigger than his smallest fingernail – the cog itself wasn't bent, but some of its teeth were slightly twisted.

"Mmm," said Alexos, and Harry stood there for a few minutes, watching him work. Every movement was smooth and full of confidence and ease, and seeing him repair this clock was every bit as satisfying as watching him attend his typewriter, if not more impressive because of the skill in it.

This wasn't a man knowing his own machine, after all, and how best to attend its care – this was, instead, a mechanic at work, the repair its own complex craft and vocation.

He turned the clock's key, winding back the mechanism, and Harry watched his lips shift into a slight smile as the cogs began to move as they should, ticking regularly. The anxiety still lingered with him, the ghost of it thrumming under his skin even though his heartbeat had slowed and he was no longer breathing fast.

"Harry, would you?" he asked. "I don't have a timepiece on me."

"It's past five," said Harry. "Haven't you eaten?"

"Oh, no, actually," said Alexos, blinking as though he'd just woken up, and Harry took out his watch, comparing the time against the clock as he wound it back. "My cup of tea is empty – I suppose I've been here some time."

"And Larry?" he pressed, and Alexos turned to glance at him as though only just realising he was there.

"Ah," he said quietly. "He followed me out here, and I told him to fuck off, but then he went silent, so I..." He gestured to Larry asleep in his rocking chair, and Harry carefully picked his way past Alexos and over to him.

It was a little room, far better arranged to get around, Harry wagered, for Alexos and Larry's skinny frames or even Tom's than for Harry's own, but for being so little it was warm and cosy, even surrounded on all sides by bits and pieces of machinery and metal, and it was surprisingly free of odour – there was a scent of black oil and grease, but it was faint, and evidently the furnace was very well-ventilated, because he couldn't so much as smell the coal dust.

"Mr Kidd?" prompted Harry, gently touching Larry's shoulder, and Larry shifted in his sleep, blinking as he sat forward. Upon seeing Harry's face, his own broke out in a smile, and he caught hold of Harry's forearm, loosely gripping his wrist.

"Oh," he said, looking around blearily, his eyes hazy even as his lips smiled. "Hullo, Harry. Do you know that Alexos here is quite the inventor?"

Harry took the box out of Larry's lap, where he'd been comparing it to similar boxes in the open magazine – it wasn't particularly large, about four inches on each side, and it was clumsily welded together on a few sides, with the other closed by a mechanism that had already been solved, a series of cogs turned into one another until they loosened the clasp.

Pressing it closed, he watched the cogs turn back on one another and then pushed on one of the levers, opening it again.

"Is it nearly time to eat?" asked Larry.

"Very nearly, Mr Kidd," he answered, and was about to go on when he felt a touch at his hand and turned to look at Alexos. Alexos was smiling at him as his thumb slid against Harry's palm, and as Harry stared down at him, barely comprehending, Alexos brushed his lips over Harry's knuckles.

He was going to make a habit of this, it seemed – was Harry's heart going to make a similar habit of fluttering every time? Was he going to be so affected every time, his lips tingling, his body almost surging with the want to touch him back with equal tenderness and at the same time, with none at all, an urge making itself known to bend Alexos right over his desk in this cosy shed of his and bugger him until he couldn't speak, let alone walk.

"Fairies," said Larry, his lips twisted in a funny little smile as he waggled his eyebrows. "The both of you."

"Go fuck yourself, Larry," said Alexos, and Larry's jaw dropped. Harry tried to stifle his laugh as he pulled back his hand, turning his attention back to winding Alexos' newly repaired clock.

He was successful only until Larry said in soft, disbelieving tones, "You called me Larry!"

The laughter was unbelievably relieving, after the day he'd had, unexpectedly so, but what was even more of a relief was the way that in response to Harry laughing, in response to Larry's lack of indignation, Alexos actually smiled, and kept smiling.

* * *

"So, what was wrong with it?" asked Larry, and Alexos glanced up from his meal at Larry, who was buttering his bread roll clumsily but with great enthusiasm. "The clock, I mean?"

"Repairing a clock, were you?" asked his father, and Alexos nodded his head.

"It belongs to Mrs Glover," he said.

"Who's that now?"

"The wife of Mr Glover, who I'm told is the cobbler."

"Do we know them?"

"I suppose we know Mr Glover by his work," said Alexos, "but I can't claim to know either man nor wife by sight. Nonetheless, the clock fell off her mantel – most of the cogs were just fine, but the one that was knocked loose had gone into the mechanism and bent some of the teeth, so I replaced that. Nice work on the thing too, it's beautifully made. Heirloom, I expect."

"So you're a sort of... repairman?" asked Larry. "For people in the village?"

Alexos' father started laughing, and Alexos huffed out what was almost a laugh himself, glancing down at his knees and not making eye contact with Larry or his father, or even with Harry, who was standing aside.

"I do repair things, now and then," said Alexos. "Mostly whatever amuses me, or whatever bits and pieces Mr Lloyd finds. But whenever Mr Lloyd offers to repair something for someone in town, he doesn't exactly bandy *my* name about. It's the impression of quite a lot of people in the village that Mr Lloyd is an extremely capable mechanic. Which— He is, he can normally tell what's wrong with something, even if he lacks the dexterity to repair it himself."

"Alexos had dreams of being an explorer when he was a boy," said his father affectionately. "He wanted to be able to repair his own plane and boat engines."

"Yes, thank you, Father," said Alexos dryly, but to his surprise, he didn't feel embarrassed or vulnerable, as he so often did, when this topic arose. His father had always seen the romance and the appeal in attending to engines and mechanisms, and Alexos recalled when first he had begun to take an interest, how his father would excitedly dive into the mathematic principles that spoke to the function of cogs or levers or pulleys or anything else.

His mother had never cared for it. She still made idle threats now and then, upon returning home, to clean out his repair shed, particularly when he fled a house full of guests and locked himself in to work. She didn't like that it was messy or dirty, that he got grease on his hands.

Or, he supposed, she just didn't like that he enjoyed it.

It wasn't that she didn't like Alexos enjoying things, per se: what bothered her, as far as Alexos had ever been able to determine, was the way in which he enjoyed things. He and his father both enjoyed things in too much isolation, or enjoyed things too passionately, or with the wrong sort of passion.

He'd actually been chatting to a fellow she'd invited to a party, once, a railway enthusiast, and when she'd seen him coming down from his bedroom with a copy of one of his magazines to show him an article about new pistons, she'd snatched it from him and hissed that he'd embarrass her, talking to one of her guests about something so inordinately dull. He'd only been sixteen or seventeen, and it had been a rare party that he'd actually been enjoying, but that had soured his passion somewhat. He still kept all his magazines in the shed even now, didn't even like to read them in his bedroom in case she tossed them on the fire as well.

"I think it's marvellous," said Larry enthusiastically, didn't appear disgusted by the concept of Alexos doing such menial work, but better than that, he wasn't... condescending. Alexos didn't know what it was, exactly, about the way Larry spoke about it, about the particular tone of his enthusiasm, but he wasn't treating it like a rich man's hobby, wasn't treating it as though it were something that didn't matter. "It's one thing to do such repairs and be able to do them, you know, to divine from examining a mechanism's innards the nature of its malady or injury, like a sort of clockwork doctor, but to do so in secret, using one's gardener as a mask? How splendid. What an enigma you are, Alexos Fox!"

"Shut up, Larry," said Alexos almost without meaning to, the second time such an outburst had come out unbidden today, and his father coughed as he sipped at his drink, laughing.

"I'll do no such thing," said Larry, undeterred. "Why should I?"

"I am not using Tom Lloyd as my masquerade cloak," said Alexos, unable to hold back his scorn even as his father chuckled, and he shook his head. "Tom Lloyd tells people he repairs everything because he takes money for "his" services, and I let him take said payment for the additional services he renders me in sourcing parts and mechanisms for me."

"No word about this to Georgina," said his father suddenly, putting out his hand, and Larry looked between the two of them with his eyes wide. "No sense mentioning it to her, you know."

"Oh, but Mrs Fox loves that sort of mischief, doesn't she?" asked Larry.

Alexos scoffed, sipping his drink.

"In stories," said his father, looking mildly reproachful at Alexos' expression, but not actually saying a thing about it. "She's not so approving of it happening in the house, though, let alone, ah... Well."

"My mother dislikes my lack of social habits," said Alexos dryly. "It rubs salt in the wound when I engage in such shrewd and strange business with the staff."

"Oh, well, that's not to be a concern now, is it?" asked Larry confidently. "What with the two of us being such friends?"

Alexos stared at him, swallowing the urge to immediately disagree with him. He realised, almost all at once, that he'd probably had the easiest time he'd ever had at dinner with someone tonight, that Larry had tricked him into feeling at-ease, into... relaxing, almost.

He felt an urge to suddenly say "Certainly not," and storm from the table, but he knew that this was childish, and more than childish, was unreasonable and unfair to himself as well as Larry. He glanced back to Harry, who met his gaze, and gave him the smallest smile.

"I really don't know," said Alexos, his voice sounding stunted to his own ears more than it sounded cool or disaffected, and Larry looked nervous for a moment, but then leaned forward.

"Do you repair many things?" he asked. "Other than clocks and typewriters? *Can* you fix a plane engine?"

"Larry, when would I ever have learned to repair a plane engine?"

"I don't know. When did you learn to repair clocks?"

"I couldn't always run around as a child," said Alexos, after only a moment's pause. "I never much cared for making models. If I wasn't observing Mr Sutton – not Henry here, but his uncle, Reginald, who was for many years our butler – I was observing the cook, or the chauffeur, or Mr Lloyd."

"I used to be like that," said Larry immediately. "I could walk, of course."

"... Of course," said Alexos, biting back the urge to say anything else.

"But I was always running off and watching people at their work, I used to be a terror as a child – my father or my mother would be walking to work, holding my hand, you know, to drop me off at school, and they'd turn around and I'd be gone – I'd be in someone's workshop watching them attend their craft, or I'd have walked into a theatre, or I'd be down by the docks watching the sailors work... I've always had quite a dangerous affection for sailors."

"Do you like to travel by boat, Mr Kidd?" asked Alexos' father, and Larry nodded enthusiastically.

"Oh, certainly, I do, I've gone to America, of course, and Ireland, and France, and sailed between places. I normally need a day or two to adjust, you know – I don't get sea-sickness, I'm never ill over it, but I'm ever such a clumsy man, and I'm even clumsier on boats, such that I can barely walk at all until I adjust."

Alexos didn't say anything, turning his head to meet Harry's gaze. Harry pointedly refused to respond in kind, keeping his stare facing forward, but Alexos could see his lips twitch in repressed amusement.

It was surprisingly easy, listening to Larry go on about his delight watching sailors at work, watching sailmakers, watching ropemakers, watching engineers, carpenters – he kept looking at Alexos, kept meeting his gaze, but didn't actually push him to respond, just kept chattering on to his father, which was—

Easier, actually.

It was probably the most pleasant dinner he'd ever had with a guest in the house, except for the guests who had entirely ignored him, which ordinarily, he preferred.

It was plain to him, all told, that Larry Kidd was an idiot, that he talked before he thought, that he was in some ways obsequious and a little too desperate to please, but something about that *panged* in him, triggered an echoing call from his own self. Wasn't that a damning indictment?

Larry Kidd, by no means, could be called lonely.

He wasn't lonely at all, couldn't be lonely – he spoke quite frequently of his various friends, spoke with affection and knowledge, and these friendships were not one-sided, because Alexos knew for a fact that he got some great stack of letters delivered to the house every other day, and it seemed to Alexos that a good half of what he wrote, on top of his already being an apparently prodigious author of fiction, must be replies to all this correspondence.

But there was a loneliness in him, Alexos thought, or an isolation, or some sort of vulnerability to him that felt familiar, as familiar as looking at himself in the mirror, although he wouldn't like to admit it. He wouldn't like to admit to any of this, or talk about any of this, didn't much like even thinking of it.

Alexos had felt a strange sort of peace earlier that afternoon, knowing that Larry was there fiddling with different things, even knowing that Larry was asleep behind him – it had reminded him, strangely enough, of how much of his childhood he had spent in the presence of Reginald or Brydon or Lloyd or someone else, not actually being attended to or looked at, but simply there in the same room as he entertained himself.

He rather wanted more of that peace.

Listening to Larry talk, watching him gesticulate wildly as he told some story about his friend who was an illustrator and had apparently helped a man climb in through his window at university when said man was fleeing a murderous girlfriend, he wondered what that might be like, actually being—

Friendly with him.

Being friends with him.

Having a friend.

When Larry cheerfully bade him good night, Alexos responded with a polite smile and a nod of his head – when Larry suddenly said, "Oh, do you need help on the sta—," Alexos said, "No, Larry, my cane is more reliable than a clumsy man's arm, as well you know."

To which Larry laughed, quite contentedly, and said, "Oh, yes. I suppose that's true, isn't it?"

Harry didn't say anything right away as he helped Alexos undress, putting aside his clothes and hanging them up. Alexos was lost in his thoughts, thinking of Larry, thinking of the way he talked, the way he ate, the way he smiled.

"The ice thaws," said Harry.

"Only because he's so willing to accept someone being so awful to him."

"I'll find you a dozen men willing to accept far worse," Harry promised, and Alexos laughed, shaking his head, but he found that the smile lingered on his face.

"Will you stay a while?" he asked quietly, and Harry nodded his head.

"Yes," he said. "If you like. I dreamt last night that you came into my room through the wall."

"Oh," said Alexos, looking to the wall between their two rooms, thinking of how Harry's could only be accessed if you came up from the servants' stairwell, the corridor on the other side of the house.

"When you first came here, you know, I sometimes dwelt on how you were on the other side of that wall when I got into bed."

"I did the same," said Harry.

Alexos felt himself smile, and he pulled Harry closer, put his hands on Harry's chest, slid his palms against his chest, felt the heat that radiated from him.

"How's the pain?" asked Harry, and Alexos sighed, leaning in closer, basked in the warmth from his body, the strength of him, the weight of Harry's hands when they settled on his arse.

"Fairly bad," said Alexos. "I got too into what I was doing – I'm stiff as a board."

"Massage?"

"Would you?"

"Why wouldn't I?"

"You're really quite wonderful, aren't you?"

"I like to think so," said Harry, and Alexos laughed, setting his cheek against his chest. "Do you think you'd like to fuck him?"

"Larry? I hadn't given it much thought. I— don't know."

He didn't know. He'd like to know. He wanted to know, wanted to touch him just to be sure, because it felt all too overwhelming, the idea that he *could* touch, experiment, that Larry would let him – encourage him, even. Kiss him back, explore back.

What sort of ridiculous, accidental insults could be manage seeing Alexos naked, rather than just seeing him limp around?

Harry kissed him, and his mind went gloriously blank.

"Let's think about it tomorrow," Harry murmured, and pushed him back toward the bed.

Chapter Fifteen

There was a fair in town, and Harry had insisted that all the other staff in the house take the opportunity for a group evening off. Felix and Betty were naturally excited about it, and that was even before Mr Brydon had, upon gentle pressure from Harry in his ear, said that he would go about teaching them the tricks of some of the carnival games.

"His father used to run them," Alexos had told him when there'd been word of the fair in town. "Ring tosses and coconut shies and skittles and all that sort of thing — he was a bookie, ran a betting shop, but he'd do that sort of thing for the village fête."

He hadn't known exactly what to make of Harry's expression when he'd taken this in, but he had seemed to be at least somewhat intrigued, and not at all displeased; it was natural, and only to be expected, based on what Alexos had learned of Harry's personality so far, that he should immediately put the new information to use, and leverage it in some manner.

Brydon would not have gone otherwise, would have lingered in the house — now, it was just the three of them, because Alexos' father had gone into town to the pub, was going to eat there.

They were all in Alexos' room, and Alexos felt fluttery and hot under his clothes, watching Larry bend over and examine the books he had on the shelves in his bedroom, as well as examining the various little pieces he had on display — small busts of different Greek philosophers, statuettes of the Kritios Boy, of Apollo, of Dionysus.

They were each fully dressed, and yet somehow, Alexos felt as though every stitch of clothing had been stripped from him already as Harry crossed the room, having locked the door.

"... heard they're so much bigger in person," Larry was saying, his hands on his hips as he leaned in and looked very closely indeed at the rows of statuettes — Alexos' mother sometimes brought them back with her from here or there, although she hadn't brought one for years, not since he'd been at university. She'd thought, with that, that he'd go on to travel further, and he'd always got the impression that was part of the reason she bothered buying him gifts at all. "Do you think when they were making them that transporting them was ha — Oh, hullo, Harry."

Larry was turning in surprise as Harry's hand slipped under his jacket to touch his waist, pressing against the wool there; his lips were parting, and Alexos thought there'd be more, that there'd be a conversation, that there'd be *something*, but Larry just turned and leaned in and then they were kissing.

Alexos' mouth felt dry observing, seeing Larry slowly turn in Harry's arms, seeing his mouth open to let Harry dexterously tongue into his mouth, tongue against tongue, lips against lips. It was all soft, wet sounds, and then Larry's breathless moan as Harry did something — sucked on his lower lip — and started to ease the jacket off his shoulders.

Alexos felt frozen in time, perhaps even in amber, as he watched the two of them work each other over — Larry's jacket was eased off his shoulders and hung clumsily over the back of Alexos' desk chair; his shirt was unbuttoned and dropped over the same, his braces unbuttoned, his trouser fronts unfastened. The whole time they were kissing, Larry's hands coming up to touch Harry's breast, the sides of his neck, his cheeks, as they moved around the room, over to the bed.

There was a very distant twinge of jealousy, or if not jealousy, simply hyper awareness, of the fact that he couldn't do the same, not with both hands whilst still being able to stand.

Alexos let out a breathless noise as Harry shoved Larry back onto the bed, tilting back to see him sprawl next to Alexos with his shoulders to the mattress as Harry unlaced his shoes and eased them off.

Larry looked up at Alexos, and Alexos stared down at him, at the flush on his features, the sweat glistening on the side of his neck, and Alexos had thought vaguely that he would just watch, that he'd just observe, but now Larry was laid out on the bed beside him, stripped down to his vest and then to his drawers as Harry pulled off his trousers, and he didn't want to just watch any longer. Larry was hairier than Alexos was, curling hairs showing on his shoulders and his arms, and he was thin, but not as thin as Alexos either.

Alexos turned to kiss him, shifting on the bed to put pressure on his better knee, and he rested his elbow on the bed beside the other man to ensure he had enough support — the noise Larry let out was muffled against his mouth, so much so that Alexos could taste it, could taste the mints that Larry was so fond of.

He didn't kiss like Harry did.

There was far more tongue from Larry than Harry, Larry's mouth was smaller, and most of all, Larry seemed to cede ground to Alexos in a way that Harry didn't. It occurred to Alexos that he was the one controlling things, that he was the one *in charge* here, and just because he could, he bit down.

Larry yelped into his mouth, and one of his knees nudged Alexos' hip as he spread his legs apart — Alexos hadn't bitten hard enough to draw blood, but he'd put pressure on Larry's lower lip, and he could hear Harry laughing quietly behind him.

"What's so funny?" Alexos asked, pulling back. Larry's pupils had dilated quite widely, though probably not quite as much as when he'd been high on cocaine, his lips were parted and wet, and he was reaching up to put his hands on Alexos' body, his chest, touching his waist.

"Alexos," said Larry breathlessly. "Won't you do that again?"

"What's so funny?" Alexos repeated, turning to look back at Harry, and when Larry surged to meet him, he acted almost reflexively, pushing Larry down by his shoulder to the bed.

Larry's breath hitched audibly in his throat, and Alexos' stomach flipped, his whole body feeling warm under the skin; Harry was smirking at him as he rubbed his hands back and forth over Larry's thighs, Larry's cock standing to attention just under Harry's mouth.

"We find in the young master, Mr Kidd," he rumbled, "a burgeoning sadist."

"I wish he'd burgeon some more in my direction," said Larry, and Alexos caught Larry's mouth under his own, shoving him down onto the bed and pinning him in place. Larry's body shuddered, and then he tried to lurch off the bed but found himself pinned in place by Alexos' hand on his shoulder — his hips raised, though, and when Alexos glanced down, he saw that the reason for this was the fact that Harry had buried Larry's cock down his throat. "Fuck," Larry whimpered. "You're rather strong for a cripple."

"Call me a cripple again, Larry, and see what happens," Alexos retorted, and Larry stared up at him with his eyes big as dinnerplates, his lips parted.

"Sorry," he said breathlessly. "Won't do it again, old chap, cross my heart."

Alexos bit down on the side of his neck, as low down as he could to ensure the mark was under the line of his collar once Larry was dressed again, and Larry let out a sharp howl, his legs falling apart, his body arching as best it could off the mattress when the two of them were pinning him down.

Alexos trailed his mouth over the front of Larry's chest, feeling the hair there — Harry shaved a good deal of his body to keep the hair from pinching in his tight clothes, and the parts he didn't shave he kept the hair trimmed down significantly. There was a neatly-groomed patch over his cock and a little dusted on his back, growing a little thicker on his arms and legs. For such a big man, though, he didn't grow that much hair in the first place, particularly on his chest and back; Larry, in contrast, had light, thin patches of hair smattered almost all over him.

The little hairs tickled under Alexos' lips as he mouthed down underneath Larry's neck, at the hollow of his throat, then further down — when Alexos swiped his tongue over Larry's nipple, pinching the other between thumb and forefinger, Larry shuddered, letting out a sharp noise.

His hips were twitching and shifting, and Alexos glanced down as he sucked Larry's nipple into his mouth, matching gazes with Harry, who had his mouth similarly full. Perhaps he oughtn't have been surprised, with the size Harry was, but even a big man couldn't have such a capacious throat as to suck a cock with this much ease, could he?

Harry had played with Alexos' cock with his hands and even his lips and tongue, but most of his attention had been concentrated on the head of it as they talked and teased with one another. He was remarkably skilled, circling his tongue around Alexos' cockhead, swiping the tip of it into the hole, even as he worked over the shaft of his cock and Alexos' bollocks with his hands, but this?

Alexos flicked Larry's nipple back and forth under his tongue as he watched Harry relax his throat and sink his head down like it was a fucking magic trick, taking Larry's cock to the root, his lips parted around its base.

Harry winked at him, and Alexos pulled back before he could laugh right into Larry's chest.

"Can I—"

Alexos blew cold air over Larry's nipple, watching the pink, wet skin stiffen, and Larry cut himself off with a strangled moan.

"Do you want his mouth or his arse?" asked Harry casually — he'd pulled back, and was now idly stroking his cock with one hand, the other stroking up and down Larry's thigh. The tip of Larry's cock was shining with spit and his own wetness, and Alexos' own cock gave a jerk in his trousers as he realised that the same slickness was shining on Harry's lips.

Larry's cheeks were red, his body trembling, and Alexos couldn't help the smirk that pulled at his lips as he took in the look on Larry's face, eager and yet entirely submissive, his eyes flitting between Alexos and Harry.

He got off on this, Alexos supposed, the two of them discussing him as though he were a piece of meat, a toy shared between them, as if he had no input whatsoever into the decisions that came next.

"Which would you rather?"

"His arse," said Harry. "And his mouth will be easier for you to access, lying back."

"No need to obfuscate the issue," Alexos retorted, feeling heady, warm, his skin hot, sweat shining on his own skin. His cock was hard in his trousers, and he had to concentrate to resist the urge to thrust and grind himself against Larry's side, although he put his palm down to subtly adjust himself. "If you want his arse, you can say that without pretending it's for my comfort."

"I'll take his mouth if you're going to be a brat about it."

"Why don't we both take his arse?"

Larry whimpered underneath them, and Alexos sharply turned his head away so that Larry couldn't see Alexos' composure break, couldn't see him laugh. *Giddiness* didn't exactly fit into the coolly dominant persona he was attempting to embrace, and giddy was precisely what he was feeling.

Leaning up on his elbow so that Larry couldn't see Harry's face, Alexos looked down at Harry — Harry, whose plummy cheeks had turned a darker shade of red, who had a little more sweat gleaming on his own chest and the sides of his neck, whose lips were parted. There was a line of saliva connecting his lips to the head of Larry's cock, the sight so abruptly arousing that it made Alexos feel dizzy.

Harry delicately wiped his lower lip with his thumb, smearing the spit away, and asked, "You want to fuck his arse the both of us at once?"

"*I don't think I can,*" Alexos mouthed at him even though Harry's wry question made his body jerk, his cock giving an eager bob, and Harry almost laughed — Alexos kicked him in the shoulder, although half bent over Larry's body, he wasn't posed at the best angle to do it very hard.

"But then," Harry said at the same volume so that Larry could hear, "I don't think he's earned that."

"N… No," Alexos agreed after a moment, schooling his expression into something sterner as he looked back at Larry, who was looking up at Alexos rather as though Alexos was God himself. "I don't think he has, has he?"

"Any way that I could?" asked Larry, and Alexos allowed himself a chuckle as he caught him in a kiss one more time, then pulled himself up.

Harry came up to help Alexos out of his clothes as Larry hurriedly slicked his fingers with a bit of wax and slid them into himself, and even as Harry peeled his shirt and jacket off, setting them neatly aside, and then undid Alexos' trousers, Alexos could scarcely take his eyes away from him.

Larry was not the most handsome man Alexos had ever laid eyes on by any means, was not ever the sort of man Alexos dreamed of, when he was alone, when he was thinking, and yet here they were now, and Alexos was utterly compelled by him, by the planes of his body, his gangling limbs, his overlarge ears and overlarge eyes, the way he beamed so widely. There was something about the sheer earnestness of him, the way he radiated eagerness, the way he was so fully, utterly engrossed in this, and so desperate to please — to please Harry, yes, and to please Alexos, too.

Harry slid his hands over Alexos' body, kissing his neck and encouraging Alexos to lean back into the heavy weight of Harry's chest: they were both watching Larry, watching him slide his fingers into his arse, fucking himself on them, rocking his hips down into his own hand.

"What position will be best for you?" Harry asked in an undertone in Alexos' ear.

"Probably if I sit back against the pillows with him on all fours, if I'm taking his mouth and you're having his arse," Alexos murmured.

"You're sure you don't want his arse?" Harry's voice was warm, full of affection, one of his hands settled loosely on Alexos' hips, and at the same time, Alexos felt annoyed at him and more importantly, utterly overwhelmed by him.

"His mouth will do for now," Alexos decided, and turned his head to catch Harry in a kiss. It was a little more yielding than usual, Harry letting Alexos control more of it, and Alexos couldn't hold back his laugh as he leaned into him, then dropped onto the bed and crawled forward on his good knee.

Alexos stared down at Larry a few minutes later, his right drawn up and his left one loosely extended — Harry had carefully guided Larry on where to put his elbow so as not to put weight on Alexos' bad knee, how and where to brace himself without doing Alexos any damage.

It wasn't really the sort of thing one imagined when considering romance, one's partner guiding a third party on how best to suck one's cock without undue injury, and yet something about it struck Alexos as so romantic he could weep over it.

He stared at Harry as he braced himself behind Larry, Larry on his elbows and knees between them, his head down in line with Alexos' cock, his arse in the air and tucked underneath the weight of Harry's belly, the front of Harry's thighs against his backside.

Harry groaned aloud as he lined up his cock, and Alexos almost cursed the position, wondered at the idea of seeing Harry on his back with Larry lowering himself onto him — like that, he'd be able to get a good view of it, wouldn't he? Of Harry's big cock sliding into Larry's arse, of the way it forced the muscle to give away, to stretch?

As it stood, what he did have a good view of was Larry's face, the stunned expression of his jaw agape, his eyes wide and then squeezing shut as Harry sank inch by inch inside him.

"Oh, God," Larry choked out.

"How are those piercings treating you?" asked Alexos, and Larry let out a wordless, desperate noise against the inside of Alexos' good thigh. Alexos acted on the spur of the moment, putting his hand out and touching it through Larry's hair — his heart beat faster in his chest, warmth flooding through him, at the way Larry's eyes fluttered closed, how soft his expression was as he tipped his head into Alexos' palm.

"Good," Larry grunted, and then whined when Harry gave a powerful thrust forward, his body making a slapping sound against Larry's. "*Christ*, how do you — ah, how do you take this, Alexos? I feel full to the brim!"

"Make yourself a bit more full, would you, Larry?" asked Alexos in the politest tones he could manage, just to see the way that tone of voice made Larry's lips quiver. "Put yourself to work."

With his hand in Larry's hair, he guided his head down to Alexos' cock, and couldn't hold himself back from moaning aloud as Larry sucked the head into his mouth. He was clumsy about it, dropping his head forward to try to take Alexos down his throat the same way that Harry could — Larry was more skilled than Alexos might be at it, but he was not blessed with Harry's prodigious ability.

The sensation of him choking, the way his body jumped, his eyes watering, made Alexos feel like a fucking hero victorious, a thrill running right through him, and he gripped Larry's hair a little tighter, keeping hold of it as Harry started to thrust into him.

There was something unreal about it, something dream-like and larger-than-life, about Larry being pinned between them like an animal on a spit, Harry rocking his hips into him from behind and Alexos with his cock buried in his mouth. Larry bobbed his head down, taking as much of Alexos' cock as he could into his mouth without catching the back of his throat, and it was sublime, the heat and wetness going to Alexos' head.

"You are something, aren't you?" he heard himself say, aware of the strain in his voice as he touched the side of Larry's cheek, his thumb trailing over the line of his cheekbone. "I had no idea you were so desperate for it."

Larry suddenly dropped his head down entirely, taking Alexos to the hilt even though it did make him choke, and Alexos moaned, tipping his hips up and into the wet heat, into the slide of his tongue against the base of his prick, the tightness around the head of his prick.

Alexos was swearing, "Fuck, *fuck*, perfect fucking tongue, fuck—", couldn't stop himself, as he thrust up and into Larry's mouth, in time with Harry's thrusts into him.

"That's it, that's a lad," Harry murmured, gripping loosely at Larry's hips to keep him steady, and then began to fuck into him so hard that the bed was rocking beneath them, Larry shoved forward each time by the weight of each thrust. He tried to pull back, but Alexos gripped his curls as tightly as he could, keeping his head down.

Larry choked, choked again, but didn't actually pull back even though there were tears on his cheeks, just *moaned* at the same time, and he forced himself to relax into him, swallowing around Alexos' cock.

"Ought I let up?" he asked, the question more at Harry than at the man pinned between them.

"He's leaking like a faucet," said Harry. "Mr Kidd doesn't care to be whipped or beaten, sir, but this sort of treatment makes the easiest slut of him there is." Larry moaned even louder around his cock, his body shuddering, and Harry groaned. "See, there?" he asked, dropping his weight over Larry's body and bounding into him. "He's coming."

"Fuck," whispered Alexos, and closed his own eyes, dropping back into the pillows and concentrating on the sensation of Larry's mouth. Just the thought of him coming like this had Alexos' bollocks drawing up, and within a minute or two he was coming and Larry was just swallowing it down.

It was actually overstimulating after a few more moments, Larry still sucking and tonguing at him, and Alexos shoved Larry's head off him, staring at him blearily as Harry dragged him back onto his prick and shoved his head down into the mattress between Alexos' legs.

Alexos stared, spellbound, at the way Harry pinned him down, at the way he fucked into Larry brutally, roughly, and Alexos was reminded dry-mouthed of certain schoolboy fantasies of Patroclus and Achilles, of one pinning the other into the dirt and riding him as though he meant to tear him to shreds.

Harry's whole body was gleaming, each tattoo looking vital and alive as though each of those animals was about to leap directly off of his skin, his muscles working in his neck, across his chest, in his arms and shoulders; his lips were curled in a snarl as he breathed heavily, fucking Larry into the bed beneath him and grunting as he sped up, became almost feral with it, and then finally thrust to the hilt and moaned, his head dropping against Larry's back.

His forehead resting between Larry's shoulders, he thrust more lightly now, and Larry whimpered breathlessly underneath him, his hands fluttering, his body utterly relaxed even with Harry crushing him.

Alexos envied him — he envied Harry, too. He wished he could be both of them at once, and still have the view he was enjoying now.

"Good lad," said Harry, and patted the side of Larry's shoulder, pushing himself up and off the bed — as he stood to his feet, Larry melted like butter into the sheet, and Alexos couldn't help but laugh at the way he flattened out, boneless, between Alexos' legs.

Did he look like that, once Harry was done fucking him?

"I'll run a bath, I think," said Harry, and leaned over the exhausted body of Lawrence Kidd as though he barely even mattered, as though he wasn't even there, cupping Alexos' cheek and giving him a small smile. "Do you need anything?"

"I have rather more than I need already," Alexos murmured, pecking him on the lips, and as Harry drew away, Alexos put his hand in Larry's hair and pulled his head up off the mattress.

Larry looked up at him, slack-jawed and dazed and grinning as though he'd just had the fuck of his lifetime.

"Shall we go out for dinner tonight?" asked Larry, tilting his head to the side.

"What, the three of us?"

"Oh," said Larry. "I don't know that we can all go together. I just meant you and I."

"No, I don't think so, not tonight," Alexos murmured.

"You'll come to the dinner tomorrow night, though, won't you? Come down to Brighton and meet the cast of the play?"

"Oh, Larry, I really don't think—"

"Of course he will," said Harry from the doorway, and Alexos glared at him, but Harry grinned at the both of them, undeterred. He was a vision, soaked with sweat and with his cock wet and softening between his muscular thighs, steam from the hot water behind him gathering around his head and shoulders like a stage curtain. "I've already booked our tickets for the train."

"Have you indeed," said Alexos through gritted teeth, but he didn't have time to be anxious about it — Larry had crawled forward and begun to nuzzle again at the base of Alexos' still mostly-soft cock, and it became difficult to concentrate on anything else.

Chapter Sixteen

Alexos dozed on the train. He didn't often travel by train, but then again, he didn't often travel at all – certainly, when he did travel, it was either with his mother and father, or entirely alone.

He wasn't accustomed to sharing a booth with a fellow passenger, least of all, several – when travelling with Brydon, he normally stayed alone and read or napped or edited through his own notes whilst Brydon found someone more interesting to chat to in another of the carriages.

With the four of them in here, it was just a little bit cramped – when getting onto the train, Larry had made a fuss of wanting him to be nearest the door, so that he could have more leg room, but Alexos had taken one look at Larry's already distractible air and fidgeting fingers and knew that he'd be up and down the whole journey, and had little faith that he'd be able to consistently hop over Alexos' extended legs without jarring or knocking them.

Alexos sat nearest the window, Sutton sitting on the bench to his left, Riggs across from him; Larry took the other opposite bench, and four or five times over the course of the few hours down to Brighton, he got up to stretch his legs, or repeatedly go to the bathroom, or chat to other people.

Harry Sutton had big, broad shoulders, and he was a fat, barrel-chested man packed with meat, muscle, and healthy insulation – were he alone in a carriage, Alexos expected that no stranger would ever choose to sit beside him, to settle himself into the small gap between Sutton and the carriage's side wall or window.

Sutton well-knew how to move and distribute his weight, moved with the keen and clear control of his body and its bulk that many large men in service learned to, let alone men with military training – initially, in sliding into the carriage to settle onto the bench beside him, he'd been very careful, ensuring he wasn't hurting Alexos... And then, seeing that Alexos was quite fine, his legs outstretched, his face tipped toward his butler, Sutton had relaxed his body.

Suddenly, Alexos was pressured on both sides, sandwiched with the window frame on his right side and the much warmer wall of Sutton's shoulder on his left, half-crushed.

Larry had said, "Oh, Alexos, there's plenty of space between Riggs and I!"

"Why, so I can be assailed by two men's sharp edges instead of one man's blunted ones?" Pleasantly blunted ones. More than pleasant – as he sniped at Larry, he made the softest eye contact he could with Harry, and Harry's returning smirk was subtle, but more than visible up close like this. Alexos could smell his cologne, feel the woollen weave of his travelling suit – like this, the hand not loosely gripping his cane could touch the meat of Harry's thigh with his fingertips without seeming suspicious or even noteworthy whatsoever.

"I don't know how I feel about being referred to as a blunt instrument, sir," Harry said mildly, arching one eyebrow.

"Feel free to express your feelings in any diary entry or musical lament you like, Mr Sutton, so long as you do the latter out of my earshot," Alexos retorted, and across from them, he saw Riggs let out a noise of some surprise, almost a laugh before he managed to clamp down on it and hold it back.

"My edges aren't so sharp," said Larry earnestly, and Alexos rolled his eyes, leaning back with his arms crossed loosely over his chest – without asking, Harry laid his coat over Alexos' thighs, the fabric a pleasant warmth in his lap, and he softly sighed at the weight of it, at the comfortable compression of his shoulders and his sides, of the coat serving as blanket.

It wasn't even difficult to doze, under these conditions, warm and comfortably confined with the movement of the train over the tracks - Larry tried to make conversation with him a few times, no matter his closed eyes, but Alexos didn't find it too much trouble to tune the man out.

* * *

Harry normally enjoyed sitting on a train bench without anyone sat beside him, usually had the luxury of a bench to himself unless he was on a packed train, but sitting so close to Alexos was a luxury in itself, albeit a different one – with Larry and Riggs across from them, making it something of a full carriage, there was a more than plausible deniability in their physical intimacy.

Within a few minutes of them coming aboard and the train beginning to move, Alexos was not merely dozing, as he'd advised he likely would – he was quite asleep, his cheek rested on Harry's shoulder, and what a warm, pleasant weight it was.

Larry had gotten up to walk down the corridor, and Harry leaned his head back against the carriage wall, looking across at Riggs, who'd removed his copy of *The Man Who Laughs* from his bag and was paging through it, scanning the pages. He'd been wringing his hands this morning, only a few chapters before the end but voicing aloud that he felt terrible about the idea of taking a library book out of the Foxes' house and Alexos, who'd been limping past in search of grease for some contraption he'd been up working on early in the morning in the kitchen, had all but rolled his eyes at the younger man and said he couldn't give a toss if he stole the thing and sold it on Brighton's literary black market.

Riggs had flushed bright pink, and Sutton had watched Brydon assure him a bit more gently that it would not be an issue for him to take the book with him given that they were going to be coming back so soon – and even were they not, that they would have more than enough faith in Riggs' ability to dispatch any borrowed book back by post if there was a need to return it urgently.

Now, Riggs was glancing across the carriage at both of them, and Harry reached across to ensure the carriage doors were properly closed.

"You're one of us, are you not, Mr Riggs?"

"One of you, Mr Sutton?" Riggs repeated, his lips parting, and Harry smiled faintly at him. He liked Riggs very well, thus far – the young man was somewhat bland in his manner and affect, but he was dutiful and sensible, and he seemed to do very well at managing Lawrence Kidd. He was timely and very well-organised, had insisted on travelling at a time of day where there wouldn't be too much of a crowd at the station – Larry became very nervous in crowds – and he kept copious and prodigious notes.

Some years ago, when Harry had first been tutoring him in the ways of valeting at the Bisphams' house, he'd already had that habit in hand. He had begun his habit of taking notes as a footman, apparently, set for him by the first butler under which he'd served as an exercise to encourage him to improve his handwriting. Harry had no idea what it had looked like before he'd taken up the affectation, but when first he'd observed the habit, he'd rather admired the young man's beautifully exquisite hand, and it was no less impeccable now, although he didn't write out his daily notes in full any longer.

Riggs kept a diary and a pocketbook, these days both written out in a personalised shorthand, and Harry had noticed this quality of his, had immediately thought of Alexos' own tendency to write out his diaries in Greek, making them illegible to any who didn't have his background of study. It didn't seem that Riggs used his pocketbooks for any failure of his own memory, because he tended to remember most details off the top of his head, but Harry did occasionally see him page through one to check a detail – ordinarily an allergy or a peculiarity about a friend or guest's preferences, or a particular date he and Kidd had been somewhere. He was a very good cook, according to Larry, and served him good and varied meals; he was a musician, played guitar as well as singing; and of course, he was very well-read.

They'd talked a little in the house, of course, chatted pleasantly over the servants' hall table over the past few weeks, but Riggs was no more effusive in conversation now than he had been when first Harry had met him.

Back then, those years back, Harry had thought him laconic simply because he was listening keenly for instruction and information, taking his education seriously, and in all honesty he hadn't given it much thought. His own health had been less than rude at the time, his nightmares worse, his sleep more lacking.

Now, it was clear to him that Riggs' quiet was his nature as much as anything else.

Riggs had no particular vices that Harry had made out, or none that made him inappropriate as a valet, anyway – he had a tendency when he was overtired to curl locks of his hair about his fingers, but that was just endearing, and he didn't do it outside of the servants' quarters.

If anything, Harry felt the young man was overly self-effacing, and too modest – he seemed shy about beginning conversations with Brydon and Harry at first, but he was getting better at it. He didn't in general seem to start conversations with anybody, usually just waited for someone to speak to him, and Harry got the impression that the young man wasn't accustomed to people doing so, that he enjoyed his relative solitude, or at the very least, sought it out.

"You don't smoke, do you, Mr Riggs?"

"No, sir, my mother abhors tobacco."

"Are you very close with your mother?"

"Quite close, sir. I write to her regularly, I visit her on my days off."

"Does she have that silent and unspoken sense, as some mothers do, that her son is an invert?"

Riggs' jaw dropped, his eyes widening, and he looked immediately to Alexos, who was now fast asleep and even snoring softly, his cheek a warm weight on Harry's shoulder. There was no excellent way for a man like him to recline in a train seat, tall and lanky as he was, and Harry knew that later in the evening, he would no doubt want to give him a massage and do his best to work the tension out of his body from being folded in his place.

"Mr Sutton—"

"One of us, I said," Harry repeated quietly. They had never discussed this, those years ago, Harry more haggard from lack of sleep, Riggs with bigger eyes and more youth in his features. Harry didn't readily recollect if he'd truly even noticed when first he'd been training Riggs under him, if he'd extended the barest thought as to Riggs' inclinations one way or another – his mind had been on other matters. "Mr Kidd and I are acquainted outside of our circles as young gentleman and butler, Mr Riggs – and I am well-familiar with the crowd he socialises with in Brighton."

Riggs' lips remained parted as he looked between Harry and Alexos both, searching Harry's face and then carefully examining Alexos' own slack features, as though he might infer from his expression in sleep some truth he wouldn't or couldn't whilst the man was awake.

Harry knew the feeling. It occurred to him in a faint and distant way that the vision he was permitted of Alexos sleeping on his shoulder, visible in the reflection of the carriage window, was not one he would soon be able to enjoy again. He ached to be able to move into his bedroom at any hour of the day without reproach or commentary – he had seen Alexos sleeping, and would continue to, but he wished he could simply sit and be in the room with him, see him so relaxed.

When would Alexos be able to observe Harry as he slept? See Harry's expression slack in unconsciousness, hear his tired mumblings, and all the rest? He supposed they were as yet only affianced – such mutual appreciation for a partner in sleep was for the already-married.

"Did Mr Kidd tell you?" Riggs asked quietly. "About me?"

He was still a young man – thirty or so, himself, a little younger than Alexos.

"He told me some things about you," Harry said. "He said he was very frustrated with you at first – I met his previous valet, Mr Habberley, I don't know that you ever had the pleasure. He was a rather scatterbrained and older gentleman, and somewhat workshy – this worked very well for Larry, going unnoticed. He was very nervous about you, about your professionalism, your devotion to the work. He's not excellent at judging the social cues of relative strangers, of course, lacks the unspoken instinct that many men have for understanding without it being said that they are of a kindred inclination – or that which some women have for their sons."

"Oh," said Riggs, seeming somewhat anxious as he repeated, "Frustrated?"

"It was short-lived, I assure you," Harry said. "Once he realised you were no threat to him, that you could be trusted."

"I would never betray him," Riggs assured him – he'd gently laid his bookmark in with the pages of the book, and was now holding it against his chest, clutching at it in the way some children might hold a stuffed bear or doll. "But I'm not, ah... He invites me to parties, sometimes. Or, or social gatherings intended for..." He subtly bit the inside of his lip. "My mother is quite frightened of my getting arrested, Mr Sutton. Her brother was arrested when she was a young woman, he got sentenced to hard labour, and he died still in a camp, it was awful, I... I never met him, but his ghost hovered over me like a shade when I was a boy.

"She knew before I did. Long before – she used to impress upon me how important it was that I perform my duties very well, she wanted me to enter service from the out, she didn't want me working in a factory or even an office. I didn't really understand why she was so strict with me, or... not strict, she wasn't punitive or angry, more that she really impressed on me a work ethic that I realised she didn't on my sisters, or seem to expect of other young men. When I was a little older, once I was twelve or thirteen, the first time a boy..." He trailed off, his eyes becoming distant for a moment, and then said, "It's not that I fear reprisal from her, Mr Sutton, she's not my keeper or my gaoler, but I can't lie to her, and there's nothing that gives her such fear as the idea of my suffering as her brother did. I may have made implications to Mr Kidd that I am, um... Celibate."

"Yes," Harry said quietly. "He mentioned that one evening you were in the same bar as him by happenstance, and he got that impression from you."

Riggs' thumb slid across the cover of the book, stroking down its leather binding, over the gilt writ into it. He looked to Alexos, still asleep, and Harry saw the expression in his face, studied it, ached at the sight of it – there was a want there, a craving, hardly deep enough to be called love or affection, but the quiet yearning was damn-near palpable.

"The two of you are involved?" he asked softly.

"My uncle arranged that Mr Fox and I should be affianced to one another, after a fashion," Harry said. There were few men, even other like-minded ones, that he would be so frank with – he hadn't even explained the particular arrangement to Larry, and had no desire nor intention to, but Riggs was a different sort of soul, a different man entirely. "There are no marriages between men like us, Mr Riggs, but we can get as close as we can – as your mother desired that you should enter service for its relative camouflage, my uncle safeguarded both myself and Mr Fox in arranging a like match for us."

There was a mistiness in Riggs' eyes as he took this in, his desire softer now, broader in its scope – and at the same time, inspired with a little more hope and warmth.

"I've no doubt it must be difficult, being so close to the light, so to speak, and not being able to step within it for fear of how it might burn you. Working for a man like Mr Kidd, being in and around his social circles, and that of their servants, too."

"Somewhat," Riggs allowed, "but it's not wholly bad. There's a soothing element to it, knowing that that world is there, within such easy reach."

"And seeing that they're not suffering unduly, either," Harry said, inclining his head. "That the world is not quite so catastrophic as your mother might fear, so long as people take care not to be caught."

"Would that it were only care that ensured one's safety," Riggs said. "Mr Sutton?"

"Mr Riggs?"

"Are there many men out there like Mr Fox?"

"Sleeping on a bigger man's shoulder, you mean?"

Riggs' lips twitched, and he looked down at his lap. "Men who speak so... I don't know, so frankly, of their desires, their opinions."

"He's a coarser man than one would expect of him, being a young gentleman and a scholar, isn't he?"

"Coarse, yes, but not violent," Riggs said quietly. "I might find a coarse man on any dock, but Mr Fox's eloquence, his handle on his own feelings..."

Harry smiled faintly at the idea of Alexos not being violent.

"Mr Fox is well-accustomed to being treated somewhat cruelly by the world – as a consequence, he works as best he can to be gentle. He's aware of his own power and influence as a gentleman: he is conscious that he might wield this over you very easily, and he has no wish to."

Riggs' brow knitted together, and he looked at Alexos again, more critically now, pensive, considering.

"But to answer your question, yes, I've no doubt there are other men you might find that please you in the way that he does, that make you feel seen, assured, considered, in the way that he does."

There was a faint pinkness in Riggs' cheeks.

"Sorry," he whispered.

"Mr Riggs, I'm not jealous, nor angry with you. At such a time as you feel safe to, I wouldn't discourage you from making your own advance on Mr Fox – I don't know if he would engage or not, but he's not untouchable."

Riggs seemed baffled. "But your... marriage...?"

"We're not a man and wife, Mr Riggs – the rules are different for a matelotage like ours beyond the need for secrecy or the peculiarities of our sex."

"I don't know that I want such things," Riggs said. "Not to insult, merely— Merely that I think I should like something more... traditional. Were it available."

"It may well be," Harry said. "I wish you every luck and consideration, Mr Riggs – and you can always reach out to me for aid or advice, if you'd wish."

"Thank you, sir," said Riggs. "It means the world, I hope you know."

Harry smiled at him, reaching across and very gently touching his knee, just for a moment – not gripping at it, but touching his kneecap with the backs of his knuckles, an assuring touch without any further intimacy. Riggs' smile was full of warmth as he inclined his head, then cracked open his book again.

"Hullo," said Larry loudly a few minutes later, opening the door with a clatter that shocked Harry out of his own slight doze. "Would anyone like to play canas—"

"Shut *up*, Larry," Alexos growled, opening bleary eyes only for a moment, and then crossed his arms loosely over his chest to go back to sleep, leaning against the back wall again.

Larry settled quietly into his seat again, and Harry said, "If you keep your voice down, Larry, I'll play Blackjack with you."

"You'd feed bacon to a dog even the fifth time he came begging," Alexos muttered under his breath.

"Judging by the width of Aristaeus, so would you," Harry retorted, and Alexos barked out a sleepy laugh, shaking his head.

Across the space between them, Harry shared a smile with Andrew Riggs, and then Riggs looked back to his book as Larry set out a tray and the cards between them.

Chapter Seventeen

They arrived at Brighton in the early afternoon, and Harry led the way to their hotel, which was near to the beachfront. He was not pleased, upon arriving, to be given a room on the third floor, and for the lift to be out of order. It took him a few minutes to convince them to swap their rooms over, arguing with the young man behind the desk that Mr Fox was hardly capable of traipsing up and down the stairs.

Initially, he could see that the gentleman assumed he was a veteran – there was something in his tone and the twist of his lips as he began offering rooms farther back from the main reception, at a longer distance, that made it clear he was assuming Alexos was like as not visibly scarred, or otherwise an eyesore, unpleasant to look at.

Harry showed only as much of his anger at the concept as was necessary to frighten the other man into quicker acquiescence, and when he came back to Larry and Alexos, it was to find that Larry was chattering happily away to some nearby friend about one of his most recent books.

"What were you arguing with the receptionist about?" Alexos asked, not standing yet to his feet, his hands loosely clasped about the top of his cane and his chin rested on top of them.

"An unsatisfactory room, although I've repaired matters."

"The lift is out-of-order, I notice."

"We have a ground floor room."

"*We?*"

"The rooms on the upper floors have separate servants' quarters – these ground floor ones have small adjoining bunks for attending valets or lady's maids."

"Bunks scarcely big enough to accommodate a grown man, let alone one grown to your proportions," Alexos said coolly, standing to his feet, and Harry's lips twitched, watching the other man's face as he looked toward the desk. He studied Alexos' posture as he rolled his shoulders slightly, adjusting the set of his hips. "Are you going to be comfortable?"

"Your concern is flattering, sir, but I'll make do," Harry murmured. "Here is your key – I'll go and unpack our things. Would you like for me to run you a bath?"

"Not particularly, though regretfully I would concede I ought to have one before this awful dinner imposes," Alexos said in an undertone, and he looked down to Larry. "This dinner is at a restaurant, I take it?"

"Felicitus, a few streets over, we ought be able to walk it," Larry said, and then looked down at Alexos' legs. "Or, erm—"

"We can walk it, Larry, don't be precious," Alexos broke in impatiently. "Felicitas, surely?"

"What?"

"Felicitas?"

"Felicitus. -TUS."

"But that doesn't mean anything, that's nonsense."

"No, it means, ah, happiness, or good luck, or. Something."

Alexos made no attempt to hide his disdain as he limped across the hall and began to follow the line down the corridor, and Larry stared after him with an abruptly miserable expression on his face. Bidding the stranger he'd been speaking with a pleasant farewell, he stood to his feet and walked alongside Harry down the corridor, adjusting his hat.

Ahead of them, Alexos cut rather a figure – Harry had never seen him have cause yet to wear a travelling suit, and its dark maroon wool suited him rather well, paired with a grey hat. Harry was hoping that given more time – not to mention exposure to the young ingenues of England he was about to make contact with tonight – that he might feel more up to experimenting with his wardrobe.

"Something I said?" Larry asked.

"Mr Fox is an academic, Mr Kidd, not a socialite," Harry said mildly. "I recall warning you time and time again he would not be an easy friend. In any case, he's not angry at you – he's angry at someone making a Latin mistake."

"Oh." Larry put his hands in his pockets as he watched Alexos ahead, opening the door to their room and going inside – Riggs had already gone with Kidd's possessions up the flights of stairs to set things away. "Do you think he's going to have a terrible time this evening?"

"Not as terrible as he'll make it out."

"He's being very, ah..." Larry trailed off as their room door closed shut, and he looked nervously at Harry, pressing his lips together. "I'm not making too much of it, am I, that he's being rather coarser of late than he was? Or— or cooler, sort of... nastier?"

"Mr Kidd," Harry said quietly, and when Larry looked at him pleadingly and he had ascertained the coast was clear in the corridor, he reached out to adjust his collar. He wasn't even making an excuse to touch the other man, either – it needed adjusting. "Larry," he amended in a kinder tone. "That Alexos is being so harsh with you is an indication of his trust and his relaxation in your presence."

"... Really?" Larry asked, but Harry could see the shift of his expression, the part of his lips and the frankly ridiculous smile as he cast another look down the corridor. "Oh, it is, isn't it? He's a sort of grumpy sailor by his basest nature. It's hardly his fault he lives his life crippled and chained to a typewriter instead of hanging from a mainsail on the stormy high seas."

"Phrase it like that to Mr Fox, Larry, and you'll find in short order that he can throw quite the punch, when it suits him."

Larry cringed, and Harry smoothed down the front of his suit for him.

"Will you tell him, um," Larry started, and then hesitated. "This lot, these actors, they're all... I mean, bright young things, the most of them, sort of young party folk, quite free, quite liberal, if you take my meaning."

"I do."

"Liberal with everything."

"Yes."

"You know, the drink and the powder and the body and all the rest."

"I follow you implicitly, Mr Kidd."

"Free with the words, too. Catty, they are, with each other and without – I sort of go through it in the affable and stupid manner I do all else," Harry's lips twitched, and he glanced down between them, "but I certainly can't keep up with it – he'll be able to, though. Say to him that he should, that's all. He'll drive these boys and girls wild for him, if he's mean in the right way."

Harry considered the idea of Alexos being in a room of young people *wild* for him – Harry really wasn't certain if he'd love or hate that, but in either case, he wouldn't expect it. "I'll pass the advice along. You're going to change and dress?"

"Mm, and I might sit and write a bit. Should I hire a car to take us over? It's a walk of fifteen minutes, maybe twenty."

"I'll send word with Riggs once Mr Fox is out of his bath. Larry, if I might advise you?"

Larry exhaled. "I wish you would."

"You really piss the man off when you ask these hundred questions about if he's certain and if he wants it. What he needs, he'll ask for – and you've seen by now he's quite confident in asking for what he wants, when he wants it."

Larry sighs. "I just want him to like me," he muttered.

"He's come to Brighton at your invitation, Larry," Harry said. "He wouldn't do that for a man he didn't."

"Only because you engineered it."

"Only because he *let* me," Harry pointed out, letting a little mild fatigue come through in his voice, and Larry looked pensive at this, even before Harry went on, "If Alexos truly didn't want to be on that train this morning, Mr Kidd, no power on Earth would have compelled him to board it."

He squeezed Larry's shoulder before heading down the corridor, following Alexos into their rooms – he was sitting on a stool in the bathroom, placidly watching hot water fill the tub. Harry pulled the latch across and said as he slipped off his coat, "People will think I'm a terrible valet, letting you draw your own bath and undress yourself whilst I chat with your friends in the corridor."

"He's your friend, not mine," said Alexos pleasantly, and Harry gave him a flat look that made the other man laugh as Harry took up Alexos' suit from the bed and hung it up on the outside of the wardrobe to be washed, drawing off his own suit jacket and hanging that up on the handle of the door that led into the servants' bedding area. "Is he alright? Was I too foul with him on the train?"

"I advised him that your cold demeanour is a sign of your burgeoning affection for him."

"You're an adept deceiver."

"And an honest man, when it suits me," Harry retorted, and as he set Alexos' folded clothes away into the chest of drawers waiting for them, he rolled his shoulders. Alexos was watching him sidelong through the open door to the bathroom – this one a good deal smaller than the ones upstairs, Harry expected, as well.

"Stiff from the train?"

"Why, eager to do something about it for me, Mr Fox?"

"Depends entirely on where you're stiff, Mr Sutton."

Harry's lips twitched at the tone in his flirtation, at the up-and-down look and smirk that accompanied it, and he slowly strode into the bathroom, nudging the door shut with his hip. The bath, much smaller than Alexos' at home, was made of an astonishingly ugly blue ceramic, contrasting with the minted green of the bathroom tile, and the terrible décor did little to make the bathroom feel any larger.

As he unbuttoned his braces and Alexos leaned his cane against the wall, reaching to unfasten the front of his trousers, he said, "Larry wanted me to pass on that you should let loose a little with his actor friends."

"Larry thinks everyone should let loose with all and sundry," Alexos muttered, sliding Harry's trousers down to his thighs, but he certainly seemed intrigued by the prospect, looking thoughtful. "Do you know any of them?"

"I know Cherry Flintman, one of the supporting cast."

"What sort of name is *Cherry*?"

"A pickled fruit's," Harry said, sighing as Alexos pulled his boxers down and wrapped a hand around his already hardening cock, his eyes closing shut as he leaned forward and into the grip of Alexos' hand. "He's a very vibrant man, often drunk, frequently imbibing other substances as well."

"Well, I can't begrudge a man his substances," Alexos said. "I was about to ask you for some aspirin to go with my bathwater. Some whiskey wouldn't go amiss, either."

Harry considered telling him that aspirin and whiskey weren't considered advisable bedfellows – as though he didn't know – but his focus was spirited away by the slide of Alexos' tongue on the underside of his cock, and he groaned quietly, gripping at Alexos' hair.

"You won't be the only addict or drunkard at the table tonight, no," Harry said softly, and Alexos' laugh was low and almost entirely muffled by the cock stuffing his handsome little mouth open. "You'll be surrounded by actors – I can't make promises, but I would expect at least a few of them will know their Aristophanes from their Euripedes, even in subpar translation." He groaned at the sweep of

Alexos' tongue into his slit, the gentle part of his lips around the skin of Harry's foreskin whilst at the same time he twisted his grip and squeezed the base of his cock. "You're becoming quite the admirable cocksucker, I hope you know."

Alexos responded by opening his mouth wider and attempting to invite Harry further into his mouth, and he choked with the head of Harry's cock flat against the back of his tongue, but he didn't stop. He'd been practising, Harry thought, or maybe just focusing the power of his keen and dangerous mind on his gag reflex, battering its protests into submission in a way he couldn't the traitorous nerves and muscles that made up the rest of him.

He choked again, Harry gripping tighter at his hair as he felt the flutter of Alexos' throat, and Alexos let out a soft whimper as Harry adjusted his stance, enabling him to lean and turn off the tap before the bath made to overflow.

"Don't get too good at this, mind you," Harry murmured, and he sank forward – Alexos' gag this time was harsher, came with a soft but spluttering keen, and his eyes opened wide and wet as he stared up at Harry, Harry's cock forced to the root inside his mouth. "I enjoy rendering you somewhat desperate – enjoy seeing the water in your eyes, those quivering lips, that shaking body."

Alexos' eyebrows shifted slightly, his eyes showing a bit of defiance in them, and Harry thrilled with it, the way that he had Harry's prick buried in him, gagging him, and yet still did not want to concede that Harry was the authority in this moment, the power between them.

Harry shoved forward with his hips, pushing his knee between Alexos' thighs at the same time he gripped even tighter at his hair, and Alexos whimpered with the weight of Harry's belly pressed into his face – it had been a long day, he was a picture like this, a *picture*... Harry didn't take long to reach his peak, and Alexos grabbed helplessly at him as he swallowed it down, pulling at his thighs, touching his belly.

When Harry drew back, he was left gasping like a beached fish, one palm rested on Harry's belly, and Harry stroked through his hair, scratching gently at the other man's scalp.

"So," Alexos said, only slightly hoarsely as he tried to look casual, reaching across and testing the bathwater with his fingers, "be nasty to the actors, get drunk, have fun?"

"Don't be too nasty or have *too* much fun," Harry murmured. "But effectively, yes. You're someone different, interesting – a friend of Larry's they haven't met before. A handsome, intelligent, well-educated man with no small amount of inheritance awaiting him."

"A cripple," Alexos added, lips flattening, although he'd made a face at being referred to as handsome. "A drunk cripple. With no friends to speak of."

"With at least one friend," Harry corrected him, "and a mutual one at that. In any case, a gentleman who stands to inherit significant wealth lacking in friends is far more exciting than one with lots of friends to compete with."

"Oh, so they'll want me for my *in*significant wealth?"

"Teach them curse words in dead languages, if you don't know what else to do."

"I've never liked the phrase "dead language"," Alexos mused out loud, wiping his mouth with the back of his hand before standing to his feet with a quiet noise of pain, and once Harry had refastened his braces, he went to help him off with his shirt and underclothes, supporting him as he stepped out of them. "There's a profound grief in something like that. Lost civilisation, dead language, extinct people."

"There's little an actor loves like profound grief," Harry pointed out, and Alexos huffed out a laugh, leaning his face against Harry's shoulder for a moment before he pulled back. "Are you sure you only want aspirin, not codeine?"

"Oh, you and your desire to give me codeine, Harry," Alexos said, but it was undercut by the mask of pain on his face. Alexos could see Harry's own expression once the pain receded, and he exhaled as he braced his palms on the side of the bath – now naked, Harry could see the way he was favouring his better side, how much he was favouring it.

"Alexos..."

"I'll consider it, but the bath will help," Alexos muttered. "I want to be able to drink, to excess, even. Not to mention to be able to take any other hospitality I'm offered."

"Have you had cocaine before?"

"No, why, don't you recommend it?"

"You'll probably like it better than I do," Harry said honestly, supporting him under his arm and easing him down into the hot bath, and Alexos' sound of pleasure was much louder now – he took in a breath through his teeth, but the heat of the water didn't deter him enough to stop him from relaxing back into the water. Once the initial shock of the heat had passed, Harry could see the bliss on his features, the slackness of his jaw as his head tipped back against the wall of the bath. "I... have nightmares. Tendencies to panic at times. Cocaine is no real aid to such things."

Alexos' eyes opened, and his gaze was keen as it settled on Harry, studying him intently.

"Shell shock?"

"Not so extreme as that," Harry demurred, but he kept his tone serious as he took the stool Alexos had vacated, reaching across and running a warmed cloth over his shoulders. Alexos moaned quietly as water trickled wet down his back, and he leaned into Harry's touch, shifting his position in the water. "But yes. Sometimes I hear the rain at night and I still think I hear gunfire."

"I'm sorry," Alexos murmured, idly rubbing his left knee in the hot water, squeezing at the tired muscle around the weak and atrophied thigh muscle. When Harry cupped his cheek, he leaned his face into the warmth of his palm, his eyes fluttering closed as Harry stroked his thumb against Alexos' skin. "You've mentioned having poor nights of sleep, nightmares. You hallucinate, as well?"

It felt odd, speaking about it so explicitly – and yet sleeping so close to each other, with barely a wall between them, he felt he needed to express it. The both of them had their own issues with sleeping, he knew that, but his could be more... volatile. "Less discrete hallucination, per se, and more a continuation of vivid dreams. You'd know all about that, of course."

"Your uncle really matched us well, didn't he?" Alexos asked, raising his eyebrows, and then he gently pulled away from Harry's touch, beginning to scrub himself clean. "Speaking of sleeping—"

"You want me to tie you down tonight?"

"You could," Alexos said, pausing a moment. "Or you could simply share the bed with me. I wasn't joking about not particularly wanting to cram you into a cupboard, Harry – for your comfort alone, I would rather you sleep in bed with me than in that little closet that amounts to a servant's sleeping quarters... but of course, it isn't about your comfort alone. I'm sure I'll be quite comforted by your presence beside me."

Harry was quiet, and Alexos glanced at him sidelong, his lips parted.

"You needn't, if you wouldn't like to—"

"I would," Harry interrupted him. "I would like to."

"I've never slept with anyone before," Alexos said. "Shared a bed with someone, I mean. You might still have to tie me to the bedpost."

"To keep you from sleepwalking, sir, or just for fun?"

Alexos laughed, and dunked his head under the water, pushing his fingers back through his hair.

"I'll prepare your suit for you," Harry murmured, but before leaving him to stew in his waters, he set the aspirin and some whiskey in a tray on the side of the bath.

Chapter Eighteen

Virtually upon sight, Alexos had decided he did *not* like Cherry Flintman.

When they arrived at the poorly named restaurant, it was Flintman who ushered he and Larry through the restaurant proper and upstairs. He did not introduce himself, nor ask after Alexos' name – he chattered loudly to Larry and Alexos both about costuming and cigarettes and an argument he'd apparently had with a moth the night previous and other such gallimaufry as that.

Picking their way through the somewhat busy restaurant, Flintman led them through a painfully narrow doorway, and although Larry was careful not to let the heavy door knock Alexos in the shoulder or hip, the base of the stairs was narrow enough he had to move out of the way to give Alexos space to actually follow him.

These stairs, Alexos would guess, had once been service stairs, because they were very narrow and very steep, with not enough space in the hall for even an inlaid banister. He was very slow-going up the stairs, and Larry kept glancing back at him nervously and apologetically as he led the way after Flintman to the next floor.

Felicitus had apparently been converted over from a house before – downstairs Alexos had noticed the old crown moulding and the light sconces, let alone the carpet, seemed rather out of place in an eatery rather than a domestic dwelling. Upstairs, a wall had been knocked through to make one private dining room of what had previously been two rooms, probably servants' dorms judging by the low ceilings and lack of natural light.

"Sorry," Alexos muttered to the man behind him on the stairs who had followed them into the restaurant, finally looking back and getting a good look at the fellow's face.

Unlike Flintman, who was tall, skinny, and strangely square, with stubble spattered over his face like so much dirt and greased back hair, this man was... was very different.

Slim and willowy, he had a halo of thick, blond-brown curls, and his eyes were a striking blue, his lips painted red, blush on his cheeks, his eyes lined and shadowed in heavy black and a pair of hearts printed on the outer side of his left eye. He smiled as he took off his hat, looking up and into Alexos' eyes – as he gave Alexos a look up and down, his thick, mascaraed lashes fluttered.

"Please, don't apologise," he said – he had a faint lisp and an Italian accent, and while he was obviously of the *theatrical* lilt, his manner of enunciation didn't seem put on in the way that Cherry's did. "I'm just grateful your boncove helped you with your coat off before you started your way up the stairs, all the better to give me a good view of the dish."

"Dish?" Alexos repeated, and the other man stepped up the last of the stairs and stood level with Alexos. He was shorter than Alexos by nearly a head, but tilted his head back to look Alexos in the eye and at the same time give him a few down the Italian's shirt – his tie was untied, the top two buttons undone, and Alexos was treated with a look underneath it at the creamy white flesh of his breast.

He was wearing a woman's perfume instead of a cologne – it was powdery and floral, sweet, with elements of vanilla in it, and Alexos couldn't resist the urge to inhale deeply and take it into his lungs, which made the Italian's eyes light up, the blue in his eyes seeming to shine.

"Those two ripe plums stretching out your back netting, ducky," said the Italian, and when Alexos stared down at him, stunned and strangely charmed, he gave a wink and slid past him into the room, and as he went past he pinched Alexos' right arse cheek, making him jump and then laugh breathlessly. His face felt warm, and he was somewhere between scandalised and absurdly delighted as he stepped off the landing, looking back and forth to see if anyone had noticed his and the Italian's physical contact, but no one seemed to be looking their way.

"Mr Fox, why don't you sit over here, pride of place?" said Flintman loudly, gesturing to a seat on the other side of the large table that dominated the room – if anything, it was a bit too big for the room it was in, let alone the chairs around it.

"Testa di cazzo, Cherry, are you fucking stupid or what?" demanded the Italian, changing his tone to speak to Flintman as he slid prettily into the seat Flintman had just offered to Alexos. "What, you want him to walk around this table every time he needs to piss, eh? It's bad enough he has to go up and down a ladder to go to the lavatory!"

Larry flushed pink, looking anxiously between Flintman, who was standing stock still with his mouth ajar, his cigarette hanging from his fingers and looking nearly ready to drop to the carpet, and the Italian, who had pulled in his chair slightly and immediately commenced to chatting to one of the ladies already sitting at the table.

"Erm, sorry, Al— Mr Fox," said Larry, "Mr Garibaldi can be... testy."

"Mr Garibaldi, is it?" Alexos asked, and the Italian looked his way, all white teeth and pretty eyes and those two pretty black hearts beside his gaze, but didn't rejoin their conversation again, kept talking about the book he'd been reading with the woman beside him – she, too, was observing the three of them with mild interest. "He's right – it makes a lot more sense for me to sit on this side of the table."

"Oh, Mr Garibaldi is right, is he?" asked Flintman, putting one hand on his cocked hip and tapping ash off his cigarette to the tray on the table – he missed some of it, and Alexos looked at the dark grey curls of ash staining the white tablecloth. "What, do you think I'm stupid as well, Mr Fox?"

"By all means, exhibit evidence to the contrary, Mr Flintman," said Alexos pleasantly as he took his seat, and then immediately put weight on his good leg, his elbows on the table, to ensure Larry didn't jar him badly as he clumsily tucked his chair in behind him. "I'm always happy to change my opinions."

Flintman stared at him, uncomprehending, and then started to laugh loudly and obnoxiously, dropping into the seat at the head of the table. "Where have you been hiding him, Larry? He's tall, he's handsome, and he's got a tongue on him."

"Mr Fox is a recent new f— erm, acquaintance, of mine," said Larry, and Alexos looked at him side-on, reading the planes of his face, the furious nerves that were suddenly apparent across his features.

"Is he often tended to this sort of over-formality when nervous?" Alexos asked.

"I'm afraid so," said Flintman, reaching across and patting the side of Larry's face, making him laugh and relax slightly, leaning away from him. "He either corrects one way or the other, goes too far. Like when a ship starts leaning one way and then keels right over the other."

"*Cherry*," Larry hissed.

"Larry and I are recent friends," Alexos said. "He's been staying with us a little while – we're much closer to Brighton than he is in Oxford, we're not far from Crawley."

"How did you come to know each other?" Flintman asked. "He was desperately frightened of putting you off him when he came to stay with you."

"Yes, you're the responsible party for the cocaine he took, I take it," Alexos muttered, sliding his cane down onto the floor and ensuring it wasn't in anyone's way. "Larry is acquainted with my mother – Georgina Fox, she writes mystery novels."

"Oh, I *love* your mother's work," said the actress beside Garibaldi – she was a handsome woman, wore a straight bob of chestnut hair, and he wondered at what product she must put in it, to make it move as such a fine and shining curtain. "I saw an excellent adaptation of her first book, the one with all the morse code, when I was in New York last! They did all this wonderful stuff with the signaller up in a box apart from the main stage in his uniform, and all the lights..."

"I *love* how your mother writes murders," said Larry, and Alexos looked at him. "If you told me she were a brutal axe killer in her spare time, I might even believe you!"

"I might believe it myself," Alexos replied faintly, rather aching to change the subject. "As it doesn't appear our companions are going to introduce us – my name is Alexos Fox."

"Hullo, Mr Fox, I'm Annette Bear," said the woman with the bob, and she stood up and leaned across the table to shake his hand to save him having to stand himself, and Alexos smiled at her. "Two predators, the two of us, hm?"

"Two calculated feeders on carrion, you might say otherwise," said Alexos, and that made her laugh, her eyes crinkling, her hair sweeping dramatically from side to side as she sat back in her seat.

"Fell Garibaldi," said the Italian, leaning forward – Alexos automatically leaned forward to take his hand, but Fell didn't shake his. He put his hand forward limply, resting over Alexos' own, and Alexos glanced across at him expectantly, raising one eyebrow. "Oh, *please*, Mr Fox, you don't have manners either, hm? You don't kiss a lady's hand?"

"I wasn't aware I was in the presence of *ladies*," said Alexos, and Fell and Annette both gasped dramatically, giving one another twin looks of indignation, and Alexos laughed faintly as he leaned forward, brushing his lips across the back of Fell's hand.

He had pretty hands, very delicate for a man – they were utterly hairless and very pale, and his pink nails were longer than he might expect, painted with a shining gloss.

"What is that short for, Fell?"

"Felice," said Fell. "Alexos, it's a Greek name, hm? I should call you Alexo?"

"Getting people to call me Alexos instead of *Alex* is difficult enough – I'm not about to start introducing vocative declensions into the ordeal."

"Oh, a man who talks about declensions at the dinner table," Fell purred, rolling his delicate little shoulders and leaning back in his seat. "How filthy is he, Larry?"

"Alexos?" asked Larry – there was a slight nervousness on the name, and he looked sideways at Alexos with a shy smile as he did it, and seemed bolstered when Alexos smiled encouragingly at him in response. "Why, he's squeaky clean, Fell, I assure you!"

"Larry," said Alexos out of the corner of his mouth. "You're ruining my reputation, and it's as yet so *new*."

They all laughed, and Alexos' skin felt as if it was burning off the back of it – it was nice, genuinely, but he was grateful indeed when the door opened behind them and more of the company began to filter in.

* * *

It was meant to be harder than it was, it seemed to Alexos. It should have been difficult, awkward, since the last time he'd gone out for a dinner with strangers... And God, when had that been? Ten years ago, when he was still at university, with the scattered other cripples and defective left behind from the war?

It should have been difficult, and yet somehow, it was easy.

The various actors were very free and open people – they were bold and catty with one another, and it was clear that they were all fairly intimate with and involved with one another's lives. Several of them appeared to be sharing rooms or lodgings together, had worked together on other projects, and even the ones who weren't cohabiting were, one might infer, in and out of each other's beds.

They treated Alexos' presence at the table as no occasion at all, and Alexos supposed that was part of what felt like such a relief.

Cherry Flintman was an Etonian and Cambridge graduate, and three or four of the others of the company were publicly educated themselves, but Alexos was surprised to find that wasn't the case for all of them, and pleasantly so. He sipped at his wine and listened as Annette and Nina regaled Fell with tales of growing up in England.

Nina and Annette kept laughing as they talked about different things their parents had done to keep their houses warm – stealing coal from work, hot water bottles, cooking indoors, purchasing a large mastiff dog who was indeed warm and cuddly, but hogged the blankets and farted continuously.

"What about you, Alexos?" Fell asked, laying his hand on his chin and looking flirtatiously across the table at him. "What – or who – keeps you warm at night?"

"We have a dog as well," Alexos said mildly. "He's a basset hound, and his name is Aristaeus. I don't generally let him into the bedroom with me, but he's an amiable and dutiful footwarmer in the library."

"You have your own library?" Nina asked, raising her eyebrows, her lips parting. "Gosh, Mr Fox, are you terribly rich?"

"We're more than comfortable," Alexos said honestly, resisting the urge to laugh at the question – it wasn't a stupid one to ask, merely that he couldn't remember ever hearing someone ask it and not be gasped at or immediately told to hush, told how rude it was. Neither Fell nor Annette seemed to have any interest in such a thing – they were as intrigued at the prospective answer as Nina was. "I'm not in line for some sort of inherited seat or a title or anything like that, and we don't have a great deal of land or acreage. We have our home, and then my father's stakes are in factories; my mother's, of course, in her books."

"And yours? What are your stakes in?" asked Nina – her hand touched Alexos' on the table, and Alexos felt himself stiffen just slightly, unable to hold it back. She looked faintly apologetic, drawing her hand back, and she laid her hands in her lap.

"Larry's mentioned you're a scholar?" Annette prompted him.

"I'm a classicist," Alexos said. "I've most recently finished a work on Seneca's *Thyestes*."

"Oh, how devilish," Fell said enthusiastically, his eyes flashing with intrigue. "Do you think the meat of his children was very tender when he feasted unknowingly upon it, Mr Fox?"

"I expect it was like veal," said Nina, wrinkling her nose. "*Not* to my taste."

Alexos laughed, and he looked between the three of them, glancing up the table at the rest of the company as they want on chatting with one another, playing a game of trying to balance one of the cut flowers on the table on their noses.

"Have you played many ancient Greek parts?"

"Clytemnestra," said Annette, and Alexos felt his eyebrows rise.

"You aren't a bit young to have played her?" he asked, and he was delighted at the way she laughed – she had a hoarse and throaty laugh, made deep by cigarettes.

"Oh, I like *you*, Alexos," she murmured. "And Nina does a tremendous Antigone, I must say. I'd not met her yet, the first time I saw her on stage – how old were you, 18, 19? I wept my bloody eyes out, came to chat to her at an afters with all my make-up run down my face. Everyone thought my boyfriend must have cheated me something awful to put me in such a state!"

"Oh, Nettie," Nina said shyly. "Fell here has no care for tragedy, of course."

"No, I don't," said Fell primly. "I did some vignettes when I was younger – we adapted some of the Socratic dialogues, and I think I was quite the dashing Alcibiades, although we'd never get away with something so blatant on the stage here."

"No?"

"Oh, no. I put rouge on my nipples," said Fell, and Alexos laughed. "What? I expect the good general himself would have done the same, had he thought to!"

"Who's to say he didn't?" Alexos replied, and the four of them looked sidelong up the table as Cherry Flintman let out a loud roar of triumph, balancing a cut rose on his nose, his head tilted right back to allow for it. "I really dislike him."

"Oh, we all do," mused Annette. "He is marvellous in bed though."

"Has about an average set of equipment, but rides like a stallion," agreed Fell. "One is best advised to check him for sores and pustules before one saddles and reins him though. I must take a short journey to the powder room. Join me, darling?"

"Of course, dear," said Annette, and Fell took her arm once they were around the narrow part of the table, although they had to go single file down the stairs.

"Sorry," Nina said softly. "I, erm— Well, I got the impression you were a Greek sort, even before you were chattering a bit more with Felice. I've always been drawn more to men like you – I don't know what it is."

"Perhaps that we're a bit cleaner than our... What's the opposite of Greek, in this context?" Alexos asked faintly, feeling a sort of rush in his ears at the strange vulnerability of the question, of the conversation between them. "French?"

"Oh, God," said Nina, wrinkling her nose, and Alexos laughed.

He was hesitant before he said, "I must say, I'm not... I wouldn't say I'm tremendously worldly, Nina. I don't often leave my home – I've been critiqued of late for being something of a recluse."

"You should come to the theatre more often," said Nina warmly. "I can't promise you no one will ever be a nuisance, but in a place like that – in a theatre, in an auditorium, all eyes are on the stage. No one to stare at you."

"The staring doesn't bother me as much," Alexos murmured. "It's no great compliment, of course, but at least I can ignore it. Comments, assumptions..."

"Did it embarrass you?" Nina asked. "When Fell snapped at Cherry like that?"

"No," Alexos said, huffing out a noise, and he rubbed the back of his neck before he said, "you know, what embarrassed me more was Larry apologising for him – the awkwardness at Cherry having made a thoughtless error, an assumption, and being more embarrassed at Fell's accurate correction, however emotional, than at the error itself."

"Oh," said Nina, furrowing her blond brows, and she nodded her head very seriously, her lips pressed loosely together. "That makes sense. Sorry."

"It's alright," Alexos said. "What is it about me?"

"Sorry?"

"You guessed I was of a *Greek lilt*, as you put it, once you laid eyes on me – I'm not as blatant as Cherry, and I don't have a lisp like Fell's, I'm not as pretty as he is, as delicate. For an academic, I'm something of a coarse man – I've coarse hands and strong wrists. I've been recognised, and recognised like-minded men in turn, but it never occurred to me what precisely made me..."

Nina was looking at him consideringly, her head tilted to one side, and she drummed her fingers against her knees. She wore the same glossy polish on her nails that Fell Garibaldi did, and Alexos wondered if they shared the bottle, if they painted one another's nails.

"I don't know," said Nina. "I know it's not very helpful, but, um... I don't know that I've got the sense for it that Nettie and Fell do – the observation and the little clues, the tiny inferences and deductions. I'm not as clever as they are – Nettie says it's something I'll hone as I get older, but I don't think I'll get it that honed."

"What clued you in, then?"

"Well," said Nina, and sighed, crossing her skinny arms over her breast and slumping back slightly in her chest. "If I'm honest with you, me liking any man at all is a sign that he might be that way. Bit of a useless sixth sense, if you ask me."

Alexos laughed, but not without sympathy. "That is a tough one," he said. "Particularly if the options you're left with are the likes of Cherry over there."

"Right?"

"Mr Fox," said Fell as he and Annette came up to the top of the stairs, and his pretty hand alighted delicately on Alexos' shoulder, his thumb pressing pleasantly into the meat of it. "Us girls are going to make a break for it – want to join us?"

"You expect me to run?" Alexos asked dryly, leaning back to look up at the other man – he touched his cheek against the warm back of Fell's hand, felt how soft the skin was, smelt the cream he probably rubbed into them every night.

"Oh, Nettie's basically an Olympian, she can carry you fireman style, and I'll carry your cane," Fell suggested, and Alexos and Nina both laughed, even before Annette made a furious no gesture behind Fell's back. "No, ducky, we can probably just creep away without having to put those poor legs of yours to undue labour."

"Were you a soldier?" asked Nina.

"No," said Alexos.

"Rickets?" Annette asked.

"Polio."

"Oof, hard luck," said Annette. "My cousin got it bad – a few of her friends died, and there's one boy in an iron lung, but she's mostly alright. Uses a chair. Mind you, the doctors say her snoring is from the polio."

"Snoring?" Fell repeated sceptically. "From polio? You're not sure they're just making excuses for her?"

"Apnea," Alexos supplied, trying not to laugh. "Polio causes wasting of the muscles, including around the throat and lungs – her airways close up while she sleeps. The worst that can come of that, of course, is death, not to mention interrupted sleep, but in the meantime... Snores."

"I wish she would die sometimes," Annette said, with such a serious expression that Alexos felt his mouth drop open. "If only so I can get some shut-eye while she's in the house."

"You're so *awful*, Nettie," Nina said, and then the three of them started laughing, and Alexos almost couldn't believe he was laughing himself – there was something in the way the three of them leaned into one another, the way they laughed a similar laugh despite having such different voices, different faces.

Annette and Fell's eyes both crinkled in the same ways despite their features being so different, Fell's so pretty and rounded, Annette's so square and handsome; Nina had big, brown eyes that glittered just like Fell's did despite being such a different colour; Nina and Annette held their hands similarly when they laughed, pressed their knees together in the same manner.

It was rather like meeting three sister-brothers, what with the blending of gender between each of the three – the sort of thing one ought expect of actors, he supposed. Bright young things, bohemians, and all of that.

"I don't know that I'm up for further excitement tonight," Alexos said reluctantly – his body was aching from sitting in the dining chair, and his bladder was uncomfortably full. He'd been avoiding taking the stairs downstairs, and he was dreading it now, knew that the descent would be so much more painful than walking up them, and so much the slower.

"You're at the Sun, right?" Fell asked. "We'll walk with you. Why don't you start heading down the stairs, and we'll collect our things and make our excuses." He hesitated, and then said, "Would you rather that, or would you like one of us to support you a bit?"

"I would rather descend alone, yes," said Alexos softly, feeling the warmth in his smile rise up to his own cheeks, and Fell winked at him again, blowing him a kiss before he went to fetch his hat and coat.

An agonising twenty minutes later, having gotten down the stairs and then had to fight his way to the facilities and back, Alexos walked very slowly, and Fell Garibaldi walked at his side with his hand curled through Alexos' arm. He was leaning into him, although not enough to put any weight on Alexos' body.

It was really—

It was really quite lovely. Unexpected.

"Are they tattooed, those hearts by your eye?"

"They are, yes," Fell said. "I've other tattoos, here and there – a few of my sea-queen friends kicked up such a fuss at the idea of it, me with ink right on my face, but people are always rather charmed by it."

"You're sure they aren't charmed by you?"

"Oh, I *know* they're charmed by me, ducky," said Fell. "They were a gift from my husband – I wore mine on my face, and he wore his over his heart."

"Oh," said Alexos, and he felt himself tense, looking sideways at Fell. "That's... That's lovely. Your husband, he's...?"

"Oh, darling," said Fell, giving Alexos a small, sad smile. "Don't you worry about infidelity – I'm a war widow, I'm afraid."

"I'm sorry."

"Oh, me too. But he said it wasn't enough being my hero – he had to go and be king and country's as well."

Alexos held his tongue in response to that, didn't see the value in denigrating whatever the man's legacy was, in Fell's eyes.

"Am I going to fuck you when we get back to my hotel, Mr Garibaldi?" Alexos asked.

"Oh, you *are* a bold one," Fell said. "Would you like to play the Socrates to my Alcibiades, Mr Fox?"

"I'm sure you're as impossible to teach."

"I make a point of it," Fell whispered. "But I've got some lovely things to teach *you*."

Fell was wearing a woman's coat – it was russet brown, the sort with a removable fur stole, and he was wearing a cream-coloured silk scarf around his neck, the same colour as his hat.

It occurred to Alexos as they moved through the hotel to his room, Fell no longer on his arm, that the others in the hotel lobby didn't even seem to realise Fell *wasn't* a woman, what with the sway of his hips, how small he was, how pretty.

Alexos hung a tie on the handle of the door as they stepped inside, and then went to help Fell off with his coat.

"Oh, you *are* a gentleman," Fell murmured, and tugged Alexos by the shirt collar down into a kiss.

Chapter Nineteen

It was a pleasant evening, and Harry whiled it away down by the sprawl of the pier, sipping at his drink and enjoying the bustle and laughter of the men around him, listening to the clink of glasses, taking in the scent of beer and ale and all the rest. Whenever the door opened up and men filed in or out, he could smell sea salt from the air outside, smell vinegar and frying oil from people's fish and chips.

"You don't think he'll be offended at not having been invited this evening?" Harry asked, and Ulysses gave Harry a very serious look, tapping out his cigarette.

"Good Lord, no," said Ulysses in his rich, serious voice, ash falling into the tray. "You and I could offer as much money as we might think of – forget ten shillings, forget a pound. You might offer the man a guinea, and you couldn't get my employer in the same room as Cherry Flintman once forewarned he might be present."

"You and I both know young Samuels is best left allowing you to manage his purse strings anyway," Harry replied.

They both laughed, Harry leaning back in his seat and drinking from his glass, and across from him, and Ulysses eased off into a wry chuckle. He'd been far more expressive once upon a time, Harry well-remembered – was always laughing and joking when they were each still young, and neither of them tried and tested – and scarred – by war.

Harry had known Ulysses Valentine since he was first coming up as a hall boy years ago – when he'd been just a young lad starting out in the most junior position there was serving the Darnels, Valentine had seemed a towering and mammoth figure compared with Harry, sleeping in a draughty corridor and awake hours before dawn every day, tiny compared to all the grown men and women about him. Valentine was not, of course, the vision of towering wisdom Harry had thought him to be at that age of nine or ten – at the absolute eldest upon their meeting, he would have been eighteen.

Less than a decade separated them in age, and yet there was something tremendously comforting, even paternal, about the man, even now. There were pints between them on the table, and a ripped open packet of pork scratchings, but some part of Harry still felt the cherished warmth of the fire in that first house of his heating his back, Valentine showing him some new task element by element, teaching him how to polish shoes or repair a shirt collar or brush a coat.

Every other man he'd learned from in that house was dead now. John Denton, the butler, dead of a heart attack at the age of fifty-nine; Thomas Carr, the under-butler, and John Hound, the gardener, both dead by mustard gas; Anthony and Raymond and Robert and Liam, footmen or valets, at different times, otherwise dead in the trenches.

There had been three of them at the end of the war itself – Ulysses and Harry had each come home from the trenches and so too had Tristan Short, a butcher's third son, who had been a senior footman and had been training eagerly to be a chauffeur before the war.

He'd been a suicide.

"I visited your uncle this month past," Ulysses said in a quieter voice now – they could hear one another around all the chatter about them, each of them keen-eared as they were, though it was a close thing. "On my day off when Mr Samuels was a guest of the Darnels. Retirement suits him."

"It does," Harry agreed. "Suits him better than it does many a man of our profession, I will say – which isn't to say the man is idle. Every letter he sends me seems to indicate some new scheme or other, managing his garden, involving himself in one of my brothers' or cousins' embarkations, or gardening, or whittling – that was short-lived, he's never been of an artistic nature, no matter what they say about men like us—" (Ulysses laughed from deep in his chest, muffling the sound with another drink.) "—or reading a good deal. And posing for *pictures*, I'm given to understand?"

"And very grateful for the model Mr Samuels was too," said Ulysses. "There are few things he enjoys more than flirting with someone posing for an illustration. Few things other, of course, than—"

"Yes, yes, thanks kindly, but I hardly need to hear about your employer and his attempts to seduce my uncle, unsuccessful, I should hope," Harry stopped him, and Ulysses smirked, his jowls shifting and shadowing about his lips. "I've never much liked feeling I'm in competition with the man – not in this area, at least."

"Mr Samuels enjoys a commanding figure," Ulysses said. "As does your Mr Fox, I wouldn't wager."

"He does, although he's more flexible in that arena than Samuels is," Harry said quietly. "He's a student of classics rather than any complex science, but there is a great hunger in him, a curiosity, for all the mysteries of intimacy and the bedroom, of all the games and dialogues as might pass between such men as us."

Ulysses' expression was one of not at all disguised disapproval as he shifted slightly in his seat, setting his powerful knees together under the surface of the table. "I wondered what might compel you to introduce him to, of all people, Larry Kidd."

"You've a soft spot for Larry, and you'll hardly convince me otherwise," was Harry's accusation, and Ulysses made a dismissive sound, but in the turn of his head Harry could see the hidden shadow of his smile. "What *does* bring the two of you down here, dare I ask, if not this party?"

"Oh, he's here for the theatrical crew, certainly, he just deftly avoided an invitation to dinner. He's painting the poster for the show."

"Ah, in the same style as the covers he does for Mr Kidd's novels?"

"Precisely." Now when Ulysses smiled it was a faint thing, but there was a heavy depth of emotion in it, and Harry felt himself smile slightly himself. On their return from the front, Ulysses had taken time to recover from the injuries to his feet – he'd lost most of the toes on his left and two, if Harry remembered rightly, on the right – and had been a little slow at first to return to work.

Harry recalled that he'd been anxious – as anxious as Ulysses ever appeared – to find a new position, uncertain he would find one appropriate to his skills. Friends and old coworkers had tried their best to find him positions in big houses – two different acquaintances of the Bisphams had actually mentioned to Harry whilst he was in their employ that they had heard Mr Valentine was still in fine fettle, and asked if he might pass on their interest in taking on his employment.

As a child, Harry had looked on Ulysses and thought him a butler ready-made, so tall and square and imposing as he was, and it was no surprise to him that so many others had the same expectations of him, but Ulysses had had no interest in returning to a big house after the constant noise and bustle of the trenches.

Being a valet suited him, he'd said at the time, and a valet he would be.

He'd worked in an agency for a while, covering other valets' work as they went away – particularly working with veterans of war slow to recover, or more retiring young men – and the work had hardly seemed appropriate to a professional of his skill and dedication.

Harry had been there on the night the two of them had crossed paths with Vincent Lucas Samuels – the young gentleman had been drunk and flushed pink with it, his hands still stained with his paints, as he'd laid a banknote on the bar top and insisted on paying for a round for all in attendance.

It had hardly been an illicit place, only a quiet little pub in Selby – Ulysses had been working there, and Vincent had just painted a young woman's portrait and finished the job, taking payment for it.

"I don't know that it's entirely wise to throw your money around in that manner, sir," Ulysses had said, and Samuels had leaned on the bar and looked up at him, blinking quite coquettishly – even more unwisely.

"Is it not, my friend? Well, seeing as how you are neither a parent of mine, a nanny, nor even my valet, I hardly see why it's up to *you* to keep my unwise behaviour in check."

"Who *is* your valet, if I'm to charge a man with the responsibility?"

"I'm between men, I'm afraid. The war has yet to harden a man enough to take up the challenge of valeting for me."

"You don't strike me as too difficult to whip into shape," Ulysses had said quietly, and Samuels' eyes had widened, his mouth opening in delighted astoundment.

"I *beg* your pardon, sir?" he'd demanded in a hushed tone, all but quivering with drunken excitement, and he'd stood away from the bar and stumbled on his feet – Harry had jumped to help him, but despite being farther away and with his own scarred and imbalanced feet, Ulysses had been faster.

Samuels had looked up wonderingly at Ulysses' face from where he was held in his arms.

"I'm a valet in need of employ, you know, between men myself," Ulysses had said richly, and his smile, in that moment – that was the first time Harry had *seen* him smile, since the war had finished. It had been genuine and warm, and in the moment a cold shock had run down his spine like someone had poured ice water down the back of his collar. He'd realised he was witnessing a moment of stars reaching alignment.

Ulysses had been Samuels' devoted valet – and rather more than that – ever since that night.

"He's enjoying the work," Ulysses said now. "Much as he abhors Cherry Flintman, he doesn't mind sketching him from afar."

"Most of us find him more bearable from afar," Harry said, and Ulysses laughed.

"Quite," he murmured. "You seem content in life of recent, Harry. As content as I have been in mine for some years – your Uncle Reg has played the cards on the table quite rightly, it seems to me. You're a man in love."

Harry's heart fluttered in his chest, and he thought of Alexos laying kisses on the backs of his knuckles, on the palm of his hand, thought of Alexos' hands sliding over his chest, not only to cup his breast or squeeze admiringly at the swell of his generous belly, or touch worshipfully over his tattoos and piercings, but also to settle over his heart and rest there, feeling the beat of it under his palm.

Whether his hand was there or elsewhere, whether his hands were on Harry's body or buried in the guts of one of his machines, it seemed to Harry that Alexos ever had Harry's heart in his hands, these days.

"Is it so obvious?" Harry asked.

"To an old friend, I think so," Ulysses said softly. "Reg did mention that your letters are quite soppy over the man, as he'd hoped they might be – but I wouldn't have needed your uncle telling me about his plans to know something had been set in motion. One sees it in the set of your features, your shoulders, even the light in your eyes, old friend."

Harry's heart went from fluttering to heating from within, the warm spreading throughout his chest, and Ulysses let out a long sigh of satisfaction.

"How does he feel about the ink under your clothes?"

"Adores it," Harry murmured. "I thought he might be shocked, even horrified – the first he saw me not even undressed, but rolling up my sleeves—" When Ulysses raised his eyebrows, Harry muttered, "Well, I don't always have my sleeve cuffs attending the young master in his bath, do I? He was ensorcelled. Rather forgot about intimacy for a while – nothing compared, of course, to his response to my piercings."

"Oh, of course, you mentioned he has a fondness for machinery and putting bits of metal in his hands," said Ulysses dryly, sardonic in his judgement, and Harry made a dismissive noise, nudging him under the table. "Did he even remember what he was looking at, or just get so distracted by the barbels he got a screwdriver in one hand and...?"

Harry made no attempt to hold back the shift of his expression, and when Ulysses saw the affirmative writ across his features he nearly fell over himself laughing, his chair creaking under his weight and his hand falling to his belly as it ripped right through him, his head tossed back. Not such an expressive man any longer, it was something to see him laugh so openly and obviously – and more than that, it warmed him that Ulysses so easily took on second-hand affection for a man he'd never met.

To Ulysses Valentine – like-minded and like-hearted as Harry himself – this was no matter of perversion, but a quirk of personality that evoked love and charm. Harry well-recollected Ulysses frustrated fondness early in his relationship with Samuels, that he was so often interrupted in trying to drag his lover into bed, or attend petty errands in the intimacy of their household alone, because of the insistence he should stop still and let Samuels commit his expression or a particular angle of his body to paper or canvas.

"I did have to remind him of the *purpose* of the organ, and indeed, our shared intention with it," Harry said, and Ulysses sighed, wiping tears from his eyes.

"What a beautiful idiot your uncle has affianced you to," he said with tenderness and sentiment many of Samuels' friends never believed him capable of – this sort of softness was for the domain of men he loved and was truly friendly with, not the genuine idiots Samuels liked to fill his home with, though not so complete in their idiocy, perhaps, as Flintman. "You've long deserved one of your own."

"It's him that deserves it," Harry murmurs. "He was so closed off when I first came to serve at the Foxes', but with time and care, he's opened to it, bit by bit. To me, to Lawrence Kidd – and now, at a party of actors. Even Cherry Flintman among them."

"You might experience a recession in his openness to social engagement following that particular pill," Ulysses commented dryly, and then turned his head. His expression was serious, but not unfriendly as he said, "Ah, there you are, Andrew, I wondered if you might be joining us. Come along and sit down – would you prefer a cup of tea, or will you assent to something stronger?"

"A half-pint of cider, perhaps, Mr Valentine, thanks much," said Riggs as he came to take his seat to Harry's right, and Harry gave the young man a smile as Ulysses stood to his feet to order the three of them another round.

"All errands attended to, Mr Riggs?"

"Yes, sir, thank you," Riggs said as he settled down. He was holding his book to his breast, and now laid it down on his knees, his palm resting on top of it. "I appreciate the invitation – I had no idea Mr Valentine was also to be here in Brighton."

"Nor did I, although it was a rather happy coincidence for me, Ulysses and I are old friends."

"Ah," said Riggs, and then said in barely more than a whisper, not much of a breath behind the words, "the three of us being, erm... of a similar keel."

"A smooth and even one, at that," said Harry in slightly louder voice, although not with so much volume as to give the poor young man a conniption. "Much more to read of your book?"

"I just finished it, I only had twelve pages left before I made my way over," Riggs said, his fingers resting against the cover and stroking against the cloth-wrapped card. He sighed and then said, "I know it's Hugo, and it's not as though I expected a happy ending, but it is a profoundly sad book, Mr Sutton."

"A good read, though?" Harry asked, gentle in his invitation for the younger man to go on, and Riggs' smile was sad but genuine as he nodded his head.

"Very," he said. "What have you been talking about?"

"Oh, you know," Harry murmured. "Love and poetry, and such ridiculous matters as that."

Riggs furrowed his brow, and glanced toward the heavy figure of Ulysses at the bar, casting the other smaller men about him in shadow. "With Mr Valentine, Mr Sutton?" he asked innocently.

"I was speaking on them, in any case," said Harry diplomatically, and shared a secretive smile with Ulysses as he turned toward them, the smile showing in his eyes but not below the nose, that Riggs should neither notice nor comment on it.

"Now, Andrew," said Ulysses authoritatively as he sank into his seat. "Do tell us how you're getting on with Mr Kidd."

"Very well, Mr Valentine," said Riggs, and conversation turned to matters of craft and professionalism, and no more said about the other half of life.

Chapter Twenty

Felice Garibaldi's lips were the softest things Alexos had ever had the pleasure to touch, feeling them yield under his own, and like this, bending to kiss the other man, it was as though he was descending into a cloud made up of Fell's perfume, the sweetness engulfing him on all sides.

"You must be quiet, of course," Alexos said quietly as they broke apart, and Fell looked up at him with his beautiful blue eyes big as saucers, and held up three fingers.

"Guide's honour, Mr Fox," he said softly, quite unconvincing in his innocence, and began to unbutton his blouse. He was exquisitely dressed in a cream-coloured woman's suit, the suit jacket cinched in to create an illusion of a shorter torso, the better to make his legs seem longer in their flowing trousers, over top of a pair of heeled shoes that had clicked on the stone floors of the street.

He was not quite as slim as Alexos had thought, now disrobed – he had thin and delicate wrists and fingers and a long, graceful neck, but there was more meat beneath his clothes than Alexos anticipated. Under his clothes were expanses of soft, white skin, a plumpness at Fell's breast he might have put down to a brassiere pushing him to perkiness if it wasn't now bared to the air, a slight curve to his belly. Fell's thighs and buttocks were generous indeed, and Alexos immediately reached out and took handfuls of each side, squeezing and marvelling at the way the flesh gave way to his grip, dimpling prettily under the tips of his fingers as he felt how sublimely warm Fell was.

His cock was very small, only a little larger than Alexos' thumb whilst soft, and even as Alexos reached down and gripped it in his hand it only enlarged a little. He focused on Fell's expression as he gripped at it and squeezed gently, twisting his hand as he pulled the other man off, taking a far more tender grip than he might his own, let alone one like Harry's.

Fell's expression was beatific, his painted lips parting, his blue eyes shining prettily, and one of his hands came to rest on Alexos' chest where Alexos could best admire his painted nails.

"You are such a pretty thing," Alexos said quietly. He wondered if he ought to feel embarrassed, that the words came out of his mouth so easily, and so different in tone to the sort of compliment he might give Harry, or Harry him – this was thoughtless, easy praise, with less affection behind it, but no less desire. There was something powerful in it, too, delivering the compliment and seeing Fell's eyes widen even further, seeing the way his lips quivered, how his head tipped back as though to invite a kiss or a bite – to invite tenderness or its opposite.

"You oughtn't compliment a man so when you have his cock in your hand – you're liable to have him come apart."

"We mustn't have that," Alexos said. "It was my intention to take you apart quite deliberately."

He felt Fell's shudder as much as he saw it, and he couldn't help the laugh of triumph that tumbled from between his lips, felt the heat on his skin, burning under his clothes as he realised how easy it was, how easily he might hold the whole of Fell Garibaldi in this moment as he was his delicate little cock – how much the other man was trusting him, giving himself over to Alexos, a coarse man and a cripple.

Was this how Harry felt, knowing how much power he had over Alexos, this sense of enduring and overwhelming, exquisite victory?

"Oh," said Fell in a tiny little voice, and then adjusted himself like a bird ruffling its feathers, standing up a little straighter and doing his best to inject some more authority into his voice as he said, "Shouldn't we be getting *you* undressed, Alexos?"

"On the bed," Alexos instructed, experimentally, just to see what might happen, almost – Fell stepped slowly backward from him, immediately obedient in a way that Larry hadn't been, and Alexos followed after him, sliding his hand up the column of Felice's throat and feeling the flutter of his mouse-fast heartbeat, feeling the pump of his blood.

He'd abandoned his pretty clothes in nothing more than a heap over his shoes on the floor, but Alexos didn't care to contend with that this moment – he focused instead on easing his good knee against the mattress, between Fell's eagerly spread legs, and leant his cane against the side of the bed.

"Help me, then, if you want me undressed," Alexos said, as imperiously as he dared, and Fell's laugh was a fluttered and airy thing, his cheeks burning with a handsome red flush as his fingers went surprisingly shyly to Alexos' vest and then his shirt, unbuttoning each with dexterous movements. "You've come over rather quiet. Were I Socrates and you Alcibiades, one might expect a little more backchat."

"Do you want me bratty, do you?" Fell asked, almost breathlessly, and Alexos laughed as he laid his jacket over top of the chair, and then his waistcoat, and then his shirt. Alexos' stomach suddenly dropped when he felt Fell's gaze on him, as he looked over the very faint scars on Alexos' neck, at the top of his shoulders.

His gaze dropped then to the dug-in scars, these ones bolder and pinker, at his waist, and his hands were very gentle – in a way Alexos rather liked less – as they came to unbutton his trousers, Alexos easing the way by dropping his braces off his shoulders.

Alexos' stomach roiled as Fell's gaze followed over the lines his braces had left when he was still wearing them, where the pins had pressed in against the sides of his waist even through the cotton and leather padding, and then his eyes went lower, to the lacking muscle on Alexos' left leg, the difference between his left and right thighs quite obvious from so close up. Nausea bubbled within him, feeling Fell's gaze on him, on the ugliest parts of himself, and with such deafening silence filling the room around them, with no other man or activity to distract them, just their breathing, just Fell Garibaldi – pretty and delicate, made for the stage - and Alexos Fox, a cripple made for something else entirely.

"Does it hurt dreadfully?" Fell asked quietly.

Alexos had a vision, all of a sudden, of having this conversation with every man he would ever fuck, every man he would ever bring to bed, be undressed with, without Harry to distract them or otherwise keep them busy. It hit him with the force of a speeding train, thundering within his head, making something clench within his chest, in the base of his throat, within his guts – he felt as though he were teetering on a precipice, because where the vision of this future stretched out before him, the knowledge of his past stood in stark contrast.

No one touching him.

No man looking at him with desire or want – no man's gentle fingers sliding over his hips as Fell's were now, nor a mouth so sweet and tender as Fell's against his belly, breathing warm over his belly, up to his navel.

"I shouldn't have asked that," Fell said, his eyes downcast, and the disgust burning with weight in Alexos' chest turns itself over, and he felt his lips twitch. "Do they shame you, the signs of your illness?"

Alexos exhaled, curling his fingers into Fell's pretty hair – where it had come out from under his hat, it was gelled or held with some sort of unpleasant product rather like the brilliantine Harry set his hair with, but the majority of his hair was very soft and yielding under his grip. He asked in a dry tone that very nearly didn't quaver, "You cover your spots with make-up, I take it, when you get them?"

Fell's expression became somewhere between sultry and rebellious. "I don't *get* spots, my dear," he said severely. "Such imperfections are beyond a creature as perfect as I am."

"I believe that," Alexos said. "Being as I'm a creature quite *im*perfect, perhaps you can understand that it's rather frustrating I cannot disguise my imperfections, once undressed."

"You know what they say," Fell said, delicately shrugging his pretty shoulders. "It's not what you have – more what you do with it, hm?"

"And what would you like me to do with it?" Alexos asked, arching an eyebrow, and then groaned as Fell dipped his head and demonstrated, mouthing alongside Alexos' cock. It had softened somewhat, overtaken with his anxiety and his embarrassment, but there was no stopping it from swelling with blood now with a mouth as pretty as this on his prick. "Rather a pleasant demonstration," he managed to say despite his lacking concentration, and he put his hand deeper into Fell's hair, gripping a heavy handful of it.

The curls were tremendously soft, and he sighed and closed his eyes as he took a handful of Fell's hair in his grasp, feeling the locks of it between his fingers and then using his grip to push Fell's mouth where he wanted it, down to the base of his prick before pulling him back and feeding it into Fell's mouth.

He took it as one might take communion, looking up at Alexos with his eyes wide and focused on Alexos' face, his mouth open, his tongue waiting to receive the slide of Alexos' prick over its surface.

"I'm going to smudge your lipstick," Alexos said, pouting out his lips and making a show of seeming abashed, and he saw the flicker of snark ready itself, saw the light in Fell's eyes as he readied himself with some clever or catty comment – and then he doused that light by sliding forward.

The slight gagging noise Fell made was muffled and desperate and full of soft, aching want, and Alexos felt his anxiety burn away, replaced once more with that glow of eager triumph, that victory, that *power*.

Dominance and domination, or if not that, then the pure, primal want to fuck and be fucked – and Fell Garibaldi, it was clear to Alexos, wanted very much to be fucked.

It was easy for a little while, keeping his grip on Fell's hair and mostly moving his head rather than thrusting his own hips, keeping his good leg steady and supporting him whilst he enjoyed *this*. It added unspeakably to the moment, the way that Fell was enjoying it too – his eyes were watering and his cheeks were red, his lips slick with spittle and his lipstick prettily smudged about his chin and the sides of his mouth and the base of Alexos' prick, and his own hips were jumping and fluttering as he thrust into his own hand.

"You love this, don't you?" Alexos heard himself ask, and his voice had a stumble in it, a tension, that he wasn't ordinarily able to concentrate on when Harry was fucking him mercilessly – here, in command of the room and with Fell made quiet except for the exquisite, incredible noises he was making around Alexos' cock, his voice was filling it. He was so aroused he could barely even concentrate on the awful sound of his own voice, of its lacking strength in its distraction, of the fact that he was holding back to keep from cursing in every language he knew. "Are you ever happier than in moments like this, on your belly with a cock buried down that filthy throat of yours?"

Fell's eyes bulged, and he let out a whining, muffled noise, his hips stuttering suddenly, a hard thrust into his palm, and Alexos' own knees quaked, a weakness running down his legs as he felt a powerful rush through his cock, through the very core of him.

"Fuck," he hissed, and hauled Fell off the length of his prick.

"Hey now!" Fell protested, slightly hoarsely as he fell back as Alexos has thrown him back, his shoulders hitting the mattress, and fuck, but he was a fucking picture. His face streaked and messy, his mascara running, saliva mixed with wax on his chin, and Alexos had done that to him, turned the pretty picture he made into this one, messier and more evocative and arousing, because it was a destruction that Alexos has wrought – and Fell eagerly had wrought on him – through mutual desire alone. "I wasn't finished!"

"I decide when we're finished," Alexos said, and breathlessly laughed at the little giggle that made tumble out of Fell's mouth, at the blush in his cheeks – he laughed a little louder, then muffled the noise into his arm, as Alexos braced himself with his good knee against the mattress and hauled Fell closer to him by his gloriously plump thighs, pushing up his knees to give himself a better angle.

It was cruel of him, perhaps, not to dispense any extra oil to the matter, but he found he didn't want to, and in any case, Fell was hardly about to argue. He helpfully hoisted up his own knees and scooted his arse closer to the edge of the bed, and Alexos' mouth went dry as he admired how incredibly generous Felice Garibaldi's arse was as he lined himself up to sink inside.

It wasn't tremendously large in the way Harry's was, appropriate to the rest of his size, but it was plush, and his hands sank beautifully into the white pillow of it, very nearly as crisply clean and white as the pillowcase of the hotel sheets, but for the barest dust of blondish hair closer to his spine.

Spreading Fell's cheeks apart, he greedily took in the sight of him – Fell's cock, small and dainty and pretty much like he was, his larger bollocks supporting it to stand up against his belly, and then his hole, very pink and just slightly open, no doubt from regular use.

The thought sent quite the thrill up his spine, the thought of Fell's popularity with other men, how experienced he was, and yet how much he was enjoying *Alexos*.

"Get regular backdoor visitors, do you?" Alexos asked.

"Darling, I'm a consummate professional," Fell said, and Alexos laughed.

"How much am I expected to leave on the end table for you, after we're done?" Alexos asked, tapping the head of his cock against the slightly-open furl of Fell's hole. For all it *was* slightly open, it was really quite wonderfully small – it was going to be tight, and it was going to feel very differently to Fell's mouth, or anyone else's.

"You misunderstand me, dear – I'm an *actor*. I'd only be charging you if you were in the audience."

Alexos laughed again, and he waited for Fell to laugh himself, for his beautiful face to light up with it – and then he plunged forward, sheathed himself in one movement that forced him to readjust himself at the ache it shot down his bad leg, but that sacrifice was more than worth it, because he got to see Fell's expression crumple. His eyes squeezed shut, his lashes seeming absurdly long, his perfect lips opening in a wide O, and he didn't remember this time to stifle his long, drawn-out moan into his hand – Alexos did it for him.

Alexos groaned quietly when Fell shifted the position of his mouth to keep Alexos' hand from just a palm resting against his lips, sucking two of Alexos' fingers onto his tongue instead, and Alexos huffed out a breathless, amused noise through his sound of pleasure as he felt the tight squeeze of Fell all about him, felt how incredibly warm he was inside, felt the delicious friction.

"Fuck," he hissed, and fell forward, supporting himself on his elbows, their chests against one another, as he used his knee to let himself thrust. It fucking hurt, truth be told – he had let impatience win out over wisdom, picking this position – but he ignored the pain for now and instead concentrated on the way Fell opened to take him in, the pleasure on his face, the wet, slick heat of Fell's tongue on the underside of his fingers and his lips around them.

His eyes opened slowly and prettily, and he gazed up and into Alexos' eyes as he swallowed and sucked on Alexos' fingers, even as Alexos drove as fast and deep into his arse as he could at the same time, and fuck, but it was sublime. It was perfect, wonderful, Fell easy and eager and full of want.

"You are made for this," Alexos murmured. It wasn't so easy to be insecure about the quaver in his voice now, the sound of Fell's muffled moans and the sound of Alexos thrusting wetly against him overwhelming his hearing, not to mention the sensations – Fell's tight clutch around his cock and his fingers, Fell's pretty little prick wet and slick between them, Fell warm and eager, keeping his knees up toward his shoulders as best he could without Alexos holding them for him. "That's something you have in common with Alcibiades too, I wouldn't wonder – treacherous as he was, ever conniving, I've no doubt he was never so true as when he was on his knees or his back."

That made Fell whimper, his whole body arching, and Alexos groaned in pleasure as much as he did in slight pain, adjusting his weight, and scrambled a moment for a corner of the sheet to shove into Fell's mouth.

He took it without complaint, biting down and leaving more smeared lipstick in place – Alexos shoved one of his knees against his shoulder, using it to support himself as he gripped Fell's cock between them with his other hand. It was a tricky balancing act, but if Fell knew that, he didn't show it. He was a little overwhelmed, Alexos supposed, with Alexos fucking him as hard as he was capable.

He gripped at the sheets and fuck, but it was easy for him – how easily he came and how beautiful *that* was too, the strain on his face and then the sudden beatific relaxation, the sputter of Felice's prick between their bodies.

He tightened further, squeezing tight around Alexos' prick, and Alexos grunted because it was so tight it very nearly hurt, but it was a good hurt, well-earned.

He was breathing heavily when Fell stopped writhing, when his louder moans quieten down some, and he laid atop Fell's body and buried his face against his soft shoulder, took in the perfect scent of his skin, the sweetness of it. He'd reached some of the way to the peak, had tasted the ghost of it within reach, but it would have been too much to actually summit, and now he let himself go mostly boneless. His cock was beginning to soften, still sunk in the wonderful heat of Fell's perfect arse, and for all he wasn't going to come inside him, it was a wrench to draw away from the warmth.

"God," Fell mumbled as he tugged the sheet out of his mouth, stained with red-dyed spit. "I hope you had to get a license to go wandering about England, fucking like you do."

Alexos laughed, which fucking hurt as well, and he braced himself on Fell's body to slide forward and lie beside him on the bed on his back, and Fell sat up, looking down between Alexos' legs with an expression of mild upset.

"Oh, haven't you...? Ought I...?" Fell began to lean over, gesturing between his hand and his mouth, as if encouraging Alexos to choose between them, and Alexos caught his shoulder.

"Please," he murmured, stroking his thumb over Fell's cheek. "I'm afraid between that ladder we had to climb at the restaurant and the walk there and back on top of that *vigorous* exercise, I'm rather at my limit."

"Oh," Fell said, pouting out his lips in a very pretty moue. "You can't even bring yourself off, and let me watch?"

"Maybe put your make-up back on, let *me* watch you," Alexos suggested, although for all he liked the idea of watching Fell remake his face, part of him wanted Fell to get out and be gone as soon as humanly possible so that Alexos could find some sort of fucking painkiller. "Pour me a double first, would you?"

"Gladly," Fell said, and Alexos pointed toward the whiskey, which Fell poured him a generous measure and a half of. "You can't drink this without something to ease the taste, surely?"

"I've put far nastier things than this in my mouth," Alexos said, and Fell laughed airily as he slipped into the bathroom and filled the shaving jug with hot water.

Alexos still had his shoes on, and as he pushed himself up against the headboard, keeping his legs outstretched, he leaned forward to unlace his shoes with the very tips of his fingers, then leveraged the heels of his shoes to kick them off onto the floor, carefully kicking off his trousers pooled around his ankles as well. He was a little self-conscious of how stiffly he was holding his body, the pain that was now radiating out from his side, up from his knee, and through most of his other joints how that his body was beginning to ease off from need and desire that had overwhelmed it and remember the standard state of play.

He needn't have been self-conscious at all – Fell was focused on his reflection in the mirror, pretty little budgerigar that he was, washing off the marks of black and red and peach around his face with a damp cloth. Alexos smiled slightly as he tugged over a blanket over his lap.

Using his cane, he held it by the base and used the handle to hook his vest from the nearer chair and then his pyjama trousers, although he didn't manage the shirt as well, making it drop to the floor.

Getting the vest on was alright – getting the pyjama trousers was fucking miserable, and by the time he actually had them around his ankles, the pain of bending to wrestle with them was too much to keep on with.

"I thought you were meant to be watching this performance," Fell said archly, and Alexos looked up – he'd put on a little blush and foundation, Alexos thought, and now that Alexos was watching, he made a lovely show of reapplying his lipstick. It was quite artful, how he did it, a fluid and easy motion, well-practised.

Alexos watched as he fixed up his mascara, then applied a little something else to his brows – shadow? Some sort of highlight? Alexos was no expert in modern cosmetics, although this put him in a distant mood for... something, he didn't know.

He thought he'd enjoy seeing Fell Garibaldi play an ancient Greek role, although he supposed there wasn't money in that like there was for an adaptation of a Lawrence Kidd romantic comedy.

"How much of it is on my face?" Alexos asked fifteen minutes later, and Fell laughed as he leaned and kissed Alexos again, a gentle touch to the mouth before he drew up.

"Not as much as is on the rest of you, darling, I can assure you of that."

"Toss the tie inside on your way out, will you? My man will know it's safe to come in."

"Will do, ducky. My details are on the desk – do write me."

"I will."

Chapter Twenty-One

He wasn't generally a big drinker, and so Harry's walk back to the hotel was a little clumsy, his coat thrown over his arm to spare him from the warmth of the evening's weather combined with the heat the drink was spurring under his clothes.

Young Mr Riggs had only had one drink with them before he'd retired to his and Larry's lodgings to get things set up for his return. The conversation had been something of a gentle interview on their parts, asking him guiding questions and encouraging him to speak about his work of recent, skills he was interested in acquiring, the books he had been reading, how his mother was, and his sisters.

Afterwards, he and Ulysses had gone on talking for some time about anything and everything, in the manner of any two close friends. It was natural enough to share the foibles and strengths of their respective employers – for Harry to speak with both affection and frustration as to Alexos' mysterious disappearance with Larry before finding him in his absurdly well-outfitted mechanic's shed; for Ulysses to deplore the state of one of Mr Samuels' friends, Cricket, and his habit of letting loose all manner of creepy crawlies in their home, including worms, ladybirds, ants, and woodlice, and the fact that Samuels had an inexplicable affection for the ridiculous man.

"He's been doing full portraits of late of all his friends, has been making an album of them," Ulysses had said toward the end of their evening together, when they were finishing up the dregs of their glasses. "The one of Mr Kidd is alright – rather too accurate to be flattering, mind you."

"Am I wrong in supposing he'll be wanting to sketch me, next, or is he only drawing the gentlemen?"

"No doubt he'll want to," Ulysses had said, and he'd hesitated a moment as he loosely pulled his coat over his shoulders and buckled it at the neck as a cloak, not sliding his arms into the sleeves. "He won't speak about it, even with me, but his nightmares have been troubling him again of late. Perhaps if you might visit soon, or extend us an invitation, it's the sort of thing he and Mr Fox might talk about."

"Full portraits of his friends," Harry had said. "To remember us by, if some other catastrophe starts picking us off, as happened in the War?"

"If you want to voice that estimation in Vincent's earshot, Harry," Ulysses had said, with a sad but genuine smile, "you are a braver man than I."

Still, they'd parted with a little laughter between them, wrestling a little on exiting the pub, each of them broad enough that they eclipsed the doorway on their own, though they still played at trying to go out at the same time.

When Harry saw the tie over their hotel door, he subtly turned back in the corridor and took a seat in the lobby, reading the paper until he heard the door close down the corridor, and then he got to his feet.

The beautiful, delicate creature that slipped out from his and Alexos' room for the night was so lovely, in a pretty hat and woman's coat with a fur ruff, that Harry might even have mistaken him for a woman, if he didn't know better. He was a lovely little thing with glittering blue eyes and two little marks tattooed on his upper cheek, and he moved with a dancer's sashay on graceful, slippered feet.

"Good evening, Miss," Harry said pleasantly, touching the rim of his hat.

The young man's eyes flitted up to Harry's face from under the rim of his hat, then traced down Harry's body, lingering for a moment about his middle.

The sound he made was convincingly feminine – Harry had had his share of sea-queens, and he knew at a glance that this one was likely familiar with sailors and men at port – and quite derisive.

"I don't think so, ducky," he said in a soft, lilting voice, accented, and Harry chuckled, turning to the side to give him sufficient space to move down the corridor without so much as brushing shoulders with him.

It was something of a pleasure to watch him go, narrow as he was – his coat moved quite fluidly from its place on his shoulders, and wafting in his wake was quite a pleasant lady's perfume, subtle but impactful, mostly lilac with the barest hint of lavender.

Harry opened the door to their room and slipped inside, latching it behind him.

"Oh, Harry," Alexos said softly, smiling up at him. "You were quick. Were you waiting long?"

"Not too long at all," he said richly, pouring a glass of water and bringing it over to Alexos, who sipped at it. He was sprawled on his back in bed in just his vest and pyjama trousers, misted over with sweat, his hair mussed. A little of the pretty thing's lipstick was staining his lips, although more of it was on the side of his neck and under his ear. "Have a good time at dinner?"

"Rather a nice one," said Alexos, laughing in a faint, dazed way. He reached for Harry with his free hand, and Harry stepped closer, letting the other man slide his palm over Harry's thigh, resting with undisguised and unabashed lust on the plush meat of his side.

Harry's lips twitched, wondering how their new friend in the corridor would feel about seeing Alexos' evident desire for the body he had only just scornfully rejected, although he was more than old enough and wise enough not to take such matters to heart.

Nodding toward the door, he quirked an eyebrow. "How old was he? Nineteen?"

"Oh, God," Alexos said, looking abruptly horrified and sitting up slightly on the bed, although this made him wince. His eyes were wide as he asked, aghast, "He's surely not as young as that?"

Laughing, Harry said, "I shouldn't think so, no, though I'm surprised you didn't ask."

"It hardly came up. I was... distracted."

"No doubt. Run another bath for you?"

"Want to share it?"

"I might have a little dip, though it's all I'll manage in that tub," Harry said flirtatiously – it was quite the joy, seeing how Alexos' expression softened, how he took another gulp of his water before setting it aside and putting both his hands on Harry's hips, tilting back his head until Harry took the bait and bent down to kiss him.

Alexos' lips were a little bruised from kissing, but that only made them plumper, and he sighed in a sweet, though not entirely satisfied way. Harry was surprised indeed to find that when his hand slid between his thighs, palm resting against his crotch, he found the young master standing most of the way to attention.

"You'll forgive me if this is a stupid question," Alexos said when Harry gave him a questioning look, "but it's not so unusual to have a bit of difficulty reaching one's peak from time to time, is it?"

"Not unusual in the least," Harry said. He felt full to the brim with warmth and affection for the man before him, for the room around them, for the life ahead of him. He'd been rather satisfied before, but a night of casual chatter and good drink had done much to further bolster his spirits, and something about seeing Ulysses and talking with him, comparing his partnership with Vincent Samuels to his own with Alexos... "Did he ride you?"

"He attended me with his mouth, first. Greedy thing, he was, too – he was about ready to have a tantrum when I dragged him off me. Then, I put him down on his back and drove into him as best I was able. He's evidently something of a slut – I've hardly been up close and personal with many, but I've read a few pieces of erotica here and there, enough to recognise... He had such a greedy pinkness to him, less puckered than one might expect, the muscle just a little looser than the average man's. Such a greedy pull within him, though, tight, fiercely wet, pretty and inviting."

Harry oughtn't have expected otherwise, knowing Alexos as he did already. He didn't speak about this any differently than he spoke about poetry or baking or Aristophanes or the mechanism that moved a ribbon spool: it was casual, confident, authoritative, easy.

Alexos looked lazily up at him, smiling in a distantly satisfied way. His groan of pleasure was back in his throat, a quiet grunt, as he shifted up against Harry's hand, his grip around Alexos' cock through his pyjama trousers.

Harry was hard himself, and not just from a few ales and sympathy. Alexos' easy manner, speaking on his partner, of fucking him, was delectable. He'd wanted to ease Alexos into more social situations, wanted him to make more friends – taking a pretty actor home from a social engagement and fucking him silly was certainly a show of extroverted outreach.

It was rather more entrancing than Alexos attending a museum exhibit or lecture with a new set of friends, or joining them for morning tea or a pleasant lunch – more arousing, in any case.

"Will you tell me all?" Harry asked softly, and Alexos' smile was softer.

"Here are each of us, hard as diamonds," Alexos murmured, "and yet your voice is rich enough for reading poetry. This evening will not amount to much by way of that."

"Funny, that," Harry said, and leaned forward. He was careful about where he placed his hands, supporting Alexos close to the joint of the knee and making sure he was gripping under the stronger one and not the more injured of the two, and Alexos gasped in a breath as Harry lifted him clean from the bed, against his breath.

"Fuck *me*," Alexos hissed under his breath.

"Am I hurting you?"

"No, no," Alexos muttered – his cheeks were flushed, and he rested one hand against Harry's neck, thumb against his collar. Harry was very gentle as he carried him away from the bed and through the narrow little door to the tiny little adjoining bathroom and its little tub. Certainly, they wouldn't be sharing this one. "You're carrying me like a bride," Alexos murmured.

"I'm happy to call myself the bride between us to our friends, if you'd rather," Harry said softly. "Who carries whom can be a private matter."

Alexos' laughter was a soft and handsome thing. "You seem terribly sentimental this evening."

"I had drinks with a few friends this evening. I was accused of being a man in love."

"Were you indeed?" Alexos asked breathlessly. He grunted quietly as Harry gently set him on the stool to sit and then went to run the bath, and he was looking at Harry with interest, focus. He looked so handsome in the brighter light of the bathroom, his eyes alight, his bruised lips parted. "I might have thought to accuse you myself, had I had the opportunity."

"And you?"

"Me? In love? Quite fervently."

"With Larry Kidd, I suppose?"

Alexos' expression flattened, and Harry laughed as he poured salts into the foaming water, which was mercifully warm, late enough at night as they were, he'd been concerned there wouldn't be enough hot water left.

"With you, you great fool," Alexos said. "Though I'm sure I don't know why."

"My cock has something to do with it, I expect."

"The piercings through it, maybe."

Harry laughed, and he felt a great swelling of warmth in his breast as he went to undress.

"I enjoy how you talk," Harry said. "How you talked of fucking that young man was much akin to how you talk of anything else – I was thinking to myself what a robust and confident man you are, how you give yourself over to that which you experience and whom. Your expertise, your intellect, your curiosity. You're a frank and unforgiving man."

"And you love me for *that*?" Alexos asked disbelievingly – it was meant to be wry, that theatrical disbelief, but Harry could hear the genuine quaver of doubt in it.

"Oh, yes," Harry said, seriously, gravely. "How could I not?"

"Well, many people—"

"You know yourself," Harry interrupted him. "Know what you want out of life, what you enjoy – and you share it so... so easily. You are unabashed in it, your knowledge, when it occurs to you to share it."

"I'm arrogant, you mean," Alexos said. "And unsubtle."

"If you like," Harry said. "Use whatever words you like – I love it. I love you."

"Harry, we're meant to be tugging each other off and sloshing about in our bathwater," Alexos softly. "How are we going to do that if you have me bursting into tears from the sentiment?"

"I can tug myself off to your tears," said Harry, only half-jokingly. The shiver that went through Alexos' body was a delicious one.

"Henry Sutton, you are drunk," he said, half-laughing, and Harry grinned back at him.

"With love!"

"With ale."

"With ale," Harry admitted. "But love too."

"How was your evening?" Alexos asked. "You met with some friends, you said?"

"Andrew Cole Riggs did join us," Harry said contentedly, swilling his hand through the water to check it wasn't too hot before continuing to undress. "But he only joined us for one drink. It was mostly myself and one friend of mine of old – Ulysses Valentine. He taught me whilst I was coming up, and then we met again later. We write to one another, keep in contact."

"What an excellent name," Alexos said, and Harry laughed. "His parents are big on the classics, I suppose?"

"His mother particularly – she was a schoolmistress, and I'm given to understand he heard everything from Odysseus' journey home to the Trojan War in his nursery, from his mother's mouth. After the war, he became an agency valet for a period of time, and then went to valet permanently for Vincent Lucas Samuels."

"Oh, he's Larry's illustrator, isn't he?" Alexos asked, raising his eyebrows and shifting slightly on the stool, extending his leg a little. "Larry said he'd invited him tonight, but he wasn't able to make it. This young actress, Nina, seemed to be of the opinion he's one of the most charismatic men alive."

"He is quite charismatic," Harry allowed, because it was true, and he really did like Samuels very much. "He's a very confident creature – jubilant, almost. Big waves of beautiful blond hair, which he rarely ties up, very exaggerated red apples in his cheeks, blue eyes. In all honesty, he rather resembles one of his own illustrations."

"How old is he?"

"The same age as Ulysses, I shouldn't think, or about that age," Harry said. "Eight years older than me, twelve or thirteen older than you. But he was rejected from service after being conscripted – he has a mild case of scoliosis, which was significantly corrected as a young man with a set of braces, but he still can't run or climb, and he struggles with his breathing in constricted or dusty conditions, can't do vigorous exercise for significant periods of time, et cetera."

"Doesn't need a cane, I suppose," Alexos murmured, and Harry looked over at him – he didn't seem displeased or that upset. He was still smiling faintly. "I'm glad you had a good time. I've never been able to enjoy you so... relaxed before."

"You haven't even enjoyed me yet," Harry said richly, stepping forward, and Alexos laughed quietly at Harry in front of him, now stripped of every thread – his hands slid greedily over Harry's thighs, around his belly, gripping his sides before moving up to cup under his chest. "Tell me about him, that pretty little bird in the corridor."

"Felice Garibaldi. Fell. He's an actor – plays Luke in the production, the watchmaker's son. Has a lovely voice, knows his classics. Can rattle off a good few soliloquys not only in English or Italian, but Latin too. And very pretty, as you saw."

"Quite pretty," Harry agreed. "And a slut?"

"Such a slut," Alexos said, and Harry chuckled again, helping Alexos up and easing him down into the steaming water of the bath, settling under the swirl of the salts. He looked up at Harry lovingly as he was lowered down, cupping the side of his cheek with a tender hand. "Do you know who Alcibiades was?"

"No, I don't think so," Harry said, picking up a sponge and beginning to help Alexos scrub along his aching legs. It was wonderful, seeing the strain leak out from his body and dissipate into the water, seeing Alexos' body relax like so much more liquid, not just into the bath, but into Harry's hands, under his gaze. "A philosopher?"

"A statesman – he was an Athenian general, but then he defected to the Spartans, and after that, defected to Persia, and then went back to Athens before he was later exiled again."

"What an excellent man," Harry said immediately, feeling the warmth in his cheeks, feeling the weight of his hardening cock between his legs and looking at Alexos' in the bath as it stood up.

"The boycunts of the back-stabbing and two-faced are so often the tightest and greediest."

"I don't know how treacherous he is in his general life, but I would posit the same of Fell Garibaldi's," Alexos murmured, and then groaned quietly as Harry massaged gently under the back of his knee, then pressing down the back of his calf. "Well, Alcibiades was a student of Socrates – although as you have heard, he wasn't very keen on the Socratic moral considerations."

"Socrates fucked this Alcibiades, I take it?"

"One can only hope. He was quite an unruly student, one is given to believe."

"And Garibaldi?"

"Not unruly by half," Alexos said, and Harry watched his eyes flutter closed as Harry took his foot in hand and pressed under the soles with his thumbs, tracing the arch of the foot. "I think he had it in his head to be a brat, but he was far too eager to follow through on that – he was really quite well-behaved.

"And not like Larry, not— It wasn't about being eager to please. He was just eager for more, eager to be fucked, to be pinned down, roughed up. A born hedonist, him, as Alcibiades before him. He had such a tremendously small cock, Harry, scarcely worth more than a mouthful – pretty little thing was made to be ploughed."

"You had him on his back?"

"Mm, yes. Shoved him back and he spread his thighs wide – sucked on my fingers as though they were sweet with nectar, pinned his thigh up with my good knee, fucked him as hard as I could. A good job I put my fingers in his mouth – he might have woken up the whole building, otherwise."

"Feel powerful?"

"Very powerful," Alexos whispered. "And— and strong. I've never much concerned myself with feeling like a man. As a cripple, one is in many ways automatically emasculated, disregarded, less than, but fucking him... That melted away. Once I stopped him staring at the scars from my braces, anyway."

"You won't get that with Valentine and Samuels," Harry said, and thought for a moment about how it might feel, seeing Alexos bent over and taking Ulysses' prodigious length inside him, or better yet, seeing him moan under Samuels, seeing the two of them kiss, hold one another, fuck one another. Samuels had never been one for buggery – he wasn't a highly-sexed man, was generally more interested in being a voyeur than a participant, but when he did engage a partner, he was interested in every tactile sensation, moulding his body against another man's, rather than pursuing penetration.

It was a lovely show at any time – he should very much like to watch Samuels with Alexos.

"I've just finished with one engagement, dearest fiancé of mine," said Alexos through a soft laugh. "Do you have to fill my dance card up again so soon?"

"A man can dream, can't he? And fantasise? I *must* fantasise."

With a long-suffering but no-less-loving sigh, Alexos gestured magnanimously with one soapy hand. "You may fantasise."

"Thank you, sir," Harry said, holding Alexos' foot with one hand and saluting with the other, and Alexos splashed water into his face. With a growl, Harry pounced halfway into the bath, straddling the narrow tub and dropping the weight of his belly onto Alexos' chest, and Alexos muffled his laughter into Harry's tits as Harry kissed the top of his head a dozen times or so, then hauled him into a kiss on the mouth.

For a few minutes, they kissed and fondled one another, sloshing in their water, and Harry gripped at Alexos' cock, squeezing it and sliding his palm over the head.

"Harry," Alexos grunted against his mouth, his voice strained, and Harry laughed.

"Not a problem with not reaching your peak now, is there?" he asked, greedily kissing the other man between every other word, and Alexos gasped.

"If you want to use this bathwater after me, surely you'd rather I not, ungh, dirty it—"

"I'm sure your jism is clean enough," Harry murmured. "I know where it's been, after all."

"In and out of one hole and the next," Alexos said, and Harry squeezed, leaning back to watch the expression on Alexos' face, watch his mouth open and his head tip back, to hear the stuttered noise in his mouth and feel his prick jolt and pulse in his hand.

They kissed again, longer this time, slower, sweeter. This was less a delve of their tongues against one another and more a tender press of lips, Harry's hand gently cradling Alexos' cheek in his palm, one of Alexos' hands against his breast and the other at his hip.

"I'm very excited to spend the night in bed with you, Harry," Alexos said against their mouths when they broke apart with a quiet, wet sound, and Harry cupped his face with both hands now. Alexos gazed up at him lovingly, his lips parted. "I've dreamt of it, one time and another – the two of us in one bed together, sharing the same space, the same breaths."

"It's going to hurt your back," Harry threatened. "My weight on the mattress is not what you're used to – you're going to sink into the middle and end up drifting toward me."

"Oh no," Alexos said sarcastically, his smile a dreamy thing. "How ever shall I cope with drifting toward you?"

"And tomorrow," Harry said, "I thought we might take a walk along the pier."

"Yes," Alexos said, and his smile turned just a little shyer, his eyes flitting down for a moment. His right hand was stroking and idly squeezing Harry's thigh and hip. "I had been thinking, uh, perhaps I might... Well. How would you feel about another tattoo?"

"I was just considering that matching tattoos might be a nice engagement—"

"Fell Garibaldi matched tattoos with his husband, I was just thinking it might be pleasant for us to pursue ourselves!"

"Something Greek, perhaps, or—"

"Wine," Alexos said. "I want a wine bottle – you're a butler. It seems apropos."

"What should I have?" Harry asked, raising his eyebrows and smirking. "A corkscrew?"

"Subtle," Alexos said. "But I'm far from opposed."

"A pair of bottles, perhaps," Harry murmured, more serious now. "Separate vintages of the same grape – '88 and '93."

"Oh, Harry," Alexos said, and kissed him again, this time so tenderly Harry could weep. He closed his eyes, feeling it all, committing it all to memory – Alexos' hands on his body, Alexos' lips on his, the bathwater, the cool of the tile beneath his feet, the warmth and wetness of the room on his body, the lingering pleasure of the alcohol in his veins.

"Shall I help you out?" Harry asked.

"Unless you'd rather I suck your cock from here."

"... Well. Now that you say it..."

Chapter Twenty-Two

Alexos' body was, understandably, somewhat sore. Settled back in his seat in the train carriage, he had his good leg extended and resting on a newspaper on the opposite seat, his other foot on the floor. Harry was seated beside him and paging idly through his own paper.

Despite having been so heavily exercised, first with Felice and then with Harry, he'd slept the best he had in a long, long while. Harry hadn't even tied him to the bedpost, as Alexos had initially recommended – every time Alexos would begin to stir, Harry would simply band his arm around his chest and pull him closer, turn Alexos' somnambulistic intentions to affection instead.

He remembered, dreamily, Harry's mouth against his cheek, his hand on Harry's chest. He remembered the weight of Harry on the bed beside him – he had been right, the mattress did bow heavily, but for all his lower back ought to be aching, it was somewhat drowned out.

Most of what Alexos felt, despite all the sorenesses from one source and another, was satisfaction, and pure, unadulterated contentment.

"There's going to be an eclipse in November," said Harry, turning a page.

Alexos, his eyes closed, his arms crossed over his chest, his hat tipped forward to hide his face, hummed noncommittally. "Excited about it?"

"It's a novelty," Harry said. "Would you like to see it?"

"With you? I'd go and see anything. Even Cherry Flintman's next performance."

He heard Harry's quiet laugh, felt his arms shift with his smile.

The new tattoo on his ankle felt fresh and sore – the sharp, discomforting pain of the numerous stabs of the needle through his skin was actually in many ways rather pleasant, a distraction from the other pains in his body.

"How's your ear?" Harry asked.

"It feels fine," Alexos said. "A little uncomfortable, maybe – I'm rather uncomfortably aware of my own blood flow – but it doesn't feel inflamed. It looks alright, doesn't it?"

"It looks spectacular," said Harry in a rich, intimate tone, and Alexos opened his eyes to look sideways at him, unable not to smirk at Harry's expression. Despite the pallor of his hangover – he'd been somewhat green this morning, and Alexos had laughed at him very quietly, not wanting to worsen his headache – he was smiling in a lovestruck sort of way.

Alexos reached up and touched the ring through his ear, dangling from the lobe. He'd only had the one ear pierced, his left, and Harry was, infuriatingly, quite correct in his estimation in the conversation they'd had weeks ago – a piercing did indeed distract from the size of his ears.

It had been a whim, a silly one, whilst Harry was in the process of getting tattooed after Alexos' own tattoo was finished up. One of the young men in the shop, built like an ancient tree and with all sorts of barbels and rings tattooed through each and every spare bit of skin, had been more than happy to give it to him.

It looked quite handsome, he thought. He'd acted like some sort of peacock once they'd gone back to the hotel to get their things, unable to look at his tattoo under its protective bandage, and turned his head one way and the other, examining the dangling ring, the golden shine of it, the way it offset the brown of his eyes and brought out the lighter flecks in them.

"I look like a Victorian," Alexos said. "But for the tailoring of my suit, you'd think me born fifty years earlier than I was."

"I'd still have you."

"With five-and-fifty years between us instead of just the five?"

"Absolutely."

"You're a fool."

"A fool in love."

"Well, I'm not."

"You're not in love? Mr Fox. You wound me."

"Oh, I'm in love, alright, Mr Sutton, don't you worry about that. I'm just not a fool about it."

"A genius, are you?"

"Something like that."

"A man should kiss you."

"A man might well get us arrested."

"A man can wait until we're in private."

Alexos laughed, shaking his head – he quietened the laughter as soon as he saw Harry's expression tighten a little, his nose wrinkling, his brow furrowing.

"Is it so bad? The hangover?"

"The headache is lingering," Harry muttered, rubbing the side of his nose with his knuckle. "I used to be able to drink like a sailor and feel no ill-effect whatsoever."

"You just need practice, that's all. Why not try to keep apace with me?"

"Because I need to be able to remain standing whilst going about my duties, for one. I'd be insensible if I drank the way you did."

"Some bodies can take more punishment than others, dear butler of mine."

"Some can indeed," Harry said, voice full of implication, and even without looking, Alexos knew that his eyes were roving up and down his body. "When your mother next throws some soirée at the house, we might invite Larry and some of those actors as well – Mr Garibaldi, Ms Bear, Ms Holland."

"And Mr Samuels, perhaps," Alexos said, surprised at how easy it seemed to him, the idea of it, inviting people to his home for one of his mother's awful parties and... it not being so awful.

"Perhaps," Harry said softly. Shifting, he extended one of his own legs, and Alexos opened his eyes to look – his left leg where Alexos' tattoo was on his right. They had their tattoos mirroring one another, the same tattoo reflected, though the artist had artfully made the same design a little larger on Harry's thicker calf. Two bottles of red wine, one standing up – Harry's, vintage of 1888 - and the other on its side – Alexos', marked 1893. The bottles of wine didn't exactly match up with the ephemera on Harry's left leg, the ship's wheel and other assorted nautical tattoos, but it was a bit more cohesive than it might have been with the marine mammals and creatures on the other side.

Alexos didn't know that he had the strategy and patience to have such a beautiful set of themes and movement across his tattoos the way that Harry had – all he knew was that he wanted tattoos on every inch of him that he could keep hidden, and maybe more tattoos after that.

"Would you like an engagement ring," Harry asked in a quiet voice, and Alexos was surprised at how his heart beat faster, at how his skin felt abruptly hot, his cheeks flushing, at just those words, "or is the one in your ear good enough?"

"The one in my ear is fine, thank you," Alexos said. "Would you like an engagement ring for your finger, or should I buy you one to put... somewhere else?"

He heard Harry's intake of breath, and he was just readying himself to say something more, to tease him, but the door of the carriage opened.

"Is this seat taken?"

"By all means, sir, please," Harry said. "My employer is asleep – he needs to keep his leg extended, what with his injury."

"Oh, that's fine, fine," said the other man sitting down. "War wound, was it?"

Harry made a noncommittal noise, and Alexos feigned sleep until he wasn't feigning it any longer – the second time in as many days he'd fallen asleep at Harry's side.

They travelled home together, and when they were finally in private again, they kissed, and kissed, and kissed... until the bell sounded for dinner, and they came apart again.

"Are any of your friends builders, by any chance?" Alexos asked as Harry helped him on with his jacket. "Someone who could put a secret door between our rooms?"

"I've been making inquiries already for a month, sir."

"Very good, Harry. Very good indeed."

FIN

(for now)

Author's Notes

Thank you so much for reading, and I hope you enjoyed!

This piece started out a few years ago as a TweetFic, fixated wholly on the idea of a butler floating the idea of a betrothal to his injured master whilst he was forced to rely on the butler to shave his face. When I went to adapt it from Tweets into prose, I fleshed it out into a serial work, making the gentleman into a polio survivor, including Reginald Sutton as a character, and then adding in the piercings and tattoos.

You see it now as an eBook, and paperbacks will be available from Sunday 16th November. There'll be a physical book launch with a party at Wharf Chambers in Leeds with wine and cheese and I'll read aloud from the book, so keep an eye out for event details if you're Yorkshire-based and would like to attend.

For everyone else, physical copies will of course be available to buy online as usual.

I plan to write many more stories with these two and their various friends and acquaintances, so keep a weather eye out! There'll be more of Annette, Nina, and Fell; more of Larry; more of Valentine and Vincent Lucas Samuels; and of course, they'll meet Donald Howard and meet some of his favourite men.

Naturally, I was highly influenced by my own interest in the interwar period and particularly in similar characters – most notably, Wodehouse's *Jeeves and Wooster* in the valet/butler and gentlemen dynamics, as well as Evelyn Waugh's *Vile Bodies* when it came to taking inspiration for the actors, as well as Stephen Fry's film adaptation of the same book, *Bright Young Things*.

Ulysses Valentine is less inspired by the likes of Reginald Jeeves or *Downton Abbey's* Charles Carson, and more by the painfully sexy (to me) figure of Sam Vimes' butler in Pratchett's *City Watch* books, Willikins.

More from the Author

I now have a new website, and you can find a preponderance of information, as well as a great amount of stuff to read, upon it.

www.JohannesTEvans.co.uk

On my website, you can find:

- Hundreds of free-to-read short stories
- Dozens of free-to-read essays, guides, and other non-fiction
- Regular blog updates
- Information about collaborations and commissions
- Upcoming events and appearances

There's also a subscription service where for as low as $3 USD per month or $30 USD per year, you can access all premium stories as they're posted in addition to the free-to-read works.

If you'd like to seek out more of my work, *Heart of Stone* is a full-length novel set in the 18th century, and is a slowburn slice-of-life romance between a vampire and his secretary, the vampire ADHD and the secretary autistic. It has a lot of humour and domestic elements throughout.

www.ingramcontent.com/pod-product-compliance
Ingram Content Group UK Ltd.
Pitfield, Milton Keynes, MK11 3LW, UK
UKHW040142031125
464641UK00001B/1

9 798231 645923